THE FLOATING OPERA
and
THE END OF THE ROAD

By John Barth

JOHN BARTH

The Floating Opera

and

The End of the Road

ANCHOR BOOKS
DOUBLEDAY
NEW YORK LONDON TORONTO SYDNEY AUCKLAND

AN ANCHOR BOOK
PUBLISHED BY DOUBLEDAY
a division of Bantam Doubleday Dell Publishing Group, Inc.
1540 Broadway, New York, New York 10036

ANCHOR BOOKS, DOUBLEDAY, and the portrayal of an anchor
are trademarks of Doubleday, a division of Bantam Doubleday
Dell Publishing Group, Inc.

The Floating Opera was originally published by Appleton,
Century Crofts, Inc., in 1956. *The End of the Road* was
originally published in hardcover by Doubleday in 1958.
The 1967 Doubleday editions were revised by the author.
The Anchor Books Edition is published by arrangement with
Doubleday.

Library of Congress Cataloging in Publication Data ·
Barth, John.
  [Floating opera]
  The floating opera and The end of the road/
  by John Barth.—Anchor books ed.
    p. cm.
  I. Barth, John. End of the road. 1988.
  II. Title: Floating opera.   III. Title: End of the road.
  IV. Title: Floating opera and The end of the road.
  PS3552.A75A6   1988   87-26213
  813'.54—dc19   CIP
  ISBN 0-385-24089-9

FIRST ANCHOR BOOKS EDITION: 1988

THE FLOATING OPERA and THE END OF THE ROAD

My books tend to come in pairs, as did their author; I am half of a set of opposite-sex twins.

Our parents didn't plan it that way. Nor did the progenitor of my first two published novels, *The Floating Opera* (1956) and *The End of the Road* (1958). Insofar as I had any literary plan in the early 1950's, it was simply to write a publishable novel if I could and perhaps in the process learn who I was, at least in the medium of fiction.

As is the case with most apprentices in the arts, I had been attempting unsuccessfully for years, by trial and error, to find out what if anything my muse, like the beast in a monster movie, was trying to say to me. Such basic messages, so apparently obvious after the fact, can be far from clear to the fledgling writer. What is his essential subject matter? What will be his characteristic handle on it? Having discovered or decided (as I had by age nineteen or twenty) that your vocation is for writing instead of, say, music, and further that it is for fiction rather than poetry or drama or journalism, you may face still a number of questions the answers to which are by no means self-evident: Are you essentially a novelist or a short-story writer? Is your muse the lady with the grin or the one with the grimace? Are you a realist or a fantast? Ought you to make your art for its own sake or engage it in the service of some lofty cause? Are you more interested in the thing said than in its saying (the Windex approach to language) or vice-versa (the stained-glass approach)? Is less really more? Shall you sing white whales or scarlet letters or green extra-terrestrials or the black urban underclass or WASPs in the pink or none of the above, and shall you do so out of your private experience or avoid autobiographical fiction as one avoids flashers and confessional drunks?

Good lyric poets frequently hit their stride early: Rimbaud *stopped* writing poetry at age nineteen. Fiction writers, however—novelists in particular—often don't find their answers to these questions until later.

In my case, it happened at age twenty-four. I was living and teaching in central Pennsylvania then, inadequately supporting a wife and three small children on an entry-level academic salary and not quite facing the fact that, after five years of industrious literary apprenticeship, things weren't panning out, muse-wise. I had published a couple of stories in ephemeral literary magazines, but my first two book-length efforts—an *ersatz* Faulkner novel and a projected Boccaccian cycle of one hundred

Chesapeake tidemarsh tales—had justly failed to find a publisher. Their author was neither a Faulkner nor a Boccaccio. Once before, after high school, I had discovered (at the Juilliard School of Music) that I had not a certain talent that I'd hoped I had. But I had been single then, a callow kid with the smorgasbord of college waiting for him down the road; changing career plans was no big deal. The situation this time was more consequential, and the pressure was on: The family could not make ends meet, and with neither substantial publication nor the Ph.D., I had no academic future. Moreover, while I'd previously thought I wanted to be a musician, I *knew* I wanted to be a writer. Indeed, in some gut way and despite ample evidence to the contrary, I knew I *was* one—that was perhaps the only thing I knew about myself for sure—as clearly as I knew that nothing I'd written thus far was "for real." "*Vocation*" implies both a summons and an able response; I had the call, but not yet the calling.

My problem, I believe in retrospect, was how to integrate on home grounds—the tidewater Maryland area where I had grown up, and where my imagination was still rooted like marsh grass—the two large sources of literary inspiration exemplified in those abortive early projects: the great Modernists like Joyce and Faulkner on whom I had cut my apprentice teeth, and the old tale-tellers like "Scheherazade" and Boccaccio whom I had devoured extracurricularly. But the clock was running. It appeared that I would be obliged to resign my Penn State instructorship, borrow money from God knows where, and return to Johns Hopkins to complete if I could the doctorate in literary aesthetics that I'd abandoned earlier to try my luck with the muse. Before I made that unhappy decision, however, I had a season (the spring of 1955) to attempt one "final" literary project.

High and dry in the Pennsylvania uplands, I used to pore nostalgically over albums of Marylandia by the Baltimore photographer A. Aubrey Bodine. In one of them I found shots of Captain James Adams's Original Floating Theater, a tug-towed showboat that I remembered having seen as a boy at the municipal wharf in my hometown (Edna Ferber spent a season aboard while writing her novel *Showboat*, the basis of Jerome Kern's musical; but Capt. Adams's homely, sturdy Chesapeake vessel was a far cry from Mississippi Riverboat Gothic). Its portentous name suggested allegory; I made notes toward a fiction in the form of . . . well, a philosophical blackface minstrel show. I had picked up from the postwar *Zeitgeist* some sense of the French Existentialist writers and had absorbed from my own experience a few routine disenchantments. I imagined myself something of a nihilist—but by temperament a smiling nihilist, not the grim-faced kind. I would write some sort of nihilist minstrel show.

It turned into a novel, *The Floating Opera*, because I found the minstrel-show conceit too artificial to sustain and because, while dreaming up a tidewater story of which the showboat show might serve as climax, I discovered by happy accident the turn-of-the-century Brazilian novelist

Joaquim Machado de Assis (*Epitaph of a Small Winner, Philosopher or Dog?*, *Dom Casmurro*, etc.). Machado—himself much under the influence of Laurence Sterne's *Tristram Shandy*—taught me something I had not quite learned from Joyce's *Ulysses* and would not likely have learned from Sterne directly, had I happened to have read him: how to combine formal sportiveness with genuine sentiment as well as a fair degree of realism. Sterne is pre-Romantic; Joyce is late or post-Romantic; Machado is both Romantic and romantic: playful, wistful, pessimistic, intellectually exuberant. He was also, like myself, a provincial, though his novels are set in the sophisticated ambiance of late-nineteenth-century Rio de Janeiro, as was his adult career. Machado's tone and manner, as much as his narrative technics, showed me how I might get my disparate gods together on a tidewater showboat.

Whatever its shortcomings, *The Floating Opera* came together more surely and quickly than anything I'd written before. I drafted it in the spring of '55, spent the summer revising it on location in Maryland, and in the fall drafted even more swiftly a companion piece, *The End of the Road*. The problem of economic survival did not go away: The *Opera* would take nearly a year to find its first publisher (who then would insist that it conclude on a less "nihilist" note: See my preface, below, to the 1967 Doubleday revised edition, which restores the original, apocalyptically shrug-shouldered ending). But I knew I was finally and truly on track. As the manuscript went its difficult rounds, my family skimped and did without for another semester while I finished and revised *The End of the Road*, began *The Sot-Weed Factor*, and stubbornly put off the abandonment of my writerly ambitions. Early in 1956, just when that abandonment could be postponed no longer—I had actually reapplied and been readmitted to that doctoral program in Baltimore—my agent telephoned to say he had a contract at last for *The Floating Opera*. Not so much elated as unspeakably relieved, I canceled the move and went back to my writing desk for keeps.

No doubt some of the discouragement of those raw years, masquerading as general philosophic principle, comes through in *The Floating Opera* and even more in *The End of the Road* (whose bleak title was another acquiescence to New York: My working title had been *What To Do Until the Doctor Comes;* my then editor, the late Edward Aswell of Doubleday, feared the novel would be mistaken for a treatise on first aid). The *Opera* I regarded as a nihilist comedy, *Road* as a nihilist catastrophe: the same melody reorchestrated in a grimmer key and sung by a leaner voice. Their situations have in common that they are narrated by the Other Man in a more or less acknowledged adulterous triangle complicated by an ambiguous pregnancy. The personnel of the two triangles—their ages, social positions, attitudes, and moral voltages—are dissimilar, but the narrators share a radical alienation that fascinated me at the time. "A man may smile and smile and be a villain," Shakespeare reminds us. Todd Andrews, of the *Opera*, embodies my conviction that one may smile

and smile and not only take his own life but blow up the whole show—
or, failing in the attempt, shrug his shoulders and come to a conclusion
beyond Albert Camus's (in, e.g., *The Rebel* and *The Myth of Sisyphus*):
namely, that one may go on living because there is no more justification
for suicide than for going on living. Jacob Horner, of *The End of the Road*,
embodies my conviction that one may reach such a degree of self-es-
trangement as to feel no coherent antecedent for the first-person-singular
pronoun. Horner cobbles up a "self" to deal with the crisis of the plot—
arranging an illegal abortion for his pregnant lover lest she commit calm
suicide—but his efforts lead to a mortal fiasco, and Horner abdicates
personality altogether. If the reader regards either of these egregious
conditions (as embodied by the narrators) as merely psychopathological
—that is, as symptomatic rather than emblematic—the novels make no
moral-dramatic sense.

By the time *The Floating Opera* was launched, its builder had turned
away from (what were by my standards) realism and minimalism to the
high-energy extravagancies of *The Sot-Weed Factor* and *its* sort-of twin,
Giles Goat-Boy. Though the *Opera* had the good fortune, especially for a
first novel, to be nominated for that year's National Book Award in
fiction, its hardcover run was brief; it has lived its gratifyingly long half-
life mainly in paperback editions. Ditto *The End of the Road*, though it was
made into what ought to have been an excellent movie: Stacy Keach as
Jacob Horner, James Earl Jones as the Doctor, Harris Yulin as Joe Morgan, Dorothy Tristan as Rennie Morgan. Those first-rate ingredients
failed to make a first-rate dish; the film was X-rated by the Production
Code Administration for scenes nowhere to be found in the novel (man
rapes chicken, etc.) and Z-rated by the muses. "The principal difference
between the novel and the film," remarked the critic John Simon, "is
that the novel concludes with a harrowing abortion, whereas the film is
an abortion from start to finish." Fairly said, alas.

So: 1) an unsuccessful mass-murder/suicide attempt by a middle-aged
small-town bachelor lawyer with prostate trouble and a hair-trigger
heart condition; and 2) an unsuccessful abortion, fatal to the mother,
made necessary by a failed condom in an era of unreformed abortion
laws and arranged by the adulterous antihero, a walking ontological vacuum: These are the plot armatures of my first pair of opposite-twin
novels. That *The Floating Opera* and *The End of the Road* are again in re-
print thirty years later suggests to their author that there may be more to
them than their "nihilist" materials; that the how of their telling is at
least as important as the stories told.

Truth to tell, I knew that all along.

JOHN BARTH

The Floating Opera

PREFATORY NOTE TO THE REVISED EDITION
OF *The Floating Opera* (1967)

The Floating Opera was written in the first three months of 1955; its companion piece, *The End of the Road*, in the last three months of the same year. The *Opera* was my first novel; I was twenty-four, had been writing fiction industriously for five years, and had had—deservedly—no success whatever with the publishers. One finally agreed to launch the *Opera*, but on condition that the builder make certain major changes in its construction, notably about the stern. I did, the novel was published, critics criticized the ending in particular, and I learned a boatwright little lesson. In this edition the original and correct ending to the story has been restored, as have a number of other, minor passages. *The Floating Opera* remains the very first novel of a very young man, but I'm pleased that it will sink or float now in its original design.

JOHN BARTH

Contents

I. Tuning my piano

To someone like myself, whose literary activities have been confined since 1920 mainly to legal briefs and *Inquiry*-writing, the hardest thing about the task at hand—*viz.*, the explanation of a day in 1937 when I changed my mind—is getting into it. I've never tried my hand at this sort of thing before, but I know enough about myself to realize that once the ice is broken the pages will flow all too easily, for I'm not naturally a reticent fellow, and the problem then will be to stick to the story and finally to shut myself up. I've no doubts on that score: I can predict myself correctly almost every time, because opinion here in Cambridge to the contrary, my behavior is actually quite consistent. If other people (my friend Harrison Mack, for instance, or his wife Jane) think I'm eccentric and unpredictable, it is because my actions and opinions are inconsistent with *their* principles, if they have any; I assure you that they're quite consistent with *mine*. And although my principles might change now and then—this book, remember, concerns one such change—nevertheless I always have them a-plenty, more than I can handily use, and they usually hang all in a piece, so that my life is never less logical simply for its being unorthodox. Also, I get things done, as a rule.

For example, I've got this book started now, and though we're probably a good way from the story yet, at least we're headed toward it, and I for one have learned to content myself with that. Perhaps when I've finished describing that particular

day I mentioned before—I believe it was about June 21, 1937—
perhaps when I reach the bedtime of that day, if ever, I'll
come back and destroy these pages of piano-tuning. Or perhaps not: I intend directly to introduce myself, caution you
against certain possible interpretations of my name, explain the
significance of this book's title, and do several other gracious
things for you, like a host fussing over a guest, to make you as
comfortable as possible and to dunk you gently into the meandering stream of my story—useful activities better preserved
than scrapped.

To carry the "meandering stream" conceit a bit further, if
I may: it has always seemed to me, in the novels that I've
read now and then, that those authors are asking a great deal
of their readers who start their stories furiously, in the middle
of things, rather than backing or sidling slowly into them.
Such a plunge into someone else's life and world, like a plunge
into the Choptank River in mid-March, has, it seems to me,
little of pleasure in it. No, come along with me, reader, and
don't fear for your weak heart; I've one myself, and know the
value of inserting first a toe, then a foot, next a leg, very
slowly your hips and stomach, and finally your whole self into
my story, and taking a good long time to do it. This is, after
all, a pleasure-dip I'm inviting you to, not a baptism.

Where were we? I was going to comment on the significance
of the *viz.* I used earlier, was I? Or explain my "piano-tuning"
metaphor? Or my weak heart? Good heavens, how does one
write a novel! I mean, how can anybody stick to the story, if
he's at all sensitive to the significances of things? As for me,
I see already that storytelling isn't my cup of tea: every new
sentence I set down is full of figures and implications that I'd
love nothing better than to chase to their dens with you, but
such chasing would involve new figures and new chases, so
that I'm sure we'd never get the story started, much less ended,
if I let my inclinations run unleashed. Not that I'd mind,
ordinarily—one book is as good as another to me—but I really

do want to explain that day (either the 21st or the 22nd) in June of 1937 when I changed my mind for the last time. We'll have to stick to the channel, then, you and I, though it's a shoal-draught boat we're sailing, and let the creeks and coves go by, pretty as they might be. (This metaphor isn't gratuitous —but let it go.)

So. Todd Andrews is my name. You can spell it with one or two *d*'s; I get letters addressed either way. I almost warned you against the single-*d* spelling, for fear you'd say, "*Tod* is German for death: perhaps the name is symbolic." I myself use two *d*'s, partly in order to avoid that symbolism. But you see, I ended by not warning you at all, and that's because it just occurred to me that the double-*d* *Todd* is symbolic, too, and accurately so. *Tod* is death, and this book hasn't much to do with death; *Todd* is almost *Tod*—that is, almost death— and this book, if it gets written, has very much to do with almost-death.

One last remark. Were you ever chagrined by stories that seemed to promise some revelation, and then cheated their way out of it? I've run more times than I'd have chosen to into stories concerning some marvelous invention—a gravity-defier, or a telescope powerful enough to see men on Saturn, or a secret weapon capable of dislocating the solar system—but the mechanics of the gravity device are never explained; the question of Saturn's inhabitation is never answered; we're not told how to build our own solar-system dislocators. Well, not so this book. If I tell you that I've figured some things out, I'll tell you what those things are and explain them as clearly as I can.

Todd Andrews, then. Now, watch how I can move when I really care to: I'm fifty-four years old and six feet tall, but weigh only 145. I look like what I think Gregory Peck, the movie actor, will look like when he's fifty-four, except that I keep my hair cut short enough not to have to comb it, and I don't shave every day. (The comparison to Mr. Peck isn't intended as self-praise, only as description. Were I God, creating the face of either Todd Andrews or Gregory Peck, I'd change it just a trifle here and there.) I'm well off, by most standards: I'm a partner in the law firm of Andrews, Bishop, & Andrews —the second Andrews is me—and the practice nets me as much as I want it to, up to perhaps ten thousand dollars a year, maybe nine, although I've never pushed it far enough to find out. I live and work in Cambridge, the seat of Dorchester County, on the Eastern Shore of Maryland. It's my home town and my father's—Andrews is an old Dorchester name—and I've never lived anywhere else except for the years I spent in the Army during the First World War and the years I spent in Johns Hopkins University and the University of Maryland Law School afterwards. I'm a bachelor. I live in a single room in the Dorset Hotel, just across High Street from the court-house, and my office is in "Lawyers' Row" on Court Lane, one block away. Although my law practice pays my hotel bill, I consider it no more my career than a hundred other things: sailing, drinking, walking the streets, writing my *Inquiry*, staring at walls, hunting ducks and 'coons, reading, playing politics. I'm interested in any number of things, enthusiastic about nothing. I wear rather expensive clothing. I smoke Robert Burns cigars. My drink is Sherbrook rye and ginger ale. I read often and unsystematically—that is, I have my own system, but it's unorthodox. I am in no hurry. In short, I live my life—or have lived it, at least, since 1937—in much the same manner as I'm writing this first chapter of *The Floating Opera*.

I almost forgot to mention my illnesses.

The fact is, I'm not a well man. What reminded me of it just now was that while I was daydreaming about the name *Floating Opera*, sitting here at my table in the Dorset Hotel, surrounded by the files of my *Inquiry*, I commenced drumming my fingers on the table, in rhythm with a galloping neon sign outside. You should see my fingers. They're the only deformity in a body otherwise serviceable and, it has in my life been whispered to me, not unlovely. But these fingers. Great clubbed things: huge, sallow, heavy nails. I used to have (probably still have) a kind of subacute bacteriological endocarditis, with a special complication. Had it since I was a youngster. It clubbed my fingers, and now and then I get weak, not too often. But the complication is a tendency to myocardial infarction. What that means is that any day I may fall quickly dead, without warning—perhaps before I complete this sentence, perhaps twenty years from now. I've known this since 1919: thirty-five years. My other trouble is a chronic infection of the prostate gland. It gave me trouble when I was younger —several kinds of trouble, as I'll doubtless explain somewhere later—but for many years now I've simply taken a hormone capsule (one milligram of diethylstilbestrol, an estrogen) every day, and except for a sleepless night now and then, the infection doesn't bother me any more. My teeth are sound, except for one filling in my lower left rear molar and a crown on my upper right canine (I broke it on a ferryboat railing in 1917, wrestling with a friend while crossing the Chesapeake). I'm never constipated, and my vision and digestion are perfect. Finally, I was bayoneted just a little bit by a German sergeant in the Argonne during the First World War. There's a small place on my left calf from it, where a muscle atrophied, but the little scar doesn't hurt. I killed the German sergeant.

No doubt when I get the hang of storytelling, after a chapter or two, I'll go faster and digress less often.

Now then, the title, and then we'll see whether we can't start the story. When I decided, sixteen years ago, to write about how I changed my mind one night in June of 1937, I had no title in mind. Indeed, it wasn't until an hour or so ago, when I began writing, that I realized the story would be at least novel-length and resolved therefore to give it a novel title. In 1938, when I determined to set the story down, it was intended only as an aspect of the preliminary study for one chapter of my *Inquiry*, the notes and data for which fill most of my room. I'm thorough. The first job, once I'd sworn to set that June day down on paper, was to recollect as totally as possible all my thoughts and actions on that day, to make sure nothing was left out. That little job took me nine years— I didn't push myself—and the notes filled seven peach baskets over there by the window. Then I had to do a bit of reading: a few novels, to get the feel of the business of narrating things, and some books on medicine, boatbuilding, philosophy, minstrelsy, marine biology, jurisprudence, pharmacology, Maryland history, the chemistry of gases, and one or two other things, to get "background" and to make sure I understood approximately what had happened. This took three years—rather unpleasant ones, because I had to abandon my usual system of choosing books in order to do that comparatively specialized reading. The last two years I spent editing my recollections of that day from seven peach baskets down to one, writing commentary and interpretative material on them until I had seven peach basketsful again, and finally editing the commentary back down from seven peach baskets to two, from which I intended to draw comments rather at random every half hour or so during the writing.

Ah, me. Everything, I'm afraid, is significant, and nothing is finally important. I'm pretty sure now that my sixteen years of preparation won't be as useful, or at least not in the same way, as I'd thought: I understand the events of that day fairly well, but as for commentary—I think that what I shall do is try not to comment at all, but simply stick to the facts. That way I know I'll still digress a great deal—the temptation is always great, and becomes irresistible when I know the end to be irrelevant—but at least I have some hope of reaching the end, and when I lapse from grace, I shall at any rate be able to congratulate myself on my intentions.

Why *The Floating Opera?* I could explain until Judgment Day, and still not explain completely. I think that to under-

stand any one thing entirely, no matter how minute, requires
the understanding of every other thing in the world. That's
why I throw up my hands sometimes at the simplest things;
it's also why I don't mind spending a lifetime getting ready to
begin my *Inquiry*. Well, *The Floating Opera*. That's part of
the name of a showboat that used to travel around the Virginia
and Maryland tidewater areas: *Adam's Original & Unparalleled
Floating Opera*; Jacob R. Adam, owner and captain; admissions
20, 35, and 50 cents. The *Floating Opera* was tied up at Long
Wharf on the day I changed my mind, in 1937, and some of
this book happens aboard it. That's reason enough to use it as
a title. But there's a better reason. It always seemed a fine
idea to me to build a showboat with just one big flat open
deck on it, and to keep a play going continuously. The boat
wouldn't be moored, but would drift up and down the river
on the tide, and the audience would sit along both banks.
They could catch whatever part of the plot happened to un-
fold as the boat floated past, and then they'd have to wait until
the tide ran back again to catch another snatch of it, if they
still happened to be sitting there. To fill in the gaps they'd
have to use their imaginations, or ask more attentive neighbors,
or hear the word passed along from upriver or downriver.
Most times they wouldn't understand what was going on at
all, or they'd think they knew, when actually they didn't. Lots
of times they'd be able to see the actors, but not hear them.
I needn't explain that that's how much of life works: our friends
float past; we become involved with them; they float on, and
we must rely on hearsay or lose track of them completely;
they float back again, and we either renew our friendship—
catch up to date—or find that they and we don't comprehend
each other any more. And that's how this book will work, I'm
sure. It's a floating opera, friend, fraught with curiosities,
melodrama, spectacle, instruction, and entertainment, but it floats
willy-nilly on the tide of my vagrant prose: you'll catch sight

of it, lose it, spy it again; and it may require the best efforts of your attention and imagination—together with some patience, if you're an average fellow—to keep track of the plot as it sails in and out of view.

II. The Dorchester Explorers' Club

I suppose I must have waked at six o'clock, that morning in 1937 (I'm going to call it June 21). I had spent a poor night —this was the last year of my prostate trouble. I'd got up more than once to smoke a bit, or walk about my room, or jot some notes for my *Inquiry*, or stare out the window at the Post Office, across High Street from the hotel. Then I'd managed to fall asleep just before sunrise, but the light, or whatever, popped me awake on the tick of six, as it does every morning.

I was just thirty-seven then, and as was my practice, I greeted the new day with a slug of Sherbrook from the quart on my window sill. I've a quart sitting there now, but it's not the same one; not by a long shot. The habit of saluting the dawn with a bend of the elbow was a hangover from college-fraternity days: I had got really to enjoy it, but I gave it up some years ago. Broke the habit deliberately, as a matter of fact, just for the exercise of habit-breaking.

I opened my eyes and bottle, then, and took a good pull, shook all over from head to toe, and looked at my room. It was a sunny morning, and though my window faces west, enough light reflected in to make the room bright. A pity: the Dorset Hotel was built in the early eighteen hundreds, and my room, like many an elder lady, looks its best in a subdued light. Then, as now, the one window was dappled with little rings of dust from dried raindrops; the light-green plaster walls were filigreed with ancient cracks like a relief map of the Dorchester marshes; an empty beef-stew can, my ashtray, was overflowing butts (I smoked cigarettes then) onto my writing desk—a bizarre item provided by the management; the notes for my *Inquiry*, then in its seventh year of preparation, filled a mere three peach baskets and one corrugated box with MORTON'S MARVELOUS TOMATOES printed on the end. One wall was partially covered, as it is yet, by a Coast & Geodetic Survey map of Dorchester County—not so annotated as it is now. On another hung an amateur oil painting of what appeared to be a blind man's conception of fourteen whistling swan landing simultaneously in the Atlantic during a half-gale. I don't recall now how I came by it, but I know I let it hang through inertia. In fact, it's still over there on the wall, but once while drunk my friend Harrison Mack, the pickle magnate, drew a kind of nude on top of it in crayon. All over the floor (then, not now) were spread the blueprints of a boat that I was building at the time in a garage down by the range lights on the creek; I'd brought the prints up to do some work on them the day before.

It seems to me that any arrangement of things at all is an order. If you agree, it follows that my room was as orderly as any room can be, even though the order was an unusual one.

Don't get the impression that my life, then or now, is "bohemian" or "left bank." If I understand those terms correctly, it isn't. In the first place, by 1937 I wasn't enthusiastic about any kind of art, although I was and am mildly curious about it. Neither was my room dirty or uncomfortable—just crowded. It was probably the day before the maids came to clean: they spoil my orderliness by putting things "straight"—that is, out of sight. Finally, I live too well to be called a bohemian. Sherbrook rye costs $4.49 a quart, and I use a lot of quarts.

So. It's really a quite adequate room, and I'm still here. I woke up that morning, then, slugged my rye, looked around my room, got quietly out of bed, and dressed for the office. I even remember my clothes, though that date—the 21st or 22nd—escapes me, after sixteen years of remembering: I wore a gray-and-white seersucker suit, a tan linen sports shirt, some necktie or other, tan stockings, and my straw boater. I'm sure I splashed cold water on my face, rinsed my mouth out, wiped my reading glasses with toilet paper, rubbed my chin to persuade myself that I didn't need shaving, and patted my hair down in lieu of combing it—sure, because I've done these things, in that order, nearly every morning since perhaps 1930, when I moved into the hotel. It was at some moment during the performance of this ritual—the instant when the cold water met my face seems a probable one—that all things in heaven and earth came clear to me, and I realized that this day I would make my last; I would destroy myself on this day.

I stood erect and grinned at my dripping face in the mirror.

"Of course!"

Exhilaration! A choked snicker escaped me.

"For crying out loud!"

Momentous day! Inspiration, to have closed my eyes on the old problem; to have opened them on the new and last and only solution!

Suicide!

I tiptoed from the room to join my colleagues in the hall, the charter members of the Dorchester Explorers' Club, for coffee.

Like the hotels of many small towns, the Dorset is bigger than it need be. Most of its fifty-four rooms are empty in the wintertime, and even with the addition of the several all-summer visitors who move in when the weather warms, there are enough rooms left empty on an average night to accommodate any traveling circus or muskrat-trappers' convention that might come through town unexpectedly. The owners are able to stay in business, one might guess, only because the building was paid for several generations ago, and willed to the present operators unencumbered; because overhead and maintenance costs are very low; and because a number of elderly ladies and gentlemen unfortunate enough to have outlived their welcome in this world are forced by circumstances to make the hotel their last stopover on the road to the next. These super-numeraries, especially the men among them, comprise the Dorchester Explorers' Club—meetings every morning from 6:15 until 6:45. The D.E.C., founded and named by myself, is still extant, though of the charter members only I remain alive.

That morning, as I remember, just two others were present: Capt. Osborn Jones, an eighty-three-year-old retired oyster dredger crippled by arthritis, and Mister Haecker, seventy-nine, former principal of the high school, then pensioned and, though in good health, devoid of family—the end of his line. Because Capt. Osborn had difficulty with stairs, we met in his room, on the same floor as mine.

"Morning, Cap'n Osborn," I said, and the old man grunted, as was his habit. He was dressed in a shiny gray cap, a nondescript black wool sweater, and blue denims washed nearly to whiteness.

"Morning, Mister Haecker," I said. Mister Haecker wore his usual spotless and creaseless black serge, a silk necktie, and a clean if somewhat threadbare striped shirt.

"Good morning, Todd," he answered. I remember he was lighting his first cigar of the morning with one hand and stirring coffee with the other. I had purchased a one-burner hot plate for the Club some months before, and by mutual consent it remained in Capt. Osborn's room. "Good and hot," he said, handing me a cup of coffee.

I thanked him. Capt. Osborn commenced swearing steadily, in a monotone, and striking his right leg with his cane. Mister Haecker and I watched him while we sipped our coffee.

"Can't wake her up, huh?" I offered. Every morning, as soon as Capt. Osborn dressed and sat down, his leg went to sleep, and he pounded it until the blood circulated. Some mornings it took longer than others to get the job done.

"Drink your coffee, Captain," Mister Haecker said in his very mild voice. "It will do more good than all your temper."

Capt. Osborn grew dizzy from the exertion; I saw him grip his chair arms to steady himself. He sighed, between clenched teeth, and took the coffee that Mister Haecker held out to him, grunting his thanks. Then, without a word, he deliberately poured the steaming stuff all over the delinquent leg.

"Hey there!" Mister Haecker exclaimed with a frown, for such displays annoyed him. I, too, was startled, afraid the coffee would scald the old fellow, but he grinned and struck once more at the leg with his cane.

"Smack her good," I urged admiringly.

Capt. Osborn gave up the struggle and settled back in his chair, coffee still steaming and dripping from his trouser leg onto the floor.

"Awright," he said, breathing heavily, "awright. I'm goin' to die. But I want to do it all at oncet, not a piece at a time." He regarded the leg with disgust. "God damn leg." He kicked his right foot with his left. "Pins and needles, feels like. One time I could buck and wing with that leg. Even steered my boat with 'er, standin' on the other and holdin' a donkey rope in each hand! No more, sir."

"Wouldn't be so bad if he'd die in installments," I said to Mister Haecker, who was fixing the Captain another cup of coffee. "Maybe the undertaker'll bury him a piece at a time, and we can pay him a little each month."

This about Capt. Osborn's senility was a running joke in the Explorers' Club, and as a rule Mister Haecker, for all his primness, joined in the bantering, but this morning he seemed preoccupied.

"You *are* going to die, Captain," he said solemnly, giving Capt. Osborn the fresh coffee, "just as Todd says. But not for a spell, we trust. In the meantime you're an old man, same as

I. Just old age, is all. Why buck it? There's not a thing in this world you can do about it."

"Ain't nothing I can do about it," Capt. Osborn admitted, "but I ain't got to like it."

"Why not?" Mister Haecker pressed. "That's just what I want to know."

"Why'n hell should I?" Capt. Osborn snorted. "Can't work and can't play. Jest spit tobacco and die. You take it; I don't want it." He drew a handkerchief from his sweater pocket and blew his nose violently. The cushions of his chair, the drawers of his table, the pockets of his sweater and trousers— all were stuffed with damp or drying handkerchiefs: the Captain, like many watermen, suffered from acute sinusitis, aggravated by the damp air of Dorchester County, and would have nothing to do with doctors. His only therapy was the half-tumblerful of Sherbrook that I gave him every morning before I left the hotel. It kept him mildly drunk until near noon, by which time his sinuses were less congested.

"Well," Mister Haecker said, "wise men have never run down old age. Let me read you a quote I copied down from a book yesterday, just to read you."

"Oh, my. Oh, my."

"He's going to convert you, Cap'n Osborn," I warned.

"Hee, hee!" the old man chuckled. He always thought it tremendously funny when I suggested that he was a backslider.

"No," Mister Haecker said, spreading open a folded strip of paper and holding it to the light. "This is something I copied down from Cicero, and I want you to hear what Cicero says about being old. Here's what Cicero says, now: '. . . *if some god should grant me to renew my childhood from my present age, and once more to be crying in my cradle, I should firmly refuse. . . .*' There, now. I guess Cicero ought to know. Eh?"

"I expect so," Capt. Osborn said, not daring to contradict flatly the written word.

"Well, now," Mister Haecker smiled. "Then I say let's make

the most of it. How does it go? *The last of life, for which the first was made.* Don't you think so?" He looked to me, for support. "Don't *you* think so?"

"Don't ask me, Mister Haecker; I'm still in the first."

"Listen," Capt. Osborn said, in that tone employed by old men to suggest that, having indulged long enough the nonsense of others' opinions, they are about to get down to the truth. "Ye see this here arm?" He held out his bony right arm. "Well, sir, they could tie me to a cottonwood tree this minute, and hitch a team to this here arm, and they could pull 'er out slow by the roots, God damn 'em, and I'd let 'em, if they'd make me forty again, with a season's pay in my pocket and all summer to live. Now, then!"

He sat back exhausted in his chair, but his face was triumphant.

"Do you think that's right?" Mister Haecker pleaded to me. "Is that the way you'd feel?"

"Nope," I said. Mister Haecker brightened considerably, but Capt. Osborn glared.

"Ye mean ye'd spend yer time readin' nonsense to yerself?" he asked incredulously.

"Nope," I said. Now Mister Haecker seemed disappointed too.

"Well, what's your opinion about it?" he asked glumly. "Or don't you have one?"

"Him!" Capt. Osborn snuffled with laughter and phlegm. "That one's got opinions on ever'thing!"

"Oh, I've got one," I admitted. "Matter of fact, I woke up with it this morning."

"Woke up with it, did ye!" Capt. Osborn cackled. "I bet it's a hot one, now!"

Mister Haecker waited patiently, though without much relish, to hear my opinion, but he was spared it, because Capt. Osborn's laughter turned into coughing and choking, as it sometimes did, and the two of us had to clap him on the back until, still sputtering, he caught his breath. As soon as he could breathe normally again, I left the club meeting to fetch him his glass of rye from my room, for it seemed to me he needed his medicine badly.

Light step! I wanted to dance across the hall! My opinion? My opinion? S U I C I D E ! Oh, light step, reader! Let me tell you: my whole life, at least a great part of it, has been directed toward the solution of a problem, or mastery of a fact. It is a matter of attitudes, of stances—of masks, if you wish, though the term has a pejorativeness that I won't accept. During my life I've assumed four or five such stances, based on certain conclusions, for I tend, I'm afraid, to attribute to abstract ideas a life-or-death significance. Each stance, it seemed to me at the time, represented the answer to my dilemma, the mastery of my fact; but always something would happen to demonstrate its inadequacy, or else the stance would simply lose its persuasiveness, imperceptibly, until suddenly it didn't work—quantitative change, as Marx has it, suddenly becoming qualitative change—and then I had the job to face again of changing masks: a slow and, for me, painful process, if often an involuntary one. Be content, if you please, with understanding that during several years prior to 1937 I had employed a stance that, I thought, represented a real and permanent solution to my problem; that during the first half of 1937 that stance had been losing its effectiveness; that during the night of June 20, the night before the day of my story, I became totally and forcibly aware of its inadequacy—I was, in fact, back where I'd started in 1919; and that, finally and miraculously, after no more than an hour's predawn sleep, I awoke, splashed cold water on my face, and realized that I had the real, the final, the unassailable answer; the last possible word; the stance to end all stances. If it hadn't been necessary to tiptoe and whisper, I'd have danced a *trepak* and sung a *come-all-ye!* Didn't I tell you I'd pull no punches? That my answers were yours? *Suicide!* Poor Mister Haecker, he must wait to learn my opinion (wait, wretched soul, I fear, for Judgment Day), but not you, reader. *Suicide* was my answer; my answer was *suicide*. You'll not appreciate it before I've laid open the problem; and lay it open I shall, a piece at a time, after my fashion —which, remember, is not unsystematic, but simply coherent in terms of my own, perhaps unorthodox, system.

Then, for heaven's sake, what is my system? Patience, friend; it's not my aim to mystify or exasperate you. Remember that I'm a novice at storytelling—even if I weren't, I'd do things my own way. I suggest you substitute this question for yours: Why didn't I carry Capt. Osborn's rye with me when I first left my room, so that I shouldn't need to return for it? There's a more specific question, and a more reasonable, and a less prying, and its answer involves the answer to the other. I didn't take the rye with me in the first place because it wasn't my habit to do so, and one of the results of my eye-opening answer was that this day—this June 21 (I'm almost certain) —should, because of its very momentousness, be lived as exactly like every other day of my recent life as I could possibly live it. Therefore, although I knew very well that Capt. Osborn would need his medicine, I left it in my room and returned for it after coffee, as was my practice.

Is this an answer? More to the first question than to the second; you still don't know how the practice originated, any more than I do, but you know that my system for living this extraordinary day was to live it as ordinarily as possible, though every action would necessarily be charged with a new significance. And similarly, my method in telling this story will be to set down the events of that day as barely as possible, for I know that in the telling I'll lose the path often enough for you to learn or guess the whole history of the question, as the audience to my untethered showboat pieces together the plot of their melodrama—and I swear by all the ripe tomatoes in Dorchester that when the excitement commences, the boat will be floating just in front of you and you shan't miss a thing.

So, then. I crossed the hall to my room, opened the door softly, and tiptoed inside to fetch the glass of rye. My intention was to rinse the drinking glass out, fill it half full, and leave as quickly as possible, but as soon as I turned the faucet at the washbasin, and it sounded its usual A♭ above high C, Jane Mack opened her marvelous green eyes and sat up in my bed: her hair, brown and sleek as a sable's, fell around her shoulders, and the bed sheet slid to her hips; she raised her right arm to push the hair back; the movement flattened her stomach and lifted one of her breasts in a way that flexed my thighs to watch. I was still holding the quart of Sherbrook in my right hand and the glass in my left. Jane asked me, in a sleepy voice, whether it was eight o'clock yet; I told her it was not. She scratched her head, yawned, flopped back on the pillow, sighed, and, I think, went to sleep again instantly. The sheet was still at her hips, and she lay with her back to me. I believe that a small warm breeze was moving through the room, and I remember clearly that a little ray of sunlight reflected from something outside and streaked brilliant across the sun-browned skin of her, where her waist grew smallest above the round angle of her hip, thrust up by the hard mattress of my bed. I drank Capt. Osborn's medicine myself, as was *not* my practice, poured him another dose, and tiptoed out.

III. Coitus

If you're still with me, I shan't even bother explaining why I couldn't tell you that Jane Mack was my mistress until after I'd announced that this day was a momentous one: either you're familiar with the business of climaxes and anticlimaxes, in which case no explanation is necessary, or else you know even less about storytelling than I do, in which case an explanation would be useless. She was, indeed, my mistress, and a fine one. To make the triangle equilateral, Harrison Mack was my excellent friend, and I his. Each of the three of us loved the other two as thoroughly as each was able, and in the case of Jane and Harrison, that was thoroughly indeed. As for me—well, I'll explain in a later chapter. And Harrison was quite aware of the fact that between 1932 and 1937 his wife spent many, many hours in my room and in my bed. If he didn't know that I had made love to her exactly six hundred seventy-three times, it's because Jane neglected to keep score as accurately as I did.

I'll explain it now: it's a good yarn, and Capt. Osborn can wait a chapter for his rye.

I first met Harrison Mack in 1925, at a party given by a classmate of mine from the University of Maryland Law School. It was a drunken affair held somewhere in Guilford, a wealthy section of Baltimore. At the time, I shall explain, I was in the early throes of a spell of misanthropic hermitism, which lasted from 1925 until 1930. I had, for various reasons, renounced the world of human endeavors and delights, and although I

continued my legal studies (principally through inertia), I was
having no more to do with my fellow man and his values than I
had to. Rather a saint, I was, during those five or six years—a
Buddhist saint, of the Esoteric variety. It was one of my pro-
visional answers to the peculiar question of my life, and long
after I'd outgrown it I still remembered that stance with pleasure.

For one thing, it made me appear mysterious, standing aloof
in a bay window, smoking a cigarette with an air of quiet
wisdom while all around me the party screamed and giggled.
Some quite pleasant people, Harrison Mack among them, reasoned that I must have answers that they lacked, and sought
me out; women thought me charmingly shy, and sometimes
stopped at nothing to "penetrate the disdainful shell of my
fear," as one of their number put it. Often as not, it was they
who got penetrated.

On the night of this particular party I found myself being
made friends with by a great handsome fellow who came over
to my window, introduced himself as Harrison Mack, and
stared out beside me for nearly an hour without speaking: some
time afterwards I observed that Harrison involuntarily adopts,
to a great extent, the mood and manner of whomever he happens to be with—a tendency I admire in him, for it implies
that he has no characteristic mood or manner of his own. We
talked after a while, brusquely, of several things: the working
class, prohibition, law, the Sacco-Vanzetti affair, and Maryland. Harrison, it turned out, was well off; his father, Harrison
Mack Senior, was president of a pickle company. Since the
cucumbers that were ultimately transmogrified into Mack's
Pickles were grown on the Eastern Shore, whence they were
carried as whole pickles to the Baltimore plant for fancy processing, the Macks had summer homes sprinkled about the
peninsula, and Harrison was no stranger to the haunts of my
youth. We talked aloofly of pickles and wealth.

Harrison—a fine, muscular, sun-bronzed, gentle-eyed, patrician-nosed, steak-fed, Gilman-Schooled, soft-spoken, well-tailored aristocrat—to his family's understandable alarm was a communist at the time. Not a parlor communist, either: an out-and-out leaflet-writing revolutionary who had sold his speedboat, his Stutz automobile, and God knows what else, to live on when his father disinherited him; who spent ten hours a day writing and distributing party-line penny dreadfuls among factory workers, including the employees of the Mack Pickle factories; who took his lumps with the rest when strikebreakers or other kinds of bullies—including certain salaried employees of the Mack Pickle factories—objected to his activities; who was at the moment engaged to marry the woolliest-looking specimen of intellectual Bolshevism I've ever laid unbelieving eyes upon, because she was ideologically pure; and whose only remaining streak of good sense, as far as I could see that night, was his refusal to become actually a dues-paying member of the Party, for fear it might prove a liability to the execution of his schemes.

As it happened, Harrison did precisely, if accidentally, the only thing that could possibly have induced me to like him that night: he made it obvious from the beginning that he liked me a great deal. He was an engaging fellow, still is, and I saw nothing amiss in a saint's having one friend. The sheer oppositeness of his enthusiasm from anything I myself could conceivably have been enthusiastic about at that time—though I had been interested enough in social reform not too long before—drew me to him, and, as I learned later, he was attracted by my "transcendent rejection" (his term) of the thing that meant life to him. In short, we were soon friends, and walked blindly to my rooms at dawn for more drink, singing the *Internationale* in French through the mansioned and junipered roads of Guilford.

I knew him well for the next year, or until my graduation from law school. I was a saint throughout the whole period—indeed, that mask endured for four more years—and although

we argued sometimes for days, neither of us was rational enough
to be convinced of the other's position. I say this because I
know for certain that all the major mind changes in my life
have been the result not of deliberate, creative thinking on my
part, but rather of pure accidents—events outside myself im-
pinging forcibly upon my attention—which I afterwards rationalized into new masks. And I suspect that Harrison simply
assumes, in time, the intellectual as well as the manneristic color
of his surroundings.

For example, when we said goodbye in 1926—I to set up
practice in Cambridge, he to assist a Party press in Detroit—I
thought I detected an ideologically impure attitude in him
toward his leaflet-writing colleagues. He had, in fact, come to
loathe them, and, it seemed to me, had begun to prefer refuting
the *Mensheviki* with me in my room to supporting the
Bolsheviki with them in some dirty factory. He was not at all
enthusiastic about his new assignment, and I think he would
have washed his hands of the whole business, but that such a
defection would have given his arguments for universal brotherhood a hollow ring. Our separation upset Harrison more than
me, whose nirvana could hardly be ruffled by such a mundane
circumstance as losing a friend.

I saw him next in 1932, under quite different circumstances.
I had been admitted as a partner in the firm of Andrews &
Bishop, and throughout 1927 and 1928 I enriched myself and
the firm at the rate of perhaps forty dollars a month—the
folks of Cambridge very wisely trust no new doctors or lawyers, even fifth-generation natives of the county. I was living
with my father, a widower, in his house in East Cambridge.
In 1929 Dad lost all his savings and property on the stock
market, and the next year he hanged himself with his belt from
a floor joist in the basement. After that I made more money
from the firm, despite the depression, since Dad's clients more
or less inherited me as their lawyer, and when the family
house and lot, a summer cottage at Fenwick Island, Delaware,

and one or two timber properties down the county had been sold toward meeting Dad's debts, I moved into Room 307 of the Dorset Hotel, where I've lived ever since.

And I became a cosmic cynic, although I didn't bother to mention the fact to Harrison when I saw him again, any more than I'd told him before, in so many words, that I was a saint.

He walked into my office in Lawyers' Row, next to the courthouse, one afternoon, very solemnly, and put a bottle of gin on my desk. He had grown stouter and a bit tired-looking, but was still bronzed and handsome.

"I'm back," he said, indicating the gin, and for the rest of the afternoon we drank tepid gin and walked the several streets of Cambridge, renewing our friendship.

"What happened to your revolution in Detroit?" I asked him once. "I notice they're still making cars out there."

"Ah," he shrugged, "I got fed up with the fuzzy bastards."

"And the brotherhood of man?" I asked him later.

"To hell with the brotherhood of man!" he replied. "I wouldn't want those guys for field hands, much less brothers."

"What about Miss Moscow?" I asked later yet, referring to his fiancée of 1926.

"Free lover," he snorted. "I believed all men were brothers; she thought all men were husbands. I gave the whole mess up."

And so he had, for it became apparent, as he talked, that he was in fact a saint these days, of the sort I'd been earlier. He was having little to do with the world's problems any more.

"Social justice?" I asked him.

"Impossible to achieve, irrelevant if achieved," he answered, and went on to explain that men aren't worth saving from their capitalist exploiters.

"They'd be just as bad if they were on top," he declared. "Worse, in fact: we present capitalists are gentlemanly beasts, and my comrades were beastly beasts."

It was the "inner harmony" of the "whole man," he told me, that mattered. The real revolution must be in the soul and spirit of the individual, and collective materialistic enthusiasms only distracted one from the disorder of his own soul.

"Marxism," he said, "is the opiate of the people."

He insisted I come to his house for dinner.

"To Baltimore?" I exclaimed. "Tonight?"

He blushed. "I'm living here now, Toddy." He explained that upon his recanting the Marxist heresy, his father had reinstated him in the Mack family's good graces and excellent credit ratings, and put him in charge of all the cucumber patches and raw processing plants on the Shore.

"We bought a house in East Cambridge," he said, "on the water. Just moved in. Come help us warm it."

"Us?"

"I'm married," he said, blushing again. "Loveliest thing you ever saw. Janie. Ruxton and Gibson Island, you know, but sensible. You'll love each other."

Well. I went to Harrison's house that evening, when we were good and drunk, and I recall saying "For pity's sake!" when I found that he'd bought Dad's old house—the one in which I was born and raised, and which I'd abandoned in disgust.

"Didn't know it was your family's place till I'd bought it and searched the title," Harrison claimed, beaming. He was happy about the whole thing: he'd heard since about Dad's debts and the fact that I'd lost the house along with the other property, and it gave him pleasure to have rescued it, so to speak, from unclean hands, and to be able to invite me to make it my home as often as I wished. I thanked him, and without much appetite followed him inside.

Jane, perhaps twenty-six at the time, met us at the door with an indulgent smile, and we were introduced. She was indeed "Ruxton and Gibson Island," a combination of beauty and athleticism. She wore a starched sundress and looked as if she'd just stepped from a shower after a swim. Her dark brown hair, almost black, was dried by the sun, as was her skin. That night she kept reminding me of sailboats, and has ever since. I think of her as perched on the windward washboard of a racing sailboat, a Hampton or a Star, perhaps tending the jib sheet, but certainly squinting against the sun in a brilliant blue world—a sun that heats the excellent timber beneath her thighs, and dries the spray on her face and arms, and warms the Chesapeake wind that fans her cheeks, fluffs her hair, and swells the gleaming sails. And in fact her skin, particularly across the plateau of her stomach, did indeed, I later learned, smell of sunshine, and her hair of salt spray; and the smell of her in my head never failed for five years to give me that giddy exhilaration which as a boy I always felt when I approached Ocean City on a family excursion, and the first heady spume of Atlantic in the air made my senses reel. To be sure, she insisted it was simply the result of not washing her hair as often as she should: she was in fact an ardent sailor.

For dinner we were served chicken breasts and some vegetable or other. Harrison was too drunk to bother with small talk; he ate and gave polite orders to the maid. And I was too full of gin and Jane to do much besides stare at the chickens' breasts and hers. Luckily, Harrison had told her that I was shy —his impression of my former sainthood—and so she interpreted as a timid inability to look her in the face what was actually a hushed and admiring if somewhat drunken ogling directly beneath. I've no idea what was said that evening, but I remember clearly that, as frequently used to happen when my sexual passions were aroused and unsatisfied, my ailing prostate gave me pain that night, and I was unable to sleep.

Of course I wanted to make love to her—I can't think of any attractive girl I ever saw in my youth whom I didn't wish to take to bed, and young Mrs. Mack was, if somewhat grave like her husband, a good deal more lovely and sensible than most of the women I'd encountered in my thirty-two years. Nor had I scruples about adultery—I was a cynic, remember. Still, I know that left to myself I'd never have carried my attentions beyond ogling her and telling her, half seriously, in Harrison's presence, that I was in love with her: I simply didn't choose to prejudice my friendship with Harrison, whom I really enjoyed, or to do anything which, if successful, might disturb what appeared to be a pleasant marriage. There could, I decided during the first weeks of what turned out to be a close friendship between the three of us, be no doubt that in their sober fashion Jane and Harrison were in love with each other.

But the matter was taken out of my hands one August weekend. Harrison had acquired one of his father's summer cottages, on Todd Point, downriver from Cambridge, and the three of us often spent weekends there, sailing, swimming, fishing, drinking, and talking. On the morning of the second Saturday in August he and Jane roused me out of bed in the hotel, loaded me into their roadster with themselves and two cases of beer, and set out for the cottage. It struck me during the ride that they were unusually, even deliberately, exuberant: Harrison roared risqué songs at the top of his voice; Jane, sitting in the middle, had her arms around both of us; husband and wife both called me "Toddy boy." I sighed to myself, resolved not to wonder, and emptied three bottles of beer before we finished the fifteen-mile trip to the cottage.

All morning we swam and drank, and the exaggerated liveliness and good-fellowship continued without letup. It was decided that after lunch we would load the rest of the beer into the Macks' sailboat—a beamy, clinker-built knockabout—and sail to Sharp's Island, in the Bay at the mouth of the Choptank, in order to sail back again. Harrison gave Jane a long goodbye kiss and set off to find ice, which he declared we needed in quantity; Jane set her bathing-suited self to washing the lunch dishes, and I went to sleep on the Macks' bed in the cottage's one bedroom. The absence of Harrison—the first time he'd left us alone together, as it happened, because of my supposed shyness—was conspicuous, and on my way to sleep I was acutely conscious of Jane's presence on the opposite side of the plywood partition. I fell asleep imagining her cool brown thighs—

they must be cool!—brushing each other, perhaps, as she walked about the kitchen; the gold down on her upper arms; the salt-and-sunshine smell of her. The sun was glaring through a small window at the foot of the bed; the cottage smelled of heat and resinous pine. I was tired from swimming, sleepy from beer. My dream was lecherous, violent—and unfinished. Embarrassingly. For I felt a cool, real hand caress my stomach. It might have been ice, so violently did my insides contract; I fairly exploded awake and into a sitting position. I believe it was "Good Lord!" I croaked. I croaked something, anyhow, and with both hands grabbed Jane, who sat nude—unbelievable! —on the edge of the bed; buried my face in her, so startled was I; pulled her down with me, that skin against mine; and *mirabile dictu!* I did indeed explode, so wholly that I lay without sense or strength.

Damned dream, to wake me helpless! I was choked with desire, and with fury at my impotence. Jane was nervous; after the first approach, to make which had required all her courage, she collapsed on her back beside me and scarcely dared open her eyes.

The room was dazzlingly bright! I was so shocked by the unexpectedness of it that I very nearly wept. Incredible, smooth, tight, perfect skin! I pressed my face into her, couldn't leave her untouched for an instant. I quiver even now, twenty-two years later, to write of it, and why my poor heart failed to burst I'm unable even to wonder.

Well, it was no use. I fell beside her, maddened at my incapacity and mortified at the mess I'd made. That, it turned out, was the right thing to do: my self-castigation renewed Jane's courage.

"Don't curse yourself, Toddy." She kissed me—sweetness! —and stroked my face.

"No use," I muttered into her.

"We'll see," she said lightly, entirely self-possessed now that

I seemed shy again: I resolved to behave timidly for the rest
of my life. "Don't worry about it. I can fix it."

"No you can't," I moaned.

"Yes I can," she whispered, kissing my ear and sitting up
beside me.

Merciful heavens, reader! Marry Ruxton and Gibson Island,
I charge you! Such an imaginative, athletic, informed, exuberant mistress no man ever had, I swear: she burst frequently into
spontaneous, nervous laughter. . . .

Enough. I don't really believe in chivalry any more than in
anything else—but I shan't go further. Enough to know that
we were soon able to commit jubilant adultery. Afterwards we
smoked and talked.

"How about Harrison?" I asked.

"All right."

"All right?"

"Yes."

"How?"

"He doesn't mind."

"Doesn't or *won't?"*

"Doesn't."

"He knows?" I asked incredulously.

"Approves."

"Don't you love each other?"

"Of course," she said. "Don't be silly."

"What the hell!"

"We talked it over," she explained, embarrassed again. "Harrison thinks the world of you, and I do, too. We don't see why
a woman can't make love to somebody she likes a lot, just for
the pleasure of it, without a lot of complications. Do you?"

"Of course not," I said quickly.

"That's how we felt," she said. I was becoming curious and
a bit amused. "Harrison and I love each other completely," Jane
went on, speaking very solemnly and scratching a fly bite on
one leg. "So much that neither of us could possibly ever be

jealous. If you thought for a minute that I didn't love him because of what I've done, I'd die."

"Nonsense," I assured her, just as solemnly. "I understand everything."

"Thank heaven." She sighed and rested her head on me. "We talked it over for a long time. I was scared to death. I still don't know if I should've done it, but Harrison is wonderful. He's so *objective.*"

"I've loved you since the first time I saw you," I said, and though I intended it to sound convincing, the solemnity of it made me blush.

"I wish you wouldn't say that," Jane said. "I don't think there's got to be any love in it. I like you a lot, as a friend, but that's all, Toddy."

"Not for me."

"I mean it," she said. "I enjoyed making love to you, and I hope you liked it, too. That's plenty enough, I think, without falsifying it with any romance."

"I agree, if that's how you want it," I said sedately. "You were the finest thing in the world."

She cheered up a lot, then. She went to the icebox for beer —I noticed there was at least fifty pounds of ice inside—and when I came up behind her, held her against me, and nuzzled the back of her neck, she laughed and pressed my hands more tightly against her with her own.

"I don't know how I'll be able to face Harrison," I said, in order to please her.

"Oh, you mustn't be embarrassed, Toddy. He's wonderful about this. He was as eager as I was. He really thinks you're fine."

"He's amazing," I said. She seemed afraid that I wouldn't appreciate his marvelousness. "He's a regular saint."

"He admires you a lot." Her back was toward me while she opened the beer.

"But he's better in every way than I am," I declared to the calendar on the wall. "How can I ever pay him back?"

Now I confess that this last was a loaded question; barrister that I am, I was curious to learn the extent to which Harrison had suggested to his wife that she go to bed with his friend.

"He doesn't expect any payment," she assured me. "I mean, I don't either. You mustn't feel obliged at *all*, Toddy. The thing is to not make much of it; it was just for the pleasure of it; that's all."

"I can't believe that any man could go on liking another man, though, after that," I said doubtfully.

"I swear he will, Toddy!" Jane cried, very urgently for one determined to make light of the whole matter. "How can I convince you? Honest, it was as much his idea as mine!"

I shook my head to indicate either the difficulty anyone might have in comprehending such an unorthodox situation, or the awe that an ordinary, unthinking, weak-willed mortal such as myself necessarily felt before such saintly generosity as Harrison Mack's.

"Cheer up," Jane smiled, and kissed me on the nose as she handed me my beer. I was certain my attitude had been the best possible one. She was in control, sheltering and encouraging me. Somewhat self-consciously, but apparently for my benefit, she slipped off the robe she'd covered herself with and began donning lithely the bathing suit she'd stripped off to come to me earlier. The show, I supposed, was part of the gift from Saint Harrison. It was a dazzlingly good show, and I drank it in with my beer.

After I'd calmed a little from the shock of being seduced, I sat in an old glider on the little screened porch of the cottage to watch the Choptank through the pines. Jane came through, smiled at me as though to say again, "Please don't worry, now; I swear Harrison approves," and walked down the lawn and out on the pier to the sailboat. I watched her then with pleasure as she pumped the bilge, sponged the hull and deck, and bent

the mainsail and jib to the spars. Everything she did was graceful, efficient, and lust-provoking. I shook my head in astonishment at the whole business.

I heard the car drive up, and a moment later Harrison entered through the rear of the cottage. He made a noisy business
of putting the unnecessary ice away, and after a while came
out on the porch with me, handed me yet another beer, and sat
on the glider. He was, of course, embarrassed, and despite himself made an exaggerated show of everything: lighting his cigarette and mine, taking deep draughts of the beer, stretching out
his legs, sighing, yawning. No question but that he knew very
well I had made love to his wife. We rather avoided looking
either at each other or at Jane, whose rangy body was much
before us. I smiled at the notion of Harrison's pulling a revolver
from his shirt and laying me out with three slugs of lead. I began recalling all the violent consequences of adultery I'd ever
heard of as a lawyer and a reader of tabloid newspapers. Was
this hospitable prostitution something novel, or did one simply
never hear of it?

"Well," Harrison croaked, in a voice that I believe was meant
to be hearty, "we can either keep quiet about it, like gentlemen, or talk frankly about it, like I'd like to, to make sure we
understand each other."

"Sure," I said, and began peeling the label off my beer bottle.

"She makes love well, doesn't she?" Harrison grinned.

"Oh, yes indeed!" I said.

There was a silence that Harrison didn't let last more than
an instant.

"I want you to know it's all right with me, Toddy," he said,
his voice still unnatural. "I approved of it as much as Janie did.
She likes you a lot, you know, and I do too. I think it was a
swell idea she had."

I was certain now that it had been Harrison's idea.

"Janie and I love each other completely," he went on, wishing I'd help him. "We're not stupid enough to be affected by

things like jealousy or conventions. [*Pause*] You can have sexual attractions apart from love. We both enjoy love-making. [*Pause*] If I was attracted to any girl, Janie wouldn't be silly enough to object to me going to bed with her, because she knows there wouldn't be any love in it."

"Of course not," I said.

"It's like playing tennis," Harrison laughed. "Just for the fun and exercise. Some guys would get jealous if their wife played tennis with another man, or danced with him. Actually, I guess kissing is a more serious offense than love-making, because it's no fun in itself, but just a symbol of something else."

I shook my head in apparent awe.

"*Don't feel obligated,*" Harrison laughed. "For Christ's sake don't thank me for anything. Just enjoy it. The thing is, don't make too much of it. It gets all out of proportion."

Well, I wasn't making anything out of it.

"Are any of us any different than we were?" he went on.

"I am," I said solemnly. It was clear to me that whether he realized it or not, Harrison very much wanted thanking and being obliged to; I decided to make him feel very good.

"Oh, sure," he grinned. "But you know what I mean."

"But you don't know what *I* mean," I said. "It was my first time."

"What?"

"That's right." I stared at my peeled beer bottle. "I was a virgin."

"No!" he breathed, realizing that this enormous fact was not to be laughed at. "How old? Thirty?"

"Thirty-two," I said. "I had prostate trouble for a long time."

Harrison glanced out to where Jane was walking back up the pier toward the cottage.

"Well say," he said, "I hope we didn't do anything you didn't like." He was extremely impressed and flattered.

"No," I said. "It was fine, Harrison. Of course I've nothing to compare it with."

"Well listen," he said quickly, for Jane was coming near. "For Christ's sake don't feel obligated to me. I thought it was a swell idea. I did it—we did it—because we like you. And don't get the idea—I've heard of guys like this don't get the idea I'm the kind of guy that has to push his wife off on his friends."

"Of course not."

"Well, here comes Janie," he said, relieved. "Cheer up, now. And for Christ's sake *don't feel obligated.*"

"All right," I said.

The breeze that afternoon was stiff, and a quietude settled on the three of us. For my part, I did a lot of staring at nothing, as though preoccupied with my thoughts. Harrison and Jane assumed that I was meditating on the great thing that had happened to me, and they were flattered and uneasy, and spoke in cheerful voices about nothing. Harrison, I could see, was bursting to tell Jane I'd been a virgin. Both behaved protectively and with exaggerated consideration for my feelings: it was, let me assure you, a real and thoroughgoing generosity in the Macks that I smiled at inwardly—nothing false about it except the manifestations, and that falsification was due to the strained situation, which I was aggravating by my silence. I could pretty much see where the thing was leading.

May I explain?

Really, you see, Harrison and Jane were quite ordinary people, only a little more intelligent and a lot better-looking and richer than most. They had few friends, by their own choice, preferring to be on intimate terms with just one or two people. There was nothing affected in Jane's warmth—she was naturally disposed to affection—and Harrison's intelligence, while somewhat disoriented and not really keen, was capable of convincing both of them that most social conventions are arbitrary. Yet I knew Harrison well enough to know that his emotions were often at variance with his intelligence—he realized the irrational nature of race prejudice, for example, but couldn't bring himself to like Negroes—and I supposed Jane had similar conflicts. Doubtless they'd thought about this move for a long time, each titillated with the adventure; perhaps they'd discussed it in bed together, in the dark, where their embarrassment—or eagerness—wouldn't show. Neither would want to appear overenthusiastic, I imagine, for fear of making the other suspicious—that Jane was dissatisfied or Harrison perverted, neither of which suspicions was true. I'm sure they'd worked out every detail, savoring the deed before it was committed, imagining my surprise and pleasure, and my gratitude. I really liked Harrison, and for that reason I was sorry he'd initiated the affair, because I anticipated certain unpleasant consequences from it. But it was done: Jane was officially my mistress for a while—I was sure she'd be back for more—and I resolved to enjoy the thing while it lasted, for she was all that a man, shy or otherwise, could want in a bed partner.

These were the things I thought as we rounded Todd Point and sailed on a close reach directly for Sharp's Island. Jane was at the tiller—an excellent helmsman, of course—I tended the jib sheet, and Harrison lay supine in the bilge beside the centerboard trunk, his feet forward, the mainsheet in one hand and a cigar in the other, talking to Jane, on whose bare feet his head rested. We took a swim when we reached the island, got stung by sea nettles, talked a bit about politics, and smoked cigarettes. After a while I pled fatigue and lay down to sleep on a blanket on the sand. Jane and Harrison declared they were going to walk around the island.

The time came when I felt her hand, but I had heard her returning up the beach, and so lost no manliness through surprise. I pulled her down beside me at once and kissed her.

"Where's Harrison?" I asked her.

"Other side of the island," she said, and I had the bathing suit half off her before she could add, "he's getting firewood."

"Let's go in the trees," she said, a little nervously. "They could see us from Cook's Point if they had field glasses."

"Never mind," I said. "Let's oblige me."

"Don't say that," she said.

Harrison came back as it was getting dark, dragging after him a roped bundle of firewood, and found us sitting dressed and talking on the blanket. He was not so cheerful as before, and set about silently and busily to build the fire, his stooped back half-accusing me of letting him do all the work. I let him do all the work. He remained morose throughout the rest of the evening and during the run back to the cottage. Jane made some attempt at cheerfulness, but lapsed into silence when she got no response. I watched them benignly, wondering what had happened to everyone's objectivity.

By next day the mood was gone, replaced by Harrison's usual cheerfulness; but its existence, though short-lived, was, I thought, indicative of chinks in the saintly armor. Of course, I tend to see significances in everything.

"*It was just for the pleasure of it; that's all,*" Jane had told me.

"*You can have sexual attractions apart from love,*" Harrison had told me.

Yet: "The truth is, I do love you in a way, Toddy," Jane said a week later in my hotel room. "Not the same way as I love Harrison, but it's more than just friendship; and it makes love-making more fun, doesn't it?"

"Of course," I said.

And: "A woman can love two or several men in the same way at the same time," Harrison declared after that, one night at dinner at his house, "or in different ways at the same time, or in the same way at different times, or in different ways at different times. The 'one-and-only-and-always' idea is just a conventional notion."

"Of course," I said.

Nor was I being especially hypocritical, although I'd just as readily agreed earlier to the proposition that love is separable from copulation, and copulation from love. The truth is that while I knew very well what copulation is and feels like, I'd never understood personally what love is and feels like. Are the differences between, say, one's love for his wife, his mistress, his parents, his cats, his nation, his hobby, his species, his books, and his natural environment differences in kind, or merely in degree? If in kind, are the kinds definable to the point of intelligibility? If in degree, is the necessarily general definition which can cover them all so general as to be meaningless? Is this thing a fact of nature, like thirst, or purely a human and civilized invention? If he is in love who simply decides to say, "I am in love," then love I'd never known, for often as I'd said, "I am in love," I'd said it always to women who expected to hear it, never to myself. As for copulation, whether between humans or other sorts of animals, it makes me smile.

Despite which fact, I could assent without qualm to either of the Macks' sets of propositions, for they speak only of "a person," not of everybody; who was I to say that "a person" can or cannot divorce love from copulation, when I didn't comprehend love? That "a person" can or cannot love several others at once, when I didn't comprehend love? Assenting even simultaneously to contradictory propositions has never especially troubled me, and these of the Macks weren't simultaneous. I was not and am not interested in the truth or falsehood of the statements.

What I *was* interested in, when I thought of it now and then in the weeks that followed, was the fact that the Macks had so changed their minds, because it corresponded to my speculations about the course of the affair. I scarcely regarded myself as involved in it at all: my curiosity lay entirely in the character of Harrison and, to a lesser degree, of Jane. When I'd got home that August weekend after losing my chastity, I did a bit of conjecturing, supplementing my conjectures with notes. Here is one of the outlines I wrote of Harrison's psychic process:

ANTE COITUM FELIX

I Desire for adventure.

II Titillation at idea of extra-marital sex.

III Reluctance to suggest idea to wife.

IV Love for friend—suggests idea of ex.-mar. sex for wife with friend.

V Titillation at idea.

VI Objective discussion with wife of jealousy, adultery, *etc.*

VII Planning of actual affair betw. friend and wife.

THE ACT

VIII Desperate objectivity: *"Don't feel obligated!"*

IX Real wrestling with jealousy, despite intellectual tolerance. Unusual demands on wife's affections.

X Moodiness at wife's enjoyment of affair, and refusal to hear of her canceling it.

XI Insistence that wife continue affair with friend, and mounting jealousy when she does.

XII Desultoriness except when wife asks what's up; then cheerfulness and objectivity, necessarily, or wife will end affair and chance for martyrdom.

Stages I through X, if not XII, were matters of history, easily enough inferred by the time I wrote the list. But I went on as follows:

POST COITUM TRISTE

XIII Wife, to reassure herself, decides she loves friend "in a way."

XIV Husband doubts friend appreciates enormity of his good fortune.

XV Both h. & w. become more demanding of friend; he is their property. Jealous of him, if not of each other.

XVI Want declarations of love from friend.

XVII *Friend refuses*—friendship cools.
XVIII Active dislike of friend for his ingratitude.
XIX Suspension of affair.
XX Period of mutual silence: h. & w. love each other more
than before, in self-defense.

This was as far as I could see with any certainty, but from there I outlined a number of possible directions that the business might take:

I Permanent disaffection (probable)
II Resumption of affair on original basis (quite possible)
III Resumption of affair on part of wife, against husband's will (very doubtful)
IV Resumption of qualified affection, but no more sex (quite possible)

I made other outlines, as well, in the days that followed, but this one, at least as far as Stage XX, proved the most accurate. First of all, as I have already suggested, when the horns on Harrison's brow were but a few days old, Jane and I contrived to lengthen them a bit, whether at his instigation or not I can only guess. I had returned to my room for a nap after lunch, as was my practice even then. She was waiting for me, and not long afterwards she said, "The truth is, I do love you in a way, Toddy. Not the same way as I love Harrison, but it's more than just friendship; and it makes love-making more fun, doesn't it?"

"Of course," I said.

I was sitting on the edge of my bed. She was standing directly in front of me. I believed she wanted me to tell her that I loved her.

"I love you," I said. I was right: she did want to hear it.

During the next year or so the affair went on strongly. Janie actually began spending every Tuesday and Friday night in my room—fantastic, so to schedule it!—and Harrison dropped into

the office at least twice a day. They insisted that I take dinner
with them every night, and Harrison even suggested that I
move in with them.

"You can have your old bedroom back," he said. "I've always felt it was the Andrews' house, and that we were the
guests."

The mention of my old bedroom, where I'd slept from age
zero to age seventeen, reminded me of a certain adventure, and
I laughed.

"I can't help it," Harrison smiled, a little abashed.

"No, no, it's not that," I grinned. But I turned his proposal
down, to be sure. Incredible! Yet he was, I'm sure, more manly
in every way than I—it was a matter of sheer generosity, I
swear!

Well, the thing soon commenced getting out of hand, as I'd
feared. Jane was as lovely and skillful as ever, but she was too
loving, too solicitous. Harrison was planning a summer trip to
the Bahamas for the three of us. Jane spoke vaguely for a while
of my marrying some *intelligent* girl, but soon spoke of it not
at all. Harrison mentioned it once too, with the implication that
the four of us would live precisely like one happy family. All
this out of the excess of their love for me. It was time to take
measures.

Once he stopped in my office when I happened to be preparing a suit *a vinculo matrimonii* for Dorothy Miner, a plump
Negro girl of eighteen, who picked crabs at one of the seafood
houses. She was an entirely uneducated girl, a friend of mine,
and she was arranging a divorce from her husband of a month,
one Junior Miner, who had abandoned her. Dorothy's skin,
teeth, and eyes were excellent, and she snapped her gum. Our
relationship was Platonic.

"Hi, Harrison," I greeted him. "This is Dorothy."

Dorothy grinned hello and snapped a salute.

"How d'you do," Harrison said, scarcely noticing her.
"Coming for lunch, Toddy?"

Recently he'd been taking me to lunch uptown.

"In a few minutes," I said. "Dorothy here is divorcing her husband, and I'm handling her suit."

"Oh?" He sat in one of the chairs, lit a cigar, and prepared to read a magazine.

I peered into the waiting room. The secretary had already gone to lunch.

"She's poor," I went on, "so I take it out in trade."

Harrison flinched as though I'd slapped him and, blushing deeply, looked at me with a twisted smile.

"Are you kidding?" He looked surreptitiously at Dorothy, who at my statement had clapped her hand over her mouth to hold down laughter and chewing gum.

"No indeed," I grinned. "I'm getting to be real good at this business. Isn't that so, Dorothy?"

"Whatever you say, Mister Andrews," Dorothy giggled; it was a tremendously funny joke.

"What the hell, Toddy!" Harrison laughed sharply.

"As a matter of fact," I said, moving toward her, "I believe her bill is overdue right now."

Dorothy giggled and fussed with her hair. But she rose uncertainly from her chair, brushed her skirt flutteringly, and stood facing me.

"Aw, say, Toddy!" Harrison croaked, getting up from his chair.

"Excuse me," I said. "You go on to lunch; I'll be along in a minute."

"What the hell, Toddy!" Harrison exclaimed, aghast and angry. "I'll see you later!" He left the office as fast as he could, actually perspiring from his humiliation and embarrassment. I went to the window and watched him hurry up the sidewalk.

Dorothy, meanwhile, watched my face for some clue. "What you up to, Mister Andrews?" she demanded, bursting into giggles after the question.

I don't recall my answer, but I'm sure Dorothy laughed at

whatever it was, since she thought me mad. I went to join Harrison.

"What the hell, Toddy!" he said during lunch, for perhaps the third time. "I'd have felt cheap!"

He was apologizing for what he feared I'd call his prudery, to be sure, and perhaps even chastising himself for having missed his chance; but more than that he was, I saw, deeply insulted.

"I'm not prejudiced; I just couldn't have anything to do with a Negro girl," is what he said, but "*You've been unfaithful to Jane and to me; you've defiled yourself and us in that black hussy*" is what he meant.

"Do you make a practice of that?" he asked me.

"Some of 'em pay in eggs," I said blithely. "But a man can use just so many eggs."

"Aw, hell, Toddy."

"What's the matter, man?" I laughed. "Don't you want me to put what I've learned into practice?"

"You may do anything you want to, of course," Harrison said. "I've said that all along."

"Hell, Harrison, you knew I wasn't a virgin, and Jane did, too. What did you think I'd been doing for thirty-two years?"

But of course they didn't know; they'd believe anything I told them. Harrison could only shake his head. His appetite was gone.

"You mustn't take things seriously," I said cheerfully. "No matter how you approach it, everything we do is ridiculous." I laughed again, as I do every time I remember what happened in my bedroom when I was seventeen.

"Friendship's not a ridiculous thing," Harrison said, full of emotion. "I don't see why you've decided to hurt Jane and me."

"Friendship may or may not be ridiculous," I said, "but it sure is impossible."

"No, it's not," Harrison said. He was very near tears, I think, and it looked ridiculous in a robust fellow like him. "I just wish you hadn't hurt us. There wasn't any reason to. I'm not angry. I just wish you hadn't done it."

"Nonsense," I said. "I didn't say anything."

"Do you think love is ridiculous?" Harrison asked.

"Everything is ridiculous."

"Why'd you lie about being a virgin? There wasn't any reason to."

"You deserved that for expecting to hear it, and being pleased when you heard it," I said.

Harrison practically slumped on the table. I really believe I had destroyed his strength.

"You don't like us," he declared hopelessly.

"Buck up, man, this is degrading!" I said. "What difference does anything make? Of course I was acting, but you all wanted an act. How do you think Jane would've felt if I'd told her the truth? I'm on your side."

"The hell you are," Harrison grumbled; he was angry enough at me now to get up and walk out of the restaurant. He even left me with the check.

It was Tuesday, and there was a good chance that Jane was in my room, waiting for me to come up for my nap. I took my time, strolling down to Long Wharf before heading toward the hotel, so that Harrison could rescue her from my clutches. When finally I went in, no one was there, but I thought I detected the smell of her skin in the air. Perhaps it was my imagination. I sighed and, for the first time since that August weekend, really relaxed. It was a pity: the Macks were agreeable people, and they would have a bad day.

IV. The Captain's confession

Now, what was I doing? I believe I didn't explain how Jane got to be back in my bed again by 1937, did I? Well, I'll finish the story later, as we go along: I've stayed close to the plot for a good long time now. Wait: looking back I see that the whole purpose of the digression was to explain why it was that I was incapable of great love for people, or at least solemn love. And I see I didn't explain it yet, at that. Good Lord! The last half of this book, I'm afraid, will be nothing but all these explanations I've promised and postponed. Let's forget all this for the moment and get Capt. Osborn his glass of rye, which I've been holding all this time, before he dies of thirst and old age.

Very well: I tiptoed from my room, so as not to disturb Jane again from her slumbers, and took the old rascal his drink, which he threw down neat with much sputtering and fuming.

"Ah, that's a good boy, son," he grinned upon finishing. Already his face was regaining its color. "If yer headed out, why I'll jest take yer arm, sir."

Mister Haecker had watched us listlessly all this time. That morning he seemed more nervous and preoccupied than usual, and—I swear this isn't all hindsight—I believe I suspected just then that for some reason or other this June 21 or 22 was going to be as momentous a day for him as for me.

"I'm headed out right now, Cap'n," I said. Capt. Osborn wheezed to his feet and limped over to take my arm, so that I could help him down the steps.

"Going out today, Mister Haecker?" I asked.

"No, son," Mister Haecker sighed. He looked as if he would say more; as if, in fact, the "more" were filling his head to bursting. One terrible look he flashed me, of pure panic; I've not forgotten it. I waited a moment for it to come. "No," Mister Haecker said again, flatly this time, and rose to return to his room.

Capt. Osborn and I left then, and started the slow descent of the stairs. I tried carefully to feel every step, so full was I of the wonder of this day; of my new and final answer, and my stupidity at not having thought of it years ago.

But I am not a thinker, nor have I ever been. My thinking is always after the fact, the effect of my circumstances, never the other way round.

"This is step number nine," I said to myself. "Isn't it a nice step? This is step number ten, as you go down, or eighteen as you come up. Isn't it grand? This is step number eleven, or seventeen . . ." and so on. There was plenty of time to enjoy each step for its particular virtues, because of Capt. Osborn's lameness. I was having a fine time.

On step number seventeen going down, or eleven coming up, Capt. Osborn pinched my arm, the one supporting him, and chuckled softly. "How was it last night, Toddy boy?"

I looked at him in amused surprise. "What?"

The Captain chortled. "Ye don't s'pose a nosy old dog like me don't know what's up, do ye?" He poked me with his elbow, and actually winked.

"You lecherous old bastard!" I grinned. "I bet you've been listening at my door!"

"Naw, boy, I got ears for that kind o' carryin's-on. Shucks! Don't think I give a durn about it, boy. I'd have 'em up to my room by the clutch if I weren't most dead."

I said nothing, wondering only why he'd bothered to tell me about it.

"I been listenin' to you and her for a right smart while now," he said seriously, but with his eyes twinkling. "She's a fine gal, and a frisky-lookin' one. You know how it is when yer old."

"How is it?"

Capt. Osborn snorted and smacked me on the shoulder. "Well, sir, I jest couldn't go on a-listenin' to ye any more, Toddy boy, without ye knew about it. 'Tweren't noways fair. I even left my door open some nights, now that's how wicked I am. Ye can think what ye like; I done told ye now and it's off my chest."

He seemed really relieved—of course he was a little drunk, too.

"How long have you been listening?" I asked him. "Since 1932?"

"Durn near," Capt. Osborn admitted glumly. "I swear I never did no more'n leave my door open, though. I don't care, Toddy; ye can hate me if ye want."

Now he didn't dare to look me in the eye. He was unable to speak for shame. We were near the bottom of the steps.

"So you think she's frisky-looking, do you?" The change in my voice gave him courage, but he still felt bad.

"I've had a bunch o' women, Toddy," he whispered to me solemnly. "My wife, God rest her poor soul, was a fine woman, despite she weren't no beauty; and a waterman—well, ye run into lots o' floozies round the boats, want to help a drudgeman spend his wad. Some of 'em was mighty lively, too, for a small town, sir! And I been to the city, and the fancy houses, I won't lie." He smiled at the memory, then grew solemn again. "But I swear to God as I'm standin' here before ye this minute, may He smite me dead if I'm a-lyin', I never in my life seen a woman could hold a candle to that gal o' yourn, Toddy. She's a beauty, I declare!"

"You old goat," I said after a minute.

"I shan't do it no more, Toddy," he said wretchedly.

"Indeed you shan't." I laughed, and his spirits were soon restored. I had had a magnificent idea, an idea such as one should have every day. Oh, it was going to be a lovely momentous day. "Good morning to you, Cap'n," I said when we reached the lobby. "I may go by your corner later on today. I'm going to pay my bill now."

But Capt. Osborn wasn't ready to let me go yet. He held on to my arm and chewed his coffee-stained mustache for a minute, composing what he had to say. I waited respectfully, for I was in no hurry at all.

"Do you believe that malarky o' Haecker's?" he asked finally, a little suspiciously. " 'Bout how nice it is to git old?"

"No."

"I sleep light," he said after a moment, looking past me to the street door. "Some days I don't sleep a wink from one day to the next, sir, but I don't git tired, or I guess I'm the same tired all the time, sleep or no. Ye git that way when yer old; ye don't need sleep 'cause ye ain't able to do nothin' when yer awake to tire ye out no more'n ye already are. An old man hears what he ain't s'posed to hear, and don't hear half what he ought to. I've heard you and that young lady till I wanted to holler, if my head wasn't clogged up with the catarrh and my lights a-burnin' with the bronchitis and my joints stiff with the rheumatism, and I'd cuss myself for listenin', and couldn't stop to save me. I'd cuss myself for not gittin' up to close the door, but when yer old as me, gittin' up is a chore, and ye got to sort o' collect yerself, and then ye jest wait all day to git back in bed, but can't sleep 'cause ye know that sooner or later that there bed ye was so hot to crawl into is goin' to be the last time ye'll crawl into it. That ain't no fit lullaby to git sung to sleep with, Toddy! And when I'd git up and go to the door, why I could jest hear ye all the plainer, and I'd tell myself that right there was somethin' I'll never do again on this earth!"

He paused for breath; I was astonished at his volubility.

"Well, sir, Haecker might be right; he's a sight smarter'n me, but I swear I can't see one durn thing to this *old* business. The sinus keeps a-fillin' yer nose till yer fit to drown, and yer eyes water, and yer legs go to sleep if ye set still, and yer bones pain ye if ye move. I'd rather be forty and feel good and be dumb as a post, and be fit to do work, than to feel all day like I weren't rightly alive, and hurt all the time and have to blow my nose till it's sore, and crack a cane on my legs to keep the blood a-goin', even if I knew all there was to know."

"Mister Haecker's just a kid," I smiled, delighted to hear Capt. Osborn talk.

"He ain't but seventy and fit as a fiddle," the old man snorted. "I'd of said the same thing at seventy if I'd of commenced to think about it, which I didn't commence to think about it till I was eighty. And I can tell you today it's an awful thing to think about, this *dyin'*, and I would rather be chokin' from the sinus, and not fit to git out o' bed no more, and use a bedpan and eat dry toast, than to be dead, sir! Any man tells ye yer goin' to git to like the idea jest 'cause yer old, he's lyin' to ye, and I want to tell ye right now, when the time comes I am goin' to cuss and holler."

Well, he went on in that vein, and I remember it all, but that's enough of Capt. Osborn for now—perhaps you don't enjoy old men as I do. When he had said his piece—and completely forgotten, I'm certain, what he'd been apologizing for —he went out into the street to take his place on the loafers' bench uptown with his cronies in the sunshine. I loved him, if I loved anyone, I think; death for him would be the hyphenated break in a rambling, illiterate monologue, a good way for it to be if you're most people. He was fooling himself and not fooling himself about it, so that ultimately he wasn't fooling himself at all, and hence it wasn't necessary to feel any pity for him. I felt much sorrier, in my uninvolved way, for Mister Haecker, with his paeans to old age and gracious death: he was really fooling himself, and one could anticipate that he would someday have a difficult time of it. In the meanwhile, he must spend all his energies shoring up his delusion, and do it, moreover, alone, for his intensity and prudishness found him no friends; Osborn, on the contrary, sniffed and wheezed and creaked and spat, and cursed and complained, and never knew a gloomy day in his life.

I remembered my little plan and went to the registration desk. Jerry Hogey, the manager, was on duty. He was a friend of mine, and it was due to his understanding of the world that Jane had been able to come to my room despite hotel policy at any time for the last five years. I bid him good morning as usual, and borrowing a sheet of hotel stationery from him, scribbled a note to Jane.

"This is for the young lady, Jerry," I said, folding it and giving it to him.

"Sure."

Then, as I had done every morning since 1930 (and still do), I wrote out a check for one dollar and fifty cents payable to the Dorset Hotel, for the day's lodging.

V. A *raison de coeur*

That's right, I pay my hotel bill every day, and reregister every day, too, despite the fact that the hotel offers weekly and monthly and even seasonal rates for long-term guests. It's no eccentricity, friend, nor any sign of stinginess on my part: I have an excellent reason for doing so, but it is a *raison de coeur*, if I may say so—a reason of the heart and not of the head.

Doubly so; literally so. Listen: eleven times the muscle of my heart contracted while I was writing the four words of the preceding sentence. Perhaps six hundred times since I began to write this little chapter. Seven hundred thirty-two million, one hundred thirty-six thousand, three hundred twenty times since I moved into the hotel. And no less than one billion, sixty-seven million, six hundred thirty-six thousand, one hundred sixty times has my heart beat since a day in 1919, at Fort George G. Meade, when an Army doctor, Captain John Frisbee, informed me, during the course of my predischarge physical examination, that each soft beat my sick heart beat might be my sick heart's last. This fact—that having begun this sentence, I may not live to write its end; that having poured my drink, I may not live to taste it, or that it may pass a live man's tongue to burn a dead man's belly; that having slumbered, I may never wake, or having waked, may never living sleep—this for thirty-five years has been the condition of my existence, the great fact of my life: had been so for eighteen years already, or five hundred forty-nine million, sixty thousand, four hundred eighty heartbeats, by June 21 or 22 of 1937. This is the enormous question, in its thousand trifling forms (Having heard tick, will I hear tock? Having served, will I volley? Having sugared, will I cream? Itching, will I scratch? Hemming, will I haw?), toward answering which all my thoughts and deeds, all my dreams and energies have been oriented. This is the problem which, having answered it thrice before without solving it, I had waked this one momentous morning with the key to, gratuitously, gratis, like that! This question, the fact of my life, is, reader, the fact of my book as well: the question which, now answered but yet to be explained, answers, reader, everything, explains all.

Well, perhaps not all, or at least perhaps not clearly. It doesn't directly explain, for example, why I chose and choose to pay my bill daily, every morning, instead of weekly or seasonally. Don't think, I beg you, that I fear not living to get my money's worth if I pay too far ahead: lose money I might, but fear losing it, never. There's nothing in me of Miss Holiday Hopkinson, my ninety-year-old neighbor and senior member of the D.E.C., who buys her one-a-day vitamin pills in the smallest bottles—for her, the real economy size—and sleeps fully dressed, her arms folded funereally upon her chest, so as to cause, by her dying, the least possible trouble for anybody. No, I pay my buck-fifty every morning to remind myself—should I ever forget!—that I'm renting another day from eternity, remitting the interest on borrowed time, leasing my bed on the chance I may live to sleep on it once more, for at least the beginning of another night. It helps me maintain a correct perspective, reminds me that long-range plans, even short-range plans, have, for me at least, no value.

To be sure, one doesn't want to live as though each day may be his last, when there is some chance that it may be only his next. One needs, even in my position, something to counter-balance the immediacy of a one-day-at-a-time existence, a life on the installment plan. Hence my *Inquiry*, properly to prepare even for the beginning of which, as I see it, would require more lifetimes than it takes a lazy Buddhist to attain Nirvana. My *Inquiry* is timeless, in effect; that is, I proceed at it as though I had eternity to inquire in. And, because processes persisted in long enough tend to become ends in themselves, it is enough for me to do an hour's work, or two hours' work, on my *Inquiry* every night after supper, to make me feel just a little bit outside of time and heartbeats.

So, I begin each day with a gesture of cynicism, and close it with a gesture of faith; or, if you prefer, begin it by reminding myself that, for me at least, goals and objectives are without value, and close it by demonstrating that the fact is irrelevant. A gesture of temporality, a gesture of eternity. It is in the tension between these two gestures that I have lived my adult life.

VI. Maryland beaten biscuits

Now you know my secret, or an important part of it. No one else—except Dr. Frisbee, I suppose—ever knew it, not even my excellent friend Harrison. Why should I have told him? I never told him I was a saint, and yet he became one himself soon enough afterwards. I never told him in so many words that I was a cynic, and yet he's one today, as far as I know. If I had told him of my heart condition he'd only have tried to acquire one too, and I've no particular wish to make anyone unhappy. No, I long ago learned that one's illnesses are both pleasanter and more useful if one keeps their exact nature to himself: one's friends, uncertain as to the cause of one's queer behavior and strange sufferings, impute to one a mysteriousness often convenient. Even Jane never suspected my ailing heart, and though she well knew—from how many painful nights!— that something was wrong with me, I never told her about my infected prostate, either. As a result, she often attributed to herself failures in our intercourse that were incontestably mine, and Jane—proud Jane—is never lovelier or more desirable than when contrite.

Enough: I paid my hotel bill, then, and stepped onto High Street just as the clock on the People's Trust building struck seven. Already the air was warm; it promised to be a blistering day, like the day before, when temperature and humidity both were in the nineties. Very few people were about yet, and only an occasional automobile wandered down the quiet expanse of the street. I crossed diagonally against the traffic—to the corner of Christ Episcopal Church, whose lovely stones were softly greened, and strolled from there down the left side of High Street toward Long Wharf, eating my breakfast as I walked.

I recommend three Maryland beaten biscuits, with water, for your breakfast. They are hard as a haul-seiner's conscience and dry as a dredger's tongue, and they sit for hours in your morning stomach like ballast on a tender ship's keel. They cost little, are easily and crumblessly carried in your pockets, and if forgotten and gone stale, are neither harder nor less palatable than when fresh. What's more, eaten first thing in the morning and followed by a cigar, they put a crabberman's thirst on you, such that all the water in a deep neap tide can't quench—and none, I think, denies the charms of water on the bowels of morning? Beaten biscuits, friend: beaten with the back of an ax on a sawn stump behind the cookhouse; you really need a slave system, I suppose, to produce the best beaten biscuits, but there is a colored lady down by the creek, next door to the dredge builder's. . . . If, like a condemned man, I had been offered my choice from man's cuisine for this my final earthly breakfast, I'd have chosen no more than what I had.

Few things are stable in this world. Your morning stomach, reader, ballasted with three Maryland beaten biscuits, will be stable.

High Street, where I walked, is like no other street in Cambridge, or on the peninsula. A wide, flat boulevard of a street, gently arched with edge-laid yellow brick, it runs its gracious best from Christ Church and the courthouse down to Long Wharf, the municipal park, two stately blocks away. One is tempted to describe it as lined with mansions, until one examines it in winter, when the leaves are down and the trees gaunt as gibbets. Mansions there are—two, three of them— but the majority of the homes are large and inelegant. What makes High Street lovely are the trees and the street itself. The trees are enormous: oaks and cottonwood poplars that rustle loftily above you like pennants atop mighty masts; that when leaved transform the shabbiest houses into mansions; that corrugate the concrete of the wide sidewalks with the idle flexing of their roots. An avenue of edge-laid yellow bricks is the only pavement worthy of such trees, and like them, it dignifies the things around it. Automobiles whisper over this brick like quiet yachts; men walking on the outsized sidewalk under the outsized poplars are dwarfed into dignity. The boulevard terminates in a circular roadway on Long Wharf—terminates, actually, in the grander boulevard of the Choptank. Daniel Jones, upon whose plantation the city of Cambridge now rests, put his house near where this street runs. Colonel John Kirk, Lord Baltimore's Dorchester land agent, built in 1706 the town's first house near where this street runs. There are slave quarters; there are porch columns made of ships' masts; there are ancient names bred to idle pursuits; there are barns of houses housing servantless, kinless, friendless dodderers; there are brazen parades and bold seagulls, eminence and imbecility; there are Sunday pigeons and excursion steamers and mock oranges—all dignified by the great trees and soft glazed brick of the street. The rest of Cambridge is rather unattractive.

As was my custom, I strolled down to the circle and over beside the yacht basin. The river was glassy and empty of boats, too calm to move the clappers of the bell buoy out in the channel, a mile away. A single early motor truck inched across the long, low bridge. The flag above the yacht club predicted fair weather. With a great sense of well-being I tossed the last hard half of my breakfast biscuits at a doubler crab mating lazily just beneath the surface. As was *their* custom, the gentleman did the swimming while the soft lady beneath, locked to him with all her legs, allowed him his pleasure, which might last for fourteen hours. Crabbers refer to the male and female thus coupled as one crab, a "doubler," just as Plato imagined the human prototype to be male and female joined into one being. My biscuit landed to starboard of the lovers, and the gentleman slid, unruffled, six inches to port, then submerged, girl friend and all, in search of the missile that had near scuttled his affair. I laughed and made a mental note to make a physical note, for my *Inquiry*, of the similarity between the crabbers and Plato, and to remind Jane that there were creatures who took longer than I.

I lit my first cigar and completed the circle, coming around to the side nearest the creek. Work was commencing in the lumber mill and shipyard across the creek mouth from where I stood: a weathered bugeye, worn by forty or fifty years of oyster-dredging, was hauled up on the railway, and a crew of men scraped barnacles and marine growth from her bottom. I surveyed the scene critically and with pleasure, but no more intently than usual, despite the fact that I might never see it again, for I was determined to preserve the typicality of this great day. I had knocked the first ash from my cigar and was preparing to walk part way up High Street to the garage where my boat lay a-building, when my satisfied eye caught something new in the picture: a brightly lettered poster tacked to a piling at the farthest corner of the wharf, where the creek joined the river, and at the foot of the piling a small package or bale tied with a string. I walked over to investigate.

ADAM'S ORIGINAL & UNPARALLELED FLOATING OPERA, announced the poster; *Jacob R. Adam, Owner & Captain.* 6 BIG ACTS! it went on to declare: DRAMA, MIN-STRELS, VAUDEVILLE! *Moral & Refined!* TONIGHT TONIGHT TONIGHT TONIGHT! *Admissions:* 20¢, 35¢, 50¢! TONIGHT TONIGHT! FREE *Concert Begins at* 7:30 *PM! Show Begins 8:00 PM!*

The bundle at the foot of the piling contained printed hand-bills advertising the show in more detail; it was obviously dumped there temporarily by the showboat's advance man. I took a handbill from the bundle, stuck it into my coat pocket to read at my leisure, and continued my morning walk.

I smoked my way back onto High Street, the handbill folded

in my pocket and my mind preoccupied with scampering ideas as flitting as idle mice. In thirty seconds I'd forgotten all about the poster, the handbill, and ADAM'S ORIGINAL & UN-PARALLELED FLOATING OPERA.

VII. My unfinished boats

When I think of Cambridge and of Dorchester County, the things I think of, understandably, are crabbing, oystering, fishing, muskrat-trapping, duckhunting, sailing, and swimming. It is virtually impossible, no matter what his station, for a boy to grow to puberty in the County without experiencing most of these activities and becoming proficient in one or two of them.

Virtually, but not entirely. I, for example, though I was not a sheltered child, managed to attain the age of twenty-seven years without ever having gone crabbing, oystering, fishing, miskrat-trapping, duckhunting, sailing, or even swimming, despite the fact that all my boyhood companions enjoyed these pursuits. I just never got interested in them. Moreover, I've never tasted an oyster; I can't enjoy crabmeat; I'd never choose fish for dinner; I detest wild game of any sort, rodent or fowl; and although Col. Henry Morton, who owns the biggest to-mato cannery on God's earth, is a peculiar friend of mine, the tomatoes that line his coffers upset my digestion. But lest you conclude too easily that this represents some position of mine, let me add that I *have* done some sailing since I set up my law practice here in 1927—though I still can't handle a sailboat myself—and I'd become, as a matter of fact, something of an expert swimmer by the time of this story. And this *does*, in a small way, reflect a philosophical position of mine, or at least a general practice, to wit: being less than consistent in prac-tically everything, so that any general statement about me will probably be inadequate. To be sure, many people make such statements anyway—I get the impression at times that doing so constitutes a chief activity of the town's idle intelligences— but I have the not-inconsiderable satisfaction of knowing that they're wrong and of hearing them contradict one another (and thereby, I conclude, cancel one another out).

All this, deviously, by way of introduction to my boatbuilding, for my next step, after completing my morning stroll around Long Wharf, was to turn off High Street into an alley running down to the creek. There, in a two-car garage loaned me by a friend and client of mine, every morning I did an hour's work on the boat I'd been building for some years.

My boats—what shall I say of them? In my life I've built two. The first I started when I was perhaps twelve years old. I had devoured every yachting magazine I could lay my hands on, had "sent away" for blueprints and specifications, had tossed and dreamed of hulls and spars and sails until I was dizzy with yearning. To build a boat—that seemed to me a deed almost holy in its utter desirability. Then to provision it, and some early morning to slip quietly from my mooring, to run down the river, sparkling in the sun, out into the broad reaches of the Bay, and down to the endless oceans. Never have I regarded my boyhood as anything but pleasant, and the intensity of this longing to escape must be accounted for by the attractiveness of the thing itself, not by any unattractiveness of my surroundings. In short, I was running *to*, not running *from*, or so I believe.

But I could never be content with anything even remotely within my power to achieve. My father, delighted at the idea of my building a boat, suggested various types of skiffs, scows, prams, dinghies, and tenders, and even a simple catboat: he would help me, of course, with the steaming of the frames and strakes. But what! Go to Singapore in a dinghy? Cap the black growlers of the northern ocean in a row-skiff? For me it was more a problem of choosing between a fifty-foot auxiliary sloop and a fifty-foot auxiliary schooner. The sloop rig, I remember arguing to myself, lent itself more readily to one-man cruising, and I'd not need to rely for help on the indistinct young girls I somehow saw lying about the deck; on the other hand, if in a typhoon, say, I should be dismasted, that would be all, brother, were I to put my eggs in one basket as the sloop rig does. A divided rig—schooner, yawl, or ketch, in the order of my preference—would leave me some hope of limping bravely to port under the remaining mast. To be sure, these delicate arguments had to be kept to myself. I allowed my father to buy me enough lumber for a skiff, and I remember quite clearly regretting then that he and Mrs. Aaron, the current housekeeper, weren't dead, so that I could commence work on my schooner without their scoffing to embarrass me.

Finally I more or less began work on the skiff, declaring it to be a lifeboat for my schooner. Alas! I was clumsy with tools, if deft and ingenious with daydreams. My measurements were wrong, my lines out of plumb and out of symmetry, my saw cuts rough and crooked, my nails askew. All summer I worked on the thing, correcting one error with another, changing the length and shape of a miscut strake to fit a mismeasured frame, laying a split batten over a gaping seam, ignoring fatal errors into nonexistence, covering incompetence with incompetence, and pretending that the mere labor and bulk of the thing would somehow rectify all the fundamental mistakes implied in the very first step (rather, misstep) of construction. I made it known that I desired neither help nor advice, and my father, chalking the cost of the lumber up to my education, left me alone.

When autumn came I lost interest in boatbuilding. Why labor so on a dinghy, when what I wanted was a schooner? And a schooner, of course, I could never build where there were people to watch and scoff. Left to myself, absolutely to myself, I was certain I could build one and surprise everybody with the finished product. But it must be only the finished product that they judge me by, not the steps of construction: there would be a grandeur in the forest, so to speak, transcending and redeeming any puny deficiencies in the individual trees. All through the winter the half-framed hull weathered untouched in the back yard, like a decomposing carcass whose ribs are partly exposed; by spring I was interested in nothing but horses. The skiff remained in the yard, a silent reproach to my fickleness, for perhaps six years. Then one year, while I was in the Army, a hurricane blew the boat off its sawhorses, and the rotting planks sprang from the frames. My father used it for firewood, I believe.

I tell you this story because it's representative of a great many features of my boyhood. My daydreams, my conceptions of how things should be, were invariably grandiose, and I labored at them prodigiously and always secretly. But my talent for doing correctly the small things that constitute the glorious whole was defective—I never mastered first principles—and so the finished product, while perhaps impressive to the untutored, was always mediocre to the knowledged. To how many of my young achievements does this not apply! I dazzled old ladies at piano recitals, but never really mastered the scales; won the tennis championships of my high school—a school indifferent to tennis—but never really mastered the strokes; graduated first in my class, but never really learned to think. And so on: it's a painful list.

Now a deficiency like this, which doubtless stems from over-eagerness to shine in the eyes of one's neighbors, can be hard to throw off, and I'm confident I should have it yet, but that the Army cured me of it.

Not the Army as such—heavens no. The Army as such was a terrible experience in every way. I enlisted impulsively in 1917 and realized before the bus left Cambridge what a really distasteful experience I was going to have. And I had it, too: every unpleasant thing that could happen to a soldier in that insane army happened to me, except being gassed and being

killed. Certainly I wasn't patriotic. I had no feelings at all about
the issues involved, if there were any (I've never been curious
enough really to find out).

Well, this isn't a book about my war experiences, though I
could write a good long book about them, and it wouldn't resemble any war book you've ever read, either. Except for a
single incident—and I mean to tell you about it at once—my
Army career was largely without influence on the rest of my
life. This one incident, during the battle in the Argonne Forest,
I find significant in two ways, at least: it in some manner
cured the tendency described above, and it provided me with
the second of two unforgettable demonstrations of my own
animality.

The Argonne fighting was well under way before my outfit
was sent in to replace a rifle company that had been destroyed.
It was my first and only battle. I was, of course, inadequate
fighting material—what intelligent boy isn't?—but I was no more
afraid as the lorries drove us to the front than were any of my
fellows, and I've never been cowardly, to my knowledge, in
matters of physical violence. It was late afternoon when we
arrived, and the Germans were laying down an incredible barrage on our positions. We were hustled out of the lorries onto
the ground, and it was much as I imagine jumping from an
airplane would be: relative calm, and then bang! horrible confusion. We were all paralyzed. None of us remembered anything, not anything that we'd been told. Frightful! Horrifying!
The air, I swear, was simply split with artillery. The ground—
you couldn't stand on it, no matter how loudly your officers
shouted. We all simply fell down: fortunately for us, I guess.
I suppose most of you, if you are men of this century, have
experienced the like, or worse.

I've no idea what we did. Indeed, I've often wondered, if
there were many soldiers like me, how the Allies won the war.
God knows how much the government had spent on my train-
ing, hurried as it was, and then I—all of us—simply collapsed.

No cowardice, no fear (not yet); we were simply robbed of muscle by the noise.

Just before dark, I remember, I found myself belly-down on a sort of ridge. All around were splintered tree stumps, three feet high. I had no idea what I was doing there. The sun was almost down, and there was a great deal of smoke in the air. A number of uniformed figures seemed to be attending to some business of theirs in a hollow below me. The barrage, I think, had ceased, or else I was totally deaf.

"Why," I said to myself, rather drunkenly, "those men are German soldiers. That is the enemy."

I could scarcely believe it. For heaven's sake! German soldiers! It occurred to me that I was supposed to kill them. I didn't even look around to see if the rest of the United States Army was with me; I simply fired my rifle any number of times at the men working in the hollow. None of them dropped dead, or even seemed to notice their danger. It seems to me they should have counterattacked, or taken cover, or something. No, sir. I remember very carefully reloading and firing, reloading and firing, reloading and firing. It was a hell of an easy war, but how in the world did you go about killing the enemy soldiers? And where was everyone else?

The next thing that happened (for scenes changed in this battle as in dreams) happened in the dark. Suddenly it had been nighttime for a while. This time it was I who was in a hollow, on all fours in a shell hole half full of muddy water. I still had my rifle, but it was empty, and if I owned any more ammunition I didn't remember how to put it in the rifle. I was just there, on hands and knees, my head hanging down, staring at the water. Everything was quiet again; only a few flares made a hissing noise as they drifted down through the air. And now there came real fear, quickly but not suddenly, a purely physical sensation. It swept over me in shuddering waves from my thighs and buttocks to my shoulders and jaws and back again, one shock after another, exactly as though rolls of flesh were undulating. There was no cowardice involved; in fact, my mind wasn't engaged at all—either I was thinking of something else or, more probably, I was just stupefied. Cowardice involves choice, but fear is independent of choice. When the waves reached my hips and thighs I opened my sphincters; when they crossed my stomach and chest I retched and gasped; when they struck my face my jaw hung slack, my saliva ran, my eyes watered. Then back they'd go again, and then return. I've no way of knowing how long this lasted: perhaps only a minute. But it was the purest and strongest emotion I've ever experienced. I could actually, for a part of the time it lasted, regard myself objectively: a shocked, drooling animal in a mudhole. It is one thing to agree intellectually to the proposition that man is a species of animal; quite another to realize, thoroughly and for good, your personal animality, to the extent that you are actually never able to oppose the terms *man* and *animal*, even in casual speech; never able to regard your fellow creatures except as more or less intelligent, more or less healthy, more or less dangerous, more or less adequate *fauna*; never able to regard their accomplishments except as the tricks of more or less well-trained beasts. In my case this has been true since that night, and no one—not my father, nor Jane, nor myself— have I been able even for a moment to regard differently.

The other part of the incident followed immediately. Both armies returned from wherever they'd been hiding, and I was aware for the first time that a battle was really in progress. A great deal of machine-gun fire rattled across the hollow from both sides; men in ones and twos and threes stalked or crawled or ran all around, occasionally peering into my shell hole; the flares blazed more frequently, and there was much shooting, shouting, screaming, and cursing. This must have lasted for hours. With a part of my mind I was perfectly willing to join in the fighting, though I was confused; if someone had shouted orders at me, I'm certain I'd have obeyed them. But I was left entirely alone, and alone my body couldn't move. The waves of fear were gone, but they'd left me exhausted, still in the same position.

Finally the artillery opened up again, apparently laying their fire exactly in the hollow, where the hand-to-hand fighting was in progress. Perhaps both sides had resolved to clean up that untidy squabble with high-explosive shells and begin again. Most of the explosions seemed to be within a few hundred feet of my hole, and the fear returned. There was no question in my mind but that I'd be killed; what I feared was the knowledge that my dying could very well be protracted and painful, and that it must be suffered alone. The only thing I was able to wish for was someone to keep me company while I went through with it.

Sentimental? It certainly is, and I've thought so ever since. But that's what the feeling was, and it was tremendously strong, and I'd not be honest if I didn't speak of it. It was such a strong feeling that when from nowhere a man jumped into the mudhole beside me, I fell on him instantly and embraced him as hard as I could. Very sensibly he assumed I was attacking him, and with some cry of alarm he wrenched away. I fell on him again, before he could raise his rifle, but he managed, in our tussling, to run the point of his bayonet into the calf of my left leg, not very deeply. I shouted in his ear that I didn't want to fight with him; that I loved him; and at the same time—since I was larger and apparently stronger than he—I got behind him and pinioned his arms and legs. He struggled for a long time, and in German, so that I knew him to be an enemy soldier. How could I make everything clear to him? Even if I were able to talk to him and explain my intentions, he would certainly think me either a coward or a lunatic, and kill me anyway. He had to understand everything at once.

Of course, I could have killed him, and I'm sure he understood that fact; he was helpless. What I did, finally, was work my rifle over to me with one hand, after rolling my companion onto his stomach in the muddy water, and then put the point of *my* bayonet on the back of his neck, until it just barely broke the skin and drew a drop of blood. My friend went weak—collapsed, in fact—and what he cried in German I took to be either a surrender, a plea for mercy, or both. Not wanting to leave any doubts about the matter, I held him there for several minutes more, perhaps even pressing a trifle harder on the bayonet, until he broke down, lost control of all his bodily functions, as I had done earlier, and wept. He had, I believe, the same fear; certainly he was a shocked animal.

Where was the rest of the U. S. Army? Reader, I've *never* learned where the armies spent their time in this battle!

Now read this paragraph with an open mind; I can't warn you too often not to make the quickest, easiest judgments of me, if you're interested in being accurate. The next thing I did was lay aside my rifle, bayonet and all, lie in the mud beside this animal whom I'd reduced to paralysis, and embrace him as fiercely as any man ever embraced his mistress. I covered his dirty stubbled face with kisses: his staring eyes, his shuddering neck. Incredibly, now that I look back on it, he responded in kind! The fear left him, as it had left me, and for an hour, I'm sure, we clung to each other.

If the notion of homosexuality enters your head, you're normal, I think. If you judge either the German sergeant or myself to have been homosexual, you're stupid.

After our embrace, the trembling of both of us subsided, and we released each other. There was a complete and, to my knowledge, unique understanding between us. I, in fact, was something like normal for the first time since stepping out of the lorry. I was aware, now, with all my senses. A great many shells were whistling overhead, but none were bursting very near us, and the hand-to-hand fighting had apparently moved elsewhere.

The German and I sat on opposite sides of the shell hole, perhaps five feet apart, smiling at each other in complete understanding. Occasionally we attempted to communicate by gestures, but for the most part communication was unnecessary. I had dry cigarettes; he had none. He had rations; I had none. Neither had ammunition. Both had bandages and iodine. Both had bayonets. We shared the cigarettes and rations; I bandaged the wound in his neck, and he the wound in my leg. He indicated the seat of his trousers and held his nose. I indicated the seat of my trousers and did likewise. We both laughed until we cried, and fell into each other's arms again—though only for an instant this time: our fear had gone, and normal embarrassment had taken its place. We regarded each other warmly. Perhaps we slept.

Never in my life have I enjoyed such intense intimacy, such clear communication with a fellow human being, male or female, as I enjoyed with that German sergeant. He was a little, grizzled, unlovely fellow, considerably older than I; doubtless a professional soldier. I saw him more clearly as the day dawned. While he slept I felt as jealous and protective—I think *exactly* as jealous and protective—as a lion over her cub. If any American, even my father, had jumped into the shell hole at that moment, I'd have killed him unhesitatingly before he could kill my friend. What validity could the artifices of family and nation claim beside a bond like ours? I asked myself. What difference did it make that we would go our separate ways, never having learned even the other's name, he to kill other Americans, I perhaps to kill other Germans? He and I had made a private armistice. What difference (I asked myself) did it make even if we were to meet each other again, face to face, in the numberless chances of war, and without a smile of recognition, go at each other with bayonets? For the space of some hours we had been one man, had understood each other beyond friendship, beyond love, as a wise man understands himself.

Let me end the story. My rhetorical questions, as you may have anticipated, raised after a while the germ of a doubt in my mind. To be sure, I understood perfectly how *I* felt about our relationship. But then, I had instigated it. My companion had indeed responded, but from beneath the pointed end of my bayonet, his face down in the mud. Again, he'd not turned on me, though he'd had many opportunities to do so since our tacit truce; but, as I remarked, he looked like an old professional soldier, and I, remember, was only eighteen. How could I be certain that our incredible sympathy did not actually exist only in my imagination, and that he was not all the while smiling to himself, taking me for a lunatic or a homosexual crank, biding his time, resting, smoking, sleeping—until he was good and ready to kill me? Only a hardened professional could sleep so soundly and contentedly in a mudhole during a battle. There was even a trace of a smile on his lips. Was it not something of a sneer?

In the growing light everything seemed less nightmarish. Doubtless the fighting had moved considerably away from our position. Was I in German territory, or was he in Allied territory? He was indeed an unlovely fellow. Common-looking, and tough. No intelligence in his face. Heaven knows he looked incapable of conceiving or appreciating any such *rapport* as I'd envisioned. Hadn't he speared my leg? Of course, I'd jumped him first. . . .

I grew increasingly nervous, and peered out of my hole. Not a living soul was visible, though a number of bodies lay in various positions and degrees of completeness on the ground, in the barbed wire, on the shattered stumps, in other holes. The air was full of smoke and dust and atmospheric haze, and it was a bit chilly. My leg hurt. I sat back in the hole and stared nervously at the German sergeant, waiting for some sign of his awakening. I even took up my rifle (and moved his away), just to be safe. I was getting jumpier all the time, and began to worry that the fear might return.

Finally I decided to sneak quietly out of the hole and make my way to the Americans, if I could find them, leaving the

German asleep. A perfect solution! I rose to my feet, holding my rifle and not taking my eyes from the German soldier's face. At once he opened his eyes, and although his head didn't move, a look of terrible alarm flashed across his face. In an instant I lunged at him and struck him in the chest with my bayonet. The blow stunned him, and my weight on the rifle held him pinned, but the blade lodged in his breastbone and refused to enter.

My God! I thought frantically. *Can't I kill him?* He grasped the muzzle of my rifle in both hands, trying to force it away from him, but I had better leverage from my standing position. We strained silently for a second. My eyes were on the bayonet; his, I fear, on my face. At last the point slipped up off the bone, from our combined straining—our last correspondence!—and with a tiny horrible puncturing sound, slid into and through his neck, and he began to die. I dropped the rifle—no force on earth could have made me withdraw it—and fled, trembling, across the shattered hollow. By merest luck, the first soldiers I encountered were American, and the battle was over for me.

That's my war story. I told it—apropos of what? Oh yes, it cured me. In fact, it cured me of several things. I seldom day-dream any more, even for an instant. I never expect very much from myself or my fellow animals. I almost never characterize people in a word or phrase, and rarely pass judgment on them at all. I no longer look for the esteem or approbation of my acquaintances. I do things more slowly, more systematically, and more thoroughly. To be sure, I don't call that one incident, traumatic as it proved to be, the single cause of all these alter-ations in me; in fact, I don't see where some of them follow at all. But when I think of the alterations, I immediately think of the incident (specifically, I confess, of that infinitesimal punc-turing noise), and that fact seems significant to me, though I'll allow the possibility of the whole thing's being a case of *post hoc, ergo propter hoc*, as the logicians say. I don't really care.

So, when I was mustered out of service in 1919 and entered Johns Hopkins University, I began to relearn, correctly, a number of things that I'd half-learned before—among them the technique of thinking clearly. I found, for example, that when I handled a tennis racket correctly, I had little aptitude for tennis. On the other hand, my golf game improved considerably. I gave up playing the piano. And, when in 1935 I again took a mild interest in boats, I did everything correctly right from the beginning. Not that I believe, as many people do, that there is some intrinsic ethical value in doing things properly rather than improperly. I don't subscribe, as an ethical premise, to the proposition that anything worth doing is worth doing well. It's simply that I've been incapable, temperamentally, of doing things otherwise than correctly since 1918, just as prior to then I was very nearly incapable of doing anything just right.

My boat is a thirty-five-foot work boat, "torpedo-backed" and narrow-beamed in the manner of the tong boats used hereabouts. Her frames, keel, and floor timbers are of stout white oak, and her side, deck, and bottom planking of good white cedar. A very seaworthy little craft, carefully, slowly, and correctly built. By this morning in 1937 I'd been working on her for two years, doing pehaps an hour's work each day. Many mornings I remember, I simply sat in the garage and stared at her, thinking out the wisest next move, or at the wall, thinking of nothing.

On this particular morning I laid some floor planking: I'd finished planking the sides and bottom and had turned the hull right side up. As usual, I didn't bother to change my clothes or even roll my sleeves; in hat, coat, and tie I set to work laying $3/4"\times3"$ tongue-and-groove cedar planks to the floor beams, fastening them with bronze screws and galvanized wire nails, countersunk and puttied over. I'd cut the planks the day before, so that at the end of my hour most of the deck was laid and I wasn't even sweating. I brushed the knees of my trousers (they weren't dirty, for I kept my wood clean), lit my second cigar of the day, surveyed my work for several minutes, and then left for the office, closing the garage door behind me. If anyone ever took the trouble to finish my boat, I reflected without sorrow, he'd have himself an excellent vessel.

VIII. A note, a warning

A note, a warning, if I may?

I got from my father the habit of doing manual work in my good clothes. Dad always made a fetish of it, like the nineteenth-century surgeons who affected evening clothes in the operating rooms and prided themselves on executing difficult surgery without bloodying their starched and studded shirt fronts.

"It teaches a man to be careful," Dad declared, "and to work easily. Hard work isn't always good work."

In the same attire he'd worn that afternoon in court, boutonniere and all, Dad would spade the vegetable garden before supper, spray the catalpa trees for caterpillars (mixing the unslaked-lime spray himself), and perhaps whitewash the foundation piers of the house or hose off the car. He never got dirty or wet, or even ruffled. When one day in 1930 I came home from the office and found Dad in the cellar, one end of his belt spiked to the floor joist and the other fastened around his neck, there was not a smudge of dirt anywhere on him, though the cellar was quite dusty. His clothes were perfectly creased and free of wrinkles, and although his face was black and his eyes were popped, his hair was neatly and correctly combed.

I agree with Dad that doing manual labor in one's office clothes teaches one to work carefully and neatly, and I follow his practice almost consistently. But I suspect that he attributed to the habit some terminal value; it was, I think, related to some vague philosophy of his. With me that is not the case, and I caution you against inferring anything of a philosophical flavor from my practice. There is in my daily routine a great deal that legitimately implies my ideas about things, but you mustn't work from the wrong things or you'll go astray. Perhaps I shouldn't even have mentioned working on my boat in my good clothes.

IX. The handbill

I didn't choose the practice of law as my career, except perhaps passively; it had been assumed from earliest memory that I was to study for the Maryland Bar and enter Dad's firm, and I never protested. Certainly I've never been dedicated to anything, although as with many another thing I've always maintained a reasonable curiosity about the meanings of legal rules and the workings of courts.

May I say that I am perhaps the best lawyer on the Eastern Shore? Perhaps I shouldn't, for you'll take the statement as self-praise. If I thought the practice of law absolutely important, then my statement would indeed be as much a boast as a description; but truthfully I consider advocacy, jurisprudence, even justice, to have no more intrinsic importance than, say, oyster-shucking. And you'd understand, wouldn't you, that if a man like myself asserted with a smile that he was the peninsula's best oyster shucker (I'm not), or cigarette roller, or pinball-machine tilter, he'd not be guilty of prideful boasting?

I am the legal equivalent of a general practitioner in medicine. I handle criminal cases, torts, wills, deeds, titles, bonds, articles of incorporation—everything that a lawyer can get his fingers into. I've argued in orphans' courts, circuit courts, federal courts, admiralty courts, and appellate courts—once in the United States Supreme Court. I seldom lose cases; but then I seldom plead a case that I'm not fairly happy about to begin with. I must confess that I pick and choose among my possible clients, not to find easy cases, but to find interesting ones.

My partners, fortunately for the firm, are not so choosy; they keep fairly busy and earn good incomes. Harry Bishop, of the original Andrews & Bishop, was sixty-three at the time of this story (he died in 1948). He and Dad founded the firm in 1904, when both were fairly young men. Jimmy Andrews—no relation to me—is the other partner. In 1937 he was perhaps twenty-seven or -eight, just beginning his practice, and I'd suggested bringing him into the firm if only for the convenience of being able to use the same letterhead we'd used before Dad hanged himself.

Our office, whither I went at last after my hour of boat-building, is a little frame building. We each have a private office, but we share the same waiting room, lavatory, and secretary.

The last-mentioned, Mrs. Lake, a lady of fifty, was typing when I entered and paid my usual respects.

"No one waiting for me, I suppose?" I asked.

"Mrs. Mack was in," Mrs. Lake said.

"Oh? What for?"

"She left a note," Mrs. Lake said. "I put it on your desk." I straightened my tie, using the waiting-room mirror.

"No word yet from Charley this morning?"

"Not yet."

Charley was Charley Parks, an attorney whose office was next door to ours. He was an old friend and poker partner of mine, and currently we were on opposite sides in a complicated litigation that had developed out of a trifling automobile accident. The suit was several years old already and hadn't even been tried yet: both parties being wealthy and "litigious," as we barristers say, Charley and I were having a field day fencing with procedural disputes. I'll describe the case eventually.

"How about the pickle barrel?" I asked, stubbing out my cigar in Mrs. Lake's ashtray and picking up my mail from her desk.

"I think there's a letter there from Baltimore," she said.

This had to do with my major case at the moment, another venerable one, involving the contested will of Harrison Mack Senior, the pickle king, who had died in 1935. It too was a labyrinthine affair: suffice it for the moment to say that Harrison had retained me to rescue his jeopardized millions (nearly three million, in fact), and that since January things had been looking up for our adversaries, much to Harrison's concern, if not mine.

I took my letters into my office then and began my last day's work at the law. Two of the letters were advertisements; I threw them out unopened. Another was a check for one thousand seven hundred dollars from William Butler, my client in the automobile litigation mentioned before—an installment on his bill. I put it aside for Mrs. Lake to handle. Another was a personal note from Junior Miner, the ex-husband of the girl in Chapter III, whose divorce I'd handled five years before. It read, in part:

I will kill you m———g son of a bich if come on Pine street m———g son of bich you now why. J.M.

I've no idea why Junior deleted that word in his weekly letter to me; perhaps he was prudish. He believed I arranged Dorothy's divorce in order to make her my mistress, and sent me threatening letters of this sort every six or eight days for a number of years. I put this one aside for Mrs. Lake to file with the others, hoping, as I always did on these occasions, that Junior would not be foolish enough to carry out his threat. Our State's Attorney, Jarman James, was an avid Negro-hanger, and it would have distressed me to present him with such an easy case. To be sure, if Junior didn't carry out his threat within the next several hours, he would be safe.

The next letter I recognized at once from my own handwriting on the envelope—I'd addressed it to myself. It was postmarked *Baltimore*, and it was, or could be, tremendously important. But I wasn't ready to read it yet; I propped it against my desk lamp.

The other letters had to do with various works in progress. I read them, spending some minutes after each to stare out of my window at the county jail and make mental notes. Then I put them aside and read Jane's message.

Darling, if you hoped in some way to hurt me again with your note this morning, you failed. I'm not disturbed at all. I will do exactly what you suggest, my dear, if you will see Marvin Rose for a complete physical, to find out why you're such a pansy. Love, Jane.

Really, she had come a long way since I first met her. I must explain that Marvin Rose is a doctor and a golfing friend of mine, and that in naming a visit to him as the condition for her granting my request—remember the note I sent her earlier, by way of Jerry Hogey—Jane believed herself safe: not since 1924 had I visited a doctor except socially, and Jane knew that my refusal to do so was no less strong for its being unreasonable.

Jane's note, too, I put aside for Mrs. Lake to file, first replacing it in its envelope. I think I may safely suggest, reader, that no one—no one—in Cambridge could bring suit against me with reasonable hopes of winning. In cases where I can't persuade judge or jury with rhetoric or legal gambit, I usually have something in my files to do the trick as evidence. Certainly I could foresee no circumstances in which this note might prove useful, especially since my slight involvement in the world would be terminated that very day. Despite which fact, I put it aside for Mrs. Lake.

Then I called the doctor.

"I'd like an appointment to see Dr. Rose just before lunch," I told his receptionist.

"I'm sorry, sir, Dr. Rose will be busy until this evening."

"Would you tell him it's Todd Andrews?" I asked. "I want a physical. Maybe he can look at me during his naptime." I knew that Marvin was in the habit of napping in his office, on the examination table, before lunch.

"Hold on." I heard her cover the mouthpiece and speak to Marvin.

"Hello? Todd?" It was Marvin who spoke now.

"Yes. How about a minute of your naptime today, Marv?"

"What the hell, Toddy, you sick?" he asked incredulously.

"Nope."

"Somebody suing me?"

"Nope. I just want an examination."

He was speechless. For years he and I had argued, at golf or over highballs, about medicine and law, or rather health and justice, and although he had no inkling of my cardiac ailments, he knew that I was unhealthy and that I didn't care to consult a physician about it.

"Sure, Toddy, come on up, boy," he laughed. "Say, are you pulling my leg?"

"Nope. I want the whole works. Eleven o'clock?"

"Make it eleven-fifteen," Marvin said. "I want to sharpen my needles and things. I don't get you often."

We talked for a minute or two of other things, and then I went to my files, got out the dossier on the litigation over Harrison Mack Senior's estate, and prepared to begin work in earnest.

But again I interrupted myself. I had bitten the end off my third cigar, and finding my matchbook empty, I slapped my coat pockets to search for another. What I found was the handbill I'd pocketed earlier on Long Wharf and had forgotten to read. I unfolded it and spread it out on my desk.

COMING

BIGGER & BETTER THAN EVER!

ADAM'S

ORIGINAL   A N D   UNPARALLELED

"Ocean-Going"

FLOATING

OPERA

Jacob R. Adam, Owner & Captain

AT: Long Wharf, Cambridge, June [21 or 22]

Tickets on Sale All Day at the Ticket Office
ADMISSIONS: 20¢, 35¢, 50¢

* * SEATING CAPACITY 700 * *

LARGEST FLOATING THEATRE ON THE EASTERN SEABOARD

($60,000 Actually Invested to Date)

A
Choice Company
of
Players,
Presenting the Finest in DRAMA,

MUSIC,

MINSTRELS,

VAUDEVILLE

ONE LONG LAUGH!

Great Moral Show
The High-Water Mark of Mirth, Melody, & Minstrelsy

A   N
L   E
L   W

Up-to-date Comedians, Dazzling Dancers,
Cultivated Singers.

MORAL AND REFINED	**GORGEOUS**	Cooled by the breezes of the sea

You Are Cordially Invited to Visit America's
Finest & Safest Floating Theatre During the Day

[On the inside of the folded sheet was more information about
the virtues of Adam's Floating Opera, and a program of the
evening's entertainment.]

*FREE Concert Begins at 7:30 PM; Show Begins 8:00 PM

PROF. EISEN'S
$7,500 CHALLENGE ATLANTIC &
CHESAPEAKE MARITIME BAND

Composed of the Finest Musicians in the *U.S.A.!*

Listen for the CALLIOPE!

Watch for the BAND PARADE!

EVERY PROMISE MADE
FAITHFULLY KEPT

Come early for the Band Concert and Stay for the
East Coast's Finest Show

✶ *SEE* ✶

THE MARY PICKFORD OF
THE CHESAPEAKE

!! MISS CLARA MULLOY !!

IN
a new, side-splitting one-act comedy

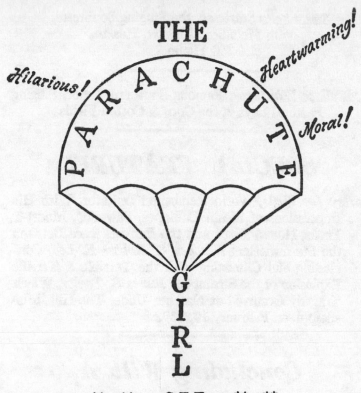

* * SEE * *
The Chaste & Inimitable

ETHIOPIAN TIDEWATER MINSTRELS

U.S.A.'s Greatest Sable Humorists

* * SEE * *
J. Strudge, the Magnificent Ethiopian Delineator,
The Black Demosthenes, in
His Original Burlesque Stump Speech

Sweet Sally Starbuck, the Singing Soubrette,
with Melodies of Heart, Hearth,
& Home.

———

T. Wallace Whittaker, Famous Southern Tenor, Singing
Pastoral Lays of the Corn & Cotton Fields

———

SPECIAL FEATURE!

Burley Joe Wells, World Renowned Imitator, With His
Impressions of Steam Calliopes, Sawmills, Model-T
Fords, Hound Dogs, and the Famous Race Between
the Sternwheelers *Natchez* & *Robert E. Lee*, Con-
cluding and Climaxing with the Terrible & Terrific
Explosion of the Steamboat *James B. Taylor*, Which
Tragedy Occurred at Natchez-Under-The-Hill, Mis-
sissippi, on February 19, 1892.

———

Concluding With A

WONDERFUL
PANITHIOPLICONICA

———

DON'T MISS IT!
KEEP YOUR EYE ON THE
DATE!

Bring the Kiddies

Approved By Press, Public, & Clergy Alike.

Well. Far be it from me to miss the Wonderful Panithiopliconica.

"Mrs. Lake," I called, "will you telephone Mrs. Mack sometime this morning and ask her if I may take Jeannine to see the showboat when it pulls in?"

"Okay," Mrs. Lake said. "What time?"

"Late this afternoon, I guess. About four? Am I supposed to do anything after four?"

"I'll look. . . . No."

The famous race between the sternwheelers *Natchez* and *Robert E. Lee*. I wouldn't miss it for anything. But I didn't keep my eye on the date, as Capt. Adam's handbill suggested; indeed, I crumpled the bill and threw it away just then, and I've never been able to remember whether all this occurred on the twenty-first or twenty-second of June. To be sure, at some time during the nine years I spent recollecting the events of this day, I could with small effort have gone to the files of the daily *Banner* and dug out the showboat advertisement to fix the date. But I've never bothered to. Is it the Navajo Indians who make it a point always to leave in their woven rugs and other artifacts some slight imperfection, an odd stitch or a bump of clay, in order not to compete with the gods? I think it is. Well, I have no gods, and so I can't justify my shortcomings as do the Navajos. But it has, I must say, seemed unwise to me from the beginning to verify that date. Perhaps I can't explain why.

Indeed, I shan't try.

X. The law

That will-o'-the-wisp, the law: where shall I begin to speak of it? Is the law the legal rules, or their interpretations by judges, or by juries? Is it the precedent or the present fact? The norm or the practice? I think I'm not interested in what the law is.

Surely, though, I am curious about things that the law can be made to do, but this disinterestedly, without involvement. A child encounters a toy tractor, winds it up, and sets it climbing over a book. The tractor climbs well. The child puts another book here, so, and angles the first. The tractor surmounts them, with difficulty. The child opens the pages of the first book, leans the second obliquely against it, and places his shoe behind the two. The tractor tries, strains, spins, whirrs, and falls like a turtle on its back, treads racing uselessly. The child moves on to his crayons and picture puzzles, no expression on his face. I don't know what you mean, sir, when you speak of justice.

It may be that, like Capt. Osborn, you have come to believe that I have opinions about everything, absurd ones at that. Very well. But of most things about which people hold some sort of opinion, I have none at all, except by implication. What I mean is this: the law, for example, prescribes certain things that shall not be done, or certain ways in which things shall be done, but of most specific human acts it has nothing to say one way or the other. Yet these extralegal acts, or most of them, are certainly influenced and conditioned, implicitly, by the laws pertaining to other things. People, for example, aren't allowed to kill us while we're performing our extralegal acts. In the same way, though I have no opinion one way or the other on whether suicide, for instance, is a sin, I have certain opinions on a few other things that made it possible for me to contemplate suicide in 1937, and actually to resolve to destroy myself.

All right. I have no general opinions about the law, or about justice, and if I sometimes set little obstacles, books and slants, in the path of the courts, it is because I'm curious, merely, to see what will happen. On those occasions when the engine of the law falls impotently sprawling, I make a mental note of it, and without a change of expression, go on to my boat or my *Inquiry*. Winning or losing litigations is of no concern to me, and I think I've never made a secret of that fact to my clients. They come to me, as they come before the law, because *they* think they have a case. The law and I are uncommitted.

One more thing, before I explain the contest over Harrison Mack Senior's will: if you have followed this chapter so far, you might sensibly ask, "Doesn't your attitude—which is, after all, irresponsible—allow for the defeat, even the punishment, of the innocent, and at times the victory of the guilty? And does this not concern you?" It does indeed allow for the persecution of innocence—though perhaps not so frequently as you might imagine. And this persecution *concerns* me, in the sense that it holds my attention, but not especially in the sense that it bothers me. Under certain circumstances, to be explained later, I am not averse to pillorying the innocent, to throwing my stone, with the crowd, at some poor martyr. Irresponsibility, yes: I affirm, I insist upon my basic and ultimate irresponsibility. Yes indeed.

It did not deeply concern me, as I said before, whether Harrison received his inheritance or not, though I stood to profit by some fifty thousand dollars or more if he did. In any world but ours, the case of the Mack estate would be fantastic; even in ours, it received considerable publicity from the Maryland press.

Old man Mack, whom I've come to admire tremendously

though I never met him, died in 1935, after years of declining physical and mental health. He left a large estate: stock in the Mack Pickle Co. amounting to 58 per cent of the total shares, and worth perhaps two million dollars in fairly good times; stock in various other business concerns, some more prosperous than others; a large house in Ruxton, another in West Palm Beach, and cottages in Nova Scotia and Maryland (including the one I was seduced in); extensive farmlands, especially cucumber farms, the crop from which was bought by the Mack Pickle Co.; perhaps a hundred thousand dollars in cash; assorted automobiles, cabin cruisers, horses, and dogs, and, through the majority stockholdings, the potential presidency of the pickle company, which office carried a salary of twenty-five thousand dollars a year. It was, undeniably, an estate that many people would consider worth going to court about.

Now of the several characteristics of Harrison *père*, three were important to the case: he was in the habit of using his wealth as a club to keep his kin in line; he was, apparently, addicted to the drawing up of wills; and, especially in his last years, he was obsessively jealous of the products of his mind and body, and permitted none to be destroyed.

You perhaps recall my saying that when I first met Harrison Junior, in 1925, he was undergoing an attack of communism, and had been disinherited as a result? It seems that disinheritance, or the threat of it, was the old man's favorite disciplinary measure, not only for his son, but also for his wife. When young Harrison attended Dartmouth rather than Johns Hopkins; when he studied journalism rather than business; when he became a communist rather than a Republican; he was disinherited until such time as he mended his ways. When Mother Mack went to Europe rather than to West Palm Beach; when she chose sparkling burgundy over highballs, Dulaney Valley over Ruxton, Roosevelt and Garner over Hoover and Curtis; she was disinherited until such time as she recanted her heresies. All these falls from and reinstatements to grace, of course, required emendations of Father Mack's will, and a number of extrafamiliar circumstances also demanded frequent revision of his bequests. His country club admits someone he doesn't like: the club must be disinherited. A pickle-truck driver runs down a state policeman checking on overloaded vehicles: the driver must be defended in court and provided for explicitly in the will. After the old man's death, when his safe was opened, a total of seventeen complete and distinct testamentary instruments was found, chronologically arranged, each beginning with a revocation of the preceding one. He hadn't been able to throw any of his soul-children into the fire.

Now this situation, though certainly unusual, would in itself have presented no particular problem of administration, because the law provides that where there are several wills, the last shall be considered representative of the testator's real intentions, other things being equal. And each of these wills explicitly revoked the preceding one. But alas, with Mr. Mack all other things weren't equal. Not only did his physical well-being deteriorate in his last years, through arthritis to leukemia to the grave; his sanity deteriorated also, gradually, along the continuum from relative normalcy through marked eccentricity to jibbering idiocy. In the first stages he merely inherited and disinherited his relatives and his society; in the second he no longer went to work, he required entertainment as well as care from his nurses, and he allowed nothing of his creation—including hair- and nail-clippings, urine, feces, and wills—to be thrown away; in the last stages he could scarcely move or talk, had no control whatever over his bodily functions, and recognized no one. To be sure, the stages were not dramatically marked, but blended into one another imperceptibly.

Of the seventeen wills (which represented by no means all the wills Mack had written, merely those written since he acquired his mania for preserving things), only the first two were composed during the time when the old man's sanity was pretty much indisputable; that is, prior to 1933. The first left about half the estate to Harrison Junior and the other half to Mother Mack, provided it could not be demonstrated to the court that she had drunk any sparkling burgundy since 1920. This one was dated 1924. The other, dated 1932, left about half the estate to Mrs. Mack unconditionally and the rest to Harrison, provided it could not be demonstrated to the court that during a five-year probationary period, 1932–37, Harrison had done, written, or said anything that could reasonably be construed as evidence of communist sympathies. This clause, incidentally, ran through most of the subsequent testaments as well.

Of the other fifteen documents, ten were composed in 1933 and 1934, years when the testator's sanity was open to debate. The last five, all written in the first three months of 1935, could be established without much difficulty, in court, as being the whims of a lunatic: one left everything to Johns Hopkins University on condition that the University's name be changed to Hoover College (the University politely declined); others bequeathed the whole shebang to the Atlantic Ocean or the A.F.L.

Luckily for the majesty of Maryland's law, there were only two primary and four secondary contestants for the estate. Elizabeth Sweetman Mack, the testator's widow, was interested in having Will #6, a product of late 1933, adjudged the last testament: it bequeathed her virtually the entire estate, on the sparkling-burgundy condition described above. Harrison Junior preferred #8, the fruit of early 1934; it bequeathed *him* virtually the whole works, on the clean-skirts condition also described above. Misses Janice Kosko, Shirley Mae Greene, and Berenice Silverman, registered nurses all, who had attended old Mack during the first, second, and third stages, respectively, of his physical invalidity, liked Wills #3, 9, and 12, in that order: therein, apparently, their late employer provided them remuneration for services beyond the line of duty. The final contestant was the pastor of the Macks' neighborhood church: in Will #13 the bulk of the estate was to pass to that church, with the express hope that the richer and more influential organized religion became, the sooner it would be cast off by the people.

It was an edifying spectacle. Mrs. Mack retained Messrs. Dugan, Froebel & Kemp, of Baltimore, to defend her legal rights; her son retained Andrews, Bishop, & Andrews, of Cambridge; the nurses and the minister retained separate attorneys. Everyone was a little afraid to carry the thing to court immediately, and for several months there was a welter of legal nonsense, threats, and counterthreats, among the six firms involved. Five of us joined forces to oust the clergyman from the sweepstakes—it was enough for the three nurses to agree that Mack was definitely insane by the time Will #13 was composed. A month later, by pretty much the same technique, Misses Kosko and Greene induced Miss Silverman to withdraw, on the solemnly contracted condition that should either of them win, she would get 20 per cent of the loot. Then, in a surprise maneuver, Bill Froebel, of Dugan, Froebel & Kemp, produced sworn affidavits from two Negro maids of the Mack household, to the effect that they had seen Miss Greene indulging in "unnatural and beastly" practices with the deceased—the practices were described in toothsome detail—and suggested to that young lady that, should she not decide the contest wasn't worth the trouble, he would release the affidavits to the newspapers. I never learned for certain whether the affidavits were true or false, but in either case they were effective: the additional attraction of several thousand dollars, payable when Mrs. Mack won the case, induced Miss Greene to seek her happiness outside the courts.

The field was cleared, then, in 1936, of half the entries, before the race even began. Only Miss Kosko, Harrison Junior, and Mrs. Mack remained. Each of them, of necessity, must attempt to prove two things: that Father Mack was still legally sane when the will of their choice was written, and that by the time the subsequent wills were written, he no longer could comprehend what he was about. On this basis, Miss Kosko, I should say, had the strongest case, since her will (dated February 1933) was the earliest of the three. But love was her undoing: she retained as her attorney her boy friend, a lad fresh out of law school, none too bright. After our initial out-of-court sparring I was fairly confident that he was no match for either Froebel or myself, and when, late in 1936, he refused on ethical grounds a really magnanimous bribe from Froebel, I was certain.

And sure enough, when the first swords clashed in Baltimore Probate Court, in May of 1936, Froebel was able, with little trouble, to insinuate that the young lawyer was an ass; that the nurse Miss Kosko was a hussy out to defraud poor widows of their honest legacies by seducing old men in their dotage; that Mrs. Mack, out of the kindness of her bereaved heart, had already offered the trollop a gratuity more munificent than she deserved (this news was ruled out as incompetent evidence, of course); and that even to listen tolerantly to such ill-concealed avariciousness was a tribute to the patience and indulgence of long-suffering judges. In addition, Froebel must have offered some cogent arguments, for surrogate courts, even in Baltimore, are notoriously competent, and the judge ruled in his favor. When Froebel then offered Miss Kosko another settlement, considerably smaller than the first, the young barrister accepted it humbly, coming as it did on the heels of his defeat, and didn't even think of appealing the judgment until it was too late.

Then, in June of the same year, Froebel filed suit for Mrs. Mack, charging flatly that Mr. Mack had been of unsound mind when he wrote Will ⚹8, Harrison's will, and never again regained his sanity. If the court so ruled, then Mrs. Mack's will, ⚹6, would become the authentic testamentary instrument, since Miss Kosko was out of the running. If the court ruled against him, then our document, ⚹8, would automatically revoke his.

There was not much difference between Mack's mental state in late 1933 and his mental state in early 1934. I introduced statements from Misses Kosko and Greene that in both years he required them to save the contents of his bedpan in dill-pickle jars, which were then stored in the wine cellar, and I got the impression that the judge—a staid fellow—believed Mack had been insane from the beginning. The newspapers, too, expressed the opinion that there was no particular evidence on either side, and that, besides, it was a disgraceful thing for a mother and her son to squabble so selfishly. All the pressure was for out-of-court settlement on a fifty-fifty basis, but both Harrison and his mother—who had never especially liked each other—refused, on the advice of their attorneys. Froebel thought he could win, and wanted the money; I thought I could win, and wanted to see.

Will #6, remember, gave all the estate to Mrs. Mack, provided she hadn't tasted sparkling burgundy since 1920. Our will left the money and property to Harrison, if he had steered clear of Moscow since 1932, and in addition, bequeathed to Mrs. Mack the several hundred pickle jars just mentioned. Both documents included the extraordinary provision that, should the separate conditions not be fulfilled, the terms were to be reversed.

Froebel's arguments, essentially, were two: (1) That a man has not necessarily lost his business sense if he provides once for a complete reversal of bequests, of the sort seen in Will #6, assuming he is really dead set against sparkling burgundy; but then to reverse himself completely in the space of a few months indicates that something has snapped in his head, since there were no dramatic external changes to account for the new will. (2) That the bequest of the pickle jars appeared in no wills before #8, and in all the wills from #8 through #16, and that such a bequest is evidence tending to show that Mack no longer understood the nature of his estate.

"Not necessarily," I suggested. "Suppose he didn't love his wife?"

"Ah," Froebel replied quickly, "but he left the pickle jars to a different person each time, not to Mrs. Mack every time."

"But remember," I said, "he saved the mess because he liked it; the bequest of it, then, is an act of love. Would you call love insane?"

"Indeed not," Froebel answered. "But if he'd loved her, he'd have given her the property as well as the—excrement."

"No indeed," I countered. "Remember that in one will he bequeathed all his money to the church because he disliked the church. Couldn't the bequest to my client be such an act, and the bequest to yours the real gift?"

"It could indeed," Froebel grinned. "Will you say that that's the case?"

"No, I shan't," I said. "I merely suggested the possibility."

"And in doing so," Froebel declared, "you suggest the possibility that Will Number Eight is as insane as Will Number Thirteen, the church will you mentioned. Anyone who bequeaths three millions of dollars as a punishment, I suggest, is out of perspective."

Oh, Bill Froebel was a lawyer. When it came to impromptu legal sophistry, he and I had no equals at the Maryland Bar.

My arguments were (1) that the inclusion of the pickle jars was hardly sufficient evidence of a sudden loss of understanding, when Mack had been collecting them since Will #3 or 4; (2) that therefore the testator was either sane when he composed both instruments or insane when he composed them; (3) that if he was sane both times, Will #8 was official; (4) that if insane both times, some earlier will was official and must be brought forward, or otherwise Mack could be deemed to have died intestate (in which case Harrison would get all the money, Mrs. Mack retaining only dower).

The judge, Frank Lasker of the Baltimore bench, agreed. Froebel appealed the decision through the Court of Appeals to the Maryland Supreme Court, and both appellate courts affirmed the lower court's judgment. It seemed as if Harrison were a wealthy man: all that remained was to wait until January of 1937—the end of his probationary period—and then to demonstrate that Harrison had kept clear of communist sympathy since 1932. He assured me that nothing could be suggested which could be called fellow-traveling, even remotely. Froebel threatened for a while to institute a new suit, in favor of Will #2, but nothing came of his threat.

The final test was in the form of a hearing. Harrison and I appeared at the Baltimore courthouse early in January; Judge Lasker read the terms of Will #8 and declared that if no one present could offer evidence of such sympathies as were therein interdicted, he was prepared to declare the matter settled and to order the will executed. Froebel then appeared, much to my surprise, and announced that he had such evidence, enough to warrant the reversal of bequests provided for by our will, and was ready to offer it to the court.

"You told me there wasn't anything," I reminded Harrison, who had turned white.

"I swear there isn't!" he whispered back, but nevertheless he began perspiring and trembling a little. I sat back to see what Froebel had cooked up.

"What will you attempt to prove?" the Judge asked him.

"That as recently as last year, your honor, while his poor father was in the grave—perhaps speeded there (who knows?) by his son's regrettable irresponsibility—that just last year, your honor, this son, who is now so eager to take from his mother what is rightfully hers, was aiding and abetting actively, with large gifts of money, that doctrine against which his father's entire life was such an eloquent argument; confident, I doubt not, that he could conceal his surreptitious Bolshevism until such time as he was in a position to devote the whole of the Mack estate toward overthrowing the way of life that made its accumulation possible!"

Froebel was a past master of the detached noun clause: judge and spectators were stirred.

"For heaven's sake!" Harrison whispered. "You don't think he means my Spanish donations!"

"If you were silly enough to make any, then I daresay he does," I replied, appalled anew at Harrison's innocence.

And indeed, the "Spanish donations" were precisely what Froebel had in mind. He offered in evidence photostated checks, four of them, for one thousand dollars each, made out to an American subscription agency representing the Spanish Loyalist government. They were dated March 10, May 19, September 2, and October 7, and all were signed *Harrison A. Mack, Jr.*

Judge Lasker examined the photostats and frowned. "Did you write these checks?" he asked Harrison, passing the pictures to him.

"Of course!" Harrison yelled. "What the hell's that—"

"Order!" suggested the Judge. "Aren't you aware that the Loyalist movement is run by the Communist Party? Directed from the Kremlin?"

"Aw, come on!" Harrison pleaded, until I poked him and he sat down.

"May I point out," Froebel continued blandly, "that not only is a gift to the Loyalists in essence a gift to Moscow, but this particular subscription agency is a Party organization under FBI surveillance. A man may donate to the Loyalists through honest, if vague, liberalism, I daresay; but one doesn't send checks to this subscription outfit unless one is sympathetic with the Comintern. Young Mr. Mack, like too many of our idle aristocrats, is, I fear, a blue blood with a Red heart."

I believe it was this final metaphor that won Froebel the judgment. I saw the newspaper people virtually doff their hats in tribute, and scribble the immortal words for the next editions of their papers. Even the Judge smiled benignly upon the trope: I could see that it struck him square in the prejudices, and found a welcome there.

There was some further discussion, but no one listened closely; everyone was repeating to himself, with a self-satisfied smile, that too many young aristocrats are blue bloods with Red hearts. *Blue bloods with Red hearts!* How could mere justice cope with poetry? Men, I think, are ever attracted to the *bon mot* rather than the *mot juste*, and judges, no less than other men, are often moved by considerations more aesthetic than judicial. Even I was not a little impressed, and regretted only that we had no jury to be overwhelmed by such a purple plum from the groves of advocacy. *A blue blood with a Red heart!* How brandish reasonableness against music? Should I hope to tip the scales with puny logic, when Froebel had Parnassus in his pan? In vain might I warn Judge Lasker that, through the press, all America was watching, and Europe as well, for his decision.

"My client, a lover of freedom and human dignity," I declared, "made his contributions to the oppressed Loyalists as a moral obligation, proper to every good American, to fight those Rebels who would crush the independence of the human spirit, and trample liberty under hobnailed boots! How can you charge him with advocating anarchy and violent overthrow, when in a single year he gives four thousand dollars to support the Spanish Government against those who would overthrow it?"

And on I went for some minutes, trying to make capital out of the Spanish confusion, wherein the radicals were the *status quo* and the reactionaries the rebels. It was an admirable bit of casuistry, but I knew my cause was lost. Only Froebel, I think, had ears for my rhetoric; the rest of the room was filled with *blue bloods with Red hearts.*

And Judge Lasker, as I think I mentioned, was famously conservative. Though by no means a fascist himself—he was probably uncommitted in the Spanish revolution—he epitomized the unthinking antagonism of his class toward anything pinker than the blue end of the spectrum: a familiar antagonism that used to infuriate me when, prior to 1924, I was interested in such things as social justice. When finally he ruled, he ruled in Froebel's favor.

"It does not matter whether there is a difference between

the Moscow and Madrid varieties of communism," he declared, "or whether the Court or anyone else approves or disapproves of the defendant's gifts or the cause for which they were intended. The fact is that the subscription agency involved is a communist organization under government surveillance, and a gift to that agency is a gift to communism. There can be no question of the donor's sympathy with what the agency represented, and what it represented was communism. The will before me provides that should such sympathy be demonstrated, as it has been here, the terms of the document are to be reversed. The Court here orders such a reversal."

Well, we were poor again. Harrison went weak, and when I offered him a cigar he came near to vomiting.

"It's incredible!" he croaked, actually perspiring from the shock of it.

"Do you give up?" I asked him. "Or shall I appeal?"

He clutched at the hope. "Can we appeal?"

"Sure," I said. "Don't you see how unlogical Lasker's reasoning is?"

"Unlogical! It was so logical it overwhelmed me!"

"Not at all. He said the subscription agency was sympathetic to communism. You give money to the agency; therefore you're sympathetic to communism. It's like saying that if you give money to a Salvation Army girl who happens to be a vegetarian you're sympathetic to vegetarians. The communists support the Loyalists; you support the Loyalists; therefore you're a communist."

Harrison was tremendously relieved, but so weak he could scarcely stand. He laughed shortly.

"Well! That puts us back in the race, doesn't it? Ha, I'd thought there for a while—Christ, Toddy, you've saved my ass again! Damned judge! We've got it now, boy!"

I shook my head, and he went white again.

"What the hell's wrong?"

"I'll appeal," I said, "but we'll lose again, I guess."

"How's that? Lose again!" He laughed, and sucked in his breath.

"Forget about the logic," I said. "Nobody really cares about the logic. They make up their minds by their prejudices about Spain. I think you'd have lost here even without Froebel's metaphor. I'd have to talk Lasker into liberalism to win the case."

I went on to explain that of the seven judges of the Court of Appeals who would review the decision, three were Republicans with a pronounced anti-liberal bias, two were fairly liberal Democrats, one was a reactionary "Southern Democrat," more anti-liberal than the Republicans, and the seventh, an unenthusiastic Democrat, was relatively unbiased.

"I know them all," I said. "Abrams, Moore, and Stevens, the Republicans, will vote against you. Forrester, the Southern Democrat, would vote for you if it were a party issue, but it's not; he'll go along with the Republicans. Stedman and Barnes, the liberals, will go along with you, and I think Haddaway will too, because he likes me and because he dislikes Lasker's bad logic."

"But hell, that's four to three!" Harrison cried. "That means I lose!"

"As I said."

"How about the Maryland Supreme Court?"

"That's too much to predict," I said. "I don't know that they've declared themselves on Spain, and I don't know them personally. But they've affirmed almost every important verdict of the Court of Appeals in three years."

Harrison was crushed. "It's unjust!"

I smiled. "You know how these things are."

"Aw, but what the hell!" He shook his head, tapped his feet impatiently, pursed his lips, sighed in spasms. I expected him to faint, but he held on tightly, though he could scarcely talk. The truth was, of course, that it is one thing—an easy thing—to give what Cardinal Newman calls "notional" assent to a proposition such as "There is no justice"; quite another and more difficult matter to give it "real" assent, to learn it stingingly, to the heart, through involvement. I remember hoping that Harrison was strong enough at least to be educated by his expensive loss.

I appealed the judgment of the Court.

"Just to leave the door open," I explained. "I might think of something."

That evening, before I left Baltimore with Harrison, we had dinner at Bill Froebel's club, as his guests. I praised his inspiration, and he my logic-twisting. Harrison was morose, and although he drank heavily, he refused to join in the conversation. He couldn't drive home. On the way, he would clutch my arm and groan, "Three million bucks, Toddy!"

I looked coldly at him.

"Hell, man," he protested, "I know what you're thinking, but you should know me better. I don't want the money like another man might, just to go crazy on. Think what we could do on three million bucks, the three of us!"

It was the first time since Jane and I had resumed our affair in 1935 that Harrison had spoken again of "the three of us," as he had used to do.

"A million apiece?" I asked. "Or a joint account?"

Harrison felt the bristles and flinched, and all the way home he felt constrained to pretend that the loss of three million dollars touched his philosophical heart not at all. I watched the effort from the corner of my eye, and marveled sadly at his disorientation.

Finally he broke down, as we were crossing the Choptank River bridge, pulling into Cambridge. The water was white-capped and cold-looking. Dead ahead, at the end of the boulevard that the bridge ran onto, Morton's Marvelous Tomatoes, Inc., spread its red neon banner across the sky, and I smiled. The town lights ran in a flat string along the water's edge, from Hambrooks Bar Lighthouse, flashing on the right, to the Macks' house in East Cambridge, its ground-floor windows still lit, where Jane was waiting.

"I give up, Toddy," he said tersely. "I'm no philosopher. I can't say I wouldn't have been happy at one time without the money—I *did* get myself disinherited a few times, you know. But once it came so close and seemed so sure—"

"What is it?" I demanded.

"Ah, Christ—Janie and I had plans." He choked on his plans. "How the hell can I say it? I just don't feel like living any more."

"You *what?*" I sneered. "What'll you do—hang yourself in the cellar? There's a twentypenny nail right there, in a joist—you'll find it. It's already been broken in. And I know an undertaker who can turn black faces white again."

"All right, all right," Harrison said. "I don't care what you think. I said I'm no philosopher."

"Forget about philosophy," I said. "You don't lack philosophy; you lack guts. I suppose you're going to ask me to marry Jane afterwards, so the two of us can remember you? You're wallowing, Harrison. It's swinish."

"I'm weak, Toddy," he said. "I can't help it. Don't think I'm not ashamed of it."

"Then cut it out."

"You can't just cut it out," Harrison protested, and I sensed that he was growing stronger. "I'm past believing that people can change."

"You don't want to cut it out."

"Sure I do. It doesn't matter whether I do or not; I can't do it. I'm weak in some ways, Toddy. You don't understand that."

I flicked my cigarette out of the ventilator in a shower of sparks. We were off the bridge then, coasting along the dual highway in the Macks' big automobile.

"I know what weakness is. But you make your own difficulties, Harrison. It's hard because you never thought of it

as easy. Listen. An act of will is the easiest thing there is—
so easy it's laughable how people make mountains of it."

Harrison had by this time actually put aside the idea of his
loss and was following the thought.

"You know better," he said. "You can't discount psychology."

"I'm not saying anything about psychology," I maintained.
"Psychology doesn't interest me. We act as if we could choose,
and so we can, in effect. All you have to do to be strong is stop
being weak."

"Impossible."

"You never tried it."

Nor, alas, did he want to just then: I could see that plainly
enough. We went into the house for a last drink. Jane had
heard the news, of course, by telephone, and she cried awhile.
I told her flatly that I had no sympathy for either of them while
they behaved like that.

"What would *you* do, damn it!" she cried impatiently.

I laughed. "I've never lost three million bucks," I said, "but
I'll tell you what I did once, after Dad hanged himself for
losing a few thousand."

I told them then, for the first time, the story of my adventures
with Col. Henry Morton—which story, reader, I'll pause to tell
you, too, sooner or later, but not just now. I had decided that
I didn't want Harrison to brood over his money: he wasn't
ready to be strong of his own choosing yet, apparently, and so
I opened the way toward turning him into a cynic, in emulation
of me. He was ripe for it anyhow, it seemed to me, and even
the one story might do the trick.

There's little need for weakness, reader: you are freer, perhaps, than you'd be comfortable knowing.

As I left, Jane asked me: "You don't have anything up your
sleeve, Toddy?"

"I shan't commit myself," I said. "But Harrison might as well
believe he's out three million bucks, at least for a while."

"What will he do?" she asked anxiously. "Did he say anything to you coming home?"

"He'll either grow stronger or hang himself," I predicted. "If he grows stronger it won't matter to him whether he gets the money or not, really, and then I wouldn't mind seeing him get it. If he kills himself over it, I'll be just as glad he's dead, frankly. Sissies make me uncomfortable. That goes for you, too. You're not ready for three million bucks yet. You don't deserve it."

Then I left. I suppose if *I* ever lost three million dollars I'd holler like a stuck hero. Or perhaps not: one really can't tell until the thing is upon one.

Well, the will case dropped out of the papers then; the Court of Appeals wouldn't hear the appeal for at least six months, though I doubted that they'd wait much longer than that. In the meantime, Lizzie Mack, Harrison's mother, couldn't use up the old man's estate (except for running expenses for the house), though it was temporarily hers.

I conducted, during the next few months, a rather intensive investigation into the characters of the appellate court judges— my findings confirmed my original estimate of the situation. As far as one with much information could guess, the decision would be four to three for Lizzie if the hearing were held when tentatively scheduled.

And if it weren't? I considered that question, sitting in my office, staring at my staring-wall opposite the desk. What advantage was there in delay, if any? And how could one delay the appeal? The advantage was negative: that is, I was certain of defeat if there were no delay; if there were any, I might very possibly still be defeated, but there would be more time for something to turn up. So, I suppose, a condemned man snatches at a day's reprieve, still hoping for a god on wires to fetch him off, and on the very gibbet, his neck roped, pleads eye-to-sky for the saving car. Who knows? Perhaps, hooded and dropped, he yet awaits in a second's agony for God's hands

on him, till the noose cracks neck and hope in one sick snap.
To be sure, ours was but a matter of money, but the principle
was the same. By September the Loyalists might be winning,
or it might become dangerous over here to like the fascists, the
way Hitler was behaving. By October Franco might win, and
the poor crushed Loyalists be pitied then, when they were no
longer a threat. Anything could happen to swing one more vote
our way. November was an off-year election month: perhaps
some party issue would ally John Forrester, the reactionary
Democrat, with his more liberal colleagues. Perhaps—

I smiled, moved my feet off the desk, and went to the file.
I looked up each of the judges, checking the length of their
incumbencies and the number of years in office remaining to
each.

"Ah, Freddie Barnes, you old whoremonger," I cooed; "so
you're up to the post again this year, are you?"

That fact mattered little, since Roosevelt was going great
guns and Barnes was a popular figure in Maryland: he'd be
re-elected without difficulty. Of the other Democrats, Forrester
had two years to go, Haddaway had four, and Stedman had
six. I checked the Republicans: Abrams had two years yet;
Stevens, six; Moore—

"Well, well, well!" I grinned. "You rascal, Rollo! Time to
run again, eh?"

Mrs. Lake, at my request, spent the rest of her afternoon
telephoning various Baltimorians for me, some eminent and some
shady, some honest and some flexible, some friendly and some
employable. By quitting time I was one of perhaps seven people who knew as a fact, beyond puny speculation, that Judge
Rollo Moore, despite the backing of Maryland republicanism,
was going to lose his coming election by a well-insured margin
to Joseph Singer, who, bless his heart, was a chronic if somewhat fuzzy liberal—a man after Harrison's own heart.

We would win, by God, almost certainly, if we could hold
off the appeal until November! No, until January of 1938,

after the new officeholders had been sworn in. Nearly a year! I racked my brain, in my thorough but unenthusiastic way, to think of some stalling maneuver, but of the few I could imagine, none was satisfactory. What I needed was something diverting, something tenuous and intricate, that I could go on complicating indefinitely, if need be. Nothing crude would do: my maneuver, whatever it was, must be subtle even if its motives were clear to the professional eye, or else I should lose the respect, and possibly the vote, of men like Judge Haddaway, for instance, whose decisions were more often influenced by such things as the symmetry and logical elegance of a brief than by more mundane considerations like the appellant's politics.

Ah, nonsense, there was nothing. The months passed; it was spring; August and judgment would soon be upon us. Harrison sweated but kept silent. Jane wept a little, and sometimes failed to come to my room when I expected her, but kept silent. They were learning; they were strengthening, or else they were naïve enough to have some canine faith in me. At least they kept silent about it, though I often caught them looking at me intently, at supper or wherever. In fact, they often stared at me, and sometimes didn't even notice when I noticed them.

As for me, I stared at my wall. I have in my office, opposite the desk, a fine staring-wall, a wall that I keep scrupulously clear for staring purposes, and I stared at it. I stared at it through February, March, April, and May, and through the first week of June, without reading on its empty surface a single idea.

Then, on the very hot June 17th of 1937, our Mrs. Lake, who is as a rule a model of decorum, came sweating decorously into my office with a paper cup of iced coffee for me, set it decorously on my desk, accepted my thanks, dropped a handkerchief on the floor as she turned to leave, bent decorously down to retrieve it, and most undaintily—oh, most indecorously, —broke wind, virtually in my coffee.

"Oh, *excuse* me!" she gasped, and blushed, and fled. But ah, the fart hung heavy in the humid air, long past the lady's flight. It hung, it lolled, it wisped; it miscegenated with the smoke of my cigar, caressed the beading oil on the skin of my nose, lay obscenely on the flat of my desk, among my briefs and papers. It was everywhere, but I had learned, even then, to live with nature and my fellow animals. I didn't flinch; I didn't move. Through its dense invisible presence I regarded my oracular wall, and this time fruitfully.

"By God, now!" I cried.

I heard a small sound in the outer office.

"Mrs. Lake!" I rushed to my door. "Where's all the crap?"

"Oh, Mr. Andrews!" she wailed, and buried her face in her arms. Harry Bishop and Jimmy Andrews peered skeptically from their doorways.

"No!" I said, patting Mrs. Lake furiously on the head. "No, I mean old man Mack's pickle jars. Where've they been all this time? Where does Lizzie keep them?"

"I don't know," Mrs. Lake sniffed, wiping her eyes.

"What was it?" I hurried back to my file, began pushing things around, and finally found the inventory of the Mack estate. "One hundred twenty-nine bottles of it, in the wine cellar!"

"Well," remarked Mr. Bishop, and returned to his work. Jimmy Andrews hung around to see what was up.

"Call 'Stacia," I said to Mrs. Lake. "No, hell no, don't. I'll run up to Baltimore." I looked at my watch. "Will you run me to the bus, Jim? I bet I can catch the four o'clock."

"Sure," Jimmy said. He drove insanely; I made the bus with two minutes to spare, and was soon off to Baltimore.

Eustacia Callader was an old Negro servant in the Mack household, whom I'd met during the course of the litigation. She had virtually raised Harrison Junior and was quietly on our side in the contest over the estate, though she grasped little of the controversy. She it was whom I sought now. Arriving in Baltimore four hours later, I stopped in a drugstore to buy envelopes and stamps, and then took a taxi out to Ruxton, getting out at the driveway of the Mack house. The sun had just set, and I actually hid myself on the grounds in the rear of the house—it was all quite theatrical—and waited, I suppose, for 'Stacia to come out of the kitchen for something. An unlikely plan, but then my whole scheme, my suspicion, was unlikely: when the great Negro woman did, as a matter of fact, come out just forty-five minutes later, en route to the garbage cans down by the big garage, I took her appearance as a good omen. Following her out of earshot of the house, I approached her.

"Lord 'a mercy, Mister Andrews!" she chuckled enormously. "What y'all doin' up here? Come see Lizzie?"

"'Stacia, listen," I whispered urgently. "I've got a five-buck question." I gave her the five, and she giggled helplessly.

"Where does Lizzie keep the old man's fertilizer?" I asked. "Is it still in the wine cellar?"

"De fertilize'?" 'Stacia chortled. "What fertilize'?" She laughed so hard that I knew she didn't understand.

"The crap, 'Stacia," I demanded. "How does Lizzie feel about all those bottles of crap?"

"Oh, dat's what you mean de fertilize'!"

"A hundred and twenty-nine jars of it," I said. "Used to be in the wine cellar. Are they still there?"

When 'Stacia regained control of her risibility, she admitted that she didn't know, but she promised to find out and tell me. I gave her a buss on the cheek and took up lodgings in a clump of forsythia bushes near the garbage cans, while 'Stacia returned to the house to question the other servants who lived in. I was prepared, if it should prove necessary, to bribe somebody heavily to destroy those pickle jars for me secretly, but I didn't look forward to taking that step, since it opened the way for blackmail. Still, it seemed highly unlikely to me that Mrs. Mack had ordered them removed herself, although it was exactly that possibility which had occurred to me on the occasion of Mrs. Lake's *faux pas*.

I was pleasantly surprised, then, when three hours later—it was after midnight—'Stacia lumbered back with the announcement that though the bottles were indeed still in the wine cellar, Mrs. Mack had observed last week to R. J. Collier, the gimpy, dusty old fellow who tended the gardens, that the seals on the jars were apparently not airtight, and had mentioned the possibility of someday disposing of the collection. Indeed, 'Stacia verified that with the coming of hot weather the jars had begun to smell noticeably, and that the odor was creeping up occasionally to the ground floor. Two days before, R. J. Collier had taken it upon himself to pile the whole stack into the far corner of the wine cellar and to cover it with a wet tarpaulin, hoping thereby to check the bouquet, but his experiment had yielded no apparent results. Mrs. Mack was growing annoyed. R. J. Collier had, that very day, broached the suggestion that his late employer's singular remains be put to work around the flower gardens—the zinnia beds, especially, could use the nourishment, he declared. All the servants considered the suggestion more touching than tactless, and I, too, sensed a seed of poetry in the gardener's practicality. But Lizzie had remained noncommittal.

"Listen, 'Stacia," I said, "you mustn't say a word about the pickle jars, or about me being here. I'm going to give you ten dollars, honey—"

"Hoo, Mister Andrews!"

"—here, ten bucks. Now I want you to keep a close watch on those jars. Make sure you know everything that Liz or R. J. Collier or anybody else does to them. Look. I'm giving you all these envelopes with stamps on them. They're addressed to me, so keep them hidden, and there's paper inside. Now, then, every time even one of those bottles is moved from where it is now, you write to me and tell me. Understand?"

'Stacia giggled and shook and grunted, but I was fairly sure she understood.

"For Christ's sake don't say a word," I cautioned her again. "If everything turns out right, Harrison will give you a brand-new car. A yellow roadster, he'll buy you. Okay?"

'Stacia could scarcely stand for laughing. But she stuck the envelopes deep between her endless bosoms and rumbled off to the house, shaking her head at my derangement. I walked out to the road and hiked two miles to a telephone. Next day I was back in my office, smoking cigars and staring at my wall. I didn't bother to tell Harrison anything about my trip—perhaps nothing would come of it after all.

And except for the infrequent parries with Charley Parks, the attorney next door, over our automobile suit—you'll recall I mentioned it earlier?—I had done nothing else, no work at all on any case, since then: nearly a week. I was waiting for 'Stacia's letter, and thinking steadily about possible alternative plans of action. I'd decided to sit thus until July 1. If nothing had happened to the jars by then, I'd take the risk of bribing R. J. Collier to destroy some of them.

Then, this morning, there was 'Stacia's letter, one of the self-addressed envelopes I'd given her. It could contain anything from nonsense to the key to three million dollars, and it was merely as a disciplinary exercise that I'd postponed reading it until after I'd read the other letters and the handbill, and had called Marvin Rose. But I shan't exact such discipline from you, reader. Here is the letter:

Mr. Andrew. Mrs. Mack, has put pickle jars in grenhouse. R. J. Coler, has put on zinas. Eustacia M. Callader. R. J. Coler, has put 72 bottles on zinas. Eustacia M. Callader.

I put the letter in the dossier with the other documents pertaining to the Mack will case, returned the dossier to the file, and locked the filing cabinets. For nearly two hours I stared at my wall, and then I left the office to stroll uptown for my appointment with Marvin.

A good morning's work, reader: I opened a few letters and put one in the file. An excellent morning's work for one's last morning on earth, I should say.

My friend Harrison is three million dollars richer for it.

XI. An instructive, if sophisticated, observation

The thermometer outside the offices of the daily *Banner* read eighty-nine degrees when I walked past it on my way uptown. Few people were on the streets. At the curb in front of a large funeral parlor a black hearse was parked, its loading door closed, and several mourners, along with the black-suited employees of the establishment, stood quietly about in the yard. As I approached, an aged Chesapeake Bay retriever bitch loped from a hydrangea bush out onto the sidewalk and up onto the undertaker's porch, followed closely by a prancing, sniffing young mongrel setter. I saw the Chesapeake Bay dog stop to shake herself in front of the door; the setter clambered upon her at once, his long tongue lolling. Just then the door opened and the pallbearers came out with a casket. Their path was blocked by the dogs. Some of the bearers smiled guiltily; an employee caught the setter on his haunches with an unfunereal kick. The bitch trundled off the porch, her lover still half on her, and took up a position in the middle of the sidewalk, near the hearse. The pair then resumed their amours in the glaring sun, to the embarrassment of the company, who pretended not to notice them while the hearse's door was opened and the casket gently loaded aboard.

I smiled and walked on. Nature, coincidence, can be a heavy-handed symbolizer. She seems at times fairly to club one over the head with significances such as this clumsy "life-in-the-face-of-death" scenario, so obvious that it was embarrassing. One is constantly being confronted with a sun that bursts from behind the clouds just as the home team takes the ball; ominous rumblings of thunder when one is brooding desultorily at home; magnificent dawns on days when one has resolved to mend one's ways; hurricanes that demolish a bad man's house and leave his good neighbor's untouched, or vice-versa; Race Streets marked SLOW; Cemetery Avenues marked ONE WAY. The man whose perceptions are not so rudimentary, whose palate is attuned to subtler dishes, can only smile uncomfortably and walk away, reminding himself that good taste is a human invention.

But it's not easy to keep one's patience in the face of the world's abundant ingenuousness. For instance, when I came to the corner of High and Poplar Streets and stopped to chat awhile with Capt. Osborn and two of his cronies, installed on their loafers' bench in front of George Melvin's store, I had to put up with a prominent MEN WORKING sign near an open manhole in the street before them; a senile clock in the store window, which, like the store and the old men, had ceased to mark the passage of time; a movie-theater poster directly behind Capt. Osborn's head, advertising a double bill —*Life Begins at Forty* and *Captains Courageous;* a pigeon perched restlessly on a NO PARKING sign—I could go on for a page. Really, to resist the temptation to use such ponderous, ready-made symbols taxes one's integrity, and I'm certain that if I were writing stories for my bread and butter, my resistance would weaken. I recall once reading a story that ended with the hero dead on the floor—was he a suicide or a homicide?— beneath a cash register announcing: THIS REGISTERS THE AMOUNT OF YOUR PURCHASE. The machine, as one familiar with life's elephantine ironies might have anticipated, registered zero, and I for one take it as a mark of the author's lack of acumen that he couldn't ignore that cash register, or make it read $4.37 or some other meaningless figure. It's too easy otherwise, like using clichés.

So, reader, should you ever find yourself writing about the world, take care not to nibble at the many tempting symbols she sets squarely in your path, or you'll be baited into saying things you don't really mean, and offending the people you want most to entertain. Develop, if you can, the technique of the pallbearers and myself: smile, to be sure—for fucking dogs are truly funny—but walk on and say nothing, as though you hadn't noticed.

XII. A chorus of oysters

Socially, as well as economically, Capt. Osborn and his colleagues of the loafers' bench were exclusively consumers. They ate food, wore clothing, and smoked cigars, but they produced nothing. They sat immobile on their antique bench like a row of crusty oysters and ingested with their eyes everything that passed, but they did not participate. The life of Cambridge passed by and through them like sea water through an oyster's gills: they strained from it what nutrition they wanted as it passed, digesting people and events with a snort or a comment, but they never moved from their position. They were a chorus of ancient oysters, stolidly regarding the fish that swam through their ken. Their infrequent voices were slow, nasal, high-pitched, and senile.

A bright blue roadster, for example, would roar by.

"Eee, there rides young Mowb Henly!" one would observe.

"'E's a hot one," another would add. "Ol' Mowb's boy. Can't do nothin' with that youngster."

"No, *sir*," a third would agree.

"Eee, ol' Mowb's boy!" the first would repeat, rumbling his way up to a wet cackle of mirth and expectoration.

"'E's bad as 'is ol' man," the second would remark.

"Ye know what they say," would crow the third. "*Like father, like son.*"

The first would choke and strangle then, his red rheumy eyes a-twinkle, his red cracked face all grinning, the small saliva spilling over his brown teeth and thin red lips, and begin the refrain again:

"Eee! Hmph! *Hawk!* Sploo! Ol'—*thoo!* Thff! Ol'—Hawk! Thff! *Thoo!* Ol' Mowb Henly! *Thooie!*"

I had a few minutes to spare, so I took a seat at the shady end of the bench—the old men liked the sun—and listened to their hoary music for a while. Presently the loaded hearse drove by from the funeral parlor, two cars with lighted headlights following behind. The procession paused at the intersection and then moved on through the red light, heading for Greenlawn Cemetery, out toward the country club.

"Whose funeral?" I asked.

"Why, that's Clarence Wampler's wife, ain't it, Osborn?" offered my neighbor, watching the hearse move off.

"Yep," assented Capt. Osborn. "Died Monday night."

"That the Henry Street one, come from Golden Hill?" asked the third.

"Naw, that's *Lewis* Wampler's wife yer thinkin' of," Capt. Osborn declared. "Yer thinkin' of ol' Jenny Fairwell."

"Ol' Jenny?" the first cackled. "Ol' Jenny?"

"Ol' Jenny," Capt. Osborn grinned, stretching his leg. "There was a hot one."

"Ol' Jenny!" the first snuffled happily.

"This here's *Clarence* Wampler's wife," Capt. Osborn explained. "Lived on Ross Street, down by the creek."

"Sure," the first said. "I b'lieve she was a Canlon, weren't she?"

"Now let's see," Capt. Osborn mused. "She was the oldest Canlon girl—must of been Louise Mae."

"Louise Mae Canlon. Hell, she weren't so durned old, was she?"

"Louise Mae Canlon," Capt. Osborn repeated. "She was the oldest—ol' Cap'n Will Canlon's girls, down to Golden Hill. Louise Mae Canlon must of been twenty when Clarence Wampler married 'er. I remember that was the year ol' Cap'n Canlon lost 'is schooner in the ice—I was just startin' out with my own boat that season, the *June Phillips*, I bought 'er off ol' man George Phillips, down to Fishin' Creek. That'd be 'bout 1885, I s'pect."

"Cap'n Canlon's schooner?" asked the third old fellow, who had remained silent. "Ye mean the *Samuel T. Brice?*"

"Naw, that was 'is *ol'* boat," Capt. Osborn declared. "I b'lieve the *Samuel T. Brice* burned up one time, tied up to Long Dock in Baltimore. This was Cap'n Will's *new* boat—what was 'er name? *LaVerne Canlon?* After 'is wife. Well, sir, Cap'n Will hadn't no more'n put 'er in the water, spankin' new, ever' line and whipstitch, 'fore we had that big freeze-up in the Bay, and be durned if 'e didn't git froze up in 'er, and the ice wrecked 'er. Weren't no icebreakers them days."

"No, sir," the others agreed.

"I durn near lost the *June Phillips* that winter, out off Sharp's Island. Durn water was icin' up so fast ye could watch it skim over, ever' time the wind let off. Then the breeze would puff up and we'd go a-scrunchin' a little farther. I had a extra-heavy chain for a bobstay, thank the Lord; I'd told Walter Jones to hang a big one on 'er when 'e was fittin' 'er out, and I mean I didn't know which would win, us or the ice. Thank the good Lord that breeze was up, kept us a-scrunchin' right through, don't no bobstay in the world would of cut that ice, I'm tellin' ye."

"Eee!" chuckled the first. "Don't freeze up no more like that!"

"Ol' Cap'n Jamie Snyder—you remember Cap'n Jamie? Cap'n Jamie Snyder says to me, 'e saw Walter Jones a-hangin' that big chain bobstay on the *June Phillips*, up in 'is yard, 'e says to me, 'Osborn,' 'e says, 'yer goin' to need six darkies in yer dinghy,' 'e says, 'jest to keep 'er sailin' trim!' Well, sir, I says to Cap'n Jamie, 'Cap'n Jamie, it looks like ice to me, this winter,' I says, 'and I'd a sight rather ship six darkies in my dinghy, than have to git out and walk home!'"

"Eee!"

"Yes, sir!"

"Well, sir, I didn't think no more about it," Capt. Osborn went on. "Then come that big ice, and the *June Phillips* come a-scrunchin' home from Sharp's Island—took us till past dark—with that big bobstay jest a-chewin' that ice like a lean hog corncobs, and a good load o' oysters piled in the bow to give 'er weight. Next day I seen Cap'n Jamie down to the creek, lookin' where the ice had ground the paint off the *June Phillips's* cutwater, all round that chain, and a-shakin' 'is head. 'Osborn,' 'e says, when 'e saw me watchin' 'im, 'I didn't think nothin' at the time,' 'e says, 'but I got to admit yer one up on me.' 'How's that?' I says. 'Why,' 'e says, 'don't ye know I left the *B. John Gore* fast in the ice yesterday, right off Horn Point, stuck like a minner in a gill net? Didn't I walk ever' step o' the way from the *B. John Gore* to Sim Riley's farmhouse, to git a horse, jest like ye said? I'm eatin' humble pie, Osborn,' 'e said. Then be durn if 'e didn't laugh it off and buy me a drink. That was ol' Cap'n Jamie fer ye!"

"Ol' Cap'n Jamie!"

"Eee! *Thoo!*"

Poor Louise Mae Canlon Wampler: the oysters would, perhaps, sing of her another day.

I rose to leave, and then the same dogs that had done honor to the late Mrs. Wampler came trotting down to the loafers' bench. The retriever waddled up to Capt. Osborn for an ear-scratching. The setter, ears back, tongue lolling, panted behind and attempted in his ardor to enter her from the side.

"Hoo there, feller!" wheezed one old man. "That ain't no way!"

"Pshaw!" snorted another, embarrassed. "Look at 'em, won't ye? Pecker's a-winkin' like the Cedar Point Light! Git on, there!"

"Don't spoil 'is fun," Capt. Osborn scolded with a grin.

" 'E'll git old soon enough, or a car'll hit 'im. Let 'im take it as it comes."

"Hee hee hee!"

"Aw pshaw! Hawk! *Thoo!*"

Capt. Osborn even assisted the setter a trifle with his foot, shoving the dog's haunches down to where his efforts might be rewarded. The setter set to with a will, while Capt. Osborn fondly scratched the retriever's ear and the oysters snickered.

I chuckled too, and would have stayed to watch, but it was almost eleven-fifteen. I chuckled all the way up Poplar Street toward Marvin Rose's office, thinking of animals *in coito* and of what had occurred in my bedroom on my seventeenth birthday. Behind my back I heard the oysters busily ingesting Cambridge:

"Hee!"

"Pshaw!"

"*Thoo!*"

XIII. A mirror up to life

My mother having died when I was seven years old, I grew up under the inconsistent tutelage of my father and a succession of maids and housekeepers. My father always expressed concern over my welfare and proper guidance, but from either necessity or disinclination he seldom gave me a great deal of personal attention. As for the maids and housekeepers, some liked me and some didn't, but all had their own affairs to mind while Dad was working, and so I was left to myself much of the time.

I was almost never an ill-behaved child. I was quiet, but not uncommunicative; reserved, but not reclusive; energetic at times, but seldom enthusiastic. There were few restrictions on my behavior, nor were many needed. I was (and am) temperamentally disposed of observing rules—my desires seldom fell without their pale. And because I so rarely gave him cause for concern, my father was incurious about my activities.

Therefore, when I really wanted to do something of which I was certain he wouldn't approve, it was not difficult for me to do it.

My sex life, reader, up to my seventeenth year, was so unspectacular as to be unworthy of mention. I did all the things that young anthropoids delight in while growing up; my high-school amours were limited to hot, open-mouthed kisses and much risqué conversation—until my *alliance* with Miss Betty June Gunter.

Betty June, at age seventeen, was a thin, almost scrawny little thing, most ungainly and sharp in the face, with good eyes, crooked teeth, coarse blonde hair, fine skin, and no hips or breasts to speak of. She was not considered unattractive in my set, though socially she was certainly of an inferior caste. Betty June was a poor student but a spirited girl, and there was a sharpness in her speech that bespoke a mind livelier than those of a number of more scholarly girls in our class. Besides— and this was her chief attraction—Betty June was sophisticated, worldly, informed, in a way that none of the thoroughly re- spectable girls of my acquaintance could approach. Her father was dead, and her mother—one wasn't sure what to think about her mother. The girl had little to do with her classmates, especially with the other girls, although there were a few notable exceptions: one or two girls of the most respectable sort claimed her as their close friend. We boys lusted after her with our eyes and our speech, of course, but before her cool, experienced manner we were clumsy and abashed. She regarded the lot of us as puppies, I'm sure.

The relationship between Betty June and me commenced when she fell in love with one Smitty Herrin, a twenty-seven- year-old bachelor who lived two houses from me. Smitty ig- nored her existence, she was devoted to him, and she got the habit that winter of spending much time in and about my house, hoping that Smitty would notice her. I was delighted. Betty June told me all her troubles—and they were dramatic, *real* troubles! Woman had never loved man, it seemed to me, as she loved Smitty, and yet he ignored her. She wouldn't have cared what he did to her—he might beat her and curse her (a thrilling notion to a seventeen-year-old!)—if only he'd acknowledge her devotion, but he ignored her. She would even have suffered torture for him (together we dreamed up the tortures she'd be willing to suffer, considering each soberly); would even have died for him (we discussed, in detail, various unpleasant deaths) for the merest crumb of reciprocal passion.

But Smitty remained oblivious. I was violently sympathetic, and helping her articulate her grievances I discovered that I could converse more easily and naturally with her than with anyone in my experience: there was no stultifying embarrassment, as there was with other girls, nor was there the necessity to impress that falsified all my communication with my male companions. Moreover, the things Betty June discussed were of a new and thrilling order—I felt mature and wise and confident, discussing them, and I found myself able to think more liberally, compassionately, and judiciously than I'd ever thought before.

In fact, reader, I should say that it was at just this point that I lost my innocence. Of what concern is it that eventually I made love to her? But Betty June, thin skinny Betty, she broke the seal of my mind, which had been before her coming an idle enough instrument; took from me my spiritual virginity, which is childishness and naïveté, and opened my eyes to the world of men and women—and this gently, and with warmth. A lucky virgin, I, to fall into those meager arms and pathetic problems; what she took from me, I lost with pleasure.

She came to the house nearly every afternoon, after school, and stayed until the housekeeper came to prepare supper. On Saturdays she often spent the whole day with me. We would sit alone, either in the living room or in Dad's study—I preferred the study—and I would fix drinks for us, often lacing them with rum or whiskey filched from the butler's pantry. And we talked and talked and talked, easily, sympathetically, wedding her experience with my articulation. I could feel myself expanding, maturing in the bath of her lean life, flexing the muscles of my rationality and my understanding. I've no real way of knowing how Betty June felt—whether she sensed the growing power in me or regarded me merely as a harmless colt.

There came times, alas, when, colt no more, I felt every inch a stone-horse! and regarded her leanness, perched on the couch, with nostrils all but quivering. Those were embarrassing times. I suspected that, should I ever approach her, our peculiar *rapport* would vanish. Besides—the chasm yawned, the mystery —what if she were to submit?

"Your ice is melting," Betty June would observe, and I would hide myself in my drink.

Up to this point—late winter, perhaps February—I had remained fairly objective about the matter. I understood that Betty June was in love with Smitty; that she found in me only a sort of spiritual brother; that both she and Smitty were people whom, at bottom, I did not really respect; that, finally, one of her chief attractions was her *possibility:* the tantalizing fact that unlike most of the girls in my set, Betty June was experienced, and that it was therefore not *entirely* impossible that—

How many aching, perspiring nights I placed on the altar of that possibility!

One afternoon she came over to where I sat in Dad's leather study chair, to light my cigarette. She held the match expertly, and while I drew on the cigarette she ran her free hand playfully through my hair. I caught her arm instantly; she laughed and fell into my lap. I took the cigarette from my mouth and crushed her lips with a violent kiss. She grew skittish, playful, but she didn't move away, and I kissed her again and again, passionately. I could scarcely believe my good fortune; I couldn't speak. Betty June still laughed softly, and kissed back—no girl had done that to me!—and pinched, and nuzzled, and caught my ears, nose, and eyebrows gently in her teeth. I began pawing her flat chest clumsily, sure I'd be slapped, but she stretched and made no objection. Incredible! I had a field day. At three-thirty she left me to marvel at my good luck.

From that day on our relationship was of a different sort. She still regarded me as harmless, I'm certain, but now we played instead of talking. It was beautiful sport; every afternoon ended with my transgressing the boundaries she'd tacitly drawn, pleading with her to surrender to me—confident in the knowledge that she would not. Then she would leave.

How my opinion changed! My objectivity was peeled off
with her chemise and tossed unwanted into the corner. I came
to loathe Smitty; to rail at him inwardly—for Betty June allowed not a word of criticism; to lay elaborate plans for his
ruin. I wept furiously whenever she spoke of her love for him,
and she pressed my wet face to her small breast. I regarded *my*
love—it had never been voiced—as a thing inviolable, out of
reach; a hot, virginal intercourse of souls. I went about looking
wan and distracted, brooding, melancholy. My friends kept a
respectful distance; none, I think, knew of Betty June's visits.
I regarded us as lost souls, condemned by the Fates (Clotho,
Lachesis, and Atropos—I remember looking them up, and weeping at the justice of their names) never to consummate our
love, separated by prior commitments and by barriers of position and caste (be sure I never mentioned *this* to her!), *et
cetera, et cetera.*

Thus until March 2, 1917—my seventeenth birthday. I wasn't
expecting Betty June until that afternoon, and I had decided to
spend the morning—it must have been a holiday—knocking
down the weathered frame of my unfinished boat, which still
stood rotting in the back yard. But no sooner had Dad gone to
court, and the housekeeper to her sister's place, as she always
did, than Betty June came running into the house, weeping
crazily. I held her tightly, and when she refused to calm herself
I shook her by the shoulders—it seemed a manly thing to do,
and it worked. She still sobbed and whimpered, but less violently.

"What's the matter with you?" I demanded, so frightened by
her emotion that I actually felt ill, and my knees trembled.

"Smitty's married!" she cried.

"What?"

She nodded, sniffing and shuddering. "He's been married
secretly to Mona Johnston for a year," she said, "and all that
time I was—"

"Shut up!" I commanded. "Don't even say it!" I had decided
to be strong.

"Now he's got her in trouble, and her folks are making them announce it."

"Good for them!" I said toughly. "Serves the bastard right!"

"No!" Betty June loosed fresh tears. "Now he's enlisted in the Army, because he can't stand Mona any more! He'll go overseas, Toddy! I'll never see him again!"

She threatened to break down completely.

"Tough luck!" I sneered, very proud of my new strength.

Betty June ran into the study and collapsed on the leather couch. I sniffed, strode into the butler's pantry, and took a good pull of bourbon, right from the bottle. It scalded to my stomach, set my blood on fire. I gave Betty June a few minutes to cry (and to wonder what I was doing); then I took another swig of bourbon, choked on it, replaced the bottle, and went to the study, walking with precision. Betty June, her eyes red, looked up at me dubiously.

I said nothing (couldn't have if I'd wanted to). I sat carefully on the edge of the couch and with one wrench opened her blouse. I was in no mood for trifling!

"Don't rip it," Betty June whimpered, recovering her composure.

"That's your problem," I growled, and gave her a bruising kiss. "If you don't want 'em ripped, take 'em off yourself."

She sat up at once and slipped off her blouse and chemise. I stood up and watched impassively.

"You quitting there?" I demanded sarcastically, as a matter of form.

Betty June regarded me for a moment with a new expression on her face. Then she stood up, and unbuttoning her placket, let her long skirt fall to the floor. Quickly she stripped off her petticoat, and without the least hesitation, her shoes, stockings, and bloomers, and stood before me nude. I very nearly swooned. Luckily I had the presence of mind to embrace her at once, so that I was out of range of her eyes.

"Take me upstairs," she whispered.

I was petrified, now that the opportunity was at hand. Take her upstairs! My mind raced for honorable excuses.

"Suppose somebody comes home?" I croaked.

"I'll run to the bathroom," she said. Obviously she was no novice at this sort of thing. "Come on, get my clothes." She broke away from me and ran, all pink skin, to the stairs. I retrieved her clothing and followed after, scared to death; soon, in my bedroom, cluttered like a museum with the relics of my boyhood, she received that boyhood happily, and kissed me, as I chose to think, for making her its custodian. I should have kissed her, for no hot bump of a boy ever had defter instruction. I have been uncommonly lucky with women, surely through no virtue of my own.

What follows is indiscreet, but it is the point of the story.

A seventeen-year-old boy is insatiable. His lust is a tall weed, which crushed repeatedly under the mower springs up again, green and unbowed. He is easily aroused and quickly satisfied, and easily aroused again. New to the manners of the business, I cried like a baby, bleated like a goat, roared like a lion. The time came, the lesson, when I was stallion indeed. . . .

And then I looked into the mirror on my dresser, beside us— an unusually large mirror, that gave back our images full-length and life-size—and there we were: Betty June's face buried in the pillow, her scrawny little buttocks thrust skywards; me gangly as a whippet and braying like an ass. I exploded with laughter!

"What's the matter?" Betty June asked sharply.

I tossed and rolled and roared with laughter.

"I don't see anything funny!"

I couldn't answer. I couldn't comfort the nervous tears that ran from her, though I swear I tried. I couldn't help her at all, or myself. I bellowed and snorted with laughter, long after Betty June had fumed out of my bed, out of my room, out of my house, for the last time. I laughed through lunch, to Dad's amusement (and subsequent irritation). I laughed that night when I undressed.

I have said that my experience in the Argonne, not very long afterwards, was the second of two unforgettable demonstrations of my animality. This was the first. Nothing, to me, is so consistently, profoundly, earth-shakingly funny as we animals in the act of mating. Reader, if you are young and would live on love; if in the flights of intercourse you feel that you and your beloved are models for a Phidias—then don't include among the trappings of your love-nest a good plate mirror. For a mirror can reflect only what it sees, and what it sees is funny.

Well. I never laughed at poor Betty June again, because a few days after my birthday I enlisted in the Army. Smitty was killed; I was not. Mona Johnston married someone else. Betty June, I learned upon my return from service, had become a prostitute during the war, first in Cambridge, and then—when after the Armistice it was no longer patriotic to sleep with soldiers—in Baltimore. When I next saw her, it was under entirely different circumstances. I've not heard anything from her for years.

Think me heartless—I could wish I were—but even as I write this now, thirty-seven years later, though my heart goes out to pitiful Betty, generous Betty, nevertheless I can't expunge that mirror from my mind; I think of it and must smile. To see a pair of crabs, of dogs, of people—even lovely, graceful Jane—I can't finish, reader, can't hold my pen fast to the line: I am convulsed; I am weeping tears of laughter on the very page!

XIV. Bottles, needles, knives

A good habit to acquire, if you are interested in disciplining your strength, is the habit of habit-breaking. For one thing, to change your habits deliberately on occasion prevents you from being entirely consistent (I believe I explained the virtues of limited inconsistency earlier); for another, it prevents your becoming any more a vassal than you have to. Do you smoke? Stop smoking for a few years. Do you part your hair on the left? Try not parting it at all. Do you sleep on your left side, to the right of your wife? Sleep on your stomach, on her left. You have hundreds of habits: of dress, of manner, of speech, of eating, of thought, of aesthetic taste, of moral conduct. Break them now and then, deliberately, and institute new ones in their places for a while. It will slow you up sometimes, but you'll tend to grow strong and feel free. To be sure, don't break *all* your habits. Leave some untouched forever; otherwise you'll be consistent.

In deciding to see Marvin Rose for a physical examination I was accomplishing two things at once: the appointment was extraordinary, and that fact gave an element of inconsistency to my last day on earth, which I'd decided to live routinely. At the same time, I was breaking a thirteen-year-old habit of not seeing doctors.

Marvin Rose had last attended me in 1924, when he prescribed for my infected prostate. At the time, I had just enrolled in law school and he was interning at the Johns Hopkins Hospital;

we had been fraternity brothers as undergraduates at the University, and were dependable, if not intimate, friends. It was a terrible morning that I went to him—drunken, bloody, half-conscious, aching—where he worked in the outpatient department of the old brown hive. He washed me up, gave me some kind of pill to swallow, perhaps even administered a needle. What he said, finally, was, "Stay here for a few days, Toddy."

I intended to refuse, but it seems I fainted; when I was conscious again I was hospitalized, and within a few hours, upon my being examined—painfully!—the infection was discovered. Although I wasn't aware of it at the time, Marvin's words had terminated a phase of my life, for upon my discharge from the hospital a month later, I was an entirely different person. I had stumbled in a drunken animal; I walked out a saint. The story is neither religious nor long.

Of the noises in my life, one of the loudest in my memory is the tiny popping puncture of my bayonet in the German sergeant's neck—that sergeant with whom I choose to think my soul had lain for a while. Were I ever so foolish as to try, I'm sure I could close my eyes and hear that puncture as distinctly now as I heard it then, and the soft slide of my metal into his throat. To a noise like that, thirty-six years is a blink of the eye.

Of the human voices I have heard, one of the very clearest in my memory is the gravelly, somnolent Missouri voice of Capt. John Frisbee, the Army doctor who examined me after a heart attack just prior to my discharge. Here are his very words:

"Ah sweah, Cawpr'l, if that isn't endocahditis yew got! How in the heyell did yew git in the Ahmy, boy? Yew too young to have a haht attack, now ahn't yew?"

He shook his head, examined me again to make sure, and then wrote his report, which he explained to me as gently as his naturally blunt manner would permit.

"The endocahditis isn't so bad, son; that's what clubbed yew fingahs, and it should of kept yew a civilian. It won't git no worse. The bad thing is that yew liable to have a myocahdial infahction—and that can very likely kill yew. Might be any second; might be a yeah from now; might be nevah. But yew just as well know 'bout it. Ah don't subscrahb to this secrecy hoss-m'nure, d'yew?"

Can you understand at once—I neither can nor will explain it—that I was relieved? To say that the puncture had deranged me would be too crude, but—well, I was relieved, that's all, to learn that every minute I lived might be my last.

My first impulse, after discharge, was to rush home as quickly as possible, in order to say farewell to Dad and my town before I fell dead. Every time the train slowed for a crossing I squirmed and fidgeted, sure I'd never reach Cambridge alive. Dad welcomed me warmly, and seemed so happy to have me safely home that I hadn't the courage to tell him the tragic news at once—though of course I mustn't wait too long, or my sudden death might surprise him, coming unprepared-for. I decided to gamble on a week, during which time I idled nervously about the big house, unable to concentrate on anything.

But at the week's end, when one night Dad called me into his study, and I resolved to tell him at once, he forestalled me by speaking first.

"Cheer up, Toddy," he laughed—I must have looked glum. "I didn't call you in to scold you, like I used to when your mother was alive! What I've got on my mind is serious, but it isn't solemn."

He was feeling affectionate. He handed me a cigar, and I sat on the leather couch and smoked it.

"Todd, the first thing I want you to do, if it's all right with you, is take a vacation—from now till fall. Don't feel obliged to stay here unless you feel like it—go anywhere you want to. For spending money you've got a pretty good wad in Liberty bonds that I banked for you while you were away."

I listened, hoping my heart would last until he finished, so that I could explain.

"Then when September comes, son, nothing could make me happier than if you'd go to school." He grinned. "I shan't specify Johns Hopkins, but I must say that that's where the bright men are coming from, lately. Then, if you *really* want to humor me, study law. And do it right, in a law school; not in an office like I did. But again, I shan't even specify the law. I do want you to go to school, though, son—after a vacation. See if you can spend your whole bank account by September!"

I must say that at that moment I felt wonderful about my father. His concern for me, the (for him) remarkable diplomacy of his approach, his generosity—all these, I see now, were ordinary sentiments, not unusual in themselves; but then I was a very ordinary sort of young man, too, at the time, and the sentiments, if commonplace, were nonetheless uncommonly strong. My ailing heart felt lodged in my throat; I couldn't speak.

Seeing my hesitation, Dad busied himself attending to his cigar. His smile perhaps set a little, but it did not disappear.

"Don't answer," he said then. "Don't say anything one way or the other, yet."

"No," I protested, "no, it's—"

"Not a word," Dad insisted, sure of himself again. "What a crude fellow I am, calling you in here without a word of notice and springing a whole life's plan on you! A fine son you'd be, come to think of it, if you ever agreed to anything that drastic without a little thought first!" His spirits were high again. "Get out now," he ordered cheerfully. "Go get a little tight or something, like a veteran's supposed to. I shan't listen to a word you say about this at least until tomorrow, if not next week. Go on, now, *git!*" And he buried his attention in pretended business on his desk.

Well, I worried for a day or so—and he did too, poor fellow, thinking I didn't like his proposal—and finally decided that, since I was after all still alive, and might be for several months, I might as well leave Dad happy by enrolling in college: he would have the satisfaction of knowing he'd done all a father could do for me. Besides, why tell him about my heart? Why make both suffer, when there was no help for it?

"I'm going to Hopkins, Dad," I announced one morning at breakfast, "and then to Maryland Law School, if it's all right with you. And I don't know if this is right or not to ask, but I'd like it if when I get out I could eventually set up here in town, like you did, maybe as a junior partner or something."

Dad didn't say a word. He was so happy his eyes watered, and he had to fold his napkin and get up from the breakfast table. I was certainly glad I'd said what I said.

So I went to Johns Hopkins, enrolled in the pre-law curriculum. At Dad's suggestion I joined a fraternity—Beta Alpha Order, a Southern outfit—and lived in the fraternity house. I must say that if one has to go to college under the conditions I went under, the early twenties was an excellent time to go. It seemed to me that nearly all of my fraternity brothers expected, like myself, to fall dead any moment, for they lived each day as though it were to be their last. Their way of life suited my feelings exactly, and I soon made myself one of them. We stayed drunk for days at a time. We set fire to the men's rooms in night clubs, ignited smudge pots in the streets, installed cows in unexpected places. We brawled and fought, made nuisances of ourselves, spent nights in jail sobering up. We kept women in the house overnight, in violation of University and chapter rules—night-club strippers, prostitutes, strange ladies, college girls—and we paid fines for it; some of us were justifiably expelled from the University. We went on adulterous weekend trips to Washington and New York, beach parties at Beaver Dam and Betterton, and once a fantastic bullfrog hunt in the Dorchester Marshes south of Cambridge. We fell from speeding automobiles, and were hospitalized; occasionally even fought honest to goodness duels, and were hospitalized. One of us

died in an automobile crash, drunk. Two of us were obliged
to marry girls inadvertently made pregnant. Three of us were
withdrawn from the University by irate parents. One of us
committed suicide with sleeping pills and was discovered at the
autopsy to be syphilitic. Three of us turned into chronic alco-
holics. Perhaps a dozen of us were dismissed from school for
failing courses.

Does this sound like a lampoon of student life in the early
twenties? It is, indeed, a thing easily lampooned, but remember
that the lampoons didn't appear out of the air: they were written
mostly by men who lived through just this sort of life. It reads
like a lampoon to me, too—but that's how it was.

One thing more, which perhaps distinguished my crowd from
similarly exuberant groups of undergraduates at other colleges
at the time: those of us who didn't flunk out got an education
—it is difficult to remain long at Hopkins and escape education.
It was we who followed the real tradition of the chapter and,
to some extent, of the University: *studentensleben,* in the manner of the old German universities. We drank hard, caroused
hard, studied hard, and slept little. We crammed for examinations, drank black coffee, chewed cigarettes, took benzedrine—
and read books, quizzed each other for days, and read more
books, and asked more questions. The ones who failed were not
really a part of us: the goal was to drink the most whiskey, fornicate the most girls, get the least sleep, and make the highest
grades. I for one am thankful that studying was part of the sport,
because otherwise I shouldn't have bothered with it, knowing
I'd not live to take my bachelor's degree. To be sure, most of
us remembered nothing two days after the final examinations;
but some of us did. It was the professors, the fine, independent
minds of Johns Hopkins—the maturity, the absence of restrictions, the very air of Homewood, that nourished the seeds of
reason in our ruined bodies; the disinterested wisdom that refused even to see our ridiculous persons in the lecture halls; that

talked, as it were, to itself, and seemed scarcely to care when some of us began to listen passionately.

I lived through 1920, through 1921, through 1922, through 1923. In the summers I lived on at the fraternity house and worked as a stonemason, a brush salesman, a factory laborer, a lifeguard at one of the city pools, a tutor of history, even, and once actually a ditchdigger. To my great surprise I was alive on commencement day, if not entirely sober, and lived to walk off Gilman Terrace with my diploma—pale, weak, educated. I had lost twenty pounds, countless prejudices, much provincialism, my chastity (what had remained of it), and my religion. I had gained a capacity for liquor and work; an ability to take beatings; a familiarity with card games, high society, and whorehouses; a taste for art and Marxism; and a habit of thinking that would ultimately lead me at least beyond the latter. My college years are as interesting, to me, as my time in the Army, but no more of them than what I've mentioned is relevant here.

Because at summer's end I was still alive and had to have something to do, I went ahead with my program and began reading the law at the University of Maryland Law School, in downtown Baltimore. I no longer lived in the fraternity house— in an adolescently idealistic moment I had proposed amending the Order's constitution to admit Jews and Negroes, and had brought the righteous wrath of Beta Alpha upon my head. Instead, I had a marvelous fourth-floor room in an ancient row house—it must once have been palatial—on Monument Street, very near Hopkins Hospital: a room suggested to me by Marvin Rose. My neighbors and companions were medical students; the atmosphere was intense, electric with work, exhausting—more deadly serious than before, perhaps (for we were no longer undergraduates), but not more sober. With Marvin I rode in ambulances on night duty, learned first aid, hardened my stomach to carnage that equaled Argonne's, made love to certain nurses and strange female patients, and drank.

I read Justices Holmes and Cardozo, and the Spanish and
Italian legal philosophers; I studied criminal law, torts, wills, legal Latin. With the medical students, achievement, competence,
even brilliance, were still part of the sport: I drove myself,
drank much, read much, slept little. When I was discharged
from the Army I'd weighed 180 pounds; on commencement
day at Hopkins I weighed 160; by the end of my first year at
law school I was down to 145.

"Less work for the pallbearers," I told myself—for no one
else suspected my Damocletian heart.

One night in mid-December of 1924 (I believe it was the
last night before the Christmas holiday at both the law school
and the medical school), Marvin and some of his colleagues proposed going out on the town, and since I happened to have
thirty dollars, I agreed. I was the more eager to drink because
all that day I'd had strange, sharp pains in my lower abdomen—
too low for appendicitis. Walking hadn't soothed them, nor
had lying down, and so I looked forward to a pleasant general
anesthesia.

"Dinner," Marvin announced, and six of us took two cabs
to Miller Brothers' for crab imperial. I ached all through the
meal.

"Drink," he announced later, and we took a bus out to a
speakeasy near the hospital, one patronized by the medical students, and got somewhat drunk. I shifted and squirmed with
pain.

"*Divertissement!*" announced someone a few hours later—
we were five, then, because Marvin had to go on duty in the
outpatient department for the rest of the night—and the whole
party adjourned to a house of joy that someone else had heard
of on North Calvert Street, about halfway to the University.

We rode out in a cab. Someone put something in the one
whiskey bottle from which most of us drank—I'm no toxicolo-
gist, and so I can't say what it was. When we disembarked we
were loud, rough, and on the verge of helplessness. Twice in

the next half hour I nearly fainted, not from liquor but from the fiery pains in my abdomen. I could scarcely wait to get a woman, for apart from the blessing of lying down, I had an inebriate notion that sex might relieve the pain.

Someone must have done my selecting for me; I'm sure I neither saw nor cared which of the girls I went upstairs with.

But "Toddy!" one of my companions hollered from down a hallway, just as my girl and I were entering a bedroom. "Hol' on!"

"No," I called back politely.

"Hol' on!" my colleague hollered again, and came lurching down the hall, pulling a girl behind him. "I got a lady here knows you from 'way back, boy."

"Oh," I said, and went into the room where my girl was waiting.

"*Oh* nothing!" the medical student cried, striding in behind me. "Why take a total stranger when right here's an ol' buddy? I'm swappin' with you."

The new girl was apologizing to my girl for being dragged in.

"You guys better get straightened out quick," my girl snapped, "or I'm callin' Cozy to bounce you."

I fell on the bed, dizzy almost to vomiting. I felt as though a hot needle, a hot bayonet, were piercing—my liver? My spleen?

Then I was standing in the center of the room, holding onto a bedpost for support, and Betty June Gunter, not a day older than she had been in 1917, was sitting on the bed, holding a cigarette in her hand, dangling a slipper from one foot, smiling mockingly at me.

I could see now; in fact I felt much more sober, but I was certainly suffering to the point of delirium.

"Glad to see you, Toddy," Betty June said sarcastically.

"I'm not going to talk, if you don't mind," I said carefully. "We'd never get it all said, and if it's all the same to you, I—"

What happened was that I collapsed then. After that Betty June had slipped off her one-piece whore's dress and I was holding her. If six years of prostitution had changed her at all, I couldn't see how. I remember wishing I were entirely sober and painless so that I could appreciate the grotesque coincidence of my meeting her, and also talk to her coherently. As far as I can tell, I was passing out every few minutes from my pain. At one point she asked me, "Do you hurt, Toddy boy?"

"I'm damn near dead," I admitted.

Then she was leaning over me, rubbing my chest and arms with rubbing alcohol.

"What the hell."

"Service of the house," she grinned.

There was a tremendous racket outside in the hall and downstairs. I believe my medical colleagues were destroying the whorehouse.

My original plan for relief occurred to me, but it was apparently out of the question: the pain unmanned me. I was perspiring.

Now Betty June was sitting perched at my feet, and was massaging my legs with the alcohol. Her business had not improved her bustline, I observed, but neither had it hardened her good eyes. I wished I were sober so that I could judge better how she felt about me. She certainly appeared affectionate enough. What an incredible coincidence! I wondered whether she knew Smitty was dead.

"You know Smitty's dead," I remarked.

Her expression, a puckered smile, didn't change. Her eyes followed her hands, rubbing my legs.

What I finally said—rather loudly, for the noise outside the door was incessant—was, "Damn it, honey, I owe you an apology. I wish this pain weren't so bad, I'd do things right for you, no laughing. That time in my room back home, I swear, I—"

That was when, still without any change of expression at all, Betty June emptied the whole bottle of rubbing alcohol in the worst possible place.

I hollered and leaped from the bed; I clutched myself and

rolled on the floor. Stupendous pain! The two together were inconceivable! To make things worse, Betty June fell upon me, still smiling. She struck at me with the alcohol bottle, coolly, putting all her small strength into each blow, and although I was able to parry nearly every assault, the crack of the bottle on my arm or elbow was punishment enough. I pushed and kicked her away, but to stand up was beyond my power. I felt on fire.

Betty June had got the bottle broken by this time, and came at me with the jagged neck of it. I rolled away and struck at her, but it was a losing fight. Every parry cost me a slash on the arm, across the knuckles, in the palm of my hand. When I finally got a grip on her right wrist, she kicked and bit. What I wanted to do, what I tried to do, was break her arm, if possible, to slow her up. That's what I was attempting when the room filled with people.

"Cozy!" Betty June cried.

There was a din. I didn't dare let go of Betty June's arm, although I was too weak to break it. Much blood was on us both. I felt like going to sleep; I had the strongest impulse to say, "Let's be friends," and go to sleep on her poor thin arm, there on the floor. *Why isn't the whole thing a sailboat?* I remember wondering through the pain that was crucifying me; then I could let go of everything, tiller and sheets, and the boat would luff up into the wind and hang in stays, and I could sleep.

Cozy must have been a competent bouncer. I daresay he rabbit-punched me, considering the circumstances and the additional pain in the back of my neck when I woke up next, but I didn't even feel the blow when it fell. Cozy had stuffed me into the back seat of somebody's parked automobile, on the floor. I had my shirt and trousers and shoes on, loosely, but no underwear, necktie, stockings, coat, or overcoat. Three-inch adhesive tape had been rolled roughly around my slashed arm

—Cozy's employer hadn't wanted me to die near the premises —and since no major blood vessels had been severed, the bleeding had virtually stopped, but not before daubing my clothes. My neck throbbed; I still burned, though not quite so severely —horrible few minutes!—and the mysterious original pain continued undiminished.

I crawled out of the car after a while. I still had my wristwatch: it was four in the morning. What part of town was I in? I kept close to the wall of row houses along the street, both to steady myself and to shelter myself from the cold, and walked to the corner gas lamp. As is usual in the poorer neighborhoods, the street signs around the lamp were broken off. I turned the corner and walked numbly for an infinity of uninhabited city blocks, all fronted with infinities of faceless, featureless, identical row houses and nightmare lines of marble steps like snaggled teeth. Then came the second coincidence of the evening: I had been walking in a lightless alleyway, quiet and black as a far cranny of the universe; I half-fell around a corner, and was on Monument Street—civilized, brightly lighted, filled with automobiles and streetcars even at four o'clock. The brown Victorian pile of Hopkins Hospital stood just across the street, disgorging frequent ambulances into the city and swallowing others. A flurry of lights and a succession of strong smells, and presently I was sitting in a hard chair in a corridor of the hospital. There was much glare; soft hustlings of carts, stretchers, nurses, orderlies; muffled clinkings of instruments and glass; laughter in the distance; activity, busyness, all around my hard chair where I sat holding my head tightly. Everybody was awake in the hospital; I felt so safe I wanted to vomit.

Marvin Rose was saying, "Stay here for a few days, Toddy."

Then I was in the ward—had slept for a long time and was in little pain—and when I opened my eyes a lean nurse was holding my left arm. Before I could explain to her whatever it was that I felt explosively needed explaining, her needle had made quite the wrong small popping puncture (more felt than heard, to be sure) in the white underskin of my forearm, and I fainted another time.

Few things, I venture, are more uncomfortable to a man than a needle biopsy. The horrid instrument opened the secret of my pain to the doctor who attended me. A severely infected prostate—most unusual in a twenty-four-year-old man. And my health was generally broken down. I remained in the ward for a month, with little to do but think.

Here are the things I thought about, lying long hours immobile with closed eyes: my imminent, instant death; the futility, for me, of plans and goals; the tight smile on Betty June's lips (she hadn't laughed); the sound of punctured skin. I thought at times coherently, at times dizzily, moving from one subject to the next and starting over again. I would not attempt to sort the causes from the effects in my month's thinking, but when I was finally discharged I had decided with my whole being that I was "out of it"; that the pursuits, the goals, the enthusiasms of the world of men were not mine. My stance had been wrong, I concluded: the fact with which I had to live was not to be escaped in whiskey and violence, not even in work. What I must do, I reasoned, is keep it squarely before me all the time; live with it soberly, looking it straight in the eye. There was more to my new attitude, but it was a matter of the rearrangement of abstractions, not important here. The visible effects on my behavior were primarily these: I still drank, but no longer got drunk. I smoked, but not nervously. I took women to bed only in the rare cases when it was they who assumed the initiative, and then I was thorough but dispassionate. I studied and worked hard and steadily, but no longer intensely. I talked less. I began in earnest what was to be a long process of assuming hard control over myself: the substitution of small, specific strengths for small, specific weaknesses, regarding the latter with the same unresentful disfavor with which one regards a speck of dust on one's coat sleeve, before plucking it quietly off. I unconsciously began to regard my fellow men variously as more or less pacific animals among whom it was generally safe to walk (so long as one observed certain tacitly assumed rules), or as a colony of more or less quiet lunatics among whom it was generally safe to live (so long as one humored, at least outwardly, certain aspects of their madness).

There have been other changes in my attitude during my life, but none altered my outward behavior and manner so markedly as this one. I was uninvolved; I was unmoved; I was a saint. I was, so I believed then, in the position of those South American butterflies who, themselves defenseless, mimic outwardly the more numerous species among which they live: appropriately, the so-called "nauseous" Danaïs, whose bad taste and smell render them relatively safe. At least when walking their streets, I had to pretend to be like all the other butterflies —but at heart I knew I was of another species, perhaps a less nauseous one.

I continued, therefore, my study of law, as part of the mimicry; at Marvin's prescription I began taking a capsule of diethylstilbestrol every day; and I awaited more quietly the moment of death. In my good time I meditated, disinterestedly, that tight, puckered smile on the face of the female human being who had intended to kill me. And, for the next thirteen years, though the prostate continued to give me frequent pain, I ceased to share that pain with physicians. Who ever heard of a saint's crying for a doctor?

"Well, well, well!" Marvin shouted (in 1937) when I stepped into his office. He rubbed his hands gleefully. "Coming home to die, are you? What'll it be, Todd? What the hell, you pregnant?"

"A plain old physical examination, Marv," I said.

"Going to buy some insurance, man? I'll lie for you. Hell, boy, I'll euthanaze you."

"None of your business. Come on, examine."

But we smoked a cigar first, and Marvin reminisced about Baltimore. When he got around to examining me, I said:

"Will you go along with me on something, Marvin?"

"Where's the body? What'd you do, Todd?"

"Examine me to your heart's content," I said, "but I don't want you to say a word about anything you see or find; don't even change expression."

"I won't even examine you if you say so, you big sissy. I'll call Shirley in here and let her look at you."

"Just write it all down," I smiled, "and either mail it to me or drop it off at the hotel. The point is that I don't want to know anything at all, at least until tomorrow. Okay?"

Marvin grinned: "You're the doctor."

He then went through the examining routine, talking all the while he checked my height, weight, eyes, ears, nose, throat, and teeth. Then I stripped to the waist, and with stethoscope, watch and sphygmomanometer he checked my heart, my pulse, and my blood pressure, keeping the expressionless face I'd asked for. Then he tapped my chest and back, listening for congestion, and felt my vertebrae. Finally I removed trousers and underwear, and he tapped my knee, testing for locomotor ataxia, felt for hernias, and looked for hemorrhoids and flat feet, all without any alteration of expression.

"How about a blood test and a urinalysis?" he asked.

I produced a urine specimen, but declined the blood test.

"How's the old prostate? Been keeping her empty?"

"No trouble," I said.

"Sure raised hell that one time, didn't it? I swear I wanted to cut her out for you, Toddy; you wouldn't have had another twinge. But that screwball Hodges—remember him? the resident?—he was having a feud with O'Donnell, the surgeon, that year, over politics, and wasn't letting anybody get cut. Goddamn Hodges! I swear he'd have tried to amputate a leg with his damn internal medicine! What a bunch!" He made some notes on an examination form and slipped it into an envelope. "Here y'are, lad, the whole sad story. How about a little old needle biopsy? Have a look at the old infection. Make you dance and holler."

"Let it go," I said, and began dressing.

"No needle? How am I supposed to know what's what? How about an X ray, raise your bill a few bucks?"

"Drop the paper off any time after today," I said, accepting from Marvin another light for my cigar, which had gone out. "Please keep everything under your hat, Marv."

"I don't blame you," Marvin said, walking me to the door with his arm across my shoulders. "I'd be ashamed, too." We shook hands. "Well, hell, Toddy. Don't wait so long next time. And listen, if the old prostate commences to hurt you, I'll cut it out. You ought to keep check."

I smiled and shook my head.

"What do you say? Come down to the hospital Monday for an X ray, and I can take her right out, clean as a whistle."

"Wait till Monday," I said. "But don't hold your breath."

We said goodbye, and Marvin went back to lie on the examination table for a nap. He was (I'm late saying it) a beefy little man with sparse blond hair, flushed skin, and tiny red veins in his cheeks. His arms and hands were so full of meat that it seemed as if the skin of them were ready to burst, like overboiled frankfurters. It would be pleasant to be able to go on and say of Marvin's great hands that, awkward as they appeared, the moment they were slipped into surgeon's gloves they assumed the deftness and delicate strength of a violinist's. This is the sort of thing one usually hears. But the truth is that those clumsy-looking hands, once slipped into surgical gloves, remained rather clumsy, depending as they did from slightly clumsy arms and ultimately from a somewhat clumsy brain. The truth is that the magnificent Hopkins does not infallibly produce faultless medicine men; the truth, alas, is that in fact I should be markedly reluctant, even were I not opposed to it on principle, to allow my excellent friend Marvin to incise me with his not-altogether-unerring knives. The fact of affection needn't preclude objectivity.

XV. That puckered smile

One doesn't move on without giving that tight smile, Betty June's puckered smile, some further attention. Mere drunkenness and pain are no excuse for my not having realized, until she was upon me with the bottle, that I had done to Betty June a thing warranting murder at her hands (I am, by the way, reasonably confident that it *was* Betty June in the Calvert Street whorehouse, although I was certainly drunk). She wanted to kill me, I see now, for having laughed that time in my bedroom.

Here's how I understand it: that morning in 1917 she had learned that Smitty Herrin, to whom she had unreservedly humbled herself, had all the while been married to Mona Johnston, from Henry Street, and had made Mona pregnant. In desperation, Betty June had come to me and had attempted— unconsciously, I daresay—to reassert her wounded ego by humbling me with the gift of her body, a lean receptacle for my innocence. But in the throes of intercourse I had laughed, so violently as to unman myself, and couldn't even stanch her injured tears for very helplessness. She had assumed that I was laughing at her, at some ridiculousness of her, although this was not *particularly* true. And then—what? Smitty and I both enlisted, he was killed, and she became a prostitute. Ordinarily, perhaps, it would have been possible for her to rationalize her behavior, first as a patriotic gesture and later as gaining a livelihood from "the oldest profession"—but she had my laughter in her ears to remind her, every time she unhooked her one-

piece gown for a new customer, that there was something
ludicrous about her and about what she was doing. For many
sorts of people, and Betty June is one of them, this suspicion
would be nearly intolerable. So: seven years later, when she's
doubtless so deeply enmired in the business and all its attendant
vices that she can't very well escape, seven years later I show up
party-drunk at her whorehouse—looking prosperous and smug
to her, no doubt—accept her as my whore without a word,
and only later, after permitting her to massage my body, refer
with vague regret to the time I laughed at her.

Don't you agree that this is probably how it was? I can't
account otherwise for her murderousness (yet I must say,
though I can scarcely explain it, that if I hadn't *mentioned* the
matter, I believe Betty June would have gone through with the
intercourse I had paid for). The remarkable thing, it seems to
me, is not at all that she wanted to kill me—even simple shame
at being thus discovered could account for that—but that I
failed to realize it at once; that I missed the obvious implication
of that puckered smile.

And this is what I wanted to say, because I consider it fairly
important (hell, even urgently important) to the understanding
of this whole story: quite frequently, things that are obvious to
other people aren't even apparent to me. The fact doesn't especially bother me, except when it leads to my not jumping clear
of dangerous animals like poor Betty. The only likely explanation I can imagine is that out of any situation I can usually interpret a number of possible significances, often conflicting,
sometimes contradictory. Why, for instance, could it not have
been that Betty June, after seven years of prostitution and
various unfortunate experiences, had come to see, as I did, the
essential grotesqueness of the whole business—the very four-
letter verb for which is wittily onomatopoeic—and upon en-
countering me had decided to demonstrate her agreement by a
rousing good copulation, at which we'd both laugh long and
loud? Or, less dramatically, why could it not have been that

she'd forgotten the affair in my bedroom, and was smiling merely at my drunkenness, or in anticipation of scorching me with isopropyl alcohol? Or, less kindly, that observing my helplessness she was smiling at the thought of earning seven dollars for giving me nothing more voluptuous than a rubdown? I'm not especially defending myself: very possibly another person would have seen factors in the situation that would preclude all these alternatives; or, possibly, another person wouldn't have imagined these alternatives in the first place. I honestly believe that to most men (and to any woman) Betty June's intentions would have been obvious. To me they were not.

On the other hand, things that are clear to me are sometimes incomprehensible to others—which fact occasions this chapter, if not the whole book.

XVI. The Judge's lunch

Harrison and I were in the habit of lunching at a confectionery store on Race Street, beside the old opera house. It was run by an orphans' court judge, an engaging fellow who refused, for purely aesthetic reasons, to serve hot platters: he disliked the smells of cooking in his store. This integrity alone would have attracted me to the place, but the proprietor had a host of such opinions; like me, he was in the habit of giving sound, unorthodox, and not infrequently *post facto* reasons for his behavior, which reasons he was wont to articulate at length to his regular customers in a loud voice, for he was slightly deaf.

It was to this place that I walked after leaving Marvin. Race Street was afire with dusty sunlight, and few people were out. A number of unclean children were playing tag on the wide cracked steps of the opera house, swinging over and under the brown brass rail that led up to the shuttered box office. On both inner walls of the arcaded façade, crusty with weathered architectural gingerbread, were plastered posters advertising *Adam's Original & Unparalleled Floating Opera*.

Not until I'd actually entered the confectioner's—until the Judge, small, dapper, bald, and boutonniered, greeted me and I remarked politely that he looked like a million dollars—did I remember that, should I choose, I was in a position to make my friend Harrison worth nearly three million. It may seem incredible that such a thing could simply slip one's mind, but it very nearly did. I believe that if the Judge hadn't prompted my remark, I'd have forgotten the matter entirely, perhaps until too late. And I was glad I'd remembered it.

You see, although Eustacia's information assured me that I could win the case (all that was necessary was to secure from Equity an order holding up the appeal until the missing portions were accounted for. The thing could be complicated indefinitely, and after the coming elections, when Joe Singer had replaced Rollo Moore on the Appellate Court bench, I was confident that the Circuit Court judgment would be reversed)— although the thing was in my hands, by no means did it necessarily follow that I would do anything about it. Very possibly I would decide to keep the new information secret, let it die that day with me instead of giving it to young Jimmy Andrews or Mr. Bishop to work with after my death. For one thing, remember that I was a fairly thoroughgoing cynic at the time, especially concerning money; also—nothing cynical about this —I believed Harrison was undeserving of the money unless he overcame his former weakness. It was my opinion that in order for him to be worthy of the inheritance, he had to demonstrate a strength of character that would make the loss of it unimportant: a pretty lofty opinion for a cynic. At any rate, I decided not to mention Eustacia's letter right away.

I was a few minutes late; Harrison was waiting for me, talking to the Judge. We went back to our table.

"Janie dropped out to the plant just before I drove in," he said. "What are you needling her for?"

"Needling her?"

"That note you sent her this morning," Harrison said mildly. "You know what I'm talking about."

"I do now," I smiled. "I'd forgotten." I gave my order to the girl who came to our table; Harrison had already ordered. "I wasn't entirely joking, Harrison. Cap'n Osborn's got a couple more years, at the most, before he dies. Suppose you were in his place: wouldn't you like a fine send-off like Janie? Hell, he couldn't do anything to her. Are you angry?"

"I wasn't before," Harrison grinned, "because I thought you were just being nasty. But if you're *serious* about her showing herself to the old buzzard, I probably ought to get mad."

I held a light for his cigar. He was doing fine so far.

"Well, if you want to," I laughed. "But Janie handled it pretty brightly, I think. Did she tell you about *her* note?"

"No."

"She said she'd do what I asked if I'd agree to let Marvin Rose look at me, to see why I'm such a pansy. Her very words."

Harrison chuckled, a little relieved. "Fair enough," he said. "What did she mean, *pansy?* Or shouldn't I ask?"

"You may ask, but a little more softly next time. The fact is, I spent most of last night looking out my window, and the rest of the time reading a book."

Harrison looked concerned. "You getting senile?"

"Quitting while I'm still ahead, maybe." I smiled. "As a matter of fact, I don't think Marvin found anything especially wrong with me, at least not below the belt. I was just up there."

Harrison's peace of mind vanished. "You did what she said?"

"Yep."

The girl brought our lunches: a bacon and tomato sandwich and iced tea for Harrison, and a chopped olive and Swiss cheese on rye for me, with iced coffee.

"Well, what now?" Harrison asked. "I don't know what to say. You sure do change your mind about things."

I shrugged. "It's not your problem; it's Jane's. Cap'n Osborn won't know the difference either way."

Harrison started to object, but then he changed his mind and bit into his sandwich instead.

"All right," he said, talking with his mouth full. "I won't worry about it."

"Good man."

Harrison then changed the subject and talked idly about a possible strike of his cucumber picklers. His mouth was still full, and there were three little flecks of mayonnaise on his lower lip. As he spoke, an occasional crumb blew over to me. I admired two things: the casual bad manners that one often encounters in finely bred animals like Harrison, and the fact that his description of the labor difficulties in his plant suggested neither a pro-union bias from his Marxist days nor an anti-union bias from his present position. He was interested in the situation, but rather cynical toward both the union leaders, who were making him out to be a slave driver, and his own administrative staff, who advocated firing the lot of them and hiring "new niggers" in their places. It seemed to me that cynicism, although he was not entirely at home with it yet, became him a great deal more than had his earlier saintliness. I listened with some interest, regarding his still-handsome face (he was forty-three, I guess, and Jane in her early thirties) and the little drops of mayonnaise, which he finally licked away.

We finished our sandwiches and smoked for a while, enjoying our drinks. The Judge's store wasn't air-conditioned, but he had three big old ceiling fans, and the place was light and cool.

"Oh, by the way," Harrison said, "Jane wasn't in when your secretary called this morning, but the maid took the message, and then apparently you were out when Jane called back. She says she'll drop Jeannine off at your office at three, if that's not too early. She's coming uptown to the hairdresser's around then."

I was a little disturbed, not at the change of hours (I had planned to take Jeannine to see the showboat at four), but because my instructions to Mrs. Lake—to call Jane—were the second thing I'd forgotten in a few hours. No, come to think of it, I'd had *three* lapses of memory: Eustacia's letter, my note to Jane, and my request to Mrs. Lake. This was a serious matter, for it could be taken as a sign of nervousness, of apprehension at my decision to destroy myself that day. I was of course not indifferent toward the resolution, but my feeling was more one of pleasure at having found the final solution to my problem than one of commonplace fear. And, pleasure or fear, I marked it an indication of imperfect control to be so touched by my feeling as to make unusual slips of memory on what I'd decided was to be a quite usual day.

"I thought I'd take her down to see the showboat when it pulls in," I said. "How's her tonsils?"

"All right, I guess. Anyhow it wasn't tonsillitis. Marvin came out and looked at her throat yesterday, and said it didn't look like he'd have to take them out, unless we wanted him to go ahead and get it over with. It was her throat that was infected, and her tonsils just swelled up on general principles. I don't know what Jane's decided. Both of us had tonsillitis when we were kids."

"Better leave them in," I suggested. "Mine used to swell up every now and then, whenever I had a sore throat, but it never amounted to anything."

There was a certain tactlessness in this remark, as I'll explain presently, and I made it for that reason, with nonchalance. Harrison took the cigar from his mouth and studied its ash.

"I don't know," he said.

"Marvin's a little quick with the knife. Once when I was in law school and he was interning, he was all set to make a eunuch out of me."

Harrison replaced the cigar in his mouth and drew on it as we got up from the table.

"That would've been too bad," he observed, and put a quarter down for the girl. Then he fetched his straw and mine, and we walked through the front of the store. Have I described Harrison? Not being a writer by trade, I sometimes neglect these details. He was heavy weighed perhaps two hundred pounds—and still well-built, though he showed signs of going to fat from lack of exercise. His features, which had been chiseled when I first knew him, had begun to round off a little, and his cheeks and belly no longer looked hard, as they had when he played much tennis and rode horses. He still had a good head of tightly curled blond hair, contrasting nicely with a complexion as much flushed as sunburned (I daresay his blood pressure registered somewhere between mine and Marvin's), and his eyes, teeth, and arms were excellent. Very wealthy-looking fellow, Harrison, and very clean and handsome. The thin, consumptive communist would justifiably loathe him, but the properly nourished parlor communist would be made uncomfortable by his charm. Those particular aspects of Harrison relevant to this story have made him look less engaging than he really was—I can't dwell on him, of course, for it's not his story. Let me repeat, if I've mentioned it before, that he was by no means either a fool or a weakling. He was a reasonable, generous, affable, alert fellow. I might even say that if this were a rational universe and if I could be any person I chose, I should not choose to be Todd Andrews at all. I should choose to be very much like my friend Harrison Mack.

"How's the pickle business, Todd?" the Judge called to me as we stepped out on the sidewalk, where he spent much of his time watching the town. He referred, of course, to the disputed will, which case he had followed with great interest. "You gentlemen in the money yet?"

Ordinarily I'd have enjoyed explaining the new development to him, for although he was not professionally trained, his mind was quick and sure, and he'd have appreciated the maneuver. But of course I could not.

"Nothing new, Judge," I said loudly. "Depends on how the war goes, maybe."

"Well, I doubt it'll go good for the Loyalists," he declared. "They've been holding their own lately, but it can't keep up. They've got the Russians, but Mr. Franco, he's got the Germans, and like it or not, the German's a better soldier than the Russian is. The German might be dumb, but he's dumb like a smart dog. Old Russian, he's dumb like an ox."

Harrison was fidgeting to leave. For my part, I was interested enough in the Judge's prognostications, for he knew how to read newspapers, and read five or six a day. It was, in fact, the Judge who had first predicted to me that Rollo Moore wouldn't be re-elected, and I'd have gone ahead with my plans on the strength of his judgment even had I not been able to confirm it in certain Baltimore Republican circles.

"You think Franco's in, then?"

"I think it'll take him a couple of years yet to wind it up," the Judge said. "By that time the whole shebang might blow."

"Well," Harrison fidgeted.

I said goodbye to the Judge—after all, I probably would not see him again, and he was one of my favorite citizens— and walked with Harrison as far as his car, which was parked on Poplar Street.

"Will you come for cocktails tonight?" he asked as he slipped behind the wheel.

I leaned down and talked to him through the window on my side. "Much obliged."

Harrison put the Cadillac in gear.

"*Don't feel obligated,*" he smiled ruefully. "Any time after four."

He slid away down the brick street, which shimmered now in the very hot sun. I walked toward the hotel for my nap, feeling fine about Harrison. There was no need for haste in making my decision, but the lunchtime had done his cause much good indeed.

XVII. The end of the outline

Climatologically, this day of which I write was rare for Dorchester County, rare for the Eastern Shore, where the same ubiquitous waters that moderate the temperatures—the ocean, the Bay, the infinite estuaries, creeks, coves, guts, marshes, and inlets—also make them uncomfortable. This day, on the contrary, was excessively warm (the temperature as I walked to the hotel must have reached 95), but extremely dry. I was wearing shirt, suit, underwear, and hat, and there was no shade on Poplar Street, but my body was dry as a white bone in the desert, and I was entirely comfortable. It was a day when one would have liked to sit alone on a high dune by the ocean—the Atlantic beach is often just this dry, given a land breeze—in air as hot and salty as Earth's commencement, the drought of precreation before the damp of procreation; to sit a dried and salted sterile saint, Saint Todd of the Beach, and watch voracious gulls dissect the stranded carcasses of sandy skates and sharks, bleached and brined to stenchlessness. The locust trees by People's Trust were dusty, and mast-truck high in the High Street poplars, locusts rasped and whirred a parched dirge for my last high noon. It was a lovely day for suicide. One felt that one would hardly bleed into such aridity; more probably a knife in the neck would be kissed with a desiccant hiss of mere dry air.

Turning the corner of Poplar, High, and Locust Streets, I found the loafers' bench empty: the old men were home to nap. The Choptank sparkled at the foot of the boulevard. *Adam's Original & Unparalleled Floating Opera* posters graced every business window on the empty streets from the Judge's place to the hotel, red, white, and blue, as though the town had been set for Independence Day and then everyone—men, women, dogs, and pallbearers—had gone to a parade somewhere else.

The hotel lobby was light and cool; a small chat with Jerry Hogey, and then I went to my room. Are you so curious as to follow me down the hall to the men's room? If you aren't (I shall be only a minute), read while you wait the story of my resumption of the affair with Jane Mack. Look back into Chapter III, and you'll find that near the end of it I reproduced an outline of the events that I imagined led up to my seduction by the Macks. In the final section of that outline I listed what I considered to be the four possible courses that my relationship with them could take after I'd broken it off by an act that, judged in the very terms that I objected to, they must regard as an insult. Now of these four courses, either I or IV (that is, permanent disaffection or the resumption of a qualified affection, one of the qualifications being a suspension of the affair) seemed the most probable to me after the incident in my office with Dorothy Miner, which terminated the friendship.

However, I was reckoning without two things, neither of which I could reasonably have been expected to predict.

In the first place, just a few weeks after the Macks had severed relations with me, Jane learned, upon being examined by Marvin Rose for chronic nausea, that she was pregnant. Moreover, she was probably three months pregnant: it was possible for her not to guess it herself only because she had always been irregular. As soon as Marvin looked at her, he said, "You're pregnant," and it instantly seemed so obvious to her (she swore later that her tummy filled out the moment he spoke the word) that she became a little hysterical at not having recognized it herself. Marvin gave her a sedative. Jane hurried home and could scarcely wait to tell Harrison when he came in from work, she was so delighted. But when he walked into the house and she opened her mouth to tell him, it suddenly occurred to her that she was *three months* pregnant, not three weeks or three days; she remembered me, burst into tears, and nearly fainted. When finally she was able to explain things to Harrison, he couldn't say a word.

The pregnancy was pretty miserable for both of them (I learned this later, of course). It would have been simple enough to arrange an abortion, but it happened that they really wanted a child, and had tried unsuccessfully for several years to have one. They both wished, too late, that Jane had been more diligent in using precautions with me, but the fact was that she hadn't; it is a mark of Harrison's saintliness that not once did he suggest a reproach for her carelessness, and a mark of Jane's that she owned up to it in the first place. Being intelligent people, they were able to talk about the matter frankly, and they tried hard to articulate their sentiments, to decide how they really felt about it.

"Look at it this way," Harrison's most frequent argument ran; "suppose I was sterile—wouldn't we sooner or later probably adopt a kid? Or suppose you'd been married before and had a kid—wouldn't we still love it after you married me? Now, this is better than adoption, because you're going to be the real mother either way. And it's better than a previous marriage, because there's a good chance I'm the real father. After all, I slept with you more than Andrews did."

That was a pretty good argument, I thought, but Harrison never could put enough conviction into his voice, and that last sentence, whether intended to do so or not, usually brought Jane to tears.

"That's all true," was her typical reply, "but no amount of reasoning can get around the fact that if I hadn't made love to Todd in the first place—or if I'd only kept my stupid head and been careful—then either I wouldn't be pregnant or we'd know you're the father." This said with her fine head in her hands, her excellent shoulders shaking.

Harrison then, quite calmly (but not kissing the sable hair or stroking the shoulders): "What the hell, hon, a fact's a fact. It was my idea as much as yours. We shouldn't have taken the step if we can't stand up to the consequences."

"But we didn't think of this!" Jane would wail.

And Harrison would shrug. "People get pregnant."

And so on. A lousy pregnancy. To make it worse, Jane was ill for most of the remaining six months. She could keep nothing on her stomach, and on several occasions required uncomfortable glucose injections to stave off malnutrition. At the same time, though, her illness had the virtue of keeping her weight down. I saw her just once, in her ninth month, from a short distance away, and she was so beautiful that I suffered a rare twinge of regret and real longing, no less intense for its being short-lived. And her moderate size eased her delivery: on October 2, 1933, in the Cambridge Memorial Hospital, after only three hours of labor, she gave birth to a six-pound ten-ounce girl, whom she named Jeannine Paulsen (Jane's maiden name) Mack.

Harrison and Jane had, understandably, been not a little fearful of the day when they must actually bring their baby home; when it would be committed totally into their hands and they would be expected to love and care for it. The care was no problem—there were bottles, formulas, and trained nurses—but they feared that the love might simply not be forthcoming. Jane especially feared this about Harrison, and Harrison about himself. But as it happened they quickly took to their daughter —she was an engaging child, luckily, right from her infancy— and found it easy to be affectionate parents. Perhaps their knowledge of the danger of any other reaction sufficed to open the buds of love in their hearts. They breathed more easily (the baby, obviously doing her best to protect her own interests, contrived to resemble neither Harrison nor me to any embarrassing degree) and wondered what they'd worried so much about.

"I swear," Harrison volunteered, "if somebody should prove to me, right this minute, that Todd was Jeannine's father, I wouldn't love her a bit less for it."

"Oh, I'm sure he's not," Jane scoffed (you understand that I heard all this later). "But I don't think I would, either. She's beautiful."

But the important statement, for this story, Harrison made sometime in the spring of 1934, about a year after I'd insulted them.

"You know," he said, "you may not agree with this, because I know how much you dislike him, but I sometimes think that that business with Todd was partly our fault, too."

"*Our* fault!"

"I mean, what the hell, we put him on the spot, when you got in bed with him; he might not even have wanted to, you know—not because he didn't want you, but because he might have thought it would hurt our marriage. But if he'd refused, we'd have been insulted, wouldn't we? And, in fact, if he hadn't done it on our terms, we'd have been insulted, I think."

"Still, he had no business telling us he was a virgin," Jane insisted.

"But you can't deny we were pleased when he did," Harrison replied. "That proves we were expecting too much of him. And we certainly had no right to expect him not to make love to other women. What the hell, he's a bachelor."

"But he was supposed to be in love with me."

"You're in love with me, too," Harrison smiled, "but you made love to Todd. You understand."

Jane sulked.

"We expected too much. We should've known him better."

"Well maybe you're right," Jane said. "But he certainly had

no right to break it off like he did, with that damned colored girl!"

Harrison grinned. "I guess he's unprejudiced. To tell the truth, the more I think about that, the more I believe he was just ad-libbing. That girl didn't know what was up any more than I did."

Jane pouted for a while, but after the ice had been broken they talked more freely about me, and less bitterly. Gradually it got to be assumed that they'd really been too demanding (a piece of objectivity that still appalls me), and that to some extent I'd been justified in showing my claws.

The next step was for Jane to say, "Hell, I forgive him; I just don't want anything to do with him any more."

And for Harrison to say, "I still like Todd all right; it's just that I can't get enthusiastic about seeing him any more. I don't bear him any grudge."

Jeannine grew and grew, and discreetly began to look like her mother.

The second thing that I hadn't predicted was that on January 10, 1935, Harrison Mack Senior would die, leaving seventeen testamentary instruments for his wife, son, and nurses to play games with. But he did, as surely as sweet Jane got herself impregnated, and as irremediably. No one needed to suggest to Harrison that he needed professional assistance, either; he consulted a lawyer a lot more quickly than Jane had consulted a physician, and the firm that he retained was Andrews, Bishop, & Andrews. The obvious necessity for legal counsel, the disturbance over his father's death, the excitement over the big estate—all these made his move seem quite natural, so that if there was anything in it of an overt act to reinstate our friendship, the overtness was effectively camouflaged, and one needn't even think of it.

There were, one can imagine, dozens of details in the litigation that required discussion, strategies to be worked out, conferences to be held, many more than could be conveniently fitted into my leisurely office schedule. It was inevitable, then, that Harrison and I should occasionally utilize our lunch hours for the purpose; even that he should eventually invite me, with aplomb, to come for late cocktails one evening, and that I, with commensurate grace, should accept.

Of that evening—at first somewhat strained, since it was my first meeting with Jane in more than two years—just one incident will do here: the Macks had put Jeannie to bed early, thinking thereby to keep discomfort at a minimum, and with the assistance of Gilbey's gin and Sherbrook rye, the three of us had contrived to reach a condition of mellow, if tacit, mutual forgiveness. We all felt relieved that the nonsense of the past two years was done, though nothing was said about it directly; our good spirits were reflected in the unusual amount of liquor consumed, in the fact that whatever legal matters had provided the excuse for our meeting never got discussed, and (most significantly) by the fact that when Jeannine, who had a slight cold, began to fret in her crib, Jane, despite a private resolve to the contrary, said spontaneously: "Come on, Toddy, you haven't met this little Mack! Come upstairs and be introduced."

She realized her slip as soon as it was out, and added at once, without changing her tone or expression, "Harrison will do the honors, won't you honey?"

The three of us went to the nursery, where Jeannine—a blond little charmer whom I must say I'd be delighted to learn I'd fathered—stood up sleepily in her crib and grinned at her parents, shyly, because I was there.

"Jeannine," Harrison said, "this is Toddy. Can you say *Toddy?*"

Jeannine could not, or would not.

"Would you like to kiss Toddy good night, honey?" Jane asked her. Jeannine hung her head, but looked up at me from under her eyebrows and chortled. When I kissed her hair—as soft as silk thread, and fragrant with baby soap—she dived into the mattress and buried her giggles in the blanket.

Jane had crossed the room to adjust the window, and Harrison and I stood side by side at the crib, where Jeannine was already on the verge of sleep. A number of obvious thoughts were in the air of the nursery—it was like a scene arranged by a heavy-handed director—and I, for one, was embarrassed when Jane, after her excellent and immediate good taste of a few minutes before, now came up behind us and grasped both our arms while we looked at the little girl. *Our little girl,* the tableau simpered, underlining the pronoun. Ah, reader, the thing was gross, sentimental; and yet I was moved, for with the Macks these sentiments are sincere. They are simply full of love, for themselves, for each other, for me.

We went back downstairs, soberly, but Harrison, sensitive by then to such solemnities, at once poured a round of cocktails and we were soon gay again, restored to grace. The evening was a success; I returned often; and soon, but for the two quiet years that sometimes hung heavy over our conversation, we spoke together as easily as ever.

Had the friendship remained at this stage of reconstruction, I should have asked for nothing more. I was content to see the Macks outgrow their unbecoming jealousy, which was as dangerous to their own relationship as it was inconsistent with their previous behavior. Nor did I see how things could tactfully become any more intimate, after my rebuff of 1933. But on the night of July 31, 1935, while I was sitting at my window reading a book for my *Inquiry* (somebody's critique of Adam Smith's economics, I do believe), there was a small knock on my door, the knob rattled, and Jane stepped in, wearing shorts.

"Hi," she said, standing just inside the closed door.

"Hello." I closed my book, threw my cigar stub out the window, and got up to give her the chair. "Sit down."

"All right." She grinned quickly and came over to the window, where I was sitting on the sill, but she forgot to sit down. I didn't want any nonsense this time—for her sake, not because I objected to nonsense on principle—and so I kept my eyes on her face, not to make it any easier for her. She mostly looked down at the street.

"We've been for a boat ride," she said. When I didn't answer, she looked at me irritably and began to fidget.

"You have to understand everything at once," she declared. "I'm not able to talk about anything just now."

"That's impossible," I said. "I can understand everything at once in about three different ways."

"You're not helping me. You're not saying any of the right things." She laughed.

I didn't smile. "That's only because I don't know what you want to hear, Jane. You should know I'll say anything I think you want to hear."

Her smile disappeared, and she regarded the dark Post Office across the street and fiddled with the curtain pull.

"That was a hard lesson, Toddy."

"I wasn't teaching anybody anything," I said sharply. "What do you think I am? I was just getting clear."

She fiddled with the cord.

"Let me ask you," I said. "Do I love you?"

"No."

"Now let's get that straight. I don't want to hurt you all."

"You don't love me and I don't love you."

This was getting as theatrical as the other. I gave it up. For ten minutes more Jane stared at the Post Office. I honestly couldn't guess what would come of it. After a few minutes, though I didn't intend any such thing, my mind—never very impressed by this sort of dramatics—wandered to other things: to the seventeen wills, to Bill Froebel, to the critique of Adam Smith. And it startled me, for I'd honestly forgotten for an instant that she was there, when Jane spun around from the window and said, "Let's get in bed, Todd." Without looking at me, she walked to the bed, unfastened her shorts and halter, and lay down, and very shortly after that I joined her.

So. Nothing remains to be told of the affair, except that after its resumption it was conducted in a manner more satisfactory to me. No schedules, no demands, no jealousy, no fictions—all was spontaneity and candor. I think that my increasingly frequent impotency after that time (by 1936, about every fourth attempt at intercourse was a failure; by 1937, about every other attempt) would have led me to call off the thing for good in time anyway, even had I not resolved on this day to kill myself. But by 1937 I could contemplate with equanimity the prospect of terminating our affair, for it left, from my point of view, nothing to be desired. Jane Mack is the finest woman I've ever slept with. Since the morning of the day at hand, when she last left my rented bed, I have desired nothing from women. She satisfied me.

Now, if you'll excuse me, I shall sleep.

XVIII. A matter of life or death

Although it was my custom to nap for an hour every day, on the day I intended to be my last I was waked almost as soon as my eyes were closed, by an urgent knock on my door.

"Come on in," I called, and pulled a robe on over my underwear.

There was no response for several moments, and I had begun to decide that my unknown caller had gone away, when I heard two or three footsteps in the hall and then another knock.

"Yes, come on in," I repeated, still tying my robe.

Another pause. I started toward the door, but it opened just before I reached it, and Mister Haecker, taut as a piano wire, stepped inside.

"Sit down, Mister Haecker!" I exclaimed, for he looked ready to faint. His smile was thin and broken like the smiles of army recruits hearing heavy artillery for the first time, and his face was white. I took his arm firmly and led him to the chair. "Let me get you a drop of rye, Mister Haecker." My first thought was that the old fellow was ill and had come to me for help.

"No thank you, Todd," he managed to say. His voice I can describe only as a prim croak. He perched on the edge of the chair as daintily as a canary on its swing, and his hands clutched his knees.

"Is anything wrong, sir?" He looked a bit better now, but still none too stable.

"No," he said shortly, closing his eyes and shaking his head. "No. I just—came in to talk to you, Todd." He looked directly at me then for the first time, and gave me a quick, sick smile. I can recall smiling at my father in just that way once at some amusement park—Tolchester, perhaps—when he put me on a carrousel much too large, loud, and rapid for my tastes, and expected me to enjoy it as everyone else did. "Are you busy?"

"Busy loafing," I said, and sat on the edge of the bed. "What's on your mind, sir?" I offered him a cigarette, which he refused with a quick shake of his head, and then I lit one myself for a change.

"I daresay you'll think me foolish, son," he began, in a tone that I at once recognized as false—a deep, head-of-the-clan tone. "A garrulous old man, like many another."

"Not unless what you say is foolish," I said flatly.

Mister Haecker blushed—a surprising thing in a man seventy-nine years old. "It may well be," he laughed nervously.

I smiled. "You don't talk nonsense as a rule."

Mister Haecker sighed, but his sigh was not spontaneous as his blush had been. And he glanced at me sharply.

"It's a not uncommon thing for quite old men—men my age—to lose their perspective," he observed. "I'm aware of that fact, and I often wonder whether we are always being fair when we call it simply senility."

He paused, but I said nothing: I was waiting for him to finish tuning his piano.

"What I mean is, there are conditions of most people's old age, other than mental failure, that could lead to the same crankiness, if you like. Disease, for example, or poverty, or isolation. Don't you think?"

"It sounds reasonable to me," I agreed mildly.

Mister Haecker looked relieved. "Now, then," he said, "the thing I actually came down here for was this—" He clenched his lean fists on his knees and stared at them. "You must tell me frankly—I think you'll be honest with me—did you think the things I told Captain Osborn this morning were entirely silly? You said you didn't agree with me, I remember."

To myself I said "Ah," and regarded my visitor's face more carefully, for the first note on the piano had been sounded. To him I said, "This morning? Oh, you mean the 'growing old' business."

I'd hoped his question was merely rhetorical, an attempt to get himself going; but apparently he expected an answer, for he remained silent, a distracted look on his really quite distinguished face.

"Well, yes and no," I answered. "If the idea you're referring to is the one I'm thinking of, that old age is the glorious finale of life—the last of life for which the first was made, and all that—then I'd say yes, it's possible that Cicero wasn't just whistling in the graveyard. After all, a good Roman fell on his sword when things got too miserable; Cicero was famous and pretty well off in his old age, and probably got a toot out of being a public figure."

"I believe he deeply loved life," Mister Haecker remarked in another false tone, a ministerial one delivered with chin thrust out and head nodding gravely. "Every stage of it for its own peculiar virtues."

"And I think the notion probably works for a number of people who actually believe in a hereafter, or who are honestly content with their careers, or who are temperamentally stoical."

"I quite agree," Mister Haecker said. "But you said *yes* and *no*."

"That's right. I think it's silly to talk about what a man's attitude *should* be, toward a thing like old age and death. Even if you start with *If he wants to die content*, you'd find that different people are content with different things. Cap'n Osborn, for example, will die content, I think; he'll be having the time of his life cussing around his deathbed, and whipping his legs for turning cold."

Mister Haecker clucked his tongue. "And what about me? I quite respect your opinion, Todd, as you should know. I've often wished I were your age"—he smiled ruefully—"or you were mine, so we could discuss things more freely. Intellectual discussion, after all, is the real joy of the winter of life, when other pleasures have flown, as it were."

I spoke as gently as I could without defeating my purpose. "If I were used to feeling pity for people," I said, "I think I'd feel sorrier for you than for anyone in this hotel, sir."

Mister Haecker's eyes grew panicky—their first really honest expression. "Indeed?"

"Don't assault me when I say this," I smiled. "I'm not by any means the truth at any price sort. But since you asked, I'll admit I consider your position the least enviable of anyone's in the Explorers' Club. Miss Holiday Hopkinson has been ready to die for so long, that when death actually gets to her it'll be an anticlimax. That could lead to hysteria, like the kid who studies diving from books all winter and then gets out on the high board and forgets everything he learned; but probably it won't. She'll die in her sleep, I'll bet. And Cap'n Osborn has known how he honestly feels about it too, for a long time, whenever he bothers to think about it, which is damned seldom. He'll just put up a whale of a tussle when the time comes. But the trouble with you, sir, if I may say so, is that you've tried to pretend you're enjoying yourself and looking forward to death as a grand finale, when actually you're not."

"Oh, that's not so!" Mister Haecker protested.

"There's nothing wrong with fooling yourself," I said soothingly. "Lots of times it's that or the insane asylum. But it doesn't work if it doesn't work. The trouble is that you're *not* fooling yourself; you know very well it's an act. What the hell's glorious about your old age? What's wrong with facing the fact that things are pretty bleak, and complaining like hell about it?"

When Mister Haecker slipped anger onto his face then, I began to weary of the colloquy and wish I were alone. Had he been sincerely angry I'd not have objected, but his anger was another of his wardrobe of masks.

"You're being quite frank, young man!" he cried.

"Forget I said anything, then." I sighed, and stretched out on the bed in my robe and slippers. "All's for the best in the best of all possible worlds."

"I'm not angry at your impertinence," he went on, "but I must say I'm disappointed in your values. They're pretty commonplace, for you."

I said nothing, and wished I'd said nothing from the beginning. After all, he was seventy-nine; even with his excellent health, he couldn't be expected to live much more than ten years, and it was no special concern of mine whether he enjoyed them or not.

"Of course my career in the public schools wasn't spectacular, if you judge it by promotions and the like," he pouted. "And I shan't deny that I'd be happier if my wife were alive, or if we'd had children—" He was watching himself being strong. He even paused before continuing in a firm voice, "—but she's not, and we didn't. Do you want me to go around in mourning, begging for pity? My friend Cicero has something to say about that, too: *In times like these, theirs is far from being the worst fate to whom it has been given to exchange life for a painless death.* And this: *If she had not died now, she would yet have had to die a few years hence, for she was mortal born.* What has happened has happened."

Was there any reason to bother pointing out to him how directly his first quotation contradicted his whole position? I flipped my cigarette out the open window.

"Of all my acquaintances," Mister Haecker went on determinedly, "I'd have expected you to be the first to recognize the happiness a mature man can get from a solitary old age, if he doesn't act childish about it. After all the hustle and bustle, one is finally able to live in the company of his thoughts, and contemplate the beauty of God's works. Isn't that what all the philosophers wanted? I can understand Osborn not realizing it; good a chap as he is, the poor fellow hasn't had the opportunity to educate himself. But *you* certainly must be aware that the life of solitary contemplation is the best—after all, you're alone, too."

"I do precious little contemplating," I said. "And if I wanted to, I could chuck the whole thing tomorrow and get married. The point is, I'm here by choice. Also, I can't quote you the lines," I added, "but your pal Cicero wasn't so enthusiastic about the contemplative life. He said somewhere that if a man could ascend into heaven all by himself and see the workings of the universe and so forth, the sight wouldn't give him much pleasure; but it would be the finest thing in the world if he had somebody to describe it to. I'm not saying I believe any of this—I think all these generalizations are asinine. But you're changing texts every few minutes."

Another mask: Mister Haecker got up from the chair and assumed an injured tone. "I see I'm keeping you from your nap," he said. "It took some courage for one my age to discuss these things with a young man. I thought you'd be interested in them."

"You're begging the question with that attitude," I said, sitting up. "If there *was* any question. You asked me how I felt about it."

"Well how *do* you feel?" he cried. "What do you want a man to do who doesn't have anything to live for? It's either pretend to be content, like a man, or go around wailing and weeping like a child."

"I don't care what anyone does," I said. "It makes no difference to me, on principle, whether you're happy or not. I'm no humanitarian. I only said I pitied you; I wouldn't want to be in your shoes. But I don't agree that the alternatives you just mentioned are the only ones."

"What else is there?" Mister Haecker cried. He was getting

worked up again, and his eyes, honest now, showed despair through any mask he donned. "Maybe you recommend suicide?" He laughed explosively. "Is that the other alternative?"

"It was for Cicero's crowd," I said. "Let me tell you something. Unless a man subscribes to some religion that doesn't allow it, the question of whether or not to commit suicide is the first question he has to answer before he can work things out for himself. This applies only to people who want to live rationally, of course. Most people never realize that there's a question in the first place, and I don't see any particular reason why they should have it pointed out to them. I'm telling you because you asked me."

"Well, I'm not a religious man," Mister Haecker declared, "but I think that's reason enough not to kill myself. If death is the absolute end, then you're better off alive under any circumstances."

"That doesn't follow. If death is the end, then it's neutral. Which is better, to be unhappy or to be neutral? It would be different if you could look forward to something better in the near future. I wouldn't commit suicide, for instance, just because the Yankees lost a ball game."

Mister Haecker stood rigid and pale, refusing to be entertained.

"You advise me to kill myself," he said stiffly.

"Not at all. I didn't say everybody *should* work out a rationale. But if you do, then you must answer the suicide question for yourself before you start, obviously. If you want to make sense, I've learned, you should never use the word *should* or *ought* until after you've used the word *if*."

"Then if I want to live rationally, I should kill myself?" he asked, his voice a thin laugh.

"You should only think about the question," I repeated. "*Whether 'tis better in the mind to suffer . . .*"

"Of course, Hamlet was either insane or pretending to be," Mister Haecker remembered triumphantly.

"You're evading the question."

"How about you?" he snickered. "Have you thought about it? I see you're still alive. Why is that?"

I smiled. "I promise I'll think about it after supper tonight, and let you know tomorrow what I decided. You do the same, and we'll compare notes and chip in for either a box of cigars or a pistol, as the case may be. But don't forget," I added seriously, "to consider every objection to suicide that you can think of. If you decide *not* to kill yourself, you can always change your mind later, but the other decision is hard to correct."

Again Mister Haecker refused to be entertained. "It's a question of values," he observed, "and life itself has a value, under any circumstances. There is an absolute value to human life that won't be denied."

"I deny it," I said. Mister Haecker smiled grimly and went to the door. His eyes were still honest; he could do nothing with the fear in them, although he covered the rest of his features with a visionary falseface when he turned at the door and said, "Life, the simple fact of life, is good, young man. Life has intrinsic value."

I was licking a cigar.

"Nothing has intrinsic value," I remarked, as coolly as though I'd known it for years, when in fact that fundamental notion had just occurred to me, between licks. Mister Haecker closed the door, and I wondered why he'd come to see me; what exactly he'd had on his mind. If it had been some sort of confession, my reaction had driven him behind his masks. No matter: if now in protest against my ideas he actually began to believe his own, that was no concern of mine.

XIX. A premise to swallow

Quantitative changes suddenly become qualitative changes. From all of Marxism, which I once thought attractive enough, I find only this dictum remaining in the realm of my opinions. Water grows colder and colder and colder, and suddenly it's ice. The day grows darker and darker, and suddenly it's night. Man ages and ages, and suddenly he's dead. Differences in degree lead to differences in kind.

When Mister Haecker had gone (Where? Up to his room, for another day of solitary confinement in the contemplative life), I donned my trousers, shirt, coat, and straw, and walked back through the great dry heat to the office. The sky was brilliant blue, the water likewise, a darker shade. Everything was still: only a few cars moved along High Street; no boats were visible on the river; the flag at Long Wharf hung limply against its staff. Everything was baking in the enormous heat, which nevertheless drew not a bead of perspiration from my skin.

What was on my mind, as I walked, was the grand proposition that had occurred to me while I was licking my cigar: that absolutely nothing has intrinsic value. Now that the idea was articulated in my head, it seemed to me ridiculous that I hadn't seen it years ago. All my life I'd been deciding that specific things had no intrinsic value—that things like money, honesty, strength, love, information, wisdom, even life, are not valuable in themselves, but only with reference to certain ends—and yet I'd never considered generalizing from those specific instances. But one instance was added to another, and another to that, and suddenly the total realization was effected—*nothing* is intrinsically valuable; the value of everything is attributed to it, assigned to it, from outside, by people.

I must confess to feeling in my tranquil way some real excitement at the idea. Need I repeat that I am not a thinker? That technical philosophy is not my cup of tea? Doubtless (as I later learned) this idea was not original with me, but it was completely new to me, and I delighted in it like a child turned loose in the endless out-of-doors, full of scornful pity for those inside. *Nothing is valuable in itself.* Not even truth; not even this truth. I am not a philosopher, except after the fact; but I am a mean rationalizer, and once the world has forced me into a new position, I can philosophize (or rationalize) like two Kants, like seven Philadelphia lawyers. Beginning with my new conclusions, I can work out first-rate premises.

On this morning, for example, I had opened my eyes with the knowledge that I would this day destroy myself (a conclusion in itself demonstrating Marx's dictum); here the day was but half spent, and already premises were springing to my mind, to justify on philosophical grounds what had been a purely personal decision. The argument was staggering. Enough now to establish this first premise: nothing is intrinsically valuable.

If you are no philosopher either, reader, take a good comfortable time to swallow that proposition—I daresay it will stick in some throats. If you can stomach it, why then you've done enough for one chapter, and so have I.

XX. Calliope music

My prose is a plodding, graceless thing, and I've no comprehension of stylistic tricks. Nevertheless I must begin this chapter in two voices, because it requires two separate introductions delivered simultaneously.

It's not so difficult, is it, to read two columns at the same time? I'll commence by saying the same thing with both voices, so, until you've got the knack, and then separate them ever so gradually until you're used to keeping two distinct narrative voices in your head at the same time.

Ready? Well: when I re-entered my office the clock in the tower of the Municipal Building was just striking two, and as if by a prearranged signal, at the same moment the raucous voice of a steam calliope came whistling in off the river: *Adam's Original & Unparalleled Floating Opera*, one could guess, had just passed Hambrooks Bar Light and was heading up the channel to the bell buoy and thence to Long Wharf. For the thousandth

It's not so difficult, is it, to read two columns at the same time? I'll commence by saying the same thing with both voices, so, until you've got the knack, and then part them very carefully until it's no trouble for you to follow both sets of ideas simultaneously and accurately.

Ready? Well: you'll recall that chapter before last I declared to Mister Haecker that anyone who wishes to order his life in terms of a rationale must first of all answer for himself Hamlet's question, the question of suicide. I would add further that if he wants my respect, his choice to live must be based on firmer ground than Hamlet's—that "conscience does make cowards of us all": that to choose suicide is to exchange unknown evils for known ones. This position (like time I blushed at the clumsy ironies of coincidence, for it happened that just as I drew from my files the nearly completed brief of a litigation involving a slight injury to the left foot of perhaps the richest man in Cambridge—who stood to be some fifteen thousand dollars richer if my client lost the case—the calliope broke into "Oh, Dem Golden Slippers," and a few minutes later, when I was reflecting on the difficulties my client would have in scraping together that sum, the melody changed to "What You Gon' Do When De Rent Comes 'Round?"

In fact, even to think of the name *Adam's Original & Unparalleled Floating Opera*—its completely unsubtle significance —when I had before me the extraordinary case of *Morton* v. *Butler*, was the greatest of accidental ironies: never did there exist such an unparalleled floating opera as the law in its less efficient moments, and seldom had the law such inefficient moments as those during which it involved itself—nay, diffused, dissipated, lost itself—in *Morton* v. *Butler*. Hamlet listed "the law's delay" as one of the things that could drive a man to suicide. That I don't accept the Prince's list, your starboard eye has already observed; that neither Morton nor Butler accepted this

Montaigne's argument against revolution) is, as the Prince admits, simply cowardly, not reasonable. On the other hand, if one chooses to die, for mercy's sake let this choice be more reasonably founded than Hamlet's, too—merely escaping "the slings and arrows of outrageous fortune" is as cowardly as is fearing dreams beyond the grave. Don't think I'm an indiscriminating promoter of suicides: I merely hold that those who would live reasonably should have reasons for remaining alive. Reasonable enough?

But I cannot accept bad luck as sufficient reason for anyone's suicide, including my father's. Indeed, it was the absence, in my opinion, of any valid reason for his hanging himself that turned me into a cynic after his death, though I had, no doubt, the seeds of cynicism in me all along. It was a sudden qualitative change, the impingement of the world onto my philosophy.

Before I tell you more about my reaction to Dad's death, and about the little adventure that followed it, let me review very briefly the case on which I spent my afternoon hour's work—what I meant to be my final hour's work as a lawyer. It will serve as an introduction to Col. Henry Morton, who plays a role in the little adventure, and at the same particular annoyance as suicidal is evidenced by their both still walking the earth. Let me review the case, a bump on the log of my story:

time keep you from assuming that I simply loafed all afternoon, when in fact I did some fruitful wall-staring. Here's a resume of the case, a bump on the log of my story:

Morton v. *Butler*, by June of 1937, was a litigation almost six years old, and at the time of this story the litigants hadn't yet even begun to try the case on its merits, but were still enmeshed, via their attorneys, in procedural disputes. Col. Henry Morton, the packer of Morton's Marvelous Tomatoes, along with his wife, was the plaintiff, and was represented by Charley Parks, my neighbor and poker partner. I represented the defendant, Mr. William T. Butler, an investment broker who happened to run the New-Deal wing of the local Democratic machine, the other, conservative, wing of which was run by Col. Morton.

What happened was simple. On October 31, 1931, Mr. Butler was driving his Cadillac sedan down Court Lane, just outside my office, and Col. Morton's only son, Allan (for whom the Colonel had a great, if overprotective, affection), was driving *his* Cadillac sedan down Gay Street, which meets Court Lane at the creek. Col. and Mrs. Morton were passengers in their son's car. The two cars met at the bottom of the hill. Butler had to make a right turn up Gay Street, and young Morton a left turn up Court Lane. Both drivers signaled their turns, and each saw the other's signal. Then (from what I gather privately) both drivers executed poor turns simultaneously, Butler turning too wide and Allan Morton too short. The automobiles collided, and both were damaged slightly. Also, Mrs. Morton broke her spectacles and scratched her face on the lenses, and the Colonel wrenched the tendons of his left foot. The drivers got out; Butler and the limping Colonel shook hands, as rival candidates for the same office might.

"Well, Bill!" the Colonel bellowed heartily. "Can't you drive that machine?"

"Not on the same street with that boy of yours!" Butler guffawed back. The two men chortled and chuckled, slapped each other on the shoulders, and then parted, having tacitly agreed that the injuries didn't seem serious, and that among responsible gentlemen such private affairs didn't go to court. Next day, Butler sent Mrs. Morton a fifteen-dollar spray of mixed flowers, and the Colonel sent Butler a quart of Haig & Haig.

Had it not been for Franklin Roosevelt, the affair might have ended there. But Roosevelt was elected in 1932, initiated the New Deal just afterwards, and in the summer of 1933 sailed up the Choptank to Cambridge, to dedicate the just-completed Harrington Bridge across that river. Both factions of the party were enthusiastic: when it was announced that the President would not come ashore, but would broadcast his dedication from the presidential yacht *Potomac*, anchored out by the bell buoy, Col. Morton took it upon himself to have razed the old freight house that stood on Long Wharf, declaring it to be a natural place of concealment for assassins with high-powered rifles. The city council nodded, and the old structure came down. The Colonel then declared that no private vessels should be permitted to leave the creek or the yacht basin while the *Potomac* was at anchor—the scene otherwise would be disrespectfully cluttered. The mayor made such a resolution, and the yacht club followed suit. Surely a magnanimous solicitude for an anti-New Dealer! But of the citizens of Cambridge, thousands of whom respectfully lined the bulkheads to see the *Potomac* and listen to the President's amplified voice, only one was invited aboard: "Old Bill" Butler, of the Butler Democrats.

One month later, for no stated reason, Mr. Butler dropped into my office and described to me his automobile accident of nearly two years before.

"I'll want you to handle it if anything comes up, honey," he chuckled (it was his habit always to speak with a chuckle, whether the thing he said was funny or not).

And not long after that (it was, in fact, on October 13, 1933, just two weeks before the statute of limitations would have run out), Charley Parks called me to say that he was filing suit against Butler for Col. and Mrs. Morton, who claimed personal injuries, and for Allan Morton, who claimed damages of $75.00 for repairs to and $600 for alleged depreciation in the value of his Cadillac. The injury claims of the Colonel and his wife totaled nearly $15,000: their hospital and medical expenses amounted to a total of $854.26, and in addition they claimed $14,000 for pain and suffering (in the case of the Colonel) and mental anguish (resulting from Evelyn Morton's permanent, if faint, disfigurement and the Colonel's perpetual limp). I guessed at once that even had Mr. Roosevelt remained in Washington, Butler's retaining me as his counsel would have been sufficient reason for the Colonel to decide, belatedly, to press the case, for as you shall see directly, between the Mortons and myself there was small love lost. I worked out my strategy at once.

Now, although Charley and I have on occasion enjoyed long sessions of legal hair-splitting over beer and seven-card stud, at no time did we ever say in so many words that we were making game out of *Morton* v. *Butler*. Nevertheless, here is what happened in the remaining two months of 1933: On November 20, the three plaintiffs filed their official complaint, charging that the collision had been due to Butler's negligence in that he took the corner at an excessive rate of speed; that he failed to have his car under proper and adequate control; and that he was guilty of other acts of commission and omission. On December 15, I filed for Butler a petition for severance of Allan Morton's action from that of the other plaintiffs. On December 29, the Circuit Court dismissed the petition. I went to Butler's New Year's Eve party and drank sloe gin.

1934: On January 9, I filed a petition to set aside the court order of December 29, which had dismissed my original petition. On April 26 the court set aside that order and granted the severance we wanted. Then, on May 4, I obtained a writ to join Allan Morton as an additional defendant, along with Butler, in the severed suit of Col. and Mrs. Morton, and filed a complaint against him—substantially identical to his complaint against Butler. On June 18, Charley Parks answered for Allan, pleading in new matter the statute of limitations, which of course had run out nearly eight months ago. On August 8, Butler replied to the new matter. On October 26, Charley filed a motion, in Allan's name, for a judgment on the proceedings relative to Butler's complaint. On December 29, exactly a year since the dismissal of my original petition for severance, the court dismissed my complaint against young Morton, and on New Year's Eve, far from committing suicide (as Hamlet would have done by this time), I got drunk at Butler's party, on vodka sours.

1935: On January 10 (while Harrison Mack Senior, by the way, was dying in his bed in Ruxton), I petitioned for permission to file an amended complaint for Butler. On January 18, the court granted its permission, and I filed an amended complaint against Allan Morton, averring that his parents, in their complaint against Butler, had charged that their $15,000 injuries were due solely to Butler's negligence; that Butler was prepared to serve a copy of that very complaint against their son; that Butler admitted neither in whole nor in part their charges; that Allan had been negligent in the operation of *his* Cadillac; that only the actual trial would determine whether Allan's own negligence had been the sole or a major contributing cause of the accident, but that it was one or the other; that Butler desired to be able to protect his right of contribution in the event the court found him to have been jointly or concurrently negligent with Allan; and that therefore Allan was jointly liable with Butler upon the causes of action declared upon by Col. and Mrs. Morton. On February 6, Allan—or rather, Charley—filed his answer along with new matter again pleading the statute of limitations. On April 8, the court, while not ruling on the accuracy of Butler's charges, dismissed my amended complaint on five grounds, all as sensible and exceptionable as are the grounds for any such ruling. Charley and I played poker a few times in March and April, and then on May 1 a stipulation of counsel was filed, agreeing to my filing a second amended complaint for Butler against Allan, and I filed the new complaint, a document differing from its predecessors only in its rhetoric. On May 21, Charley filed Allan's answer, with new matter as before. On October 21, the court dismissed the second amended complaint on the same grounds as before, and on November 12 entered orders in each of the two cases separately to the same effect. By this time I was well enmeshed in the Mack will case, but nevertheless, as Charley grinned and Butler chuckled, I took the Circuit Court's order to the Court of Appeals on November 13. That New Year's Eve I drank Sherbrook rye, first with the Macks in their club cellar, then with Butler in his club cellar, and finally with Jane in my room, but did not get drunk.

1936: The Mack will case was now involved in its own glorious intricacies, but I found time on March 17 to argue in the Maryland Court of Appeals for reversal of the Circuit Court's order. The question, for both courts, was whether, since the statute of limitations prevented our joining young Morton as an additional defendant on grounds of sole liability, we had averred in our amended complaint facts sufficient to warrant a finding of joint or concurrent liability, and the Court of Appeals agreed (on December 4) that we did not. But they quite reasonably allowed me to appeal to the Maryland Supreme Court their affirmation of the Circuit Court's order, so that the procedural question might be finally determined. That New Year's Eve, as I recall, I drank alone in my room.

1937: Now I had never agreed with the two lower courts that what they thought was the question was really the question. And so, on April 26, I argued to the Supreme Court that the *real* issue was whether a defendant in a tort action who, like Butler, was barred by the statute of limitations from joining an additional defendant (to whom he was also liable, you see) on the grounds of sole liability, might yet preserve his right of contribution by pleading joint or several liability *without* alleging facts admitting his own liability to the plaintiff (Col. and Mrs. Morton). My position was that if Butler, in order to establish Allan's joint liability, were obliged, in addition to averring facts showing Allan's negligence, to admit his *own* negligence, it amounted to denying Butler's right to bring Allan on the record at all, since any such admissions could be placed in evidence and exploited by Col. Morton when the case came to trial. Now, since in our amended complaint we alleged facts establishing Allan's negligence, all we were pleading, actually, was that if, when the thing ever came to trial, the jury should find Butler to be negligent as the plaintiffs charged, then Allan's negligence, as described in our complaint, was also a contributing cause of the collision. The Supreme Bench, reasonable fellows all, saw no justification for not allowing such a plea, especially in the case of an automobile collision, where it is always possible that both drivers were at fault. On May 24, they rendered their opinion, which reversed the order of the Court of Appeals affirming the order of the Circuit Court dismissing our second amended complaint against the additional defendant, and remanded the record to the Circuit Court with a procedendo.

There was no appealing this judgment. Charley set me up to a drink, and the suit was ready to be tried, Col. Morton in effect suing his only-begotten son. Bill Butler chuckled happily, for with Roosevelt so firmly entrenched in the White House and in public popularity as he was in 1937, the Morton wing of the local Democratic party could ill afford any bad publicity.

I wish, reader, that I could at this point announce some trump that I'd saved to play on this last day of my career, when already I'd been able to settle, as far as I was concerned, the Mack will case in favor of Harrison. But the truth is that my interest in *Morton* v. *Butler* ended with the Supreme Court's ruling, for that terminated the procedural dispute. I didn't mind missing the actual trial, which would be dull enough whoever won. I had got out the record of the case on this last afternoon only because Bill Butler, according to a note Mrs. Lake had left on my desk, was coming to see me at two-fifteen.

At two-thirty he strode in, chuckling, a bald, beefy fellow with good eyes and bad teeth, carrying a shoe box.

"What do I owe you, Todd old cod?" he sang out. "What's my bill, hon?"

"You owe me your skin," I smiled. "Charley would have hanged you. You better wait till after the trial to pay me the rest of your bill, though."

"Ain't going to be any trial," Butler chuckled.

"Does the Colonel know that?"

"Oh hell yes indeedy," Butler chuckled. "He's the one thought of calling it off, honey. Called me yesterday, day before, gives me the old family squabble routine, old party harmony song and dance. Haw! Told me if I'd let some of his boys run on my ticket next year in the primary, he'd call off the suit."

"You didn't have to take any conditions."

Butler chuckled grandly. "I told him he could have sheriff and one county commissioner if he'd call his damn state cop off my ass. You know that cop Yarberry, that the Colonel got him his job? Every time I go over the new bridge that Yarberry is after me—Colonel's got him looking for me. I could tell you plenty on Yarberry and the Colonel, hon! Old Colonel don't care about one lousy county commissioner, but he sure does want sheriff, so he promises to curb his cop and drop the suit. I already sent Evelyn another bunch of flowers."

"Hell, you didn't have to give him a thing, Bill," I said again. "He'd never sue his boy."

"Haw!" Butler chuckled. "Tell you the facts, Todd, I didn't have a sonofabitch in the stable to put up for them jobs, that I would walk on the same side of the street with, so old Colonel would of got them anyhow. That's *principles*, boy!

Give Roosevelt another go-round in '40, honey, and I'll elect you governor. How 'bout that?"

"No trial, then?"

"No trial," Butler chuckled. "Fetch in old Charleyhorse from next door; we'll try the Colonel's whiskey."

He opened the shoe box and took out a fifth of Park & Tilford.

"Call up old Charleyhorse, Julia," he chuckled to Mrs. Lake. "Come on, there, Harry Bishop; come on, Jimmy boy. We're drinking the Colonel's whiskey!"

The calliope down at the wharf broke into "Out of the Wilderness." I blushed, replaced the bulky brief of *Morton* v. *Butler* in the file, and accepted a drink of Park & Tilford.

XXI. Coals to Newcastle

When, as I said earlier, I came home from the office on the afternoon of February 2, 1930, and after searching the house for my father, finally found him in the cellar, one end of his belt spiked to a floor joist and the other fastened around his neck, there was not a smudge of dirt anywhere on him, though the cellar was dusty. His clothes were perfectly creased and free of wrinkles, and although his face was black and his eyes were popped, his hair was neatly and correctly combed. Except that the chair upon which Dad had stood was kicked over, everything in the cellar was in order.

The same could not be said of his estate. Indeed, as soon became apparent, there was no estate. It is such a commonplace story that I hesitate to tell it—and yet nothing was ever less true or pitiful for its being commonplace. Dad had had a sizable savings account; between the years 1925 and 1927 he increased it by investing in stocks. He didn't expect the boom to last, and so decided to make one big splash and quit. To make the splash he mortgaged all his property—a summer cottage and lot at Fenwick Island and one or two timber lots down the county—for as much as he could, and sank the whole wad on the market. In early 1929, when the speculative structure began to quiver, and every public official in the country began to assure us that the economy was fundamentally sound, Dad mortgaged the house and lot, borrowed on his life insurance, and contracted private notes from what few of his many friends were able to lend him money. All this, too, went on the market. No, not quite all: five thousand dollars he persuaded Harry Bishop to put in a safe-deposit box, in my name—suspecting, perhaps, that otherwise he'd not be able to resist plunging that, too.

Then the market collapsed. People were anxious enough to hire lawyers, all right, to collect debts, but they had no money to pay the lawyers with, and most debts had suddenly become uncollectable. Dad had payments falling due on at least four mortgages and countless loans, and no money to meet them with. Foreclosures threatened from all sides, lawsuits from every quarter. He would, it appeared, lose his summer cottage, his timber lots, the family home, the car, virtually everything he owned. His debts amounted to perhaps $35,000. He would have to sleep in the office, walk to court, wear his suits threadbare. Very possibly he would never reach again his former security or regain all his former respect. It was a hard pill to swallow. Instead of swallowing it anyway, he hanged himself.

Does one's father hang himself for a simple, stupid lack of money? And is one expected to set up again the chair one's father has kicked over in his strangling? Can one actually, with a kitchen knife, saw through the belt? Carry one's father up to the bed whereon one was conceived, and laying him on it, dig one's fingers into the black and ruptured flesh to release the dead neck from its collar? Reader, I still recall with shudders a summer day when I was five years old. My father (dressed in good clothes) was killing chickens in the back yard. He caught one, and holding it by the feet, laid it on the chopping block, a sawn stump; unruffled by the flailing wings, he raised the old ax, which he held close to the head, and with a soft stroke decapitated the hen. The head still lay on the stump, the little red eyes staring, the beak opening and shutting in soundless squawks. The body, once my father released it, flailed about the yard for thirty seconds and then died. I watched everything with great, uneasy absorption.

Dad picked up the chicken by its feet again.

"Will you take this in to Bessie, please?"

I held out my hand dumbly. Dad put the feet in my hand—cold, hard, dirty, stringy, scaly, dead yellow feet. I was ill then, reader, and if I think of those feet a minute longer I shall be ill now. But of this matter one *can* think, if queasily. Is one, then, expected to close the popping eyes of his father's corpse? Eyes the very veins of which are burst? Surely the dirt of the planet would cry the reason for it, the justification that would brook no questioning. I waited.

Of course there were debts. The Fenwick place; take it. The timber lots? To be sure. The house? The car? The insurance? Take them, take them. One doesn't concern oneself with trifles at one's father's grave, only with reasons. I waited.

Back at the office, Harry Bishop gave me the envelope from Dad. I took it eagerly, hoping it would contain the answer, but instead it merely had five thousand dollars in it. There was a note, too, which I must have suppressed—it's honestly, completely gone from my mind—because it said all the things I certainly didn't want to hear, in just the wrong language. Is five thousand dollars enough to pay for digging my fingers under that belt? It's not enough payment even for thinking about it! His debt to me was the last, but hardly the least debt my father escaped.

If I was demoralized by Dad's death, I was paralyzed by the five thousand dollars and the note. Certainly I sat in the office for thirty minutes with my jaw slack, staring at the bills as if I'd opened that precious last envelope and discovered inside a handful of dung, the color of a hanged man's cheeks. Five thousand dollars! After some time I replaced the crisp new thousand-dollar bills in their envelope, which was, after all, unstamped and unaddressed, and thought of all the people I knew.

The question became simple: Who was the richest man in Cambridge? Col. Henry Morton. I wrote on the envelope *Col. Henry Morton, % Morton's Marvelous Tomatoes, Inc., Cambridge, Maryland,* put a three-cent stamp in place, and snuffling like a hobbled race horse, dropped the envelope into a mailbox on my way to lunch. Next day I moved into the Dorset Hotel.

This was, I believe, in early March 1930. Very soon afterwards I received a call from the Colonel, whom I knew only slightly.

"Hello? Hello?" he shouted, as though it were not his custom to speak on telephones. "Is this Todd Andrews?"

"Yes, sir."

"Hello? Andrews? Andrews, what's this money I got from you in the mail?"

"It's a gift from me to you," I said.

"Andrews? You there, Andrews? What's going on, eh?"

"It's a gift," I repeated; "a gift."

"Huh? What? *Hello?* Andrews! Gift! Hello?"

"It's a gift," I repeated.

The day after that, the Colonel came to see me, striding unappointed into my office.

"Andrews? You Andrews? See here, young man, I don't know what you've got up your sleeve—"

"It was a gift," I explained; "that's all."

"A gift? You're crazy, son! Here, take it back, and no more foolishness!"

He did not wave anything at me—no bills under my nose.

"Of course not," I said. "It was just a gift."

"Gift? Well! Gift? What's up your sleeve, young man? What do you think I'm supposed to do?"

"Not a blessed thing, sir," I repeated. "It was a gift."

"I won't stand for tricks," the Colonel warned. "Here, take it back. No more!"

Again, he extended nothing toward me.

"I've never been obligated to any man," the Colonel said then, more calmly. "I shan't begin now."

"No obligation, sir," I insisted.

"Hmph! Whatever's on your mind, you might as well forget it. I can't be bought! If anybody was to ask me the secret of my success, I'd tell them I was never obligated to any man."

"I'd never try to obligate you, sir. It was just a gift."

"I'll teach you a lesson, son." The Colonel smiled, as though the idea had just dawned on him. "I'm going to keep half your money, and you shan't get a thing out of me in return."

"You must keep it all," I said. "I don't take back gifts."

"Hmph! You've got a lot to learn, boy. A lot to learn! Never obligate yourself to anybody."

"I shan't, sir."

"Hard times, Andrews!" the Colonel sputtered. "Bad times! Plant's laying off! A man doesn't throw his money away! What's on your mind? Eh? Eh?"

I shook my head. "Nothing, sir. No explanation."

The Colonel stood up suddenly to leave, looking grimly around my office and chewing his cigar.

"I'll teach you, boy," he said. "You'll wish you had it back!"

"No, sir."

He started out and then grinned back into the doorway.

"You'd've been better off using it to square some of your Dad's debts!" he declared and, satisfied that he'd demonstrated his independence, left. Mrs. Lake gasped at his remark.

Some time afterwards a letter came.

Dear Mr. Andrews:

By this time you are doubtless of a different mind concerning the transaction of some days ago. I am, however, a man of my word, and intend to carry out my resolution for your instruction.

Yours truly,
Henry W. Morton

I replied at once:

Dear Col. Morton:
  I have not changed my mind at all. The matter to which you refer was not any sort of transaction, and you are not obliged to me in any way. It was a gift.

Yours truly,
Todd Andrews

Within the month, Morton's Marvelous Tomatoes, Inc., became involved in a contractual dispute with a small shipping concern that ferried some of the Colonel's canned goods to Baltimore. The evidence was all in favor of the shipping company (the suit was an intricate one, and I shan't describe it here), but the Colonel had never lost a litigation before, and so he determined to spend his way to justice. An executive from MMT, Inc., called on me and announced that the Colonel wanted Andrews, Bishop, & Andrews to handle his defense.

"Sure," I said. "I'm not interested myself, but Mr. Bishop can take the case."

"I believe the Colonel is anxious for you to handle it personally," the executive said (he was Wingate Collins, a kind of vice-president); "in fact, I'm sure he is. I heard him say so."

But I declined. The Colonel took his business to Charley Parks, and ultimately obtained justice in the Court of Appeals.

Then the drivers of the Morton Trucking Company, a subsidiary of the packing house, went on strike when the Colonel refused to allow the company union to affiliate with the CIO, and Norbert Adkins, of the union, asked our firm for legal counsel. Jimmy Andrews, who had just joined us, was itching for the job, and Mr. Bishop and I saw no reason why he shouldn't take it. But Wingate Collins gave us a reason.

"I'll tell you frankly," he said, "the Colonel doesn't want any of his friends to take that job. Your outfit would be pretty unpopular if you fellows took it. You know what I mean?"

"Cut it out, Wingate," I smiled. "You've been going to the movies too much."

"I'll tell you what," he said. "You stand to come into a good thing if you don't stick up for those strikers. The Colonel's been unhappy with Matson & Parks lately—just between us, of course—and he's looking around for another law firm to represent MMT officially. That's between six and eight thousand a year extra for the firm that gets it. The Colonel's taken a liking to you, Todd, I don't mind saying. He thinks you're a very promising fellow. And I'd bet my bottom dollar you'd get that job if you'll lay off these strikers. Hell, I know you would—off the record, now—I heard him say as much yesterday."

"I guess Jim wants to handle it, Wingate," I said. "You'd better talk to him."

"I already did," Wingate sniffed. "He says he wants the union thing, but it's up to you and Harry. Harry says he don't care one way or the other."

"I don't either," I said.

"Well, I frankly think you're a damn fool, if you'll excuse me for saying so!" Wingate said heatedly. "The Colonel'll have a tough time swallowing this, I declare!"

But apparently he swallowed it. Jimmy counseled the union in the arbitration that followed, and Matson & Parks, next door, counseled the company. It was finally decided that the union would remain "independent," and, solemnly, that the strikers would pay from their treasury for the damage to six trucks that they'd overturned during the strike.

During the next year or so, the Colonel approached me, either directly or through his vice-presidents, on ten different occasions with offers of business. I declined to handle any of them personally (they were routine affairs, if lucrative); some he took elsewhere, others he rather reluctantly allowed Mr. Bishop to handle. Whenever I encountered him on the street (he rarely walked), he clapped me on the shoulder, took my arm, invited me for dinner, invited me for cruises on his yacht, invited me to membership in the Cambridge Yacht Club, the Elks, the Rotary, the Masons, the Odd Fellows (the Colonel was a joiner), and the country club (because I sometimes played golf, I was already a member). I declined his invitations politely. He fumed and stewed.

More offers for legal business came in from Morton's Marvelous Tomatoes.

"I'll say quite frankly," Wingate Collins said, "I think you're a damn fool. What you got against us? You fellows are passing up the chance of a lifetime. You got more money than you can use? I'll tell you the Christ truth, Todd, the Colonel's got ants in his pants about that money you sent him—off the cuff, now, understand. I told him you're just a damn fool, frankly, but he don't know you like I do. He can't understand it. He's got ants in his pants because he says he don't want to be obligated to any man. Now, then. You'd make him a lot easier to live with if you'd take some of this business he's throwing your way."

"The firm's not turning it down," I reminded him. "I'm just not interested personally."

"Hell, man, it's not like it's an outright gift to you!" Wingate cried. "He just wants to hire you, like anybody else might do. What you want to hold him by the tail for? Nobody else ever got him so het up before!"

"He's being childish," I said. "He knows he's not obligated to me. He even took the trouble to get it in writing."

Wingate told me frankly I was a damn fool.

Word got around town (I suspect through either Wingate or Mrs. Lake or Jimmy) about the five thousand dollars, and I was asked about it by a few extracurious people.

"It was just a gift," I shrugged.

Most people, though, had already regarded me as rather eccentric, and so were pleased enough to have their suspicions confirmed. I heard through friends that one or two of Dad's creditors were disgruntled, but of course the money was mine, not Dad's, and so they could do nothing. Some cynics wondered what I was after.

On Christmas the Colonel sent me, via his chauffeur, a case of Harvey's Scotch. When he got it back two days later, via the Cambridge Cab Company, he came again in person to my office.

"Good morning, sir," I said. "What can I do for you?"

"You can quit this damn nonsense!" the Colonel said heartily. I offered him a cigar, which he refused almost violently. I waited for him to continue.

"Do you still mean to sit there and swear to God you gave me five thousand dollars out of a clear blue sky for nothing? With times as hard as they are?"

"It was a gift," I said.

"Don't think I don't know why your father committed suicide, young man," the Colonel said. "No offense intended; you know how these things get around."

"That's right."

The Colonel sighed impatiently and tapped his cane on the floor. "I don't get it," he said.

"There's nothing to get."

"Listen," he said, rather quietly. "This needn't go beyond the two of us. Wingate Collins—you know him? Good. Wingate Collins is my vice-president unofficially in charge of labor relations. Good man, Wingate, but he's doing a lousy job. Makes everybody mad, and he's supposed to make everybody happy. Union doesn't like him, office people don't like him, I don't like him. Great fellow, you know, but makes folks mad. Well, then. Wingate's going to retire soon—he don't know it yet—and I'm going to hire a labor relations man. Want a lawyer, somebody knows people. Take you half a day, five days. Five thousand a year, and you can keep your law practice on the side."

"Nope."

"Listen," the Colonel said. "This isn't any gift. I don't know anybody else I'd rather hire. I'm just glad I got to know you."

"Thanks," I said. "I don't want the job, sir, thank you just the same."

"Don't want it!" the Colonel cried. "Men are begging for work! Don't want it!"

"No, sir."

"*Yes!*" the Colonel shouted, forgetting himself. His face was red.

"Nope," I said again.

"Take your damn money back!" the Colonel cried, but waved no bills under my nose.

"Of course not."

The Colonel actually mopped his forehead with his handkerchief.

"How about the Scotch?"

"No thank you, sir," I said.

He rose to leave, shaken.

"I shall have a great many guests in on New Year's Eve," he said softly. "You'll get an invitation; Mrs. Morton has already sent them out. It's her first big affair, and she's heard of you but hasn't met you." The Colonel had remarried perhaps a year before, his first wife having died in 1926.

"Thank you," I said.

"You needn't take the trouble to send it back, as you did the Scotch. There's no need to insult Evelyn. Just throw it in your wastebasket."

I did indeed get the engraved invitation next day, and on New Year's Eve, having drunk four double highballs in my room after supper, I decided to drop in on the Colonel's party, thinking it consistent with my policy of incomplete consistency. At eleven o'clock I took a cab out to the Morton estate on Hambrooks Bay.

The party was in full swing when I arrived. Both wings of the great brick house were bright, and perhaps a hundred and fifty people milled around inside, in tuxedos and gowns. I wouldn't have thought that there were that many tuxedos in Dorchester County. A champagne fountain had been rigged up in the main living room, and a sparkling burgundy fountain in the library. The women were drinking mostly from these. On the summer porch three white-coated Negroes tended bar, and male guests stood two deep before them. A small orchestra was playing in the basement.

The butler took my coat and my invitation at the door, but before he could do anything with the latter, the Colonel caught sight of me from across the room, where he stood laughing with some vice-presidential-looking friends. He stared for a moment, took the cigar from his mouth, and then broke into a great smile.

"Well, well, *well!*" he roared, charging toward me with hand extended. "Andrews!" He could think of nothing to say, and so pumped my arm for a minute.

"Well, well, *well!*" he roared again.

"Looks like a pleasant party," I declared.

"Well!" the Colonel said. "Ha! Say, you must meet Evelyn. *Evelyn! Evelyn!*"

Evelyn appeared from the library, near at hand. She was perhaps forty—more than half the Colonel's age—and, perhaps because she'd borne no children, her figure was still slender, and the skin on her face fairly tight. She was much better-looking than her husband.

"Evelyn, this is young Andrews, Todd Andrews; the young lawyer, you know."

"How do you do, Mr. Andrews."

"Good evening," I said.

"My husband doubted that you'd do us the honor," Mrs. Morton smiled. I guessed that she was thoroughly enjoying her first big affair: her smile was a trifle liquorish.

"Ha!" the Colonel exclaimed, and still held fast to my arm, as though afraid I'd bolt. "He's an independent young man, all right! Well, what say to a drink, Andrews? A little Scotch, eh? Ha!"

"I thank you."

"I'll be seeing you in a moment, Mr. Andrews," Mrs. Morton said. "I certainly must get to know you while we've got you. Toodleoo!"

"Toodleoo," I said.

"You've made her very pleased by coming tonight," the Colonel confided as he marched me through the crowd to the summer porch. People turned to watch us go by.

Well, it was the first party of any size that I'd been to since my saintly days prior to Dad's suicide, and I found myself reverting to that pose. As soon as I could escape the Colonel's introductions to people I already knew—there were only ten or twelve strangers at the party—I garnered two double Scotches from one of the Negroes (whom I also knew well) and retreated to the darkened basement, which had been cleared out for dancing. An auxiliary, one-tender bar had been set up across from the orchestra, and so I was able to drink uninterruptedly for some time, watching the players and the dancers. And, truth to tell, I got splendidly drunk on the Colonel's Scotch.

What followed I must tell in broken sequences, for that is how I remember it:

At midnight the place went to hell, as though every guest—there must have been two hundred then, or else all were in the basement—had decided simply to throw back his head and holler at the top of his lungs for several hours. The orchestra played on, but without audible effect, and people danced brokenly to no music. For a while someone was kissing me, and I proposed to whoever it was that we fling our glasses into the fireplace, as one should.

"There isn't any fireplace."

"Into the noise, then."

"You can't hit noise, silly."

"*Regardez,*" I said, and threw mine at the drummer.

I did indeed dance a tango with Evelyn Morton. Nay, ten, a dozen tangos, without the encumbrances of music or prior experience. And in every ill-lit corner, as his wife clung to me, I saw the Colonel smiling redly, benignly, nodding his great head, flashing his gold teeth, his gold-headed cane.

Certainly there was a floor show of drunken wives of vice-presidents, to the horror of some husbands. A cancan line. Remarkable. I recall vividly the upflung leg, the fat veined thighs of the wife of Wingate Collins, that marked man. The roaring went on, no matter how many glasses one threw at the orchestra, who played in terror. There is a picture of the drummer shielding himself behind a great cymbal, apparently carried for that purpose; of my thin, elegant highball glass glittering through the air to splinter against the wall just off his starboard ear. No matter whom one attempted to dance with, it was Mrs. Morton—slender, graceful, unattractive, drunk—and the Colonel nodded.

Then there was a tendency to take cold showers in several of the upstairs bathrooms. These showers were taken by gluts of singing men. My group sang verses of "Mademoiselle from Armentières," and I recall even now the vibrancy of my baritone, but I don't remember getting wet at all until the entrance of wet Mrs. Morton. Standing outside the shower, we had sung the line declaring that Mademoiselle had not enjoyed herself for forty years, and then between the *hinkey* and the *dinkey* my choir vanished, as in a movie, and shimmering, dripping Mrs. Morton leaped like a damp naiad from behind the shower curtain, into my arms. Her dewy bosoms, none too firm, crushed into my shirt front; her dripping hair fell over her eyes; her teeth sank into my lapel, into my boutonniere; she ground herself against my trousers. We danced a magnificent *parley-voo*, stopping with a dip that dropped us to the tiles, tapped by the tip of the Colonel's cane. Mrs. Morton caught sight of the gold teeth glinting in the light from the bathroom bulb and swooned or died, sprawling pink and sprinkled like a blushing dugong hoist from the deep.

I picked myself up and straightened my wet bow tie. The Colonel grinned feverishly and tapped his cane (seven inches from his wife's wet head) as though conversing with her spirit by Morse code.

"Mrs. Morton dances well," I said, bowing slightly to the Colonel as I stepped over Evelyn en route to the door. And then, parting, with what seemed to me a nice conjunction of wit and *savoir-faire:* "One might call her Morton's Most Marvelous Tomato, mightn't one? Good night, sir."

One was, in fact, tempted to add that it was a pity to see such a fresh tomato stewed, as it were, if not altogether canned —but one knew the line beyond which the prick of wit becomes the sting of insult, and so held one's tongue and exited gracefully.

In the new year that followed, the firm of Andrews, Bishop, & Andrews was not pressed to render its services to the Colonel, nor was I dunned with invitations to join clubs or lodges, nor confronted at every turn with invitations to parties and dinners at the Morton manor. Indeed, if there have been any parties at the Mortons' since that New Year's Eve, I've not heard of them. Jacob Matson, of Matson & Parks, became vice-president in charge of personnel for MMT, Inc., when Wingate Collins suddenly retired.

And on the rare occasions when I met Col. Morton on Race Street and tipped my hat in greeting, he flushed red, bared his gold teeth, and ignored me with the grim smile of one who is obligated in no way to any man.

XXII. A tour of the opera

At three o'clock, just after Bill Butler and Charley Parks had left my office, Jane Mack came in with her daughter. I heard Jane exchange greetings with Mrs. Lake, and then little Jeannine —three and a half years old now, and brown and lovely like her mother—came up to my desk and watched me shyly.

"Hi, Toddy," she said.

"Hi, baby."

"Honey, may I fix your pencil?"

"Sure." It was Jeannine's habit to sharpen pencils. I gave her a good long one, and she went happily to the sharpener and proceeded to grind away on it.

"Oh, my," Jane said, coming into my office, "she's happy now. How do you feel, Toddy? Any better?"

"Hello, Jane. I wasn't sick."

"Then why did you act so silly last night?" she asked, more softly, so that Mrs. Lake couldn't hear. She perched on the corner of my desk. She was wearing khaki shorts—unusual for that year—and a blue cotton blouse, and looked quite fresh and desirable.

I smiled. "I guess I just wasn't in the mood."

She smiled back and patted me on the head. "That's a stupid way to be," she said. "*I* was in the mood."

"*I* was, too," Jeannine declared from the pencil sharpener.

"Maybe I'm getting senile," I proposed. "Stamina was never my strong point, as you know."

"I know your strong point," Jane said. "Did you get my note?"

"I did."

"You sent me a dumb one, so I thought I'd send you a dumb one."

I smiled. "I don't know what Marvin found wrong with me. He'll bring the report around tonight, and we'll look at it next time you're up."

I had certainly expected some astonishment at this news, but Jane, unlike Harrison, didn't bat an eye.

"God knows it's time you went to a doctor," she said. "Well—" She jumped off the desk. "I'll be seeing you later at the house, won't I? For a Manhattan? Try not to keep Jeannine right in the sun too long, if you can help it. She's got that bonnet, but it's awfully hot out."

"All right."

"I'll be done at the hairdresser's in an hour, if you want me to drop in and pick her up. If you're finished before then and she gets on your nerves, pop her in a cab and send her home. She likes that. And for God's sake buy her an ice-cream cone."

"All right."

"'Bye, now, honey." Jane kissed her daughter. "So long, Toddy."

"'Bye, Mommy," Jeannine said.

"So long," I said, and she left. I was impressed: between the time in 1933 when I insulted her and the time in 1935 when we resumed our affair, Jane's personality had strengthened in some ways; for one thing, she was unpredictable. I wondered with quite sharp interest what she intended to do about my note, now that I'd fulfilled the conditions of hers—and when it occurred to me that I'd not be alive to find out, I experienced a small sensation of regret; the only such sensation I felt that day.

"Let's go see the showboat, honey," I suggested to Jeannine, who by this time was pushing the last fragment of the pencil into the sharpener.

"All right, honey," she said, and politely took my hand. We went out into the bright sun and walked the dry block to Long Wharf, where the showboat lay immensely along the bulkhead. Unlike its Mississippi counterparts, *Adam's Original & Unparalleled Floating Opera* was no architectural extravaganza of gilt and gingerbread. It was, by comparison with them, severely unadorned, for it had been built to withstand the tempestuous moods of Tangier Sound and the lower Bay, and even ventured into the Atlantic on occasion. The *Opera* itself was a long, narrow clapboard box mounted on a massive barge. On the bow was lettered S.S. *Thespian,* the vessel's registered name, but down both sides of the clapboards, in red letters three feet tall, was emblazoned its less modest trade name. A simple balcony affair graced either end of the theater, apparently for the employees' benefit, and lifelines ran down both sides. On the roof were ventilators, stovepipes, clotheslines, lifeboats, a trim little shed with window boxes and curtained windows, an improvised bandstand, and the steam calliope, now silent. The whole structure was braced against humping or buckling by a trusswork of piers and cables on both sides. Two tugboats moored alongside, the *Pamlico* and the *Albemarle,* provided the showboat's motive power.

"What's that, Toddy?" Jeannine asked excitedly.

"That's a showboat," I said. "Can you say showboat?"

"*Showboat.*"

"Would you like to go up close and see it?"

"All right."

Fortunately, for I'd forgotten my promise, some entrepreneur had set up a refreshment stand near the bulkhead, and so I was able to buy two vanilla ice-cream cones before we went up for a close look at the showboat. Not many people were curious enough to come out in the terrific heat; we had the spectacle pretty much to ourselves, and I set Jeannine up on a piling to get a good view.

As was her habit when excited, Jeannine slipped into the "Why?" routine.

"What's it for, Toddy honey?" she shouted, awed at the *Opera*'s size.

"It's a showboat, hon. People go on it and listen to music and watch the actors dance and act funny."

"Why?"

"Why what?" I asked. "Why do the actors act funny or why do the people like to watch them?"

"Why do the people?"

"The people like to go to the show because it makes them laugh. They like to laugh at the actors."

"Why?"

"They like to laugh because laughing makes them happy. They like being happy, just like you."

"Why?"

Of course she wasn't the least bit interested in either her question or my answers, as questions or answers; she was simply excited over the monstrous showboat and wanted to hear me talk. I could have recited the alphabet in a knowing tone, and she'd have been satisfied.

"Why do they like being happy? That's the end of the line."

"Why do the actors?"

"Why do the actors act funny? They do that so the people will pay to come see them. They want to earn money."

"Why?"

"So they can eat. They like eating."

"Why?"

"You have to eat to stay alive. They like staying alive."

"Why?"

"That's the end of the line again," I said.

"Hey there!" cried a little man on the aft balcony. "Want to look 'er over? Go on up forrard, I'll show ye round."

"Want to go on the showboat?" I asked Jeannine.

"All right."

The little man met us at the gangplank and waved us aboard.
He was tough-looking, wiry, leather-faced, with knotted hands
and the eyes of a starling, and was dressed in wrinkled black
trousers, an immaculate white shirt, and a yachting cap. Jeannine regarded him soberly while I shook hands.

"Are you Captain Adam?"

"That's a fact, sir. Jacob Adam. Bring yer little girl along
now, I'll show ye the boat. Quite a boat, ain't she?"

"She is indeed."

"Quite a boat, sir," Capt. Adam agreed. "Thirty-one years
old, and she's still sound as a dollar, if you know what I
mean—" He tugged my arm and chortled. "Dollar ain't worth
what it was in 1906!

"Quite a boat," he said again. "Had 'er built in Little Washington, North Carolina, in 1906, sir, and I had 'er built strong.
Why, you set one o' them Miss'ssippi showboats down in the
ocean for a minute, there wouldn't be a stick left fit to pick yer
teeth with."

"Why?" Jeannine demanded, gaining courage.

"Did you use to run boats on the Mississippi?" I asked.

"No, sir, I don't mind tellin' ye," the Captain declared, "I
never set foot on a boat in my life till I built the *Op'ry*. Not
even a row-skiff; now, then. I run a two-car ten-cent vaudeville
show all over the country, sir, from 1895 till 1905, and did so
good I had to quit, 'cause ever'body I hired cut out to start a
ten-cent show hisself. Next thing I knew there was so much
competition I couldn't make the nut. I figured I'd set me up in
something that takes a big wad to start with, so ever' Tom,
Dick, and Harry with ten bucks and a lot o' brass can't squeeze
in. I don't mind tellin' ye, I sunk sixty thousand dollars in this
showboat, sir, in a time when dollars was dollars, I mean. But
I wanted 'er tough, and I still got 'er."

"She looks plenty sturdy," I admitted. So far we hadn't
moved from the gangplank: there is that in me which brings out
old men's garrulity.

"She *is* sturdy, sir. Ye see them strakes along the sides there?" He pointed to the barge's side planking. "First time I saw them boards, they was trees. I walked around the Carolina woods for a year, sir, pickin' out my timber where it stood. Hundred-and-twenty-two-foot long and four inches thick, them strakes, and not a splice in 'em from stem to stern, nor a knot, either. And I got 'em drift-bolted ever' two feet with twenty-seven-inch bolts. That's for the ocean, sir! Thirty-two-foot planks across the bottom, beam to beam; not a splice. Cost me plenty, sir, but it was money well spent, let me tell *you*. One time in 1920 we was caught in a squall in Tangier Sound, and they couldn't get a boat to us. I'm not lyin', sir, for fourteen hours the waves was breakin' over the *Op'ry*'s roof. Took Mrs. Adam's pansies right out o' the window box up there, but the *Op'ry* didn't spring a plank. That's what plannin' does, sir!"

Jeannine was jumping up and down; I moved toward the shuttered box office.

"Come on inside," the Captain invited. We entered the theater, dark and cool, and Capt. Adam provided us with a running commentary on what we were observing.

"Seats seven hundred," he said. "White folks down here and in the boxes, colored folks in the balcony."

Jeannine, happily, didn't ask why.

"Used to be, couldn't get a darkie on board," he went on. "Word got around we was baitin' 'em on to send back to Africa. (That there stage is nineteen foot across; hall's eighty foot long.) Used to carry a car on board, but the salt water ruined 'er, seemed like."

"Where's *your* house?" Jeannine demanded.

"Well, little lady, I live up on the roof."

"Why?"

"*Why?* Heh! She's a fresh one, ain't she? Well, sir, come on back here with me, I'll show ye the dressin' rooms and all."

We followed the Captain behind the stage, where a row of numbered doors ran along a short hallway.

"Good big dressin' rooms," Capt. Adam said proudly. "The actors live in 'em, too. Most ever'body's into town just now, sir."

"Why?" Jeannine murmured.

"Now come on down here." We were led down a companionway. "Here's the cook's quarters and the dinin' room—we're right under the stage now—and over there's the galley. Bottle-gas stove and a nine-hundred-pound icebox. That there door leads right out to the orchestra pit. What ye think of 'er?"

"Very impressive," I said.

"Whole shebang don't draw but fourteen inch o' water, by golly. I always say, 'You give me a good-size mud puddle, I'll give you a show!' Yes, sir. Six big ventilators up on the roof. Runnin' water in all the dressin' rooms. Plenty o' heat in the wintertime. See them pipes runnin' under the stage? Heat pipes, water pipes, acetylene pipes for the footlights."

"You don't use electricity?"

"I use it for the ventilators and lights too, when I can, but ye can't depend on it. Lots o' landings ain't electrified. Ye can give a show without ventilators, but not without lights. I carry two banks o' footlights, one electric and one acetylene."

I remarked that acetylene seemed a dangerous shipmate to me.

"No sirree!" Capt. Adam denied. "Never had a speck o' trouble. Got the tanks rigged outside, where a leak won't cause no trouble, and I just run it in through this little copper line here"—he indicated with his finger a small pipe leading through a valve, from which hung a sign reading DO NOT OPEN UNTIL READY TO LIGHT FOOTLIGHTS—"and out to the foots. The rig works fine. Don't ye worry, sir; ain't nothin' about this boat that ain't been thought out plenty careful. Got a tug bow and stern, so she rides steady in a seaway. Got our circuit figured so we hit fresh water twice a year, to kill off the moss and barnacles on the bottom. Start out from Elizabeth City, North Carolina (fresh-water town), soon's it gets warm, and play up along Albemarle Sound, Pamlico Sound, through the Dismal Swamp Canal, and up the Chesapeake far as Port Deposit, hittin' all the best landings on the way. That's fresh water up by Port Deposit, so we head back home with a clean bottom again. Saves me a haulin' out."

Jeannine had begun to swing back and forth on my hand. I thanked Capt. Adam for showing us around his craft, and he ushered us through a side door that led from the dining room, where we'd been standing, to the starboard quarter of the barge.

"Did you like the showboat?" I asked Jeannine.

"All right." Her face was flushed, and I thought it best to get her out of the sun.

We passed the refreshment stand, unoccupied except for the vendor himself.

"Toddy honey, will you buy me another ice-cream cone?"

"Why?"

"I want one, honey."

"Why?"

"I want one."

"*Why* do you want one?"

"I want one."

"But why? Tell me *why*."

"I want one."

She got one, and we strolled back to the office in all the heat and light.

XXIII. So long, so long

Before we reached Court Lane, Jeannine's second ice-cream cone was dripping from brown chin and dimpled elbow, down her sundress and onto her sneakers. I paused under a great poplar tree to scrub her up a bit with my handkerchief. My head felt a little dizzy—whether from the sun or from Jeannine's questions, I couldn't say.

"Toddy, honey, I got to sit on the potty," she now remarked.

"Can you hold on a minute?" I grinned, hoping she wouldn't start asking *why*.

I picked her up and strode quickly up the sidewalk, expecting at any moment to have my coat sleeve moistened, but Jeannine chuckled and clung to my neck, her fat little arm over my mouth.

"Mmm, you smell like your mommy," I said.

This amused her. "You smell like my daddy," she countered.

"Ah."

We reached port safely, and Mrs. Lake took Jeannine to the lavatory. I spent the time writing a note to Jimmy Andrews, who stood not ten feet from me, and thinking about Jeannine, whose opinion it was that I smelled like her daddy. Possibly, of course, she was right: *I* could certainly smell some Andrews in her infant curiosity.

I finished the note (which informed Jimmy of the letter from Eustacia Callader and instructed him to institute proceedings against Harrison's mother for recovery of that part of the es-

tate which she'd disposed of) and put it in my inside coat
pocket. A few minutes later Jane came in, her hair cropped
short, and we left to go to her place for cocktails. I didn't
bother to straighten out my desk, to say a last goodbye to Mr.
Bishop, Jimmy, or Mrs. Lake, or even to take a final look at my
office, at my wonderful staring-wall. Why should I?

On the drive to East Cambridge, although I chatted amiably
with Jane and Jeannine, I was filled with my plan, which had
crystallized by then into its final form. If out of my meager
vocabulary only the term *unenthusiastic excitement* comes anywhere near describing the feeling with which all my thoughts
were suffused, you must resolve my meaning from that term's
dissonance. There remained still no small measure of the excitement which had attended my first realization that I was ready
to destroy myself; but, like all my major decisions of policy,
that resolution had been a rapid one, the effect of external impingement upon whatever was my current mask—and as in
those other cases, the resolution itself was only afterwards rationalized into some kind of coherent and arguable position.
Though it is too much to expect that I should become solemn
about it, certainly the direction of this day's rationalizing was
an awesome one—yet full of the attractiveness of desolation, the
charm of the abyss. A simple fact—that there are no ultimate
reasons—and how chilling! I heard beyond it the whistle of the
black winds of Chaos; my hackles rose, as if I had been breathed
upon by a cold sigh from the pit.

It was four o'clock; the heat lingered at its greatest intensity.
What Jane's car filled with as we drove over the creek bridge
was not the black wind of Chaos, but the stench of the crabhouses, steaming up from small mountains of red carapaces and
other nonedible parts of the crab thrown out in the sun by the
pickers. It is a smell that grabs you—I've seen many a visitor
retch while crossing the creek in summer—but like many another thing, it can be lived with: most of the natives aren't even

aware of it, and I, for one, have learned to inhale it deeply and savor it in my nostrils. I did so as we drove off the bridge, and composed a mental note for my *Inquiry*, as follows:

> Olfactory pleasures being no more absolute than other kinds of pleasures, one would do well to outgrow conventional odor-judgments. It is a meager standard that will call perverse that seeker of wisdom who, his toenails picked, must sniff his fingers in secret joy.

This meditation took its place beside my early morning's reflection on Plato and the crabbers—a good day for my *Inquiry!*—and I continued without interruption my conversation with Jane, who was as a matter of fact talking animatedly. She had announced, to my surprise, that she and Harrison were planning a trip to Italy for the fall.

"It's Harrison's idea," she said, "and I'm tickled to death with it. He wants to stay till Christmas, but I'm holding out for Easter. I was there one summer when I was a kid, and it's all beautiful! I wish we could live there."

I believe she kept glancing at me to judge my reaction, but that belief might be simple vanity. At any rate, I showed no reaction at all.

"Are you counting on the inheritance to travel on?" I asked. "It's probably wiser not to."

She looked surprised. "I thought that was out of the question. Isn't it? I'd given up hoping for that."

"I suspect you're doing the right thing."

"We're going on Harrison's salary. Hell, we can afford it." She glanced at me again. "We might even consider selling the house—if you don't mind."

"Why should I mind?"

"Well—" She shrugged her shoulders.

"Do you think Harrison will be able to swallow Mussolini's boys?"

"Oh, this isn't a political tour," Jane smiled. "I'm not even interested in politics, are you? I don't think Harrison is any more, either, the way the Spanish thing's going. He's getting cynical about political movements, I believe. He's cynical about everything nowadays, in fact, but in a sweet way. I think he got it from you."

"Not the sweetness, certainly."

"Certainly not," Jane said, and patted my leg. There was still some nervousness in her exuberance, or so I thought at least: I smelled a plan in the air, now that the crabhouses were out of range.

"When did you decide all this?" I asked cheerfully. "About the trip and the house?"

"Oh, it was Harrison's idea," she said. "About the trip. The house was my idea, because I want us to be independent. I guess it sort of popped up about a week ago. We haven't worked out any details. You don't mind, do you, if we go?" She looked at Jeannine, who was staring listlessly out the window. "You know what I mean."

"Of course I don't mind."

"I'd love it! With the money from the house we could stay there a year. Harrison can fix it with his job. God, just think— *Italy!*"

"When did you get so hot on Italy?" I smiled.

"I've always been hot on Italy. Didn't I tell you? Are you mad at me, Toddy?"

"No."

"You kind of acted like it."

We pulled up in front of the Mack house, and I lifted Jeannine down to run to Harrison, who waved from the porch.

"Were you offended by my note this morning?" Jane persisted as we walked up the lawn. "I certainly didn't think you'd take me up on going to Marvin, but I'm glad you did."

"How about *my* note?" I asked. "Harrison seemed a little

concerned when I told him at lunchtime I'd been to see Marvin, but you don't seem alarmed at all."

"Should I be alarmed? What about?"

By that time we were at the porch, and Jane skipped up the steps, kissed Harrison lightly on the forehead, and disappeared inside.

Usually we drank our Manhattans on the porch, but on this day it was much cooler in the living room. Harrison and I chatted for a few minutes about the weather, agreeing that the dull haze over the Bay prophesied a squall, and then we went inside.

"So you're going to Italy?" I remarked.

"Yes, it looks like it." Harrison fumbled at once for a cigarette in his shirt. "Did Janie tell you?"

"A minute ago. I think it's a fine idea, of course."

"Do you? Well, I wasn't so sure. It means selling the house and all—but you know how crazy Jane is about Italy, Fascists or not, and I'd like to see the place myself while there's still time. I suspect things are going to blow up over there sooner or later. Frankly, I wasn't sure how you'd feel about it," he added carefully.

"How *I'd* feel? What possible difference could it make if I objected? And I don't, at all."

"Well—"

Jane reappeared from the kitchen, and behind her came the maid with our cocktails. Jane sat down beside Harrison, on the couch; I was in an easy chair across the room, facing them.

"Well," Jane said brightly, smiling at her cocktail.

We all sipped.

"Will you be going to the showboat tonight?" Harrison asked me.

"Maybe so. I hadn't thought much about it."

"Jeannine was crazy about it this afternoon," Jane told Harrison, for my benefit. "She got two ice-cream cones, and the man took her and Todd all over the boat."

"Oh? Well," Harrison said.

"In fact, she got too excited—she's a little feverish. I called Marvin, and he says don't worry."

We sipped some more.

"Why not have supper with us?" Jane asked me. "It's just cold platters—sliced ham and potato salad."

I shrugged.

"I'll tell Louise." She jumped up and went into the kitchen again. Harrison and I sipped and sipped, and after a while I lit a cigar.

"Don't be offended by what I'm going to say now, Toddy," Harrison began, and immediately, involuntarily, I smiled around my cigar: the pressure was off.

"You can't offend me," I declared.

"Well, here's the thing. You know very well we'd like to have you come along with us to Italy"—I made a quick gesture of negation—"but I figured you had your work, and besides, the fact is, I think Jane sort of planned this thing just for the two of us. Three, counting Jeannine. You know."

"Don't even speak of it."

"Well, that's not the thing. The thing is, of course Janie won't be around here for a year, maybe two years, you never can tell. Now—I don't know how I can say this without hurting you, Toddy—the truth is, I kind of think when we come back (I don't know when that'll be) what with Jeannine getting older and all—well, it might not look too good, you know what I mean, if Janie kept on going up to the hotel."

"I agree completely," I said at once.

"Hell, I guess you're insulted, Toddy. I don't want you to take it the wrong way. You know what I think of you. But hell—"

"Sure, man. No explanation."

"Well, I want to make certain you take it right," Harrison persisted, examining his empty glass closely.

Jane came in, glanced quickly at me, then at Harrison, and

took a seat midway between us. She absorbed herself in rubbing her brown knee.

"You don't need to explain anything," I insisted firmly. "As a matter of fact—"

"I'll tell you the honest truth, Toddy," Jane broke in (I believe it was the first time she'd ever interrupted me). "If it's all right with you, I'd like to call the thing off as of now. Do you mind?"

"I was just going to suggest it," I said. Jane smiled briefly at her knee. "I'd been thinking about it for some time."

"Well, let me see if I can explain it right," Jane said, looking at me directly and pleasantly. "I'm not too good at expressing things."

"There's no need to say a word," I declared.

"Yes there is," she smiled. "I don't want to break it off unless you can understand everything."

"I understand everything."

"No, you don't," Jane said sweetly. I looked up in surprise. "If you'd understood everything, there wouldn't have been that trouble a few years ago."

"Whoa, now—" I protested.

"Let me see if I can say what I want to say, and then you can take it apart," she proposed. I grinned shortly at Harrison, who, however, didn't see me, engrossed as he was in his empty glass. "When Harrison and I got married we were as prudish as they come about extracurricular sex," Jane began. "I swore I could never look at another man, and Harrison swore he never even thought of another woman in a sexual way. Then as we got a little older we saw how dishonest that was—is that the right word?—yes, *dishonest*. I won't go into all that. Well, we decided there was nothing wrong with either of us making love to somebody else now and then, because we were absolutely sure of each other. I was very attracted to you as Harrison's friend, and as soon as we didn't have to be dishonest any more, I realized I'd like to make love to you. And except for the one bad spell, it worked out all right. It was mostly our fault, we realize, about that bad time."

"Oh, I don't know." I shrugged. This was all very embarrassing for Harrison and me.

"Well, anyhow, neither of us has any regrets that it happened."

"Or that you're calling it off," I smiled.

"Don't be bitter," Harrison said.

"I didn't mean it that way."

"You're right," Jane said. "We don't have to have any regrets about that either, if you understand why I'm doing it."

"Is it because of that note this morning?" I asked.

"The note? Oh, that stupid thing! I never did pay any attention to that. I assumed you were upset about last night, for some reason or other. I sent you my note as a joke, to get even. Heavens no, that's silly! I hadn't even considered it. Here's the thing: I don't want you to think that Harrison and I are retreating in any way to our old standards."

I raised my eyebrows.

"I can't find the damned words—what I mean is, we were unsure of ourselves when we decided to try this extracurricular business. I guess that's why we were so demanding, come to think of it. We wanted reassurance that we hadn't made a mistake. God knows that's understandable enough!"

"I think that's probably why Janie thought she was in love with you," Harrison put in, "and why I thought that was a good thing."

I pursed my lips.

"That's right," Janie agreed, looking at her husband. "Then after we started up again, after Jeannine was born, everything was fine. We all understood each other, and nobody was kidding himself. Now, then. What I want to say is that it was kind of *necessary* before to be actually carrying on affairs, to prove to ourselves that we meant what we were talking about. But we don't feel it's necessary any more. I just feel stronger, is all.

Harrison does, too. Do you understand anything I've said, Toddy?"

"I told you before, I understood everything before you said a word. I exude understanding. Didn't I say that the same thing exactly was on *my* mind? I was going to broach the subject this evening."

"He doesn't understand," Harrison observed to Jane. I turned to him at once, startled, but said nothing.

Jane sighed. "I can't make it any clearer."

The maid signaled silently from the dining room.

"Dinner's almost ready, if you want to wash up," Jane said. She got up and headed for the kitchen, paused, and came over and kissed me lightly on the mouth.

"You were wonderful a great many times," she said. "I hope this doesn't leave you with a bad taste."

I licked my lips. "Tasted fine." Jane laughed and went to help the maid, and Harrison and I went upstairs to wash.

"Did you find a buyer for the house yet?" I asked him.

"No, not yet. Matter of fact, the whole thing's been sort of tentative. All we knew for sure is that we wanted to go to Italy for a while. It's kind of crazy, I guess, but a small town can be right stultifying."

We talked for a while in the bathroom, but there was a coolness between us. And at dinner afterwards, the talk, though pleasant (even relieved), was devoid of warmth. Harrison and Jane seemed fused into one person, entirely self-sufficient. They should, it occurred to me, be permanently locked together, like the doubler crab or Plato's protohumans. I caught myself smiling inadvertently at my cold cuts all through the meal, as I thought of Jane's speech. And, I am obliged to add, I noticed several times that Harrison and Jane smiled at their cold cuts as well: for what reasons, I shan't presume to say.

A final observation: when, after dinner, I went upstairs to the bathroom before leaving the house; when, indeed, I stood there comfortably reflecting, an entirely unexpected emotion gripped me: I suddenly wavered in my resolution to die—was shaken, in fact, by reluctance. The reason was simply that my suicide would be interpreted by the Macks as evidence that their move had crushed me; that I was unable to endure life after their rebuff. And this interpretation would fill them with a deplorable proud pity. Happily, the faltering lasted only a moment. By the time I'd washed my hands, I had come to my senses; my new premises reasserted themselves with force. What difference did it make to me how they interpreted my death? Nothing, absolutely, made any difference. And, sane again, I was able to see a nice attraction in the idea that, at least partly by my own choosing, that last act would be robbed of its significance, would be interpreted in every way but the way I intended. This fact once realized, it seemed likely to me that here was a new significance, even more appropriate.

Passing down the hallway from the bathroom to the stairs, I happened to glance into my old bedroom, now a guest room, and my eye fell on a large mirror near the bed. I chuckled so hard that my eyes watered, and I walked jauntily down the stairs, more ready than ever to carry out my plan.

"Be seeing you around," Harrison called from the porch as I left; and Jane, too, added cheerful goodbyes.

"So long, so long," I called back, just as cheerfully. Looking over my shoulder as I walked down the road, I saw them standing close beside each other, talking together as they watched me leave. Perhaps—I clucked my tongue—their arms were even encircling each other's waists. I waved, but they didn't see me.

I turned and headed back toward the hotel. I believe I might even have whistled something or other, for I was as unburdened at that moment as must have been Socrates when, Xanthippe at last departed, he was free to face without distraction the hemlock that lay at the end of his reasoning.

XXIV. Three million dollars

No: there was one final matter to be settled before I could call myself really free from distracting encumbrances. I had to decide what to do about Harrison's three million dollars.

I paused halfway across the creek bridge to think about it. In order to focus the problem, I took from my billfold the letter from Eustacia Callader, and from my coat pocket the note to Jimmy Andrews, and laid them both before me on the bridge railing. Either I must put Eustacia's letter in my writing desk, where Jimmy was instructed to find it, and drop the note to Jimmy in the mailbox, or else I must drop both documents into the creek below, where fat gray gulls fed lazily on perch killed by the pollution from the packing houses. The first course would result in Jimmy's filing suit for Harrison against Elizabeth Sweetman Mack, charging that, by allowing her gardener, R. J. Collier, to spread the contents of the seventy-two pickle jars on the ailing zinnias, she had disposed of a portion of the Mack estate which was no more hers to dispose of than the three million dollars. This suit would serve to postpone the hearing of my appeal of the Circuit Court's order (to execute the will in favor of Mrs. Mack) until after Joseph Singer had replaced Rollo Moore on the Court of Appeals bench. Then Jimmy would drop the suit and argue our appeal: for the reasons explained in Chapter X, the lower-court order would almost certainly be reversed, and Harrison would get the inheritance. If, on the other hand, I decided to drop both letters into the creek, then there was little chance that the appellate court would do anything except affirm the court order.

Now, you'll recall that in the morning I had decided that the basis for my decision was to be Harrison's and Jane's strength; specifically, whether they had the strength not to care, except superficially, whether they got the money or the manure. And I must say that the morning's note from Jane and my luncheon conversation with Harrison had both inclined me in their favor. By afternoon I had, although I didn't clearly realize it at the time, more or less resolved to let the deciding factor be Jane's response to my note of the early morning, now that I'd fulfilled the conditions of hers by going to see Marvin Rose. If she chose to make Capt. Osborn the happiest old satyr in the country, I'd make her the richest woman in the county; if she was as angry and insulted by my proposal as Harrison had been by the incident in my office in 1933, then I'd destroy the letters.

But Jane had nullified this basis by choosing a third course, one difficult to evaluate. She'd been neither angry nor insulted, nor had she felt obliged to carry out her end of the bargain. She'd simply laughed at the whole thing. Was this evidence of obtuseness, insincerity, or a real and formidable strength? In fact, I no longer knew how to feel about the Macks at all, whether their new resolutions manifested a commonplace sentimentality or a strange integrity. I had no feeling about them at all.

Consequently, after inhaling deeply the fetid air of the creek for several minutes, I chose a new basis for judgment: taking a nickel from my pocket, I flipped it, caught it, and slapped it down on the letters. Heads, I preserve them; tails, they go in the creek.

My hand uncovered the skinny-assed, curly-tailed old buffalo.

Despite which fact, I gathered up the letters, dropped one in the mailbox on the corner of Academy, Market, and Muse Streets, just off the creek bridge, and put the other in my desk when I reached the hotel. Harrison had survived a double chance: that the coin would demand the destruction of the letters, and that I would allow myself, a free agent, to be dictated to by a miserable nickel.

Then, let us say, I doubtless whistled some tune or other, unburdened as must have been Socrates when, *etc.*

XXV. The Inquiry

It was a few minutes after six o'clock when I reached my room, set my straw hat on the dresser top, and prepared to put in a last evening's work on my *Inquiry*. I gathered around my writing desk the three peach baskets and one cardboard box of notes and data, put in a convenient place the empty beef-stew can, my ashtray, and began my night's work by transcribing from memory the notes I'd made that day and filing them at an appropriate depth in one of the peach baskets. Then I sat back in the chair and stared at the window for a while, deciding which aspect of the project should receive my attention.

When the clock on the People's Trust building chimed six-thirty (the Macks, as usual, had eaten early), I sat up, took a long ruled sheet of yellow legal paper from one of the pads stacked on the desk, and wrote on the top:

1. Nothing has intrinsic value.

Because I regarded this sentence for some minutes before adding to it, and because staring and regarding is duller to describe than to do, let me use the time to explain as clearly as I can the nature and history of my *Inquiry* and of the great project of which the *Inquiry* itself is only one part.

The full title of the *Inquiry*, if it ever should reach the stage of completion where a title would be appropriate, will be *An Inquiry into the Circumstances Surrounding the Self-Destruction of Thomas T. Andrews, of Cambridge, Maryland, on Ground-Hog Day, 1930 (More Especially into the Causes Therefor)*, or something of the sort. It is an attempt to learn why my father hanged himself, no more.

And no less—for it became apparent to me after a mere two years of questioning, searching, reading, and staring, that there is no will-o'-the-wisp so elusive as the cause of any human act. Easy enough to spend weeks poring over bank statements, budget books, letters from stockbrokers; to spend months examining newspaper files, stock-market reports, volumes on the theory and the history of economics; to spend years in careful, unhurried, apparently casual questioning of every person who had more than a superficial acquaintanceship with my father. All this is just more or less laborious research. But it is another thing to examine this information and see in it, so clearly that to question is out of the question, the *cause* of a human act.

In fact, it's impossible, for as Hume pointed out, causation is never more than an inference; and any inference involves at some point the leap from what we see to what we can't see. Very well. It's the purpose of my *Inquiry* to shorten as much as is humanly possible the distance over which I must leap; to gather every scrap of information that a human being might gather concerning the circumstances of my father's suicide. Say, if you wish, that the true reason for this investigation is my reluctance to admit that Dad hanged himself because he was afraid to face his creditors. Perhaps so (noble work has been accomplished for more questionable reasons), although consciously, at least, I have a different reason. At any rate, I am certainly prepared to admit that my observation of the data I collect is biased, and it's partly for that reason that even in 1937 I kept one peach basket reserved for notes on myself—it was into this basket that my two thoughts of the day, for example, were filed. It would be more accurate to say that my rejection of the stock-market losses as the cause of his suicide was the hypothesis with which I approached the *Inquiry*, the thesis that oriented my investigations.

You understand, do you, that the nature of my purpose— to make as short as possible the gap between fact and opinion —renders the *Inquiry* interminable? One could, of course, stop at some point and declare, "I have sufficient information to warrant the inference that the cause of Thomas T. Andrews' suicide was such-and-such." But my purpose is not really to leap the gap (which can be deep, however narrow), only to shorten it. So, the task is endless; I've never fooled myself about that. But the fact that it's endless doesn't mean that I can't work on other aspects of the grand project, even though the *completion* of those aspects depends ultimately on the leaping of the gap in my *Inquiry*. It doesn't follow that because a goal is unattainable, one shouldn't work toward its attainment. Besides, as I've observed elsewhere, processes continued for long enough tend to become ends in themselves, and if for no other reason, I should continue my researches simply in order to occupy pleasantly two hours after dinner.

But let's suppose that by some miracle it were given to me to know the unknowable, to *know* the cause or causes of Dad's suicide. My *Inquiry* would be complete. But my researches would not, for after supper on the day of that revelation I should draw to my desk a different peach basket—that one beside the lamp there—and after some minutes of wall-staring, resume work on a larger *Inquiry*, of which the above-mentioned is at most a relevant chapter. And this *Inquiry*, had I world enough and time, might someday be entitled *An Inquiry into the Life of Thomas T. Andrews, of Cambridge, Maryland (1867–1930), Giving Especial Consideration to His Relations with His Son, Todd Andrews, (1900–   )*. In other words, a complete study of my father's mind and life from his birth in the front bedroom of the Andrews house to his death in its cellar; from the umbilicus that tied him to his mother to the belt that hanged him from the floor joist.

A considerable task: it is my aim to learn all that can be learned of my father's life; to get the best possible insight into the workings of his mind. To do this I must, in addition to carrying out on a larger scale all the researches described in connection with the other *Inquiry*, perform extra labors as well—I must read, for example, all the books that I know my father read, looking for influences on his character and way of thinking. If one can compare infinities, this task is even more endless than the other.

I said a moment ago that the death-*Inquiry* was but a chapter in the life-*Inquiry*; in another sense, the study of Dad's life is only a necessary preliminary to the study of his death. And ultimately, I should say, they stand side by side, for they share a common purpose: what I really want to discover is the nature and extent of my father's contribution to our imperfect communication.

Imperfect communication: that's the problem. If you understand that (for to go into greater detail would enmesh us beyond hope of ever returning to the story), then it's time to pass on to the last document of all, of which my two colossal *Inquiries* combined are no more than important studies for one aspect: the *Letter to My Father*.

This document dates from the fall of 1920, when after my unsuccessful attempts to tell Dad about my uncertain heart, I enrolled in the University. I had resolved, you'll remember, not to tell him at all while I lived, because I believed that my death was imminent and that therefore I'd as well humor him during what remained of my life. Nevertheless I worried that I'd been unable to tell him when I wanted to, and (I was no cynic then) that the both of us would go to our graves without ever having understood each other.

And so I began to write a letter to my father, working on

it in snatches during my four exhausting years at college. The letter was to be found by him after my death, and its original purpose was to explain what Dr. John Frisbee had told me about my heart. But this purpose, though I never lost sight of it, was soon subsumed into a larger one: I set out to study myself, to discover why my communication with Dad had always been imperfect. I reviewed my whole life carefully, selecting and rejecting incidents for use in the letter. I spent a month, at least, attempting to explain to Dad why I'd never finished building my boat in the back yard. More than a year went to searching my muddy embrace with the German sergeant (with whom my communication had been pitifully imperfect) and to analyzing the effects on me of a certain particular popping noise. I worked, of course, irregularly, completing perhaps twenty pages of notes and one page of letter every month; seldom more than that. By the time I was installed in law school, the letter was perhaps fifty pages long, and I had a respectable stack of notes. I did not shy away from mentioning Betty June Gunter, even, although I realize now that those early attempts to understand our liaison were shallow. Especially between 1925 and 1927—the first of my saintly years—I worked with some diligence on the letter.

Then in 1927, when I set up practice in Cambridge, the letter and notes were packed into my trunk. I moved in with Dad and to my great pleasure found myself—or so I believed—closer to him than I'd ever been before. He was still garrulous and gruff by turns, but I thought I was beginning to understand him somewhat; at least I had hope that our communication was becoming less imperfect, and in this hope I abandoned the letter. I had, you see, always assumed that the source of the imperfection was in myself, and it seemed to me that perhaps as I matured (although I was twenty-seven then) my difficulty would vanish.

But Dad hanged himself, and rack my memory as I might

until sleep was a red-eyed wish, I could find no adequate reason for his act. I realized then that I had been pursuing an impossible task since 1920: to understand an imperfect communication requires perfect knowledge of the party at each end, and I'd been studying only myself. When, in the course of moving into the Dorset Hotel, my letter and notes came to light, I put the pages of the letter on my new writing desk, dumped the notes into an empty suitcase (not until later did I begin to use peach baskets), and began work on it again. I saw at once that the next step was to open an inquiry into Dad's life, in order to understand the nature and extent of his contribution to our imperfect communication; and at the same time I saw the necessity of a special and separate inquiry into the circumstances surrounding his death, this inquiry to be in the nature of a control (for unless the suicide were explained, nothing was explained) and also perhaps a key (for should I find the answer to the question of his death, the whole problem might be solved by the same solution). Thus my two *Inquiries* were initiated; but they did not close off my work on the letter and the notes on myself.

You see, then, the purposes of the three peach baskets beside my desk in 1937: one represented the life-*Inquiry*, one the death-*Inquiry*, the third the less organized self-*Inquiry*. And the cardboard box (MORTON'S MARVELOUS TOMATOES) contained the drafts of the letter to my father. To be sure, he can never now receive it. If you don't see that this fact only demonstrates further the imperfection of my communication with him, and hence intensifies the need for the letter instead of eliminating it, then between you and me, too, the communication is less than perfect. But you shall have to investigate it: I've enough to do with the three baskets and the box beside me—four parallel projects which, like parallel lines, will meet only in infinity.

On this particular evening, to be sure, their progress would cease, for the notes I took then I intended to be my last.

I. Nothing has intrinsic value.

II. The reasons for which people attribute value to things are always ultimately irrational.

III. There is, therefore, no ultimate "reason" for valuing anything.

By seven o'clock, these were the things I had written on my piece of paper, not knowing exactly which file would finally receive them. But I felt very strongly that this sequence of ideas, which represented my day's rationalizing, was of supreme importance to my *Inquiries* and my letter. In fact, when in the same list I entered the Roman numeral *IV*, without yet writing anything after it, I had a nostril-flaring sensation of the chase; I felt that some sort of answer was on the verge of being treed.

I called these ideas rationalizings, and so they were: the *post facto* justification, on logical grounds, of what had been an entirely personal, unlogical resolve. Such, you remember, had been the case with all my major mind-changes. My masks were each first assumed, then justified.

My heart, reader! My heart! You must comprehend quickly, if you are to comprehend at all, that those masks were not assumed to hide my face, but to hide my heart from my mind, and my mind from my heart. Understand it now, because I may not live to end the chapter! To be sure, each mask hid other things as well, as a falseface hides identity and personality as well as nose and mouth; but it was to hide my enigmatic heart that I became a rake, a saint, and then a cynic. For when one mask no longer served its purpose of disguise, another had perforce to take its place at once. I had been a not-very-extraordinary boy; then one day in 1919 while standing retreat I collapsed on the parade grounds at Fort Meade, Dr. Frisbee looked up from his stethoscope, and I began to eat, drink, and be merry at Johns Hopkins—my first mask. In 1924 Betty June Gunter slashed me with a broken bottle, a man named Cozy rabbit-punched me and threw me out of a Calvert Street brothel, Marvin Rose found a wicked infection in my prostate, and I became a saint—my second mask. In 1930 my father, with whom (thinking my saintliness was bringing on maturity) I had thought I was beginning to communicate, *inexplicably* hanged himself; I took the belt from his neck, mailed my legacy to Col. Morton, and became a cynic—my third mask. And each time, it did not take me long to come to believe that my current attitude was not only best for me, because it put me on some kind of terms with my heart, but best in itself, absolutely. Then, on the night of June 20 or 21, 1937—

But now you must know my last secret. In my life I have experienced emotion intensely on only five occasions, each time a different emotion. With Betty June in my bedroom I learned *mirth;* with myself in the Argonne I learned *fear;* with my father in the basement of our house I learned *frustration;* with Jane Mack in her summer cottage I learned *surprise;* with my heart, in my hotel room on the night before this last day, I learned *despair,* utter despair, a despair beyond wailing.

My despair began, not with my heart, but with two other parts of my body. Jane was in my room for the night, as you know. She had come in at perhaps ten o'clock; we'd had a drink and retired shortly afterwards. Jane had sat Turk-fashion on the bed for some time, plucking her eyebrows before we turned out the light, and I had stroked her idly while I lay beside her reading a book. We hadn't been talking at all. Then, taking my hand in hers to examine it, she said, "Did you ever ask Marvin about your fingers, Todd? My, they're ugly."

I jerked my hand away, blushing hotly. Had you forgotten that my fingers were clubbed? So had I, reader, and Jane's remark, though offered in a mild enough tone, stung me all out of proportion to my actual sensitivity about my fingers—perhaps because I'd been caressing her.

"Oh, I'm awfully sorry!" she said at once. "I didn't mean to insult you at all." She tried to kiss my fingers then, but I couldn't bear the thought. I kept them out of sight.

My subsequent failure at love-making no doubt grew out of that. For one thing, in her efforts to redeem herself Jane made all the advances, immediately, and I have rarely responded well in such situations. For another, the remark about my fingers made me irrationally disgusted with my whole skinny body, and disgust is a cold bedfellow for desire.

"Please tell me what's wrong, Toddy," Jane pleaded. "I really don't want to hurt you." (There was more to this than ordinary solicitude, as I realized next day when she announced the Italian trip.)

I assured her that I wasn't offended—after the first few minutes I really wasn't—but both her curiosity and her desire had to go unsatisfied. I got up, smoked a cigarette, went to bed, tossed and turned, sat up and read, drank another drink, and tossed and turned some more. Jane fell asleep, annoyance and injured pride still pouting from her lips. I kissed her very lightly on her frowning brow and got out of bed, resolved, since sleep was impossible, to work on the *Inquiry*.

My mood was black; I had little patience with my work. It is only in very weak moments like this that I call my project silly; I sat for an hour in the window, looking over at the Post Office and thinking how incomparably silly my thirteen years' work was. How silly, for that matter, was my whole life during those thirteen years—one feeble mask after another!

Ah, there was a symptomatic thought: it was, I think, the first time I'd ever used the term *masks* in referring to what I'd always considered to be the stages of my intellectual development. Moreover, it was not the thought of a cynic, for as soon as it lodged in my consciousness it sent out quick rootlets of despair to all corners of my mind. Indeed, as I vaguely recognized at the time, it was a sign that the mask of my cynicism—I saw then that it was a mask—was wearing thin, and no longer doing its job. If it were, would I even have thought of my heart?

And suddenly my heart filled my entire body. It was not my heart that would burst, but my body, so full was it of my heart, and every beat was sick. Surely it would fail! I clapped my hand quickly to my chest, feeling for the beat; clutched at the window frame to keep from falling; stared at *nothing*, my mouth open, like a fish on the beach. And this not in pain, but in despair!

Here is what I saw: that all my masks were half-conscious attempts to master the fact with which I had to live; that none had made me master of that fact; that where cynicism had failed, no future mask could succeed; that, in short, my heart was the master of all the rest of me, even of my will. It was my heart that had made my masks, not my will. The conclusion that swallowed me was this: *There is no way to master the fact with which I live.* Futility gripped me by the throat; my head was tight. The impulse to raise my arms and eyes to heaven was almost overpowering—but there was no one for me to raise them to. All I could do was clench my jaw, squint my eyes, and shake my head from side to side. But every motion pierced me with its own futility, every new feeling with its private hopelessness, until a battery of little agonies attacked from all sides, each drawing its strength from the great agony within me.

I can't say for how long I sat. What finally happened, when I had become sufficiently demoralized, was that my nerves, fatigued already, succumbed to the unusual strain. My body was suddenly soaked in perspiration; I trembled from head to foot. Indeed, I can't find it in me to deny that, had no other crutch been available, I should very possibly have ended that night on my knees, laying my integrity on the altar of the word *God.* But another crutch was within reach: Jane, now sleeping soundly. And the embarrassment that I feel at telling you how I went shocked and trembling to the bed; how I buried my head blindly in her lap; how I lay there shuddering until sleep found me, my knees clasped to my chest, fighting despair as one fights appendicitis—this embarrassment is not different from that I'd feel at having to confess that I'd buried myself in God. I am in truth embarrassed, reader, but in good faith I recommend this refuge to your attention. There is nothing in it of the ostrich, because the enemy you flee is not exterior to yourself.

I have no idea whether Jane was aware of any of this. At the tick of six I popped awake; my head was on the pillow, Jane's on my right shoulder. In great wisdom I inhaled the smell of her hair: sunshine and salt. There have been no women in my bed since that morning, and yet still at 6:00 A.M. I can summon to my nostrils the smell of Jane Mack. I sat up and looked around me, swelling with incipient wisdom. What had been the problem I'd buried? As was my habit, before I got up I reached to the window sill for my Sherbrook, took a good pull, and shuddered all over, but no answer came. I rose carefully from the bed, so as not to wake Jane, donned my seersucker suit, splashed cold water on my face—and realized that on this day I would destroy myself.

"Of course!"

I grinned at my dripping face in the mirror—dumb, stunned surprise. There was the end of masks!

"Of course!"

There was no mastering the fact with which I lived; but I could master the fact of my living with it by destroying myself, and the result was the same—I was the master. I choked back a snicker.

"For crying out loud!"

III. *There is, therefore, no ultimate "reason" for valuing any-thing.*

Now I added *including life,* and at once the next proposition was clear:

IV. Living is action. There's no final reason for action.
V. There's no final reason for living.

This last statement merited some minutes of expressionless contemplation, after which I capped my pen and clipped it in my pocket, put Eustacia's letter where Jimmy would find it, fetched my straw, and left my room without a shred of regret.

The *Inquiry* was closed.

XXVI. The first step

Ideally, a new philosophical position, like a new rowboat, should be allowed to sit a day or two at the dock, to let the seams swell tight, before it's put to any strenuous application. But no sooner had I taken one step into the hall than Capt. Osborn called to me from his room.

"Are ye goin' to the boat show, Toddy?"

"Yes, sir."

Capt. Osborn gave a grunt or two, hocked some vagrant phlegm into his handkerchief, and hobbled out of his room.

"I'll jest walk along with ye, if ye don't mind," he declared. "Ain't seen a boat show for years." He chuckled. "Young Haecker—I call 'im Young Haecker now—Young Haecker's been gloomin' around so lately, I figure I better have me some fun while I can. All set, boy?"

One should not have to make such decisions quickly; it's like launching a new rowboat into the teeth of a nor'easter.

"Where is Young Haecker?" I smiled.

"Oh, he ain't goin'," Capt. Osborn sniffed. "He's too old for such carryin' on! I ain't seen 'im since this mornin'. Here, I'll jest take yer arm."

Ah. As a boatwright might examine his craft for leaks, with considerable interest if little real anxiety, so I examined myself. Can he be called a builder who shies at launching the finished hull? For what other purpose was it finished?

"Of course," I said, and took my friend with me down the steps.

XXVII. The Floating Opera

Plain enough by day, the *Original & Unparalleled Floating Opera* was somewhat more ornamented as Capt. Osborn and I approached it across Long Wharf in the hot twilight. Power lines had been run from a utility pole near the dock, and the showboat was outlined in vari-colored electric lights, which, however, needed greater darkness for their best effect. On the roof of the theater Prof. Eisen and the thirteen members of his $7,500 Challenge Atlantic & Chesapeake Maritime Band were installed in their bandstand, rendering, as I recall, "I'm a Yankee Doodle Dandy" to the crowd of several hundred onlookers gathered around—many of whom, particularly among the Negroes, came only to hear the free concert and regard the "Op'ry Barge" with amazement, not having money to spare for admission to the show. The box office was open (it was nearly showtime), and a line was queued up from the ticket window down the gangplank to the bulkheads. Capt. Osborn grew excited and used his cane to nudge small running urchins out of his path, which led unswervingly to the ticket line.

The band wound up George M. Cohan and began a Stephen Foster medley. When we reached the top of the gangplank I looked around at the crowd and saw Harrison, Jane, and Jeannine just taking a place in line. They were occupied with opening Jeannine's popcorn bag, and didn't notice me.

The auditorium was already nearly half filled with the citizens of Cambridge. Capt. Osborn and I took seats about seven rows

from the rear, on the extreme starboard side of the theater—
he complaining that we hadn't arrived earlier to get really
good seats. The hall was illuminated with electric lights, each
built into a double fixture along with a gas mantle for use
at less progressive landings. Scanning the audience, I saw almost
no unfamiliar faces. Col. Morton and his wife sat in the front
row on the aisle. Marvin Rose, a showboat *aficionado*, sat a
few rows behind. Bill Butler waved cheerily to me from across
the theater. My partner Mr. Bishop was there with his wife,
whom one seldom saw in public. Harrison, Jane, and Jeannine
came in—if they saw me, they made no sign, although I waved
to them—and sat on the other side of the theater. Jimmy
Andrews, as I'd anticipated, was absent—doubtless out sailing
with his fiancée, for a mild but usable breeze had sprung up
earlier in the evening.

Above our heads the $7,500 Challenge Band concluded its
free concert with "The Star-Spangled Banner." There was
some uncertainty in the house as to whether it was necessary
to stand, since the band was outside. Some men made a half-
hearted motion to rise, hesitated, and sat down embarrassed,
laughing explanations at their wives with much pointing of
fingers toward the roof. Finally Col. Morton stood unfalteringly,
without a backward look, and the rest of us followed suit,
relieved to have a ruling on the matter. When the anthem
ended there was applause from the freeloaders outside, and
much discussion inside about whether it had really been necessary for us to stand. Soon, however, everyone's attention was
focused on the small door under the stage, from which the
members of the orchestra, resplendent in gold-braided red uniforms, began filing into the pit. When all were in their places,
and instruments had been tootled cacophoniously, Prof. Eisen
himself—lean, hollow-cheeked, Vandyked, intense—stepped to
the podium amid generous applause from orchestra and balcony,
rapped for attention, and raised his baton, on the tip of which
the whole house hung. The lights dimmed slightly, the baton

fell, and the band crashed into "The Star-Spangled Banner."
An instant's murmur and then we sprang to our feet again,
none more quickly than the Colonel—although Evelyn was a
trifle flustered.

No sooner had the final cymbal clashed than the house
lights went out completely and the electric footlights rose,
playing on the mauve velvet stage curtain. Prof. Eisen's baton
fell again, and the sprightly overture was commenced: a
potpourri of martial airs, ragtime, a touch of some sentimental
love ballad, a flourish of buck-and-wing, and a military finale.
We applauded eagerly.

Captain Jacob Adam himself stepped from behind the curtain,
bowed to our ovation, and smilingly bade us listen.

"Good evenin', good evenin', friends!" he cried. "I can't
say how happy I am to see ye all here tonight. It does my
heart good when the *Floatin' Op'ry* comes round Hambrook
Light, I'll tell ye, 'cause I know that means it's Cambridge
ahead, and I tell John Strudge, my calliope man, I say to him,
'John,' I say, 'get up a good head o' steam, boy, and let's have
"Dem Golden Slippers," 'cause that there's Cambridge yonder,'
I says, 'and ye'll sail a lot o' water 'fore ye meet finer folks
than ye'll see a-plenty in Cambridge!' Now, then!"

We cheered.

"Well, sir, folks, I'm glad so many of ye got out tonight,
'cause we got such a fine new show this year I was anxious
for all my friends and even my enemies in Cambridge to see
it." He squinted over the footlights. "Guess my friends'll be
in later," he mumbled loudly, and grinned at once lest we
miss the jest—but we were alert, and laughed especially loud.

"Yes, sir, a brand-new line-up this year, folks, from a cracker-
jack start to a whiz-bang finish! But before we haul back the
curtain and get on with the fun, I'm afraid I'll have to disap-
point ye just a wee bit."

We murmured sympathy for ourselves.

"Now I know ye was pinin' to see Miss Clara Mulloy, the

Mary Pickford of the Chesapeake, do her stuff in *The Para-chute Girl.* So was I, I got to admit, 'cause no matter how many times in a row I watch Miss Clara jump down in that there par'chute, them legs o' hers is so durn pretty I can't see my fill!"

We laughed more raucously, Capt. Osborn jabbing me in the ribs and exploding with mirthful phlegm.

"But I'm sorry to say Miss Clara Mulloy has caught a germ from someplace—must have been Crisfield, couldn't of been Cambridge—and I swear if she ain't got the laryngitis so bad she can't say a durn word!"

We voiced our disappointment, some of us resentfully.

"I know, I know," Capt. Adam sympathized. "I feel like walkin' out myself. Hey, Miss Clara," he shouted into the wings, "come on out here and show the people yer—ah—yer *laryngitis!*" He winked at us, we roared, and then Miss Clara Mulloy—brown-haired, brown-eyed, trimly corseted—curtsied onto the stage, the sequins flashing on her black gown, a red flannel scarf tied incongruously around her white neck. She curtsied again to our ovation, pointed to her throat, and moved her lips in silent explanation, while Capt. Adam looked on adoringly.

"What do ye say?" he cried to us. "Shall we call the whole thing off? I'm willin'!"

"NO!" we shouted, almost as one man—two or three rowdies cried "*Yes!*" but we glared them down.

"Do I hear *yes?*" the Captain asked.

"NO!" we roared again, our stares defying contradiction from the one or two hoodlums who are forever spoiling honest folks' fun. "No!" we pleaded, hoping Capt. Adam wouldn't judge us citizens of Cambridge by our most unfortunate element.

"*Yes!*" one of the incorrigibles snickered.

"That man should be thrown out!" I heard the Colonel declare in exasperation.

"Well, I say let's be fair and square," Capt. Adam said. "Any man, woman, or child that wants to leave can get up right now and go, and John Strudge'll give ye yer full admission money back at the box office, despite ye already heard the overture!"

We laughed at this last and applauded his generosity. The house lights came up for a moment, but no one dared move.

"All right, then, let's get on with the show!"

The house lights were extinguished, Miss Clara Mulloy rewarded our applause with a blown kiss (her eyes dewy), Prof. Eisen struck up a lively tune, and we relaxed again.

"Now, then," the Captain announced. "Instead o' *The Parachute Girl* I'm proud to present the great T. Wallace Whittaker, one o' the finest singers and actors that ever trod the boards. Ye all know T. Wallace Whittaker as the great Southern tenor—got a voice like a honeycomb in a sweet-gum stump, I swear! But what ye probably don't know is that T. Wallace Whittaker is one o' the best Shakespearian actors in the U.S.A.! Ladies and gentlemen, I have the *great* honor to present T. Wallace Whittaker, the eminent tragedian, in Scenes from the Bard!"

Uncertain applause. The band played heavy chords in a minor key, the curtain opened, and we looked into a Victorian parlor (first set for *The Parachute Girl*), in the center of which bowed T. Wallace Whittaker. He was a broad-beamed, Sunday-schooly young man, and he wore a tight black Hamlet-looking outfit. From the tone of his very first words—a lofty "I shall begin by reciting the famous speech of the duke Jacques, from Act Two of *As You Like It*"—he lost the sympathy of us men, although some wives nodded knowingly.

T. Wallace walked to the footlights, struck a declamatory pose, and closed his eyes for a moment. He did not clear his throat, but some of us cleared ours.

"*All the world's a stage,*" he declared, "*and all the men and women merely players: they have their exits and their entrances; and one man in his time plays many parts. . . ."*

Already Capt. Osborn had the fidgets, and began ticking his cane against his high-top shoe. The rest of us sat uncomfortably as T. Wallace ran through the seven ages of man.

". . . Last scene of all . . . mere oblivion, sans teeth, sans eyes, sans taste, sans every thing!"

Polite applause, especially from the ladies. I thought I heard Jeannine ask shrilly for more popcorn, but it could have been some other child. One of the rowdies made a sneering remark that I couldn't catch, but that set his neighbors chuckling, no longer so hostile to him as before, and rewarded him with a flash of T. Wallace Whittaker's eyes.

"Mark Antony's funeral oration, from Act Three of *Julius Caesar*," he announced. *"Friends, Romans, countrymen, lend me your ears. . . ."*

"Ye can have mine, boy," the hoodlum said loudly. "I've took enough!" He stalked out of the theater, and the rest of us were shamefully amused. Even some wives stifled smiles, but T. Wallace Whittaker went on, blushing, to inflame an imaginary mob against Brutus and company. The oration was long, for T. Wallace went through the whole routine of Caesar's will. By the time he insinuated his desire to move the stones of Rome to rise and mutiny, his audience was on the verge of doing likewise; we were tapping our feet, sneezing, and whispering among ourselves. When he cried at the end, *"Mischief, thou art afoot, take thou what course thou wilt!"* someone whistled and flung a handful of pennies onto the stage.

T. Wallace ignored the insult; rather, he acknowledged it with a defiant glare but refused to be bowed.

"What I shall recite now," he said grimly, "is the most magnificent thing in the whole English language. I shan't expect a noisy rabble to appreciate its beauty, but perhaps a respectful silence will be granted, if not to me, at least to Shakespeare!"

"Where's the minstrels?" someone shouted. "Bring on the minstrels!" More pennies sailed over the footlights.

"The soliloquy from *Hamlet*," T. Wallace Whittaker whispered.

"Go home!"

"Take 'im away!"

"Come on, minstrels!"

"*To be, or not to be: that is the question. . . .*"

"Ya—a—a—ah!"

The audience was out of hand now. Several young men stood on their chairs to take better aim with their pennies, which no longer merely fell at T. Wallace's feet, but struck his face, chest, and gesticulating arms until he was forced to turn half around. But he would not be vanquished.

"*To die, to sleep; to sleep: perchance to dream: ay, there's the rub. . . .*"

One pimply-faced lad, standing in a front-row seat, began aping T. Wallace's gestures, to our delight, until Col. Morton struck at him with his gold-headed cane.

"*For who would bear the whips and scorns of time, the oppressor's wrong . . .*" T. Wallace Whittaker was determined that we should have our culture. I greatly admired him.

"*. . . the proud man's contumely, the pangs of despised love, the law's delay. . . .*"

"Yahoo! Boo! Hsssss!"

It was open warfare now; T. Wallace could no longer be heard, but nevertheless he continued undaunted. Capt. Adam appeared from the wings, disturbed lest we begin taking the vessel apart, but we greeted his conciliatory wavings with more boos. He went to T. Wallace, doubtless to ask him to call it a day, but T. Wallace declaimed in his face. Capt. Adam grew panicky, then angry, and tried to drag him off; T. Wallace shoved him away, still gesticulating with the other hand. Capt. Adam shook his finger at the young man, shouted, "Yer fired!"

and signaled to Prof. Eisen to strike up the band. The $7,500 Challenge Maritime Band waltzed into "Over the Waves." T. Wallace Whittaker stepped through the closing curtains, and shaking both fists at us through a copper shower (to which I, too, contributed, standing up and flinging all my change at him), in blind defiance he screamed: *"Thus conscience does make cowards of us all, and thus the native hue of resolution is sicklied o'er with the pale cast of thought!"* Finished at last, he scooped a handful of pennies from the stage, flung them back at us, and disappeared behind the curtain.

A few more late-thrown pennies sailed after him, hit the curtain, and clicked onto the stage. We were all laughing and comparing notes, a little sheepish, but exhilarated for all that—none more so than I, for it is sometimes pleasant to stone a martyr, no matter how much we may admire him. For my part, as I believe I've mentioned elsewhere in this book, I'm seldom reluctant to assist in my small way in the persecution of people who defy the crowd with their principles, especially when I'm in favor of the principles. After all, the test of one's principles is his willingness to suffer for them, and the test of this willingness—the only test—is actual suffering. What was I doing, then, but assisting T. Wallace Whittaker in the realization of his principles? For now, surely, having been hooted from the stage and fired from his job in the cause of Shakespeare, he would either abandon his principles, in which case they weren't integrated very strongly into his personality, or else cling to them more strongly than ever, in which case he had us to thank for giving him the means to strength.

Capt. Adam appeared next from the wings, smiling thinly, and raised his hands. We were willing enough now to be silent, having made our point.

"Oh, well, who likes Shakespeare anyhow?" He shrugged cravenly, kicking a few pennies around the footlights. "If ye think yer gittin' any o' these pennies back, though, yer crazy!"

We laughed, relieved as wayward children who learn that they won't be punished after all.

"Now, then, see if ye can't be a little nicer to the next folks," Capt. Adam grinned. "At least pitch quarters at 'em. Ladies and gents: those knights of the burnt cork, the U.S.A.'s greatest sable humorists, the chaste and inimitable Ethiopian Tidewater Minstrels!"

We applauded complacently, for this was what we'd come to see. Prof. Eisen ripped into "I'm Alabammy Bound" at express-train tempo, and the curtains parted. The set for *The Parachute Girl* had been replaced by a solid blue backdrop, against which stood out the bright uniforms of a small semicircle of minstrels. There were six in all: three on each side of Capt. Adam, who took his place as interlocutor. All wore fuzzy black wigs, orange clawhammer coats, bright checkered vests and trousers, tall paper collars, and enormous shoes, and sang in raucous unison the words of the song. The two minstrels on either side of the interlocutor assisted with banjos and guitars, while Tambo and Bones, the end men, played the instruments from which their names are derived. With a great rattling and crashing the tune shuddered to its end.

"Gentle-*men-n-n-n* . . ." cried Capt. Adam, raising his arms to heaven, "BE . . . SEATED!"

Tambo and Bones, to be sure, missed their chairs and fell sprawling on the floor, accompanied by thumps from the bass drum. Knees were slapped, ribs elbowed. Capt. Osborn, beside me, strangled rapturously. Col. Morton's cane banged approval. In his new role as Mr. Interlocutor, Capt. Adam was transformed into an entirely different person—grammatical, florid, effusive— so that one doubted the authenticity of his original character. When the end men, great eyeballs rolling, had regained their seats, the classical repartee ensued, the interlocutor being tripped up in his pomposity again and again—to our delight, for our sympathies were all with impish Tambo, irrepressible Bones.

"Good evening, Mr. Tambo; you look a little down in the mouth tonight."

"Mist' Interlocutor, ah ain't down in de mouf; ah's down in de pocketbook. New hat fo' de wife, new shoes fo' de baby. Now dat no-good boy ob mine is done pesterin' me to buy him a 'cyclopedia. Say he needs 'em fo' de school."

"An encyclopedia! Ah, there's a wise lad, Tambo! No schoolboy should be without a good encyclopedia. I trust you'll purchase one for the lad?"

"No, sah!"

"No!"

"No, sah! Ah say to dat boy, ah say, ''Cyclopedia nuffin'! Y'all gwine walk like de other chillun!'"

We were led by the nose through rudimentary jokes, clubbed with long-anticipated punch lines, titillated—despite the minstrels' alleged chastity—by an occasional *double-entendre* as ponderous as it was mild. Negroes were shiftless and ignorant, foreigners suspect; the WPA was a refuge for loafers; mothers-in-law were shrewish; women poor drivers; drunkenness was an amusing but unquestioned vice; churchgoing a soporific but unquestioned virtue. Tambo and Bones deserved their poverty, but their rascality won our hearts, and we nodded to one another as their native wit led the overeducated interlocutor into one trap after another. Tambo and Bones vindicated our ordinariness; made us secure in the face of mere book learning; their every triumph over Mr. Interlocutor was a pat on our backs. Indeed, a double pat: for were not Tambo and Bones but irresponsible Negroes?

We were sung to of heart, hearth, and home by Sweet Sally Starbuck, the singing soubrette, she of the moist eyes, corn-silk hair, and flushed cheeks. What did she sing us? "I Had a Dream, Dear." "After the Ball Is Over." "A Mother's Prayer for Her Son." "Harvest Moon."

"Y'all so smaht, Mist' Interlocutor, ansah me dis, sah: whut

*got twenty-nine legs, six arms, twelve ears, three tails, twenty
feet, and a passle ob faucets, and say cockadoodledoo?"*

"*Great heavens, Tambo! What* does *have twenty-nine legs,
six arms, twelve ears, three tails, twenty feet, and a passle of
faucets, and says cockadoodledoo?"*

"*Three farmers, three milkin' stools, three Jersey cows, and
a loudmouf roostah! Ha!"*

We were preached to by J. Strudge, calliopist, ticket collector, and banjo player extraordinary, the Magnificent Ethiopian Delineator, the Black Demosthenes:

"Ladies, gemmen, houn' dawgs, bullfrawgs, an' polecats: de tex' fer today come from de forty-leben chaptah, umpteen verse —borry fo', carry three, give or take a couple, chunk in one fer good measure—ob de Book ob Zephaniah, whar de two Jedges, name ob First an' Secon' Samuel, done take de Ax ob de Romans an' cut de 'Pistles off de 'Postles fer playin' de Numbahs! Hyar how she go, bredren: *Blessed am dem dat 'specks nuffin', 'caze dey ain't gwine git nuffin'!"*

We were serenaded by banjo and fiddle, bones and tambourine.

"*Mr. Bones, I spoke to your wife today, and she tells me your
mammy's been living with you all for three years now."*

"*Mah mammy! Ah been thinkin' all dis time dat was* her
mammy!"

"*No! How can you be so consistently stupid, Mr. Bones?"*

"*Well, Mist' Interlocutor, dat ain't easy fo' a dahkie like me
dat's neber been to one ob dem fancy colleges!"*

We were supposed to hear pastoral lays of the corn and cotton fields from the vibrant throat of T. Wallace Whittaker, famous Southern tenor, but we did not, much to the disappointment of the ladies. We heard instead Sweet Sally Starbuck once more, and she sang to us this time "Just a Song at Twilight," "Beautiful Dreamer," "It's a Sin to Tell a Lie."

And Mr. Tambo! And Mr. Bones! Did they pat us the Juba?

They did. Did they cut us the Pidgin's Wing? They did. Did they scratch us the Long Dog Scratch? They did.

"Mistah Tambo, Mistah Tambo! Ah fails to unnerstan'
How a wuthless, shif'less dahkie such as you, sah,
Kin conglomerate de money fo' a Caddylac sedan,
  Jest to keep yo' yaller gal fren' sweet and true, sah. . . ."

There were banjo exhibitions, comic dances, novelty songs, more jokes.

"And now, ladies and gents," Capt. Adam announced, "for the last feature on our program: the world-renowned imitator Burley Joe Wells, all the way from New Orleans, Louisiana!"

The dead-pan banjoist seated next to Tambo stepped forward, a great black hulk, and held his arms out from his sides. Tambo and Bones stumbled up, and after some pantomimed horseplay, commenced working the arms up and down like pump handles. Burley Joe rolled his eyes and puffed out his cheeks, as though a pressure were building inside him, and when at last he opened his mouth, the blast of a steam calliope rocked the hall with "Oh, Dem Golden Slippers," the *Floating Opera*'s musical signature. A full chorus he tootled, and came whistling to the end accompanied by Prof. Eisen and our applause.

"Looziana sawmill, down in de bayou," Burley Joe grunted next. He took up a stance at one side of the stage, his back against the exit, and after some preliminary coughing, produced a hum like that of an idling buzz saw. Tambo and Bones disappeared into the opposite wing and reappeared a moment later carrying a yellow-pine plank, eight feet long and a foot wide. They tripped, they stumbled, they pulled and tugged, and finally they fed the plank in under Burley Joe's left arm. The saw whined and screamed, and the board disappeared into the wings, followed by the end men. The saw hummed on. Tambo and Bones reappeared ten seconds later with two pine planks, each six inches wide. The process was repeated again and again, the saw chunging against knots and squealing in pine resin, until at last the end men appeared with enormous satisfied smiles on their faces, each holding a single tiny toothpick in his hand; little Bones strode up to big Burley Joe and wrenched his nose as though turning a switch, and the saw's buzz slowly died away.

"Steamboat race," growled Burley Joe, who wasted none of his art on introductions. "De *Natchez* soun' like dis [*A high-pitched chugging, pumping, swishing sound. A shrill whistle*], an' de *Robert E. Lee* soun' like dis [*A low, throaty throb. A resonant bass whistle*]. Hyar dey goes, now."

It was amazing. Ship's bells clanged. Orders were shouted, soundings called. The great pumps thundered. The stern wheel spun. A deep blast of the whistle announced the *Lee*'s departure. Some moments later a deck hand cried "Steamboat 'round de bend!" and a faint shrill whistle identified the *Natchez* ahead. Prof. Eisen insinuated soft, excited music under the throb of the engines. *Toot toot!* The *Lee* flung down the gantlet. *Peep peep!* The *Natchez* accepted the challenge. A race was on! More orders, excited cries, signal bells. The engines accelerated, the music likewise.

I glanced at Capt. Osborn: he was entranced. At the house in general: enthralled. At my wrist watch: ten o'clock. A spotlight directed at Burley Joe was the only illumination in the house at the moment. Quietly, but with no particular attempt at secrecy, I left my seat, slipped down the aisle next to the starboard wall, and stepped out through a side exit, attracting little attention. Inside, the *Lee* gained slowly on the *Natchez*.

It was, of course, entirely dark outside except for the *Opera*'s lights. I found myself, as I'd planned, on the outboard side of the theater. No watchman was in sight. I walked swiftly down the starboard rail to that small companionway in the stern which I'd fixed in my mind during the afternoon's tour, and let myself into the dining room, under the stage, closing the door behind me. Over my head the *Lee* and the *Natchez* were side by side. The music was louder and faster; the minstrels called encouragement to one or the other of the ships; an occasional excited cry broke from the audience. I struck a match and lit three kerosene lanterns mounted along the dining-room walls, then went to the valve labeled DO NOT OPEN UNTIL READY TO LIGHT FOOTLIGHTS and turned it full on, feeling under my hand the rush of acetylene to the stage. Finally I entered the galley, a few feet away, put a match to one burner, and turned the others (and the oven and the broiler) full on, unlighted. A strong odor of bottled illuminating gas filled the little room at once.

Upstairs the *Robert E. Lee* forged slightly ahead of its rival, and the audience cheered. Gas hissed from the burners.

Re-entering the dining room, I glanced around carefully, checking my work. As a last touch I removed the chimneys from all three lanterns and turned up the wicks. Then I slipped out as I'd entered and took my place again in the audience, now wonderfully agitated as the *Natchez* threatened to overtake the valiant *Lee*. My heart, to be sure, pounded violently, but my mind was calm. Calmly I regarded my companion Capt. Osborn, shouting hoarse encouragement to the *Robert E. Lee*. Calmly I thought of Harrison and Jane: of perfect breasts and thighs scorched and charred; of certain soft, sun-smelling hair crisped to ash. Calmly too I heard somewhere the squeal of an overexcited child, too young to be up so late: not impossibly Jeannine. I considered a small body, formed perhaps from my own and flawless Jane's, black, cracked, smoking. Col. Morton, Bill Butler, old Mr. and Mrs. Bishop—it made no difference, absolutely.

My heart thumped on like the *Robert E. Lee*, and I smiled at the thought that I might expire of natural causes before the great steamboat explosion. The audience was wild.

"*Ladies and gentlemen!*" shouted Capt. Adam, standing in the interlocutor's chair. *"Please make ready for the great explosion of the sidewheeler* James B. Taylor! *Do not leave your seats!"*

Some women cried out, for no transition had been made at all from the one act to the other, nor did the $7,500 Challenge Maritime Band pause for a quaver: indeed, they redoubled their efforts. But the race, apparently, was forgotten. From the pit, under the frenzied music, came a slow rumbling as of tympani, its volume gradually increasing. From Burley Joe—now rising slowly from his knees, arms outstretched, eyeballs bulging—came a hackle-raising hiss like escaping steam. The drums thundered; trumpets whinnied like horses; children grew hysterical; Tambo and Bones hid behind their neighbors. From high on his chair Capt. Adam regarded his brood with an olympian smile—and calmly, more godlike than he, I too smiled.

Like some monstrous black serpent, Burley Joe poised now on tiptoe, arms overhead. The hissing and the music peaked; there was a double flash from the wings, a choked scream, a stunning explosion; the stage filled at once with thick white smoke.

After an instant of complete silence, Evelyn Morton, on the front row, quietly fainted; the Colonel caught her as she keeled. Then Prof. Eisen tore into "Lucy Long," the smoke began drifting away, and the minstrels appeared in a laughing, dancing row on the stage: Tambo, Bones, J. Strudge, Burley Joe Wells (bowing), the two guitarists, Capt. Adam himself (bowing)— and with them Sweet Sally Starbuck and Miss Clara Mulloy, dewy-eyed and blowing kisses. The audience laughed and exclaimed sharply to one another. Husbands looked at wives, wives at children, with an instant's new eyes.

"Lucy Long!" "Lucy Long!" The wonderful panithiopliconica, it turned out, was not more nor less than a grand old-fashioned minstrel walk-around—bones, tambourines, banjos, guitars. The minstrels danced, sang, leaped, cartwheeled. "Lucy Long" became "The Essence of Old Virginny"; faster and faster the minstrels cavorted, to a final, almost savage breakdown. The cymbals crashed, the performers bowed low, Tambo and Bones tumbled into the orchestra pit, and our wild applause saluted the curtains of the Original & Unparalleled Floating Opera.

XXVIII. A parenthesis

If you do not understand at once that the end of my *Floating Opera* story must be undramatic, then again I'm cursed with imperfect communication. Say what you wish about the formal requirements of storytelling; this is my opera, and I'll lead you out of it as gently as I led you in. I've little use, as a principle, for slam-bang finishes like Burley Joe's.

I helped Capt. Osborn to his feet (he was still shaken with the excitement of the steamboat race) and ushered him out with the crowd. There was still a possibility, of course, that the theater might explode—gas accumulated in the bilges of a vessel is particularly volatile—but I rather suspected that either some hidden source of ventilation (Capt. Adam had claimed the *Opera* was safe) or wandering member of the crew had foiled my plan. Need I tell you that I felt no sense either of relief or of disappointment? As when the engine of the law falls sprawling against my obstacles, I merely took note of the fact that despite my intentions six hundred ninety-nine of my townspeople and myself were still alive.

Why did I not, failing my initial attempt, simply step off the gangplank into the Choptank, where no fluke could spoil my plan? Because, I began to realize, a subtle corner had been turned. I asked myself, knowing there was no ultimate answer, "Why not step into the river?" as I had asked myself in the afternoon, "Why not blow up the Floating Opera?" But now, at once, a new voice replied casually, "On the other hand,

why bother?" There was a corner for you! Negotiated un-
awares, but like that dark alleyway in Baltimore which once
turned me dazzled onto the bright flood of Monument Street,
this corner confronted me with a new and unsuspected prospect—at which, for the moment, I could only blink.

We met Harrison, Jane, and Jeannine at the foot of the
crowded gangplank.

"How'd you like the show?" Harrison laughed. "The folks
really eat that stuff up, don't they?"

"And so do I," I said.

"Oh, well, I enjoy it too, in a sense," Harrison chuckled
briskly. "Hear those horrible old jokes again. Jeannine liked it,
anyhow." He indicated his daughter, lying like a sleeping angel
in his arms.

"We'd better get her home, I guess," Jane said pleasantly. I
believe she and Harrison both were somewhat uncomfortable
in Capt. Osborn's presence—though certainly no more so than
was that gentleman in hers. "Good night, Toddy," she smiled,
still pleasantly, but without warmth. "I guess we'll be seeing
you around."

"Of course," Harrison agreed at once, moving off.

"Certainly," I said at the same time, pleasantly but without
warmth, and we parted. I've spoken to my friend Harrison on
three separate occasions since then; to Jane only once, during
a party in 1938 celebrating the final decision of the Maryland
Court of Appeals in Harrison's favor (his presence hadn't been
necessary when I argued the case, and he sent the firm a $50,000
check via a vice-president of the pickle company); to my beautiful Jeannine, now a twenty-one-year-old debutante of Ruxton
and Gibson Island, not at all, though I note her activities occasionally on the society page of the Baltimore *Sun*. Upon their
return from eighteen months in Amalfi, Cannes, and Biarritz,
the Macks settled just outside Baltimore to live, and so there
is nothing remarkable in the fact that I don't see them any more.

Capt. Osborn and I walked back up High Street to the hotel then, and I bade him good night in the hallway.

"Hold on, Toddy," he grinned. "C'mon in my room here; I got a s'prise for ye."

I followed him in, and smiling broadly he presented me with a pint of Southern Comfort.

"There, now!"

"What's this for?" I broke the seal and sniffed appreciatively. The old man blushed. "I owed it to ye. That little business we was talkin' about this mornin', for one thing."

"Come on, then, let's drink it up," I said. "You'll need it as badly as I will, because that particular show's all over with."

"Shucks, it would've been all over with anyhow, far's I'm concerned," Capt. Osborn declared.

"How about Young Haecker?" I suggested. "Suppose we cut him in on it, too?"

I went up to the top floor to Mister Haecker's little dormer room and knocked, but though a flickering light shone under the door, he didn't reply.

"Mister Haecker?" I turned the knob, for it was doubtful that a man of his age and circumstances would be either out or asleep at ten-thirty.

The door opened onto a strange scene: a single tall white candle burned in a brass holder on the writing desk beside the bed, and flickered in the small breeze from the window. Also on the writing desk, as I saw on approaching it, were an alarm clock stopped at ten-fifteen; a volume of Shakespeare opened to Act Three, Scene One, of *Hamlet* (with, believe it or not, the words *not all* noted in the margin opposite the line *Thus conscience does make cowards of us all*); a stack of thirteen fat notebooks each labeled *Diary, 19—*(I never had nerve enough to examine those); and a glass bottle with two sleeping pills left in it. On the bed Mister Haecker lay dressed in black pajamas, his eyes closed, his arms crossed in the manner of Miss Holiday Hopkinson, next door, his features calm (*composed* is a more accurate adjective), his pulse and respiration—as I discovered upon snatching up his wrist and putting my ear to his chest—almost imperceptible.

As far as I could see there was nothing to be done in the way of first aid; I hurried downstairs and notified Hurley Binder, the night clerk, who in turn telephoned the hospital for an ambulance. Then the two of us returned to Mister Haecker's room with Capt. Osborn, who pleaded with us to help him up the stairs so that he wouldn't miss the excitement, and had our drinks there while waiting for the ambulance to arrive. Hurley Binder and Capt. Osborn clucked their tongues and shook their heads and drank their Southern Comfort, mightily impressed by Mister Haecker's elaborate preparations for departure.

"What d'ye think of that?" Capt. Osborn said several times. "And him such a educated feller!"

From time to time I felt Mister Haecker's pulse: he seemed to be losing no ground—but then there was little to lose, for pulses do not beat much more slowly. Presently the ambulance cried up past Spring Valley, and Mister Haecker was carted off to the hospital, black pajamas and all.

"Makes a man stop and think now, don't it?" Capt. Osborn said.

"It does indeed," I agreed mildly, and said good night. What I thought, personally, was that should he live through this foolishness, Mister Haecker might find the remaining years of his life less burdensome than the ones recently past, because both his former enthusiasm for old age and his apparent present despair of it were (judging from appearances) more calculated than felt, more elaborate than sincere. I should enjoy saying that history proved me correct; in fact, however, upon recovering from his generous dose of barbiturates Mister Haecker went from the hospital to a sanitorium in Western Maryland, it having been discovered that he was incipiently tubercular; there, in 1940, he attempted once again to take his life, by the same means and with as much flourish as before, and succeeded.

Alone in my room then, I sat on the window sill and smoked a cigar for several minutes, regarding the cooling night, the traffic light below, the dark graveyard of Christ Episcopal Church across the corner, and the black expanse of the sky, the blacker as the stars were blotted out by storm clouds. Sheet lightning flickered over the Post Office and behind the church steeple, and an occasional rumbling signaled the approach of the squall out over the Chesapeake. How like ponderous nature, so dramatically to change the weather when I had so delicately changed my mind! I remembered my evening's notes, and going to them presently, added a parenthesis to the fifth proposition:

V. There's no final reason for living (or for suicide).

XXIX. *The Floating Opera*

That's about what it amounted to, this change of mind in 1937: a simple matter of carrying out my premises completely to their conclusions. For the sake of convention I'd like to end the show with an emotional flourish, but though the progress of my reasoning from 1919 to 1937 was in many ways turbulent, it was of the essence of my conclusion that no emotion was necessarily involved in it. To realize that nothing makes any final difference is overwhelming; but if one goes no farther and becomes a saint, a cynic, or a suicide on principle, one hasn't reasoned completely. The truth is that nothing makes any difference, including that truth. Hamlet's question is, absolutely, meaningless.

While finishing my cigar I made a few more idle notes for my *Inquiry*, which was, you understand, open again. They are of small interest here—which is to say, they are of some interest. It occurred to me, for example, that faced with an infinitude of possible directions and having no ultimate reason to choose one over another, I would *in all probability*, though not at all necessarily, go on behaving much as I had thitherto, as a rabbit shot on the run keeps running in the same direction until death overtakes him. Possibly I would on some future occasion endeavor once again to blow up the Floating Opera, my good neighbors and associates, and/or my mere self; most probably I would not. I and my townsmen would play that percentage in my case as, for that matter, we did in each of theirs. I considered too whether, in the real absence of absolutes, values less than absolute mightn't be regarded as in no way inferior and even be lived by. But that's another inquiry, and another story.

Also reopened were the *Letter to My Father* and that third peach basket, the investigation of myself, for if I was ever to explain to myself why Dad committed suicide, I must explain to him why I did not. The project would take time. I reflected that Marvin Rose's report on my heart would reach me in next day's mail after all, and smiled: never before had the uncertainty of that organ seemed of less moment. It was beside the point now whether endocarditis was still among my infirmities: the problem was the same either way, the "solution" also. At least for the time being; at least for me.

I would take a good long careful time, then, to tell Dad the story of *The Floating Opera*. Perhaps I would expire before ending it; perhaps the task was endless, like its fellows. No matter. Even if I died before ending my cigar, I had all the time there was.

This clear, I made a note to intercept my note to Jimmy Andrews, stubbed out (after all) my cigar, undressed, went to bed in enormous soothing solitude, and slept fairly well despite the absurd thunderstorm that soon afterwards broke all around.

The End of the Road

1. *In a Sense, I Am Jacob Horner*

IN A SENSE, I AM JACOB HORNER.

It was on the advice of the Doctor that I entered the teaching profession; for a time I was a teacher of grammar at the Wicomico State Teachers College, in Maryland.

The Doctor had brought me to a certain point in my original schedule of therapies (this was in June 1953), and then, once when I drove down from Baltimore for my quarterly checkup at the Remobilization Farm, which at that time was near Wicomico, he said to me, "Jacob Horner, you mustn't sit idle any longer. You will have to begin work."

"I'm not idle all the time," said I. "I take different jobs."

We were seated in the Progress and Advice Room of the farmhouse: there is one exactly like it in the present establishment, in Pennsylvania. It is a medium-size room, about as large as an apartment living room, only high-ceilinged. The walls are flat white, the windows are covered by white venetian blinds, usually closed, and a globed ceiling fixture provides the light. In this room there are two straight-backed white wooden chairs, exactly alike, facing each other in the center of the floor, and no other furniture. The chairs are very close together—so close that the advisee almost touches knees with the adviser.

It is impossible to be at ease in the Progress and Advice Room. The Doctor sits facing you, his legs slightly spread, his hands on his knees, and leans a little toward you. You would not slouch down, because to do so would thrust your knees virtually against his. Neither would you be inclined to cross your legs in either the masculine or the feminine manner: the masculine manner, with your left ankle resting on your right knee, would cause your left shoe to rub against the Doctor's left trouser leg, up by his knee, and possibly dirty his white trousers; the feminine manner, with your left knee crooked over your right knee, would thrust the toe of your shoe against the same trouser leg, lower down on his shin. To sit sideways, of course, would be unthinkable, and spreading your knees in the manner of the Doctor makes you acutely conscious of aping his position, as if you hadn't a personality of your own. Your position, then (which has the appearance of choice, because you are not ordered to sit thus, but which is chosen only in a very limited sense, since there are no alternatives), is as follows: you sit rather rigidly in your white chair, your back and thighs describing the same right angle described by the structure of the chair, and keep your legs together, your thighs and lower legs describing another right angle.

The placing of your arms is a separate problem, interesting in its own right and, in a way, even more complicated, but of lesser importance, since no matter where you put them they will not normally come into physical contact with the Doctor. You may do anything you like with them (you wouldn't, clearly, put them on your knees in imitation of him). As a rule I move mine about a good bit, leaving them in one position for a while and then moving them to another. Arms folded, akimbo, or dangling; hands grasping the seat edges or thighs, or clasped behind the head or resting in the lap—these (and their numerous degrees and variations) are all in their own ways satisfactory positions for the arms and hands, and if I shift from one to another, this shifting is really not so much a manifestation of embarrassment, or hasn't been since the first half-dozen interviews, as a recognition of the fact that when one is faced with such a multitude of desirable choices, no one choice seems satisfactory for very long by comparison with the aggregate desirability of all the rest, though compared to any *one* of the others it would not be found inferior.

It seems to me at just this moment (I am writing this at 7:55 in the evening of Tuesday, October 4, 1955, upstairs in the dormitory) that, should you choose to consider that final observation as a metaphor, it is the story of my life in a sentence—to be precise,

in the latter member of a double predicate nominative expression
in the second independent clause of a rather intricate compound
sentence. You see that I was in truth a grammar teacher.

It is not fit that you should be at your ease in the Progress
and Advice Room, for after all it is not for relaxation that you
come there, but for advice. Were you totally at your ease, you
would only be inclined to consider the Doctor's words in a
leisurely manner, as one might regard the breakfast brought to
one's bed by a liveried servant, hypercritically, selecting this, rejecting that, eating only as much as one chooses. And clearly such
a frame of mind would be out of place in the Progress and Advice
Room, for there it is you who have placed yourself in the Doctor's
hands; your wishes are subservient to his, not vice versa; and his
advice is given you not to be questioned or even examined (to
question is impertinent; to examine, pointless), but to be followed.

"That isn't satisfactory," the Doctor said, referring to my current
practice of working only when I needed cash, and then at any job
that presented itself. "Not any longer."

He paused and studied me, as is his habit, rolling his cigar from
one side of his mouth to the other and back again, under his pink
tongue.

"You'll have to begin work at a more meaningful job now. A
career, you know. A calling. A lifework."

"Yes, sir."

"You are thirty."

"Yes, sir."

"And you have taken an undergraduate degree somewhere. In
history? Literature? Economics?"

"Arts and sciences."

"That's everything!"

"No major, sir."

"Arts and sciences! What under heaven that's interesting isn't
either an art or a science? Did you study philosophy?"

"Yes."

"Psychology?"

"Yes."

"Political science?"

"Yes."

"Wait a minute. Zoology?"

"Yes."

"Ah, and philology? Romance philology? And cultural anthropology?"

"Later, sir, in the graduate school. You remember, I——"

"Argh!" the Doctor said, as if hawking to spit upon the graduate school. "Did you study lock-picking in the graduate school? Fornication? Sailmaking? Cross-examination?"

"No, sir."

"Aren't these arts and sciences?"

"My master's degree was to be in English, sir."

"Damn you! English *what?* Navigation? Colonial policy? Common law?"

"English literature, sir. But I didn't finish. I passed the oral examinations, but I never got my thesis done."

"Jacob Horner, you are a fool."

My legs remained directly in front of me, as before, but I moved my hands from behind my head (which position suggests a rather too casual attitude for many sorts of situations anyway) to a combination position, my left hand grasping my left coat lapel, my right lying palm up, fingers loosely curled, near the mid-point of my right thigh.

After a while the Doctor said, "What reason do you think you have for not applying for a job at the little teachers college here in Wicomico?"

Instantly a host of arguments against applying for a job at the Wicomico State Teachers College presented themselves for my use, and as instantly a corresponding number of refutations lined up opposite them, one for one, so that the question of my application was held static like the rope marker in a tug-o'-war where the opposing teams are perfectly matched. This again is in a sense the story of my life, nor does it really matter if it is not just the same story as that of a few paragraphs ago: as I began to learn not long after this interview, when the schedule of therapies reached Mythotherapy, the same life lends itself to any number of stories—parallel, concentric, mutually habitant, or what you will. Well.

"No reason, sir," I said.

"Then it's settled. Apply at once for the fall term. And what will you teach? Iconography? Automotive mechanics?"

"English literature, I guess."

"No. There must be a rigid discipline, or else it will be merely an occupation, not an occupational therapy. There must be a body of laws. You mean you can't teach plane geometry?"

"Oh, I suppose——" I made a suppositive gesture, which consisted of a slight outward motion of my lapel-grasping left hand, extending simultaneously the fore and index fingers but not releasing my lapel—the hand motion accompanied by quickly arched (and as quickly released) eyebrows, momentarily pursed lips, and an on-the-one-hand/on-the-other-hand rocking of the head.

"Nonsense. Of course you can't. Tell them you will teach grammar. English grammar."

"But you know, Doctor," I ventured, "there is descriptive as well as prescriptive grammar. I mean, you mentioned a fixed body of rules."

"You will teach prescriptive grammar."

"Yes, sir."

"No description at all. No optional situations. Teach the rules. Teach the truth about grammar."

The advising was at an end. The Doctor stood up quickly (I jerked my legs out of his way) and left the room, and after I had paid Mrs. Dockey, the receptionist-nurse, I returned to Baltimore. That night I composed a letter to the president of the Wicomico State Teachers College, requesting an interview and indicating my desire to join the staff as an instructor in the prescriptive grammar of the English language. There is an art that my diffuse education had schooled me in, perforce: the art of composing a telling letter of application. I was asked to appear for an interview in July.

2. *The Wicomico State Teachers College Sits in a Great Flat Open Field*

THE WICOMICO STATE TEACHERS COLLEGE SITS IN A GREAT FLAT OPEN FIELD ringed with loblolly pine trees, at the southeastern edge of the town of Wicomico, on the Eastern Shore of Maryland. Its physical plant consists of a single graceless brick building with two ells, a building too large for the pseudo-Georgian style in which it is constructed. A deep semicircular drive runs in from College Avenue to the main entrance.

In July, when the day of my interview approached, I loaded my belongings into my Chevrolet and relinquished the key to my room on East Chase Street, in Baltimore, for I meant to take lodgings in Wicomico at once, whether I were hired or not. This was on a Sunday. The date of the interview had originally been set for Tuesday in the letter I received in answer to my application, but on the Saturday afternoon before I left Baltimore the president of the college had telephoned me and asked that I come on Monday instead. The connection was poor, but there is no doubt in my mind that he changed the date to Monday.

"I can make it either day," I recall saying.

"Well, as a matter of fact I suppose we could too," the president said. "Monday or Tuesday. But maybe Monday would be better than Tuesday for some of the Committee. Unless Monday is out of the question for you, of course. Would Tuesday be better for you?"

"Monday or Tuesday, either one," I said. I was thinking that actually Tuesday (which remember was the original date) *would* be better for me, because there might be last-minute errands or

some such for me to make before I moved out of Baltimore, and
on Sunday the stores would be closed. But I certainly wasn't going
to make an issue out of it, and for that matter an equally good
case could be made for Monday. "If Monday is better for you all,
then it's all right with me."

"I know we'd planned on Tuesday before," admitted the president, "but I guess Monday would be best."

"Either day, sir," I said.

So on Sunday I piled my clothes, my few books, my phonograph and phonograph records, whiskey, piece of sculpture, and
odds and ends into the car and set out for the Eastern Shore.
Three hours later I checked in at the Peninsula Hotel in Wicomico,
where I meant to live until I found suitable permanent quarters,
and after lunch I began looking for a room.

The first thing that went wrong was that I found an entirely
satisfactory room at once. As a rule I was extremely hard to please
in the matter of renting a room. I required that no one live above
me; that my room be high-ceilinged and large-windowed; that my
bed be high off the floor, wide, and very soft; that the bathroom
be equipped with a good shower; that the landlord not live in the
same building (and that he be not very particular about his property or his tenants); that the other tenants be of an uncomplaining
nature; and that maid service be available. Because I was so fussy,
it usually took me a good while to find even a barely acceptable
place. But as ill luck would have it, the first room I saw advertised
for rent on my way out College Avenue from the hotel met all
these qualifications. The landlady, an imposing widow of fifty
whom I just chanced to meet on her way out of the old two-story
brick house, showed me to a second-floor room in the front.

"You're teaching at the college?" she asked.

"Yes, ma'am. Grammar teacher."

"Well, pleased to meet you. I'm Mrs. Alder. Let's shake hands
and all now, because you won't see me very much around here."

"You don't live in the house?"

"Live *here*? God, no! Can't stand tenants around me. Always
pestering for this or that. I live in Ocean City all year round.
Any time you need anything, don't call me; you call Mr. Prake,
the janitor. He lives in town."

She showed me the room. Six-foot windows, three of them. Twelve-foot ceiling. Dark gray plaster walls, white woodwork. An incredible bed three feet high, seven feet long, at least seven feet wide; a black, towering, canopied monster with four posts as thick as masts, fluted and ringed, and an elaborately carved headboard extending three feet above the bolster. A most adequate bed! The other furniture was a potpourri of styles and periods—one felt as if one had wandered into the odd-pieces room of Winterthur Museum—but every piece was immensely competent. The adjective *competent* came at once to mind, rather than, say, *efficient*. This furniture had an air of almost contemptuous competence, as though it were so absurdly well able to handle its job that it would scarcely notice *your* puny use of it. It would require a man indeed, a man's man, to make his presence felt by this furniture. I was impressed.

In short, the place left nothing to be desired. Shower, maid service—everything was there.

"What about the other tenants?" I asked uneasily.

"Oh, they come and they go. Bachelors, mostly, a few young couples now and then, traveling men, a nurse or two from the hospital."

"Any students?" In Baltimore it was desirable to have students for neighbors, for they are singularly uncritical, but I suspected that in Wicomico all the students would know all the teachers rather too well.

"No students. The students generally live in the dorms or get rooms farther out College Avenue."

It was too perfect, and I was skeptical.

"I guess I should tell you that I practice on the clarinet," I said. This was untrue: I was not musical.

"Well, isn't that nice! I used to sing, myself, but my voice seemed to go after Mr. Alder died. I had the most marvelous voice teacher at the Peabody Conservatory when I was younger! Farrari. Farrari used to tell me, 'Alder,' he'd say, 'you've learned all I can teach you. You have precision, style, *éclat*. You are *una macchina cantanda*,' he'd say—that's Italian. 'Life will have to do the rest. Go out and live!' he'd say. But I never got to live until

poor Mr. Alder died five years ago, and by that time my voice
was gone."

"Do you object to pets?"

"What kind?" Mrs. Alder asked sharply. I thought I'd found
an out.

"Oh, I don't know. I'm fond of dogs. Might pick up a boxer
sometime, or a Doberman."

My landlady sighed. "I forgot you were a grammar teacher. I
had a biology teacher once," she explained.

I snatched at a last hope: "I couldn't go over twelve a week."

"The rent's eight," Mrs. Alder said. "The maid gets three dollars
a week extra, or four-fifty, depending."

"Depending on what, for heaven's sake?"

"She does laundry, too," Mrs. Alder said evenly.

There was nothing to do but take the room. I paid my landlady
a month's rent in advance, though she required only a week's,
and ushered her out to her car, a five-year-old Buick convertible.

I call this windfall a stroke of ill luck because it gave me the
whole of the afternoon and evening, and the next morning, with
nothing to do. Even checking out of the Peninsula Hotel, moving
to my new quarters, and arranging my belongings took but an
hour and a half, after which time there was simply nothing to be
done. I had no interest in touring Wicomico: it was the sort of
small city that one knows adequately at the first glance—entirely
without character. A humdrum business district and a commonplace park, surrounded by middle-class residential neighborhoods
varying only in age and upkeep. As for the Wicomico State
Teachers College, one look was enough to lay any but the most
inordinately pricked-up curiosity. It was a state teachers' college.

I drove about aimlessly for twenty minutes and then returned
to my room. The one dusty maple outside my window exhausted
its scenic potential in a half minute. My phonograph records—
nearly all Mozart—sounded irritating in a room with which I was
still too unfamiliar to be at ease. My sculpture on the mantel, a
heroic plaster head of Laocoön, so annoyed me with his blank-
eyed grimace that, had I been the sort of person who did such
things, I'd have turned his ugly face to the wall. I got the
wholesale fidgets. Finally, at only nine o'clock (but I'd been

fidgeting since three-thirty, not counting supper hour), I went to my great bed and was somewhat calmed by its imposing grotesqueness, which, however, kept me from sleep for a long time.

Next morning was worse. I slept fitfully until ten and then went to breakfast logy and puffy-eyed, nursing a headache. The interview was set for two in the afternoon, and so I had more than enough time to become entirely demoralized. Reading was impossible, music exasperating. I nicked myself twice while shaving, and ran out of polish before the heel of my left shoe was covered. Since I'd put off shining my shoes until the last minute, hoping thus to occupy those most uncomfortable moments before I left the room, there was no time to go downtown for more polish. In a rage I went down to the car. But I'd forgotten my pen and my brief case, which, though empty, I thought it fitting to carry. I stormed back upstairs and fetched them, glaring so fiercely at a nurse who happened to look from her doorway that she sniffed and closed her door with some heat. Tossing the brief case onto the seat, I left with an uncalled-for spinning of tires and drove out to the college.

My exasperation would have carried me safely into the interview had there not been a cluster of young people lounging on the front steps. I took them for students, although, it being vacation time, it is unlikely that they were. At any rate they stared at my approaching car with a curiosity no less unabashed for its being mild. My courage failed me; as I passed them I glanced indifferently at my wrist watch, to suggest that it was only to check the time that I'd slowed down. I was assisted in my ruse by the college clock, which at that instant chimed two: I nodded my head shortly, as though satisfied with the accuracy of my timepiece, and drove purposefully down the other arc of the semicircular drive, back to College Avenue. There my anger returned at once, this time directed at myself for being so easily cowed. I went again to the entrance drive and headed up the semicircle for another try. But if it took determination to approach those impassive gatekeepers the first time, with their adolescent eyes as empty as Laocoön's directing a stupid enfilade along the driveway, it took raw courage to run their fire again. I shoved the accelerator to the floor and rocked the Chevrolet around the bend, not even deigning to glance at them. Let the ninnies think what they would! The third time I did not hesitate for a moment, but drove heedlessly around to the parking lot behind the building and entered through a doorway near at hand. I was six minutes late.

I found the president's office without difficulty and introduced myself to the receptionist.

"Mr. Horner?" she repeated, vaguely troubled.

"That's right," I said shortly.

"Just a minute."

She disappeared into an inner office, from which I heard then a low-voiced conversation between her and, I presumed, Dr. Schott, the president. My heart sank.

A gray, fatherly gentleman came smiling from the inner office, the receptionist in his wake.

"Mr. Horner!" he exclaimed, grasping my hand. "I'm John Schott! Glad to meet you!"

Dr. Schott was of an exclamatory nature.

"Glad to meet *you*, sir. Sorry I'm a little late . . ."

I was going to explain: my unfamiliarity with the little city, uncertainty as to where I should park, natural difficulty finding the office, etc.

"Late!" cried Dr. Schott. "My boy, you're twenty-four hours early! This is only Monday!"

"But isn't that what we decided on the phone, sir?"

"No, son!" Dr. Schott laughed loudly and placed his arm around my shoulders. "*Tuesday!* Isn't that so, Shirley?" Shirley nodded happily, her troubled look vindicated. "Monday in the letter, Tuesday on the phone! Don't you remember now?"

I laughed and scratched my head (with my left hand, my right being pinioned by Dr. Schott).

"Well, I swear, I thought sure we'd changed it from Tuesday to Monday. I'm awfully sorry. That was stupid of me."

"Not a bit! Don't you worry!" Dr. Schott chuckled again and released me. "Didn't we tell Mr. Horner Tuesday?" he demanded again of Shirley.

"I'm afraid so," Shirley affirmed. "On account of Mr. Morgan's Boy Scouts. Monday in the letter and Tuesday on the phone."

"One of the Committee members is a scoutmaster!" Dr. Schott explained. "He's had his boys up to Camp Rodney for two weeks and is bringing them home today. Joe Morgan, fine fellow, teaches history! That's why we changed the interview to Tuesday!"

"Well, I'm awfully sorry." I smiled ruefully.

"No! Not a bit! I could've gotten mixed up myself!"

He was.

"Well, I'll come back tomorrow."

"Wait! Wait a minute! Shirley, give Joe Morgan a call, see if he's in yet. He might be in. I know Miss Banning and Harry Carter are home."

"Oh no," I protested; "I'll come back."

"Hold on, now! Hold on!"

Shirley called Joe Morgan.

"Hello? Mrs. Morgan. Is Mr. Morgan there? I see. No, I know he's not. Yes, indeed. No, no, it's nothing. Mr. Horner came in for his interview today unexpectedly; he got the date mixed up and came in today instead of tomorrow. Dr. Schott thought maybe Mr. Morgan just might happen to have come back early. No, don't bother. Sorry to bother *you*. Okay. 'By."

I wanted to spit on Shirley.

"Well, I'll come back," I said.

"Sure, you come back!" Dr. Schott said. He ushered me toward the front door, where, to my chagrin, I saw the sentries still on duty. But I threw up my hands at the idea of attempting to explain to him that my car was in the rear of the building.

"Well, well, we'll be seeing you!" Dr. Schott said, pumping my hand. "You be back tomorrow, now, hear?"

"I will, sir."

We were outside the main door, and the watch regarded me blankly.

"Where's your car? You need a lift anywhere?"

"Oh, no, thanks; my car's in the back."

"In the back! Well, say, you don't want to go out the front here! I'll show you the back door! Ha!"

"Never mind sir," I said. "I'll just walk around."

"Well! Ha! Well, all right, then!" But he looked at me. "See you tomorrow!"

"Good-by, sir."

I walked very positively past the loungers on the steps.

"You dig up that letter!" Dr. Schott called from the doorway. "See if it doesn't say Monday!"

I turned and waved acknowledgment and acquiescence, but when, back in my room at last (which already seemed immensely familiar and comforting), I searched for it, I found that I'd thrown the letter out before leaving Baltimore. Since I would not in a hundred years have been at home enough in Dr. Schott's office to ask Shirley to investigate her files, the question of my appointment date could not be verified by appeal to objective facts.

One might suppose that after such an inauspicious start I would have been less prepared than ever to face my interview, but this supposition, though entirely reasonable, does not correspond to the fact. On the contrary, I was disgusted enough not to care a damn about the interview. I didn't even bother to polish the rest of my left shoe next morning; in fact, after breakfast I sat in the park for several hours watching the children romp in the small artificial lake and didn't even think about the interview more than two or three times. When it occurred to me at all, I merely ticked my right cheek muscle. At ten minutes before two I drove out to the college, parked unhesitatingly in the front driveway, and walked through the main entrance. The steps happened to be uninhabited, but no reception committee could have daunted me that day. My mood had changed.

"Oh, hello," Shirley said brightly.

"How do you do. Tell Dr. Schott I'm here, will you please?"

"*Everybody's* here today. Just a minute, please, Mr. Horner."

I turned my smile on, and then I turned it off, so, as a gentleman might tip his hat politely, but impassively, at absolutely any lady of his acquaintance, whether she merited the courtesy or not. Shirley stepped into and out of Dr. Schott's office.

"Go right on in, Mr. Horner."

"Thank you."

Inside I was introduced by Dr. Schott to Miss Banning, teacher of Spanish and French, a dear-elderly-lady type whom one accepted on her own terms because there was absolutely nothing else to be done about her; Dr. Harry Carter, teacher of psychology, a thin scholarly old man about whom one wondered at once what he was doing in Wicomico, but not so strongly that one didn't decide rather easily that he doubtless had his reasons; and Mr. Joseph Morgan, scoutmaster and teacher of ancient, European, and American history, a tall, bespectacled, athletic young man, terribly energetic, with whom one was so clearly expected to be charmed, he was so bright, busy, and obviously on his way up, that one had one's hands full simply trying to be civil to him, and realized at once that the invidious comparisons to oneself that he could not for the life of him help inviting would prevent one's ever being really tranquil about the fact of his existence, to say nothing of becoming his friend.

Pleasantries were made about my being so eager to join the faculty that I came a day early to my interview. The Committee took a lively interest in one another's summer activities. There was joshing. Applicants for jobs at the Wicomico State Teachers College were obviously not so numerous that such meetings of the Appointments Committee were but a dull addition to the members' regular duties.

"You can count on Miss Banning's support for your application, Mr. Horner," Dr. Carter chortled. "She needs new victims to show off her mustache-cup collection to."

"Oh?" said I. This remark of Dr. Carter's was addressed not *to* me, but through me, as a grandmother teases her daughter by speaking to her grandchild.

"I have a simply marvelous collection, Mr. Horner," Miss Banning declared good-naturedly. "You'll surely have to see it. Oh dear, but you don't have a mustache, do you?"

All laughed. I observed that Joe Morgan *did* have a mustache.

"Ethel's been after me for fourteen years to grow one!" Dr. Schott guffawed at me. "Not a trim little affair like Joe's, mind you, but a great bushy one, so I can try out her collector's items! Now don't you start on Mr. Horner, Ethel!"

Ethel was poised to make a retort, in all good humor, but Joe

Morgan pleasantly interjected a question about my academic experience.

"Do I understand you're from Johns Hopkins, Mr. Horner?"

"Yes, sir."

The others nodded approval at Joe's getting so tactfully down to business. He was a find, was Mr. Morgan. He'd not stay in their little circle long. Serious attention was focused on me.

"Oh, please, not *sir!*" Dr. Carter protested. "We don't stand on ceremony out here in the provinces."

"No indeed!" Dr. Schott agreed benignly.

There ensued some twenty minutes of unsystematic interrogation about my graduate study and my teaching experience—the latter, except for occasional tutoring jobs in Baltimore and a brief night-school class at Johns Hopkins, being nil.

"What made you decide to get back into teaching, Mr. Horner?" Dr. Carter asked. "You've been away from it for some time, I presume."

I shrugged. "You know how it is. You don't feel just *right* doing other things."

All acknowledged the truth of my observation.

"Then too," I added casually, "my doctor recommended that I go back to teaching. He seems to think it's the thing I'm best at, and the thing that's best for me."

This was well said. My examiners were with me, and so I expatiated.

"I seem never to be content with ordinary jobs. There's something so—so *stultifying* about working only for pay. It's—well, I hate to use a cliché, but the fact is that other jobs are simply unrewarding. You know what I mean?"

They did know what I meant.

"You take a boy—bright kid, alert kid, you see it at once, but never been exposed to *thinking,* never been in an environment where intellectual activity was as common as eating or sleeping. You see a fresh young mind that's never had a chance to flex its muscles, so to speak. Maybe he can't speak good English. Never *heard* good English spoken. Not his fault. Not wholly his parents' fault. But there he is."

My audience was most receptive, all except Joe Morgan, who regarded me coolly.

"So you start him off. Parts of speech! Subjects and verbs! Modifiers! *Complements!* And after a while, rhetoric. Subordination! Coherence! Euphony! You drill and drill, and talk yourself blue in the face, and all the time you see that boy's mind groping, stumbling, stretching, making false steps. And then, just when you're ready to chuck the whole thing——"

"I know!" Miss Banning breathed. "One day, just like all the rest, you say the same thing for the tenth time—and *click!*" She snapped her fingers jubilantly at Dr. Schott. "He's got it! *Why, there's nothing to it!* he says. *It's plain as day!*"

"That's what we're here for!" Dr. Schott said quietly, with some pride. "That's what we all live for. A little thing, isn't it?"

"Little," Dr. Carter agreed, "but it's the greatest miracle on God's green earth! And the most mysterious, too."

Joe Morgan would not have committed himself on the matter, I believe, but that Dr. Carter addressed this last reflection to him directly. Cornered, Morgan made a sucking noise in the left side of his mouth, to express sympathetic awe before the mystery.

"I sometimes compare it to a man making fire with flint and steel," I said calmly to Joe Morgan, knowing I was hitting him where he lived. "He strikes and strikes and strikes, but the tinder lies dead under his hands. Then another strike, not a bit different from the rest, and there's your fire!"

"Very apt," Dr. Carter said. "And what a rewarding moment it is, when a student suddenly becomes *ignited!* There's no other word for it: positively *ignited!*"

"And then you can't hold him back!" Dr. Schott laughed, but as one would laugh at a sudden beneficence of God. "He's like a horse that smells the stable up the lane!"

There were reminiscent sighs. Certainly I had scored a triumph. Joe Morgan brought the conversation back to my qualifications for a minute or two, but it was plainly in the nature of an anti-climax. The other members of the Committee showed very little interest in the interrogation, and Dr. Schott began to describe very frankly the salary scale in Maryland state colleges, the hours I'd be expected to work, non-teaching duties, and the like.

"Well, you'll hear from us soon," he concluded, rising and shaking my hand. "Maybe tomorrow." I shook hands all around. "Shall I show you the back door this time?" He explained jovially my departure of the day before.

"No, thanks. My car's out front this time."

"Good, good!" Dr. Carter said heartily, for no reason whatever.

"I'm going out that way," Joe Morgan said, falling in beside me. "I live just down the block." He accompanied me across the driveway to my car, and even stood beside the front fender while I got inside and closed the door. I started the engine, but delayed putting the car in gear: apparently my colleague-to-be had something on his mind.

"Well, be seeing you around, Horner," he grinned, shaking hands with me again through the open window.

"Sure."

We released hands, but Joe Morgan still leaned against the car door, his face radiating cheerful candor. He was well tanned from his stay at camp, and had a look about him that suggested early rising, a nutritious diet, and other sorts of virtue. His eyes were clear.

"Say, were you making fun of me in there?" he asked cheerfully. "With that flint-and-steel nonsense?"

I smiled and shrugged, very much embarrassed at being thus confronted. "It seemed a good thing to say at the time."

My colleague laughed briskly. "I was afraid you'd gone out on a limb with that line of horseshit, but it looks like you know what you're doing."

Clearly he was unhappy about it nonetheless, but wasn't going to voice his criticisms.

"We'll see about that pretty soon, I guess."

"Well, hope you get the job," he said, "if it's what you want."

I put the car in reverse and eased out the clutch. "Be seeing you."

But there was a point still unsettled in Joe Morgan's mind. His face mirrored faithfully whatever was in progress behind it, and even as the car began to move backwards out of the parking space I saw a question settle itself on his pellucid brow.

"Say, we'd like to have you over to dinner—Rennie and I—before you go back to Baltimore, whether you get the job or not. I understand you've taken a room in town."

"Oh, I'll be around for a while, I guess, either way. Nothing special on the agenda."

"Swell. How about tonight?"

"Well—better not." It seemed the thing to say.

"Tomorrow night?"

"Sure, I guess so."

There was another thing, dinner invitations aside: "You know, if you weren't just being funny about that flint-and-steel, then you might as well lay off it, don't you think? There's nothing silly about working with the Scouts that I can see. You can tease me about them, or you can argue with me about them, but there's no sense just poking fun to be malicious. That's too easy."

This speech surprised me; I immediately labeled it bad taste, but I must admit that I felt ashamed, and at the same time I appreciated the subtlety with which Morgan had precluded any protest on my part by prefacing his reproof with a dinner invitation. He was still smiling most cordially.

"Excuse me if I offended you," I said.

"Oh hell, no offense! I'm not really touchy, but what the hell, we'll probably be working together; might as well understand each other a little. See you tomorrow for dinner, then. So long!"

"So long."

He turned and strode cleanly across the lawn, grown tall in the students' absence. Apparently Joe Morgan was the sort who heads directly for his destination, implying by his example that paths should be laid where people walk, instead of walking where the paths happen to be laid. All very well for a history man, perhaps, but I could see that Mr. Morgan would be a fish out of water in the prescriptive grammar racket.

3. A Turning Down of Dinner Damped, in Ways Subtle Past Knowing

A TURNING DOWN OF DINNER DAMPED, IN WAYS SUBTLE PAST KNOWING, manic keys on the thin flute of me, least pressed of all, which for a moment had shrilled me rarely.

It began with Laocoön on the mantelpiece, his voiceless groan. The set of that mouth was often my barometer, told me the weight of day; on Wednesday after my interview, when I woke and consulted him with a happening glance, his pain was simply Bacchic! That was something, now! Out of bed I sprang, unclothed, to put a dance on the phonograph while the spell should last. Against all of Mozart I owned a single Russian dance, a piece of *Ilya Mourometz*, measured and sprightly, lively and tight—there, now, Laocoön!

The dusty maple incandesced; sunshine fired the speckled windows and filled my room with a sparkle of light, and I danced like an unfurred Cossack, spinning and jumping. Once in a blue moon I felt that light—sweet manic!—and it lasted a scant three minutes, till a ring from the phone dispersed it.

I shut off the music, furious. A man with so short time to prance deserved a history of unanswered phones.

"Hello?"

"Hello, Jacob Horner?" It was a woman, and I felt naked as I was.

"Yes."

"This is Rennie Morgan, Joe Morgan's wife. Say, I think Joe already asked you over for dinner tonight, didn't he? I just called to make it official."

I allowed a pause to lie along the line.

"I mean, after your interview, you know, we wanted to make sure you'd come on the right day!

"Jacob? Are we still connected?"

"Yes. Excuse me." I was checking my barometer, who now looked dolorous enough. Batygh the Tartar had breathed on us.

"Well, it's all set, then? Any time after six-thirty: that's when we put the kids to bed."

"Well, say, Mrs. Morgan, I guess——"

"*Rennie.* Okay? My name's Renée, but nobody calls me that."

"—I guess I won't be able to make it tonight after all."

"What?"

"No, I'm pretty sure I can't. Thanks a lot for inviting me."

"But why not? Are you sure you can't make it?"

Why not? Bitch of an Eagle Scout's *Hausfrau*, you spoiled my first real manic in a month of Sundays! I spit on your dinner!

"I'd kind of planned on riding up to Baltimore this afternoon, have a look around. Something came up."

"Oh, now, aren't you just getting out of it? Come on and say so; we're not committed to each other." This from a wife? "Don't be a chicken—it doesn't make a damn to us if you don't like us."

So caught, *flagrante delicto*, I flushed and sweated. What was this beast *honesty* ridden by a woman? An answer was awaited: I heard Joe Morgan's wife breathing in my naked ear.

Very discreetly I hung up the phone. Not only that: I walked the first three steps away on tiptoe before I realized what I was doing, and blushed again to notice it.

Ah, well, the spell was broken, and I knew better than to try Glière and his *Ilya Mourometz* again. He's the fizz that makes the collins bright, is Glière, but he's not the vodka; these manics can't be teased or dickered with. Now I was not only unmanic, I was uncomfortable.

And resentful! There's something to be said for the manic-depressive if his manics are really manic; but me, I was a placid-depressive: a woofer without a tweeter was Jake Horner. My lows were low, but my highs were middle-register. So when I'd a real manic on I nursed it like a baby, and boils plague the

man who spoiled it! That was one thing. More's the damage to
have it suggested, and by a woman, that my honesty was flagging.
That it was in fact was beside the point. Great heavens, Morgans,
the world's not *that* easy!

Even as I was dressing, the telephone rang again, with a dog-
gedness that bespoke Mrs. Morgan. In a moment of lewdness (for
I was pulling up my trousers at the time) I considered allowing
that beskirted Diogenes to address her quest to my bare backside—
but I let the moment go. Rennie, girl, said I to myself, I am
out; be content that I don't commit a lewdness with your voice,
since you've aborted my infant manic. Ring away, girl scout: your
quarry's not in his hole.

Later that morning I drove the thirty miles from Wicomico to
Ocean City, there to fry my melancholy in the sun and pickle it
in the ocean. But light and water only made it blossom. The
beach was crowded with human beings whose reality I found myself loath to acknowledge; another day they might have been as
soothingly grotesque as was my furniture, but this day they were
merely irritating. Furthermore, perhaps because it was a week
day, there was not a girl on the beach worth the necessary nonsense involved in a pickup. Only a forest of legs ruined by child-
birth; fallen breasts, potbellies, haggard faces, and strident voices;
a rats' nest of horrid children, as unlovely as they were obnoxious.
When one is not in the spirit of it, there are few things less
diverting than a public beach.

When I reached the saturation point, about three o'clock, I
washed the sand off me and headed back to the car. But one
who felt as gloomily competent as I that day wouldn't leave
Ocean City without at least going through the motions of picking
up a girl, any more than one would leave Pikes Peak without
spitting—the trip were pointless otherwise. Along the boardwalk
a few girls prowled in twos and threes, most wearing T-shirts
with the name of either a college or a sorority printed on them.
They met my glowering haughtily, each of us considering the
other unworthy. I walked the three blocks to my car without
seeing a target worth the ammunition, and so, like many a hunter

nearing home, had finally to settle for even less satisfactory game or take none at all.

A woman of forty—well preserved but definitely forty—whose car was parked in front of mine, was wrenching the handle of her door in vain when I approached. She was slender, not very full-breasted, well tanned, and in no way extraordinary. I lost my taste for the hunt and walked past.

"Pardon me, sir: I wonder if you could help me?"

I turned and glared. The woman had been all brightness with her classic request, but my stare made her falter.

"You'll think I'm stupid, I guess—I locked my keys inside the car."

"I can't pick locks."

"Oh, I didn't mean that! My motel is just across the bridge. I was wondering if you'd run me over there, if you're going that way. I have another key in my suitcase."

It is small sport shooting the bird who perches on the muzzle of your gun, but what hunter could keep from doing it?

"All right."

The whole situation was without appeal, and as I drove Miss Peggy Rankin (her name) over the bridge from Ocean City to the mainland, I was made more desultory by the fact that I guessed she didn't deserve to be so severely judged. She appeared to be fairly intelligent, and indeed, had I been her husband I should doubtless have been proud that my wife still retained such trimness and spirit at age forty. But I was not her husband, and so I made no such allowances: she was a forty-year-old pickup, and only the most extraordinary charm could survive that classification.

All the way to the motel Miss Rankin chattered, and I honestly didn't hear a word of it. For me this was unusual, because, although I admired the ability to lose oneself in oneself, I was far too conscious of my surroundings, as a rule, ever to manage it. A real point against Miss Rankin, that.

"This is the place," she said presently, indicating the Surfside, or Seaside, or some such motel along the highway. I pulled into the driveway and parked. "Gee, I sure appreciate your doing this. Thanks a lot." She moved lightly out of the car.

"I'll take you back," I said, without any particular inflection.

"Oh, would you?" She was very pleased, but not overwhelmed with either surprise or gratitude. "Just a minute, while I run get my keys."

"Have you got anything cold to drink in there, Peggy? I'm pretty dry." This was as far as I was willing to go in the non-sense line just then: I decided that if she didn't ask me in, I'd take off at once for Wicomico.

"Sure, come on in," she invited, again not entirely stunned by my request. "There's no refrigerator in the room, but there's a soda fountain right next door here, and I've got whiskey. Why don't you get two large ginger ales, with lots of ice, and we'll make highballs."

I did, and we drank in her little room, she curled on the bed and I slouched in the single chair. The gloom was still on me, but it grew somewhat easier to endure; especially when we found that we could talk or not talk with a reasonable degree of ease. At one point, as might be expected, Miss Rankin asked me what I did for a living. Now, I didn't necessarily subscribe at all to honesty as a policy in adventures of this sort, and I can't imagine myself answering such stock questions truthfully as a rule; but "I'm a potential instructor of prescriptive grammar at the Wicomico State Teachers College" is so nearly the type of answer one usually dreams up at such moments that without really thinking about it I told her the truth.

"Is that so!" Peggy was genuinely surprised and pleased this time. "I graduated from WTC myself—so long ago it embarrasses me to remember! I teach English at the high school in Wicomico. Isn't that a funny coincidence? Two English teachers!"

I agreed that it was, but in fact I felt like turning in my highball and calling it quits. It was necessary to move rapidly to keep the situation from disintegrating. There was only a half inch of highball left in my paper cup: I tossed it down, dropped the cup into the wastebasket, immediately went to the bed, where my colleague lay propped on one elbow, and embraced her with some *élan*. She opened her mouth at once under my kiss and thrust her tongue between my teeth. Both of us had our eyes quite open, and I was pleased to accept that fact symbolically. *Let there be no horse manure between teachers of English*, I declared to myself, and without more ado gave the zipper of her bathing suit a meaning yank.

Miss Rankin froze: her eyes closed tightly and she clutched my shoulders, but my ungentle attack was not repulsed. The zipper undid her down to the small of her back and so gave me access to a certain amount of innocuous skin, but I could go no farther without her assistance.

"Let's take your bathing suit off, Peggy," I suggested.

This injured her. "You're in a great hurry, aren't you, Jake?"

"Well, Peg, we're old enough not to be any sillier than we have to be."

She made a noise in her mouth, and, still holding my shoulders, pressed her forehead against my chest.

"By that you mean I'm too old for you to bother being silly with, don't you?" she observed. "You're thinking that a woman my age can't afford to be coy."

Tears. Everybody was digging truth out of me.

"Why hurt yourself?" I asked over her hair to the whiskey bottle on the night stand.

"You're the one that's doing the hurting," Miss Rankin wept, looking me square in the eye. "You go out of your way to let me know you're doing me a favor by picking me up, but your generosity doesn't include wasting a little time being gentle!" She flung herself, not violently, upon her pillow, burying her face in it. "It doesn't make the least bit of difference to you whether I'm bright or stupid or what, does it? I might even be more interesting than you are, since I'm a little older!" This last piece of self-castigation, while it choked her completely for a moment, made her mad enough to sit up and glare at me.

"I'm sorry," I offered politely. I was thinking that even if she were talented as, say, Beatrice Lillie is talented, one would not pick her up in order to witness a theatrical performance: one would purchase a theater ticket.

"Sorry you wasted your time on me, you mean!" Peggy cried. "Just making me defend myself is awful enough!"

Back to the pillow. Up again at once.

"Don't you understand how you make me feel? Today is my

last day at Ocean City. For two whole weeks not a soul has spoken to me or even looked at me, except some horrible old men. Not a *soul!* Most women look awful at my age, but I don't look awful: I just don't look like a child. There's a lot *more* to me, damn it! And then on the last day you come along and pick me up, bored as you can be with the whole thing, and treat me like a whore!"

Well, she was correct.

"I'm a cad," I agreed readily, and rose to leave. There was a little more to this matter than Miss Rankin was willing to see, but in the main she had a pretty clear view of things. Her mistake, in the long run, was articulating her protest. The game was spoiled now, of course: I had assigned to Miss Rankin the role of Forty-Year-Old Pickup, a delicate enough character for her to bring off successfully in my current mood; I had no interest whatever in the quite complex (and no doubt interesting, from another point of view) human being she might be apart from that role. What she should have done, it seems to me, assuming she was after the same thing I was after, was assign me a role gratifying to her own vanity—say, The Fresh But Unintelligent Young Man Whose Body One Uses For One's Pleasure Without Otherwise Taking Him Seriously—and then we could have pursued our business with no wounds inflicted on either side. As it was, my present feeling, though a good deal stronger, was essentially the same feeling one has when a filling-station attendant or a cabdriver launches into his life-story: as a rule, and especially when one is in a hurry or is grouchy, one wishes the man to be nothing more difficult than The Obliging Filling-Station Attendant or The Adroit Cabdriver. These are the essences you have assigned them, at least temporarily, for your own purposes, as a taleteller makes a man The Handsome Young Poet or The Jealous Old Husband; and while you know very well that no historical human being was ever *just* an Obliging Filling-Station Attendant or a Handsome Young Poet, you are nevertheless prepared to ignore your man's charming complexities—*must* ignore them, in fact, if you are to get on with the plot, or get things done according to schedule. Of this, more later, for it is related to Mythotherapy. Enough now to say that we are all casting directors a great deal of the time, if not always, and he is wise who realizes that his role-assigning is at best an arbitrary distortion of the actors' personalities; but he is even wiser who sees in addition that this arbitrariness is probably inevitable, and at any rate is apparently necessary if one would reach the ends he desires.

"Get your keys," I said. "I'll wait for you out in the car."

"No! *Jake!*" Miss Peggy Rankin jumped off the bed. I was caught at the door and embraced from behind, under my arms. "Oh, God, don't go away yet!" Hysteria. "I'm sorry I made you angry!" She was pulling me as hard as she could, back into the room.

"Come on, now; cut it out. Get hold of yourself."

A forty-year-old pickup's beauty, when it is preserved at all, is fragile, and Peggy's hysteria, added to her previous weeping, left little of loveliness in her face, which normally was long, tan, unwrinkled, and not unattractive.

"Will you stay? Don't pay attention to anything I said a while ago!"

"I don't know what to do," I said truthfully, trying to assimilate this outburst. "This whole thing means more to you than it does to me. That's no criticism of anybody. I'm really afraid I might spoil it for you, if I haven't already."

I was squeezed tightly. "You're humiliating me! Don't make me beg you, for God's sake!"

By this time she stood to lose either way. We went to the bed: what ensued was, for me at least, pure discomfort, and it was of a nature to become an unpleasant memory for her, too, whether she enjoyed it at the time or not. It was embarrassing because she abandoned herself to an elaborate gratitude that implied her own humiliation—and because my own mood was not complementary to hers. Her condition remained semi-hysterical and masochistic: she did her best to make grand opera out of nature's little *cantus firmus*, and if she didn't succeed it was more my fault than hers, for she strove elaborately. Another time I might have enjoyed it—that sort of voluptuous groveling can be as pleasant to indulge as it is on occasion to indulge in—but that day was not my day. That day had begun badly, had developed tediously, and was climaxing uncomfortably, if not distastefully:

I was always uneasy with women who took their sexual trans-
ports too seriously, and Miss Rankin was not the sort whom one
could leave shuddering and moaning on the bed knowing it was
all just good clean fun.

That is how I left her, at five o'clock. At four forty-five she
had begun, as I'd rather expected, to express hatred for me,
whether feigned (this kind of thing can be sensuous sport) or
sincere I couldn't say, since her eyes were closed and her face
averted. What she said, throatily, was "God damn your eyes,
God damn your eyes, God damn your eyes . . ." in rhythm with
what happened to be in progress at the time, and I was not so
committed to my mood that it didn't strike me as funny. But I
was weary of dramatics, genuine or not, amusing or not, and
when things reached their natural *dénouement* I was glad enough
to make my exit, forgetting entirely about Miss Rankin's keys.
The lady had talent, but no discipline. I'm sure we neither wished
to see the other again.

I ate at a roadstand outside Wicomico and finally got back to
my room at six-thirty, feeling terrible. I was a man of considerable integrity within the limits of a given mood, but I was short
on endurance. I felt bad already about this Peggy Rankin—irri-
tated that at her age she hadn't yet learned how to handle her
position, how to turn its regrettable aspects as much as possible to
her own advantage—and at the same time very much sympathetic
with her weakness. I had, abstractly at least, a tremendous sympathy for that sort of weakness—a person's inability either to control his behavior by his own standards or to discipline his standards, down to the last shred of conscience, to fit his behavior—
even though in particular situations it sometimes annoyed me.
Everything that had happened with Miss Rankin could have been
high sport—the groveling, the hysterics, and numerous other things
that I've not felt like sharing by recording them—had she kept
hard control of her integrity; but her error, I feared, was that she
would recriminate herself for some time afterward for having
humbled herself in fact, and not in fun, and mine was in not
walking out when I'd started to, regardless of her hysterics. Had I
done so I'd have preserved my own tranquillity and allowed Miss
Rankin to regain hers by depising me instead of both of us. I

had remained, I think, both out of a sense of chivalry, to which I often inclined though I didn't *believe* in it, and out of a characteristic disinclination to walk out on any show, no matter how poor or painful, once I'd seen the first act.

But there was a length of time beyond which I could not bear to be actively displeased with myself, and when that time began to announce its approach—about seven-fifteen—I went to sleep. Only the profundity and limited duration of my moods kept me from being a suicide: as it was, this practice of mine of going to bed when things got too awful, this deliberate termination of my day, was itself a kind of suicide, and served its purpose as efficiently. My moods were little men, and when I killed them they stayed completely dead.

The buzzer from the front door woke me at nine o'clock, and by the time I got up and put a robe on, Joe Morgan and his wife were at my door. I was surprised, but I invited them in cheerfully, because I knew as soon as I opened my eyes that sleep had changed my emotional scenery: I felt fine. Rennie Morgan, to whom I was introduced, was by no means my idea of a beautiful woman; she looked like an outdoorsman's wife. Rather large-framed, blond, heavier than I, strong-looking, and exuberant, she was not the type of woman whom one (or at least *this* one) thinks of instinctively in sexual terms. Yet of course there I was, appraising her in sexual terms: no doubt my afternoon's adventure influenced both the nature and the verdict of my appraisal.

"Can I offer you anything to eat?" I asked her, and I was pleased to see that both of them were apparently in good spirits.

"No, thanks," Joe smiled; "we've eaten enough for three already."

"We saw your car out front," Rennie said, "and wondered whether the plane had gotten in from Baltimore yet."

"You Morgans will track a man to his very lair!" I protested.

Because we all seemed to be feeling friendly, and because Joe and Rennie had the good sense not to make a *cause célèbre* out of a *fait accompli*, if I may say so, I fetched bottles of ale from the case I had on ice down in the kitchen and told them the story of my day, omitting none but the most indelicate details (and those more from my own embarrassment than from Rennie's, who seemed able to take it straight), by way of entertainment.

We got on extremely well. Rennie Morgan, though lively, seemed to be a trifle unsure of herself; her mannerisms—like the habit of showing excruciating hilarity by squinting her eyes shut and whipping her head from side to side, or her intensely excited gestures when speaking—were borrowed directly from Joe, as were both the matter and the manner of her thinking. It was clear that in spite of the progress she'd evidently made toward being indistinguishable from her husband, she was still apprehensive about the disparity between them. Whenever Joe took issue with a statement she'd made, Rennie would argue the point as vigorously as possible, knowing that that was what he expected her to do, but there was in her manner the same nervous readiness to concede that one might expect in a boy sparring with his gym teacher. The metaphor, in fact, if you add to it a touch of Pygmalion and Galatea, pretty well covers everything about their relationship that I could see that evening, and though I'd no ultimate objection at all to such a relationship—after all, Galatea *was* a remarkable woman, and some uneasy young pugilists grow up to be Gene Tunney—the presence of two so similarly forceful people was overwhelming: I several times caught myself whipping *my* head from side to side as they did, at some especially witty remark, or gesticulating excitedly after their fashion while making a point.

As for Joe, the first hour of conversation made it clear that he was brilliant, one of the most brilliant people I'd met. He spoke slowly and softly as a rule, with a slight Southern accent, but one had always the feeling that this slowness did not come naturally to him; that it was a control which he maintained over his normal ebullience. Only when the turn of the conversation excited him did his speech rise in volume and rapidity: at these times he was likely to scratch his head vigorously, jab his spectacles hard back on his nose, and gesture eloquently with his hands. I learned that he'd taken his bachelor's and master's degrees at Columbia—the one in literature, the other in philosophy—and had completed all the requirements except the dissertation for a doctorate in history at Johns Hopkins. Wicomico was Rennie's home town and WTC her alma mater: the Morgans were staying there while Joe made a leisurely job of the dissertation. Talking with him for an evening was tremendously stimulating—I was continually impressed by his drive, his tough intellectuality, and his deliberateness—and, like any very stimulating thing, it was exhausting.

We took to each other at once: it was clear in a very short time that if I remained in Wicomico we would be friends. My initial estimate of him I had completely to revise; it turned out that those activities of his and aspects of his personality about which I had found it easy to make commonplace criticisms were nearly always the result of very careful, uncommon thinking. One understood that Joe Morgan would never make a move or utter a statement, if he could help it, that he hadn't considered deliberately and penetratingly beforehand, and he had, therefore, the strength not to be much bothered if his move proved unfortunate. He would never have allowed himself to get into a position like Miss Rankin's, for example, or like mine when I was circling around the college driveway on Monday. Indecision of that sort was apparently foreign to him: he was always sure of his ground; he acted quickly, explained his actions lucidly if questioned, and would have regarded apologies for missteps as superfluous. Moreover, four of my least fortunate traits—shyness, fear of appearing ridiculous, affinity for many sorts of nonsense, and almost complete inconsistency—he seemed not to share at all. On the other hand, he was, at least in the presence of a third party, somewhat prudish (he didn't enjoy my story) and, despite his excitability, seemingly lacking in warmth and spontaneity, though he doubtless had as clear reasons for being so as he had for being a scoutmaster—he was a man whom it was exceedingly difficult to criticize. Finally, for better or worse he seemed completely devoid of craft or guile, and in that sense ingenuous, though by no means naïve, and had no interest in any sort of career as such.

All this was exhausting, most exhausting, to encounter. We talked concentratedly until one-thirty in the morning (I could not begin to remember what about), and when the Morgans left

I felt that the evening had been the pleasantest I'd spent in
months; that in Joe I'd found an extremely interesting new acquaintance; and that I had no special wish to see this interesting
new acquaintance of mine again for at least a week.

As they were leaving, Rennie happened to say, "Oh, Jake, we
forgot to congratulate you about your job." (This sort of over-
sight, I later learned, was characteristic of the Morgans.)

"You're jumping the gun, aren't you?"

"What do you mean?" Joe asked. "Didn't Dr. Schott ever get
hold of you?"

"Nope."

"Well, you got the job. The Committee met this morning and
decided. I guess Schott called while you were in Ocean City, or
while you were asleep this evening."

They both congratulated me, awkwardly—for they were unable
to express affection, friendship, or even congratulation easily—and
then left. I still felt too fine to sleep, so I read my *World Almanac*
for a while and listened to Mozart's *Ein Musikalischer Spass*
on the record player. I was beginning to feel at home in my room
and in Wicomico; the Morgans pleased me; and I was still in an
unusual state of excitement from the afternoon's sexual adventure
and Joe's intelligence. But I must have been thoroughly fatigued
by these things, too, and from my day on the beach, for at six-
thirty in the morning I woke with a start, having dropped un-
intentionally into a sound sleep. The *World Almanac* was still
in my lap, open to page 96: "Air Line Distances Between Principal Cities of the World"; *Ein Musikalischer Spass* was playing for what must have been the fiftieth time; and the sun, just
rising between two dark brick houses across the street, shot a
blinding beam directly over my lap into Laocoön's face, contorted
noncommittally in bright plaster.

4. *I Got Up, Stiff from Sleeping in the Chair*

I GOT UP, STIFF FROM SLEEPING IN THE CHAIR, showered, changed my clothes, and went out for breakfast. Perhaps because the previous day had been, for me, so unusually eventful, or perhaps because I'd had relatively little sleep (I must say I take no great interest in causes), my mind was empty. All the way to the restaurant, all through the meal, all the way home, it was as though there were no Jacob Horner today. After I'd eaten I returned to my room, sat in my rocker, and rocked, barely sentient, for a long time, thinking of nothing.

Once I had a dream in which it became a matter of some importance to me to learn the weather prediction for the following day. I searched the newspapers for the weather report, but couldn't find it in its usual place. I turned the radio on, but the news broadcasters made no mention of tomorrow's weather. I dialed the Weather number on the telephone (this dream took place in Baltimore), but although the recording described the current weather conditions it told me nothing about the forecast for the next day. Finally I called the Weather Bureau directly, but it was late at night and no one answered. I happened to know the chief meteorologist's name, and so I called his house. The telephone rang many times before he answered; it seemed to me that I detected an uneasiness in his voice.

"What is it?" he asked.

"I want to know what weather we'll be having tomorrow," I demanded. "It's terribly important."

"There's no use your trying to impress me," the meteorologist said. "No use at all. What made you suspicious?"

"I assure you sir, I just want to know what the weather will be tomorrow. I can't say I see anything suspicious in that question."

"There isn't going to be any weather tomorrow."

"What?"

"You heard me. There isn't going to be any weather tomorrow. All our instruments agree. No weather."

"But that's impossible!"

"I've said what I've said," the weatherman grumbled. "No weather tomorrow, and that's that. Leave me alone; I have to sleep."

That was the end of the dream, and I woke up very much upset. I tell it now to illustrate a difference between moods and the weather, their usual analogy: a day without weather is unthinkable, but for me at least there were frequently days without any mood at all. On these days Jacob Horner, except in a meaningless metabolistic sense, ceased to exist, for I was without a personality. Like those microscopic specimens that biologists must dye in order to make them visible at all, I had to be colored with some mood or other if there was to be a recognizable self to me. The fact that my successive and discontinuous selves were linked to one another by the two unstable threads of body and memory; the fact that in the nature of Western languages the word *change* presupposes something upon which the changes operate; the fact that although the specimen is invisible without the dye, the dye is not the specimen—these are considerations of which I was aware, but in which I had no interest.

On my weatherless days my body sat in a rocking chair and rocked and rocked and rocked, and my mind was as nearly empty as interstellar space. Such was the day after the Morgans' visit: I sat and rocked from eight-thirty in the morning until perhaps two in the afternoon. If I looked at Laocoön at all, it was without recognition. But at two o'clock the telephone rang and startled into being a Jacob Horner, who jumped from the chair and answered it.

"Hello?"

"Jacob? This is Rennie Morgan. Will you have dinner with us tonight?"

"*Why*, for God's sake?" This Jacob Horner was an irritable type.

"Why?"

"Yes. Why the hell are you all so anxious to feed me dinner?"

"Are you angry?"

"No, I'm not angry. I just want to know why you're all so anxious to feed me a dinner."

"Don't you want to come?"

"I didn't say that. Why are you all so anxious to feed me a dinner? That's all I asked."

There was a pause. Rennie was one who took all questions seriously; she would not offer an answer simply to terminate a situation, but must search herself for the truth. This, I take it, was Joe's doing. Another person would have asked pettishly, "Why does anybody ask anybody for dinner?" and thereby cloaked ignorance in the garb of self-evidence. After a minute she replied in a careful voice, as though examining her answer as she spoke.

"Well, I think it's because Joe's pretty much decided that he wants to get to know you well. He enjoyed the conversation last night."

"Didn't you?" I interrupted out of curiosity. I didn't really see how she could have, for we had talked of nothing but abstract ideas, and Rennie's determined but limited participation had been under what struck me as a tacit but very careful scrutiny from her husband. I don't mean to suggest that there was anything ungenuine in Rennie's interest, though it was awfully *deliberate*, or anything of the husband embarrassed by his wife's opinions in Joe's concern about her statements; his attention was that of a tutor listening to his favorite protégé, and when he questioned her opinions he did so in an entirely impersonal, unarrogant, and unpedantic manner. Joe was not a pedant.

"Yes, I believe I did. Do you think that there ought to be a kind of waiting period between visits, Jacob?"

I was amazed. "What do *you* think?"

Again a short pause, and then a solemn opinion.

"It seems to me that there wouldn't be any reason for it unless one of us just happened to feel like not seeing the other for a while. I think sometimes a person feels that way. Is that how you feel, Jake?"

"Well, now, let me see," I said soberly, and paused. "It seems to me that you do right to question the validity of social conventions, like waiting a certain time between visits, but you have to keep in mind that they're all ultimately unjustifiable. But it doesn't follow that because a thing is unjustifiable it's without value. And you have to remember that *dispensing* with a convention, even a silly one, always involves the risk of being made to feel unreasonably guilty, simply because the conventions *do* happen to be conventions. Take drinking beer for breakfast, for instance, or going through red lights late at night, or committing adultery with your husband's approval, or performing a euthanasia . . ."

"Are you making fun of me?" Rennie demanded mildly, as though asking purely for information.

"I am indeed!"

"You know, it seems to me that lots of times a person makes fun of another person because the other person's opinions make him uncomfortable but he doesn't really know how to refute them. He feels that he *ought* to know how, but he doesn't, and instead of admitting that to himself and studying the problem and working out a real refutation, he just sneers at the other person's argument. It's too easy to sneer at an argument. I feel that way a lot about you, Jake."

"Yes. Joe said the same thing."

"Now you *are* making fun of me, aren't you?"

I was resolved not to let Mrs. Rennie Morgan make me uncomfortable again. That was too easy.

"Listen, I'll come eat your dinner tonight. I'll come at six o'clock, after you've put your kids to bed, as you said."

"We neither one want you to come if you don't feel like it, Jake. You have to be——"

"Now wait a minute. *Why* don't you want me to come even if I don't feel like it?"

"What?"

"I said why don't you want me to come even if I don't feel

like it? You see, the only grounds you'd have for breaking the custom of waiting a proper interval between visits would be if you took the position that social conventions might be necessary for stability in a social group, but that they aren't absolutes and you can dispense with them in special situations where your end justifies it. In other words, you're willing to have me to dinner tonight anyhow as long as that's what we all want—social stability isn't your end in this special situation. Well, then, suppose your end was to have another conversation and you had reason to believe that once I got there I'd talk to you whether I'd really wanted to come or not—most guests would—then it shouldn't matter to you whether I wanted to come or not, since your ends would be reached anyway."

"You're still making fun of me."

"Oh, now, that's too easy an out. It's beside the point whether I'm making fun of you or not. You're evading the question."

No answer.

"Now, I'm coming to dinner at six o'clock, whether I want to or not, and if you aren't ready to answer my argument by then, I'm going to tell Joe."

"Six-thirty is when the kids go to bed," Rennie said in a slightly injured voice, and hung up. I went back to my rocker and rocked for another forty-five minutes. From time to time I smiled inscrutably, but I cannot say that this honestly reflected any sincere feeling on my part. It was just a thing I found myself doing, as frequently when walking alone I would find myself repeating over and over in a judicious, unmetrical voice, *Pepsi-Cola hits the spot; twelve full ounces: that's a lot*—accompanying the movement of my lips with a wrinkled brow, distracted twitches of the corner of my mouth, and an occasional quick gesture of my right hand. Passers-by often took me for a man lost in serious problems, and sometimes when I looked behind me after passing one I'd see him, too, make a furtive movement with his right hand, trying it out.

At four-fifteen Dr. Schott telephoned and confirmed my appointment to the faculty of the Wicomico State Teachers College as a teacher of grammar and composition, at a starting salary of $3200 per year.

"You know," he said, "we don't pay what they pay at the big

universities! Can't afford it! But that doesn't mean we're not choosy about our teachers! We're a pretty dedicated bunch, frankly, and we hired you because we believe you share our feelings about the importance of our job!"

I assured him that I did indeed share that feeling, and he assured me that he was sure I did. I was not pleased at being asked to teach composition as well as grammar—I was supposed to be strictly a prescriptive-grammar man—but, pending advice from the Doctor, I thought it best to accept the job anyway.

As a matter of fact I drove out to the Morgans' place at five-thirty, for no particular reason. My day was no longer weather-less, but I was quiescent. I found Joe and Rennie having a leisurely catch with a football on the lawn in front of their house, although the afternoon was fairly warm. They showed no great surprise at seeing me, greeted me cordially, and invited me to join their game.

"No, thanks," I said, and went over to where their two sons, ages three and four, were throwing their own little football at each other—adeptly for their age. I sat on the grass and watched everybody.

"I didn't mean to get upset on the phone today, Jake," Rennie said cheerfully between passes.

"Ah, don't pay attention to what I say on telephones," I said. "I can't talk on telephones."

I've never seen a girl who could catch and throw a football properly except Rennie Morgan. As a rule she was a clumsy animal, but in any sort of strenuous physical activity she was completely at ease and even graceful. She caught and threw the ball in the same manner and with the same speed and accuracy as a practiced man.

"What have you changed your mind about that you said, then?" Joe asked, keeping his eyes on the ball.

"I don't even remember what I said."

"You don't? Rennie remembers the whole conversation. Do you really not remember, or are you trying not to make her uncomfortable?"

"I really don't remember at all," I said, with some truth. "I've learned by now that you all don't believe in avoiding discomfort.

The fact is I can never remember arguments, my own or anybody else's. I can remember conclusions, but not arguments."

This observation, which I thought arresting enough, seemed to disgust Joe. He lost interest in the conversation and stopped to correct the older boy's way of gripping the football. The kid attended his father's quiet advice as though it were coming from Knute Rockne; Joe watched him throw the ball correctly three times and then turned away.

"Here, Jake," he said, tossing me the other ball. "Why don't you pitch a few with Rennie while I put supper on, and then we'll have a drink. No use to wait till six-thirty, since you're here."

I was, as I said before, quiescent. I would not voluntarily have joined the game, but neither would I go out of my way to avoid playing. Joe went on into the house, the two boys following close behind, and for the next twenty minutes Rennie and I threw the football to each other. Luckily—for as a rule I dreaded being made to look ridiculous—I was no novice at football myself; though not so adept a passer as Joe, I was able to throw at least as accurately and unwobblingly as Rennie. She seemed to have nothing special to say to me, nor did I to her, and so the only sound heard on the lawn was the rush of passing-arms, the quiet spurts of running feet on the grass, the soft smack of catches, and our heavy breathing. It was all neither pleasant nor unpleasant.

Presently Joe called to us from the porch, and we went in to dinner. The Morgans rented half of the first floor of the house. Their apartment was very clean; what furniture they owned was the most severely plain modern, tough and functional, but there was very little of it. In fact, because the rooms were relatively large they seemed quite bare. There were no rugs on the hardwood floors, no curtains or drapes on the polished windows, and not a piece of furniture above the necessary minimum; a day bed, two sling chairs, two lamps, a bookcase, and a writing table in the living room; a small dining table and four metal folding chairs in the kitchen; and a double bunk, two bureaus, and a work table with benches in the single bedroom, where the boys slept. Because the walls and ceiling were white, the light pouring through the open venetian blinds made the living room blindingly bright. I squinted; there was too much light in that room for me.

While we drank a glass of beer, the children went into the bedroom, undressed themselves, and bathed themselves without help in the water that Joe had already drawn for them. I expressed surprise at such independence at ages three and four. Rennie shrugged.

"We make pretty heavy demands on them for physical efficiency," Joe admitted. "What the hell, in New Guinea the kids are swimming before they walk, and paddling bamboo logs out in the ocean at Joey's age. We figured the less they're in our hair the better we'll get along with each other."

"Don't think we drive them," Rennie said. "We don't really give a damn. But I guess we demand a lot tacitly."

Joe listened to this remark with casual interest.

"Why do you say you don't give a damn?" he asked her.

Rennie was a little startled at the question, which she had not expected.

"Well—I mean *ultimately*. Ultimately it wouldn't matter one way or the other, would it? But *immediately* it matters because if they weren't independent we'd have to go through the same rigmarole most people go through, and the kids would be depending on all kinds of crutches."

"Nothing matters one way or the other ultimately," Joe pointed out. "The other importance is all there is to anything."

"That's what I meant, Joe."

"What I'm trying to say is that you shouldn't consider a value less real just because it isn't absolute, since less-than-absolutes are all we've got. That's what's implied when you say you don't *really* give a damn."

Well, it was Rennie's ball—I watched them over my beer much as I'd watched them out on the lawn—but the game was interrupted by the timer bell on the kitchen stove. Rennie went out to serve up the dinner while Joe dried the two boys and assisted them into their pajamas: their physical efficiency apparently didn't extend to fastening their own snaps in the back.

"Why don't you have them snap each other up in the back?" I suggested politely. Rennie flashed me an uncertain look from the kitchen, where she was awkwardly dishing out rice with a spoon too small for the job, but Joe laughed easily and unsnapped both boys' pajama shirts so that they could try it. It worked.

Since there were only four chairs in the kitchen, Rennie and the two boys and I ate at the table while Joe ate standing up at the stove. There would have been no room at the table for one of the sling chairs, and anyhow it did not take long to eat the meal, which consisted of steamed shrimp, boiled rice, and beer for all hands. The boys—husky, well-mannered youngsters—were allowed to dominate the conversation during dinner; they were as lively and loud as any other bright kids their age, but a great deal more physically co-ordinated and self-controlled than most. As soon as we finished eating they went to bed, and though it was still quite light outside, I heard no more from them.

The Morgans had an arrangement with their first-floor neighbor whereby they could leave open a door connecting the two apartments and listen for each other's children if one couple wished to go out for the evening. Taking advantage of this, we went walking through a clover field and a small stand of pines behind the house after the supper dishes were washed. The Morgans tended to walk vigorously, and this did not fit well with my quiescent mood, but neither did refusing to accompany them. Rennie, an amateur naturalist, remarked on various weeds, bugs, and birds as we bounded along, and Joe confirmed her identifications. I can't say I enjoyed the walk, although the Morgans enjoyed it almost fiercely. When it was over, Rennie went inside the house to write a letter, and Joe and I sat on the lawn in the two sling chairs. Our conversation, by his direction, dealt with values, since they'd come up earlier.

"Most of what you told Rennie on the phone this afternoon was sensible," he granted. "I'm glad you talked to her, and I'm glad you told her it was beside the point whether you were making fun of her or not. That's exactly what she needs to learn. She's too sensitive about that."

"So are you," I said. "Remember the Boy Scouts."

"No, I'm not, really," Joe denied, in a way that left you no special desire to insist that he was. "The only reason I caught it up about the Scouts was that I'd decided I wanted to know you a little bit, and it seemed to me that too much of that might stand in the way of any sensible talking. It doesn't matter at all outside of that."

"Okay." I offered him a cigarette, but he didn't smoke.

"What really pleases me is that in spite of your making fun of Rennie you seem willing to take her seriously. Almost no man is willing to take any woman's thinking seriously, and that's what Rennie needs more than anything else."

"It's none of my business, Joe," I said quiescently, "but if I were Rennie I'd object like hell having anybody so concerned over my *needs*. You talk about her as if she were a patient of yours."

He laughed and jabbed his spectacles back on his nose. "I guess I do; I don't mean to. When Rennie and I were married we understood that neither of us wanted to make a permanent thing of it if we couldn't respect each other in every way. Certainly I'm not sold on marriage-under-any-circumstances, and I'm sure Rennie's not either. There's nothing intrinsically valuable about marriage."

"Seems to me you put a pretty high value on *your* marriage," I suggested.

Joe squinted at me in disappointment, and I felt that had I been his wife he would have corrected me more severely than he did.

"Now you're making the same error Rennie made a while ago, before supper: the fallacy that because a value isn't intrinsic, objective, and absolute, it somehow isn't *real*. What I said was that the marriage relationship isn't any more of an absolute than anything else. That doesn't mean that I don't value it; in fact I guess I value my relationship with Rennie more than anything else in the world. All it means is that once you admit it's no absolute, you have to decide for yourself the conditions under which marriage is important to you. Okay?"

"Suits me," I said indifferently.

"Well, do you agree or not?"

"Sure, I agree." And, so cornered, I suppose I *did* agree, but there was something in me that would have recoiled from so systematic an analysis of things even if I'd had it straight from God that such happened to be the case.

"Well," Joe said, "I'm not a man who needs to be married under any circumstances—in fact, under a lot of circumstances I couldn't tolerate being married—and one of my conditions for preserving any relationship at all, but particularly a marriage relationship, would be that the parties involved be able to take each other seriously. If I straighten Rennie out now and then, or tell her that some statement of hers is stupid as hell, or even slug her one, it's because I respect her, and to me that means not making a lot of kinds of allowances for her. Making allowances might be Christian, but to me it would always mean not taking seriously the person you make allowances for. That's the only objection I have to your making fun of Rennie: not that it might hurt her feelings, but that it means you're making allowances for her being a *woman*, or some such nonsense as that."

"Aren't you regarding this take-us-seriously business as an absolute?" I asked. "You seem to want you and Rennie to take each other seriously under any circumstances."

This observation pleased Joe, and to my chagrin I noticed that I was unaccountably happy that I'd said something he considered bright.

"That's a good point," he grinned, and began his harangue. "The usual criticism of people like me is that somewhere at the end of the line is the *ultimate* end that gives the whole chain its relative value, and this ultimate end is rationally unjustifiable if there aren't any absolute values. These ends can be pretty impersonal, like 'the good of the state,' or else personal, like taking your wife seriously. In either case if you're going to defend these ends at all I think you have to call them subjective. But they'd never be *logically* defensible; they'd be in the nature of psychological *givens*, different for most people. Four things that I'm not impressed by," he added, "are unity, harmony, eternality, and universality. In my ethics the most a man can ever do is be right from his point of view; there's no general reason why he should even bother to defend it, much less expect anybody else to accept it, but the only thing he can do is operate by it, because there's nothing else. He's got to expect conflict with people or institutions who are also right from *their* points of view, but whose points of view are different from his.

"Suppose it were the essence of my nature that I was completely jealous of Rennie, for instance," he went on. "Now it happens that that's not the case at all, but suppose it were true that because of my psychological make-up, marital fidelity was one of the *givens,* the subjective equivalent of an absolute, one of the conditions that would attach to any string of ethical propositions I might make for myself. Then suppose Rennie committed adultery behind my back. From my point of view the relationship would have lost its *raison d'être,* and I'd probably walk out flat, if I didn't actually shoot her or shoot myself. But from the state's point of view, for example, I'd still be obligated to support her, because you can't have a society where people just walk out flat on family relationships like that. From their point of view I should be forced to pay support money, and I would have no reason to complain that their viewpoint isn't the same as mine: it couldn't be. In the same way, the state would be as justified in hanging me or jailing me for shooting her as I would be in shooting her—do you see? Or the Catholic Church, if I were officially a Catholic, would be as justified from their point of view in refusing me sacred burial ground as I'd be in committing suicide if the marriage relationship had been one of the *givens* for my whole life. I'd be a fool if I expected the world to excuse my actions simply because I can explain them clearly.

"That's one reason why I don't apologize for things," Joe said finally. "It's because I've no right to expect you or anybody to accept anything I do or say—but I can always *explain* what I do or say. There's no sense in apologizing, because nothing is ultimately defensible. But a man can act coherently; he can act in ways that he can explain, if he wants to. This is important to me. Do you know, for the first month of our marriage Rennie used to apologize all over herself to friends who dropped in, because we didn't have much furniture in the house. She knew very well that we didn't want any more furniture even if we could have afforded it, but she always apologized to other people for not having their point of view. One day she did it more elaborately than usual, and as soon as the company left I popped her one on the jaw. Laid her out cold. When she came to, I explained to her very carefully why I'd hit her. She cried, and apologized to me for having apologized to other people. I popped her again."

There was no boastfulness in Joe's voice when he said this; neither was there any regret.

"What the hell, Jake, the more sophisticated your ethics get, the stronger you have to be to stay afloat. And when you say good-by to objective values, you really have to flex your muscles and keep your eyes open, because you're on your own. It takes *energy*: not just personal energy, but cultural energy, or you're lost. Energy's what makes the difference between American pragmatism and French existentialism—where the hell else but in America could you have a cheerful nihilism, for God's sake? I suppose it was rough, slugging Rennie, but I saw the moment as a kind of crisis. Anyhow, she stopped apologizing after that."

"Ah," I said.

Now it may well be that Joe made no such long coherent speech as this all at once; it is certainly true that during the course of the evening this was the main thing that got said, and I put it down here in the form of one uninterrupted whiz-bang for convenience's sake, both to illustrate the nature of his preoccupations and to add a stroke or two to my picture of the man himself. I heard it all quiescently; despite the fact that I was accustomed to expressing certain of these opinions myself at times (more hopefully than honestly), arguments against nearly everything he said occurred to me as he spoke. Yet I would by no means assert that he couldn't have refuted my objections—I daresay even I could have. As was usually the case when I was confronted by a really intelligent and lucidly exposed position, I was as reluctant to give it more than notional assent as I was unable to offer a more reasonable position of my own. In such situations I most often adopted what in psychology is known as the "non-directive technique": I merely said, "Oh?" or "Ah," and gave the horse his head.

But I was interested in the story of Rennie's first encounter with the Morgan philosophy, and the irresistible rhetoric Joe had employed to open her eyes to the truth about apologies. It demonstrated clearly that philosophizing was no game to Mr. Morgan; that he lived his conclusions down to the fine print; and Rennie became a somewhat more interesting figure to me. Indeed, I should say that that particular little anecdote was doubtless the main thing that made me amenable to a proposal which Joe made later on, after Rennie had joined us out on the lawn.

"Do you like horseback-riding, Jake?" Rennie had happened to ask.

"Never rode before, Rennie."

"Gee, it's fun; you'll have to try it with me sometime."

I raised my eyebrows. "Yes, I suppose it would be better to do that before I tried it with a horse."

Rennie giggled, whipping her head from side to side, and Joe laughed loudly, but not, I think, enthusiastically. Then I saw his frowning forehead suddenly illuminate.

"Hey, that's an idea!" he exclaimed to Rennie. "Teach Jake how to ride!" He turned to me. "Rennie's folks have riding horses on their farm, down the road, but I seldom get a chance to ride and Rennie hates to ride by herself. I'm busy nearly all day reading for my thesis before school starts. Why don't you let Rennie teach you to ride? It'll give her a chance to get outdoors more, and you all will be able to do some talking."

I was embarrassed both by Joe's deliberate enthusiasm for his project and by his poor taste in implying that talking to me would do Rennie good. It pleased me, perversely, to see Rennie squirm a little, too: she was apparently not yet so well educated by her husband that his ingenuousness did not sometimes embarrass her, though she was careful to conceal her discomfort from Joe.

"What do you think?" he demanded of her.

"I think it's a swell idea, if Jake wants to learn," Rennie said quickly.

"*Do* you?" Joe asked me.

I shrugged. "Doesn't make a damn to me."

"Well, if it doesn't make a damn to you, and Rennie and I think it's a good idea, then it's settled," Joe laughed. "In fact, whether you want to learn or not it's settled, if you're not willing to refuse, just like this dinner business!"

We all chuckled, and the subject was dropped, Joe explaining to me happily that as a matter of fact my statement on the telephone (that I would come to dinner whether I wanted to or not) was unintelligible.

"Rennie would've told you if you hadn't flustered her by making fun of her," he smiled; "the only demonstrable index to a man's desires is his acts, when you're speaking of past time: what a man did is what he wanted to do."

"What?"

"Don't you see?" asked Rennie, and Joe sat back and relaxed. "The idea is that you could have conflicting desires—say, the desire not to have dinner with us and the desire not to offend us. If you end by coming to dinner it's because the second desire was stronger than the first: other things being equal, you wouldn't want to eat with us, but other things never are equal, and actually you'd rather eat with us than insult us. So you eat with us—that's what you *finally* wanted to do. You shouldn't say you'll eat with us whether you want to or not; you should say you'll eat with us if it satisfies desires in you stronger than your desire *not* to eat with us."

"It's like combining plus one hundred and minus ninety-nine," Joe said. "The answer is just barely plus, but it's completely plus. That's another reason why it's silly for anybody to apologize for something he's done by claiming he didn't really want to do it: what he *wanted* to do, in the end, was what he did. That's important to remember when you're reading history."

I observed that Rennie colored slightly at the reference to apologizing.

"Mmm," I replied to Joe, non-directively.

5. The Clumsy Force of Rennie Was a Thing That Attracted Me

THE CLUMSY FORCE OF RENNIE WAS A THING THAT ATTRACTED ME during the weeks following this dinner of shrimp, rice, beer, and values that the Morgans had fed me. It was a clumsiness both of action and of articulation—Rennie lurched and blurted—and I was curious to know whether what lay behind it was ineptitude or graceless strength.

At least this was my attitude when we began my riding lessons. My mood was superior, in that I regarded myself as the examiner and her as the subject, but it was not supercilious, and there was a certain sympathy in my curiosity. That I felt this special superiority is fortunate, because it got me through the first lessons on horseback, which otherwise would have been difficult to face indeed. I hated not the work but the embarrassment of learning new things, the ludicrousness of the tyro, and I can't imagine ever having learned to ride horses (for I had only the most vagrant interest in riding) without this special curiosity and special superiority feeling to salve my pride.

Rennie was an excellent rider and a most competent teacher. We rode mostly in the mornings, fairly early, and occasionally after supper, and we rode every day unless it was raining very hard. I would drive to the Morgans' place at seven-thirty or eight in the morning, sometimes earlier, and have breakfast with them; then Joe would begin his day's reading and note taking, and Rennie, the boys, and I would drive the four miles out to her parents' farm. Mrs. MacMahon, her mother, took charge of the children, and Rennie and I went riding. Her horse was a spirited

five-year-old dun stallion of fifteen hands (her description) named
Tom Brown, and mine a seven-year-old chestnut mare with a
white race down her face, sixteen hands high, named Susie, whom
both Rennie and her father described as gentle, although she was
plenty lively enough for me. Rennie's father kept the two horses
for his own pleasure but rarely had a chance to exercise them
properly, and so was pleased with Joe's project. The first thing
he said to Rennie when he saw us approach in our riding outfits
(Rennie had insisted that I purchase cotton jodhpurs and riding
boots) was "Well, Ren, I see Joe recruited you a companion!"

"This is Jake Horner, Dad," Rennie said briskly. "I'm going to
teach him how to ride." She was aware that her father's remark
had told me something I wasn't especially intended to know—
that Joe's project hadn't occurred to him on the spur of the
moment, but had been premeditated—and being conscious of this
made her awkward. She moved off immediately to the paddock
where the two horses were grazing, leaving her father and me to
shake hands and make pleasantries as best we could.

There is no need for me to go into any detail about my instruction: it is uninteresting and has little to do with my observation of Rennie. About the only prior knowledge I had of horses
was that one mounted them from the "near," or left, side, and
even that little piece of equine lore I found to be not so invariably true as I'd believed. I was introduced to the mysteries of
Pelhams and hackamores, snaffles and curbs, of collected and
extended gaits, of the aids and the leads. I made all the mistakes
that beginners make—hanging on by the reins, clinging with my
legs, lounging in the saddle—and slowly corrected them. That I
was at first very much afraid of my animal is irrelevant, since
I'd not under any circumstances have shown my fear to Rennie.

She herself was a "strong" rider—she applied the aids heavily
and kept frisky Tom Brown as gentle as a lap dog—but most
of her abrupt instructions to me were aimed at making me use
them lightly.

"Stop digging her in the barrel," she'd blurt out as we trotted
along. "You're telling her to go with your heels and holding her
back with your hands."

Hour after hour I practiced riding at a walk, a trot, and a

canter (both horses were three-gaited), bareback and without holding the reins. I learned how to lead a horse who doesn't care to follow; how to anticipate and prevent shying and bucking and running away; how to saddle and bridle and currycomb.

Susie, my mare, had a tendency to nip me when I tightened her girth.

"Slap her hard on the nose," Rennie ordered, "and next time hold your left arm stiff up on her neck and she won't turn her head."

Tom Brown, her stallion, liked to rear high two or three times just out of the stable. Once when he did this I was horrified to see Rennie lean as far back as she could on the reins, until Tom was actually overbalanced and came toppling over backwards, whinnying and flailing. Rennie sprang dextrously out of the saddle and out of the way a second before eleven hundred pounds of horse hit the ground: she caught Tom's reins before he was up, and in a few seconds, by soft talking, had him quiet.

"That'll fix him," she grinned.

But "It's your own fault," she told me when Susie once tried the same trick. "She knows you're just learning. No need to flip her over; she'll behave when you've learned to ride her a little more strongly." Thank heaven for that, because if Rennie had told me to flip Susie over, my pride would have made me attempt it. I scared easily; in fact, I was extremely timid as a rule, but my vanity usually made this fact beside the point.

At any rate, I became a reasonably proficient horseman and even learned to be at ease on horseback, but I never became an enthusiast. The sport was pleasant, but not worth the trouble of learning. Rennie and I covered a good deal of countryside during August; usually we rode out for an hour and a half, dismounted for a fifteen- or twenty-minute rest, and then rode home. By the time we finished unsaddling, grooming, and feeding the animals it was early afternoon: we would pick up the boys, ride back to Wicomico, and eat a late lunch with Joe, during which, bleary-eyed from reading, he would question Rennie or me about my progress.

But the subject at hand is Rennie's clumsy force. On horseback, where there are traditional and even reasonable rules for one's posture every minute of the time, it was a pleasure to see her strong, rather heavy body sitting perfectly controlled in the saddle at the walk or posting to the trot, erect and easy, her cheeks ruddy in the wind, her brown eyes flashing, her short-cropped blond hair bright in the sun. At such times she assumed a strong kind of beauty. But she could not handle her body in situations where there were no rules. When she walked she was continually lurching ahead. Standing still, she never knew what to do with her arms, and she was likely to lean all her weight on one leg and thrust the other awkwardly out at the side. During our brief rest periods, when we usually sat on the ground and smoked cigarettes, she was simply without style or grace: she flopped and fidgeted. I think it was her self-consciousness about this inability to handle her body that prompted her to talk more freely and confidentially during our rides than she would have otherwise, for both Morgans were normally unconfiding people, and Rennie was even inclined to be taciturn when Joe was with us. But in these August mornings we talked a great deal— in that sense, if not in some others, Joe's program was successful— and Rennie's conversation often displayed an analogous clumsy force.

One of our most frequent rides took us to a little creek in a loblolly-pine woods some nine miles from the farm. There the horses could drink on hot days, and often we wore bathing suits under our riding gear and took a short swim when we got there, dressing afterwards, very properly, back in the woods. This was quite pleasant: the little creek was fairly clean and entirely private, shaded by the pines, which also carpeted the ground with a soft layer of slick brown shats. I remarked to Rennie once that it was a pity Joe couldn't enjoy the place with us.

"That's a silly thing to say," she said, a little upset.

"As all politeness is silly," I smiled. "I feel politely sorry for him grinding away at the books while we gallop and splash around."

"Better not tell him that; he hates pity."

"That's a silly way to be, isn't it?" I said mildly. "Joe's funny as hell."

"What do you mean, Jake?" We were resting after a swim; I

was lying comfortably supine under a tree beside the water, chewing on a green pine needle and squinting over at Susie and Tom Brown, tethered nearby. Rennie had been slouched back like a sack of oats against the same tree, smoking, but now she sat up and stared at me with troubled eyes. "How can you possibly call Joe silly, of all people?"

"Do you mean how can I of all people call Joe silly, or how can I call Joe of all people silly?"

"You know what I mean: how can you call Joe silly? Good God!"

"Oh," I laughed. "What could be sillier than getting upset at politeness? If I really felt sorry for him it would be my business, not his; if I'm just saying I feel sorry for him to be polite, there's even less reason to be bothered, since I'm just making so much noise."

"But that kind of noise is absurd, isn't it?"

"Sure. Where did you and Joe get the notion that things should be scrapped just because they're absurd? That's a silly one for you. For that matter, what could be sillier than this whole aim of living coherently?"

Now I know very well what Joe would have answered to these remarks: let me be the first to admit that they are unintelligible. My purpose was not to make a point, but to observe Rennie. She was aghast.

"You're not serious, Jake! Are you serious?"

"And boy oh boy, what could *possibly* be sillier than his notion that two people in the same house can live that way!"

Rennie stood up. Her expression, I should guess, was that of the Athenians on the morning they discovered that Alcibiades had gelded every marble god in town. She was speechless.

"Sit down," I said, laughing at her consternation. "The point is, Rennie, that anybody's position can be silly if you want to think of it that way, and the more consistent, the sillier. It's not silly from Joe's point of view, of course, granted his ends, whatever they are. But frankly I'm appalled that he expects anybody else to go along with him."

"He doesn't!" Rennie cried. "That's the whole idea!"

"Why did he cork you once for apologizing, then—twice, I

mean. Just for the exercise? Why wouldn't you dare tell him you felt sorry for him even if you did?"

I asked these things without genuine malice, only as a sort of tease, but Rennie, to my surprise, burst into tears.

"Whoa, now!" I said gently. "I'm terribly sorry I hurt your feelings, Rennie." I took her arm, but she flinched as if I too had struck her.

"Whoops, I'm sorry I said I'm sorry."

"Jake, stop it!" she cried, and I observed that the squint-eyed head-shaking was used to express pain as well as hilarity, and this it did quite effectively. When she had control of herself she said, "You certainly must think our marriage is a strange one, don't you?"

"Damnedest thing I ever saw," I admitted cheerfully. "But hell, that's no criticism."

"But you think I'm a complete zero, don't you?"

Ah. Something in me responded very strongly to this not-especially-moving question of Rennie's.

"I don't know, Rennie. What's your opinion?"

By way of answer Rennie began what turned out to be the history of her alliance with Joe. Her face, chunky enough to begin with, was red and puffy from crying, and in a more critical mood I would have found her unpleasing to look at just then, but it happened that I was really impressed by her breakdown, and the curious sympathy that I'd felt from the time I first heard of her knockout—a sympathy that had little to do with abstract pity for women—was now operating more noticeably in me. This sympathy, too, I observed impersonally and with some amusement from another part of myself, the same part that observed me being not displeased by Rennie's tearful, distracted face. Here is what she told me, edited and condensed:

"You know, I lived in a complete fog from the day I was born until after I met Joe," she said. "I was popular and all that, but I swear it was just like I was asleep all through school and college. I wasn't really interested in anything, I never thought about anything, I never even particularly wanted to *do* anything—I didn't even especially enjoy myself. I just dreamed along like a big blob of sleep. If I thought about myself at all, I guess I lived on my potentialities, because I never felt dissatisfied with myself."

"Sounds wonderful," I said, not sincerely, because in fact it sounded commonplace. It interested me only because it fitted well with the unharnessed animal that I had sometimes thought I glimpsed in Rennie.

"You shouldn't say that," Rennie said flatly. "It wasn't anything, wonderful or otherwise. When I got out of college I went to New York to work, just because my roommate had a job there and wanted me to go along with her, and that's where I met Joe—he was taking his master's degree at Columbia. We dated for a while, pretty casually: I wasn't much interested in him, and I didn't think he saw much in me. Then one night he grinned at me and told me he wouldn't be taking me out any more. I asked him why not, and he said, 'Don't think I'm threatening you; I just don't see any point to it.' I said, 'Is it because I don't sleep with you?' and he said, 'If that was it I'd have gotten a Puerto Rican girl in the first place instead of wasting my time with you.'"

"A good line," I remarked.

"He said he just didn't feel any need for female companionship in itself: companionship to him meant a real exchange of everything on the same level, and sex meant sex, and I wasn't offering him either. You'll have to take my word for it that he wasn't just feeding me a line. He meant it. He said he thought I could probably be wonderful, but that I was shallow as hell as I was, and he didn't expect me to change just for his sake. He couldn't offer me a thing in return that would fit the values I had then, and he wasn't interested in me as I was, so that was that."

"Did you fling yourself at him then?"

"No. I was hurt, and I told him he wasn't so hot himself."

"Good!"

"You're silly to say that, Jake."

"I retract it."

"Don't you see that right now you're doing all the things that Joe would never do? Those pointless remarks, half teasing me. Joe just shrugged his shoulders at what I said and walked off, leaving me on the bench—he didn't give a damn for courtesy."

"On the bench?"

"I forgot to tell you. The night all this happened my roommate
and I were having a party for some reason or other, and all our
New York friends were there—just ordinary people. We'd been
drinking and talking silly and horsing around and all: I can't
even remember what we did, because I was still in my fog then.
About halfway through the evening Joe had said he wanted to go
walking, and I hadn't especially wanted to leave the party, but I
went anyhow. We walked around in Riverside Park for a while,
and when we sat on the bench I thought he was going to neck.
He'd never bothered much with that before, and I was kind of
surprised. But he came out with this other instead and then
walked off. I realized then for the first time what a complete
blank I was!

"I went back to the party and got as drunk as I could, and the
drunker I got, the more awful everybody seemed. I discovered
that I'd never really listened to people before, what they said,
and now when I heard them for the first time it was amazing!
Everything they said was silly. My roommate was the worst of all
—I'd thought she was a pretty bright kid, but now that I was
listening to her she talked nothing but nonsense. I thought if I
heard another word of their talk I'd die.

"Finally, when I was good and drunk, my roommate tried to
get me to take a fellow to bed with me. Everybody else had gone
but two fellows—my roommate's boy friend and this other guy—
and they'd made up their minds to sleep with us. My roommate
was willing if I was willing, and you know, I was disgusted with
her, not because of what she wanted to do but because she was too
dumb to do anything clearly. But Joe had made me feel so awful
and useless, once he'd opened my eyes, that I just didn't give a
damn what happened to me; I assumed he was gone for good.

"It was funny as hell, Jake. I was a virgin, but that had never
meant anything to me one way or the other. This fellow wasn't a
bad guy, just a thin, plain-looking boy who worked in an office
somewhere, and with the liquor in him he was pawing and poking
me like a real he-man. When I decided I didn't care what
happened to me I grabbed him by the hair with both hands and

rubbed noses with him. I was bigger than he was, and he fell
right off the couch!

"My roommate and her boy friend were already in the bedroom,
so I helped the guy take his pants down right in the living room.
He was scared to death of me! He wanted to turn off the lights
and turn on the music and undress me in the dark and spend a
half hour necking before he started and this and that and the
other—I called him a fairy and pulled him right down on the rug
and bit him till the blood came. You know what he did? He just
lay there and hollered!"

"Lord, I don't blame him!" I said.

"Well, I knew if he didn't do something quick it would be too
late, because I was hating myself more every second. But the poor
boy passed out on the floor. I thought it would be fun to straddle
him as he was and give him artificial respiration——"

"My God!"

"I was drunk too, remember. Anyhow, I couldn't make it work
right, and to top things off I got sick all over him."

I shook my head.

"Then I was so disgusted I walked out of the place and went
over to Joe's room—I lived on a Hundred and Tenth and he
lived on a Hundred and Thirteenth, right near Broadway. I
didn't give a damn what *he* did to me then, after this other guy."

"I won't ask you what he did."

"What he did was take one look at me and throw me in the
shower, clothes and all: remember I'd vomited all over myself.
He turned the cold water on and let me sit there while he fixed
some soup and tomato juice, and then he put pajamas and a robe
on me and I ate the soup. That was all. I even slept with him
that night——"

"Hey, Rennie, you don't have to tell me all this."

Rennie looked at me, surprised.

"No, I mean *slept*. He didn't make love to me, but he'd never
have slept in a chair all night just for propriety's sake. Don't
you want to hear this?"

"Sure I do, if you want to tell it to me."

"I do want to tell it to you. I've never told anybody this stuff
before, and Joe and I have never even mentioned it, but nobody

ever suggested to me before that our marriage might look silly, and I think it's important to me to tell you about it. I don't believe I ever even thought about it until you started making fun of us."

"I admire Joe's restraint," I said uncomfortably.

"Jake, he *is* a Boy Scout in some ways, I guess, but he had another reason, too. When I was sober he told me he just wasn't so hard up he had to take advantage of me when I was helpless. He said he'd like to make love to me, but not just for that—anything we did together we had to do on the same level, understanding it in the same way, for the same purpose, nobody making allowances for anybody else, or he just wasn't interested. But he told me he'd like a more or less permanent relationship.

"'Do you mean marry me?' I said. He said, 'It doesn't make a damn to me, Rennie. I'd rather get married, because I don't like the horseshit that goes with most mistress-lover relationships, but you'd have to understand what I mean by a more or less permanent arrangement.' What he meant was that we'd stay together as long as each of us could respect everything about the other, absolutely everything, and working for that respect would be our first interest. He wasn't much interested in just having a wife or a mistress, but this other thing he was intensely interested in.

"Do you know what we did? We talked about it almost steadily for two days and two nights, and all that time he wouldn't touch me or let me touch him. I didn't go to work and he didn't go to class, because we both knew this was more important than anything else we'd ever done. He explained his whole attitude toward things, all of it, and asked me more questions about myself than I'd ever been asked before. 'The world is full of tons and tons of horseshit, and without any purpose,' he said. 'Only a few things could ever be valuable to me, and this is one of them.' We agreed that on every single subject, no matter how small or apparently trivial, we'd compare our ideas absolutely impersonally and examine them as sharply as we could, at least for the first few years, and he warned me that until I got into the habit of articulating very clearly all the time—until I learned *how* to do that—most of the more reasonable-sounding ideas would be his. We would just try to forget about my ideas . . . He wanted me to go back to school and learn a lot of things, not because he thought scholarship was so all-important, but because that happened to be his field, and if I stayed ignorant of it we'd just get farther and farther apart all the time. There was to be no such thing as shop talk, no such thing as *my* interests and *his* interests. What one of us took seriously both ought to be able to take seriously, and our relationship was first on the list, over any career or ambition or anything else. He told me that he would expect me to make the same heavy demands on myself and on him that he made on himself and would make on me, and that they always had to be the same demands."

"God!"

"Do you see what that meant? Joe had no friends, because he would expect a lesser degree of the same kind of thing from a friend—expect them to be sharp and clear all the time. So I scrapped every last one of my friends, because you had to make all kinds of allowances for them; you couldn't take them as seriously as all that. I had to completely change my mind not only about my parents, but about my whole childhood. I'd thought it was a pretty ideal childhood, but now I saw it as just so much cottonwool. I threw out every opinion I owned, because I couldn't defend them. I think I completely erased myself, Jake, right down to nothing, so I could start over. And you know, the thing is I don't think I'll ever really get to be what Joe wants—I'll always be uncertain, and he'll always be able to explain his positions better than I can—but there's nothing else to do but what I've done. As Joe says, it's all there is."

I shook my head. "Sounds bleak, Rennie."

"It's not!" she protested. "Joe's wonderful; I wouldn't go back if I could. Don't forget I chose to do this: I could walk out any time, and he'd support the kids and me."

But it seemed to me that she chose it as I choose my position in the Progress and Advice Room.

"Joe's remarkable," I agreed, "if you go for that sort of thing."

"Jake, he's wonderful!" Rennie repeated. "I've never seen anybody anything like Joe, I swear. He thinks as straight as an arrow about everything. Sometimes I think that nothing Joe could think about would ever be worth the sharpness of his mind. This will

sound ridiculous to you, Jake, but I think of Joe as I'd think of
God. Even when he makes a mistake, his reasons for doing what
he did are clearer and sharper than anybody else's. Don't laugh
at that."

"He's intolerant," I suggested.

"So is God! But you know *why* Joe's intolerant: he's only
intolerant of stupidity in people he cares about! Jake, I'm better
off now than I was; I wasn't anything before. What have I lost?"

I grinned. "I suppose I should say something about your individuality. People are supposed to mention individuality at times
like this."

"Joe and I have talked about that, Jake. God, please of all
things don't accuse him of being naïve! He says that one of the
hardest and most essential things is to be aware of all the possible
alternatives to your position."

"How did he mention it?"

"First of all, suppose everyone's personality *is* unique. Does it
follow that because a thing is unique it's valuable? You're saying
that it's better to be a real Rennie MacMahon than an imitation
Joe Morgan, but that's not self-evident, Jake; not at all. It's just
romantic. I'd rather be a lousy Joe Morgan than a first-rate Rennie
MacMahon. To hell with pride. This unique-personality business
is another thing that's no absolute."

"To quote the gospel to you, Rennie," I said: "it doesn't follow
either that because a thing's not absolute it isn't valuable."

"Stop it, Jake!" Rennie was getting upset again.

"Why? You could just as well take the position that even
though Rennie MacMahon wasn't intrinsically valuable, she was
all there was. Let me ask you a question, Rennie: why do you
think Joe is interested in me? He must know I'm not going to go
along with any program of his. I make allowances for everybody,
most of all for myself. God, do I make allowances for Joe! And
certainly *he's* been making allowances for that. Why was he so
anxious to have me talk to you? Didn't he know I'd tell you I
think this whole business is either funny or appalling, depending
on my mood?"

"Jake, you haven't seen how strong Joe is, I guess. That's the finest thing of all: his strength. He's so strong that he wouldn't want me if anybody could convince me I was making a mistake."

"I don't see much strength in this premeditated horseback-riding thing. Anybody who didn't know better would think he was trying to fix me up with you."

Rennie didn't flinch. "He's so strong he can afford to look weak sometimes, Jake. Nobody is as strong as Joe is."

"He's an Eagle Scout, all right," I said cheerfully.

"Even that," Rennie said; "he's so strong he can even afford to be a caricature of his strength sometimes, and not care. Not many people are that strong."

"Am I supposed to be a devil's advocate, then? I'd be a damned good one."

Now Rennie was uneasy. "I don't know. I guess this will insult you, Jake. I honestly don't know why Joe's so taken with you. He's never been interested in anybody before—we haven't had any friends, or wanted any—but he said after your interview that he was interested in you, and after your first few conversations he was pretty much excited. What he told me was that it would be good for me to get to know a first-rate mind that was totally different from his, but there must have been more to it than that."

"I'm flattered," I said, and to my mild annoyance I really was. "You think there must be more to it than that because you can't see anything first-rate about me?"

"Never mind that. What scares me sometimes is that in a lot of ways you're *not* totally different from Joe: you're just like him. I've even heard the same sentences from each of you at different times. You work from a lot of the same premises." Rennie had been getting more nervous all the time she spoke. Now she shuddered. "Jake, I don't like you!"

This calmed me: my own discomfort disappeared at this pronouncement, and my mood changed as if by magic. I was now a strong, quiet, half-sinister Jacob Horner, nothing like the wise-cracking fop who'd heard the earlier part of Rennie's history. I smiled at Rennie.

"I wish Joe hadn't thought of this idea," she said. "I don't like anything about it. I don't want to be unfair to you, Jake, but I think I was much happier a month ago, before we met you."

"Tell Joe about it."

The squint-eyed head-whipping, not in hilarity.

"Joe thinks I've come farther than I have," she said tersely. "Already I feel guilty about telling you so much. That was weak; almost like I've been dishonest with him."

"I'll tell him we've talked about it," I said.

Rennie breathed shakily and shook her head.

"That's it, see? I can't tell you not to tell him, but if you did I'd be lost. I'd never catch up again."

I could see that easily enough: it was a little germ of Rennie MacMahon that had made the confidences.

"You must have realized that some people would think the whole Morgan plan was just plain funny."

"Of course I did. But they were just 'some people.' What scares me is that anybody could grant all of Joe's premises—our premises—understand them and grant them and *then* laugh at us."

"Maybe that's what Joe was after."

"It could be, but if it was he overestimated me! I can't take it. He could take it and not worry—you remember when he was talking about the kids' physical efficiency and you suggested that they snap each other's pajamas? That's what I meant when I said he's strong enough to be a caricature of himself—all the things about him that you've made fun of. When you suggested that, it scared me, really scared me. I didn't know what he'd do. God, Jake, he can be violent! But he just laughed and had the kids do what you said."

"He's got you scared to death, Rennie. Is it because of the time he socked you?"

Every time I mentioned this Rennie wept. That blow had struck harder than God imagined.

"I'm not that strong, Jake!" she cried; "it's my fault, but I'm not strong enough for him."

Said I, "I understand that God is a bachelor."

Like Joe's earlier disquisition on values, this history of the Morgans' domestic problems was not delivered to me all in so handy a piece as I've presented it here. What happened was that, once it got started, our daily equitations changed their character. Now we generally rode silently and with amusing purposefulness directly to the little creek in the pine grove for our talk, and spent as much as an hour there instead of twenty minutes. It is interesting to note that Rennie never spoke of the matter while riding: in fact it was with ill-concealed lack of relish that she mounted Tom Brown every morning. But we always headed for the grove—the horses would doubtless have gone there without our direction, and I will admit that more than once Susie and I took the initiative in heading that way.

Back at the Morgan apartment Rennie would clam up completely unless Joe questioned her directly about our morning. This he did often, and when it became necessary Rennie would lie grimly to him about the nature of our conversation. Grimly and clumsily: it was not pretty to watch. Joe listened carefully, and, as a rule, noncommittally, and sometimes smiled. Probably he knew she was lying, although it is hard for one who is aware of the truth to judge effectively its disguise. But if he knew, it didn't worry him. He was indeed very strong.

He and I got along better all the time. He argued exuberantly with me about politics, history, music, integrity, logic—everything; we played tennis and gin rummy together, and I proofread two or three improperly split infinitives out of the manuscript of his dissertation—an odd, brilliant study of the saving roles of innocence and energy in American political and economic history. My attitude toward Joe, Rennie, and all the rest of the universe changed as frequently as Laocoön's smile: some days I was a stock left-wing Democrat, other days I professed horror at the very concept of reform in anything; some days I was ascetic, some days Rabelaisian; some days super-rational, some days anti-rational. Each time I defended myself vehemently (except on my uncommunicative days), and Joe laughed and took me to pieces. It was a pleasant enough way to kill the afternoons, I thought, but Rennie grew increasingly morose as August progressed. At the pine grove she shuddered, rationalized, talked, and wept.

She was caught.

As for me, I was still undecided whether what I had learned

of her unusual self-effacement evidenced a great weakness or an extraordinary strength; there is no way to gauge such things when they are carried out so completely. But I found her altogether, if inconsistently, more attractive, I believe, and the observing part of me now thought that it pretty well understood the attracted part (many, many other "parts" were totally unaffected one way or the other): I think Rennie's attraction for me lay in the fact that, alone of all the women I knew, if not all the people, she had peered deeply into herself and had found *nothing*. When such is the case, the question of integrity becomes meaningless.

On August 31, 1953, her attitude seemed to have changed. It had rained until early afternoon, and so we took our ride after supper, while Joe was at his Boy Scout meeting in Wicomico. That evening she held Tom Brown to a walk—rode him almost apprehensively, I thought, without force or style, and chatted idly about nothing during the ride. But in the pine grove she was calm.

"Everything's okay, Jake." She smiled, not warmly.

"What's okay?"

"I'm still sorry I ran at the mouth so, but that's over with now."

"Oh?"

"You know, I really was frightened at you for a while. Sometimes it seemed to me that I couldn't really say to myself that Joe was stronger than you. Whenever his arguments were ready to catch you, you weren't there any more, and worse than that, even when he destroyed a position of yours it seemed to me that he hadn't really touched *you*—there wasn't that much of you in any of your positions."

"You're getting very sharp," I laughed.

"That, right there," she said, catching me up: "all you'd do was laugh when he took the props out of your argument. Then just lately I began to wonder, 'If his opinions aren't him, what *is* him?'"

"Bad grammar."

Rennie ignored me. "You know what I've come to think, Jake? I think you don't exist at all. There's too many of you. It's more than just masks that you put on and take off—we all have masks.

But you're different all the way through, every time. You cancel yourself out. You're more like somebody in a dream. You're not strong and you're not weak. You're nothing."

I thought it appropriate to say nothing.

"Two things have happened, Jake," Rennie said coolly. "One is that I'm pretty sure I'm pregnant again—my period is a week late, and I'm usually regular. The other thing is that I've decided I don't have to think about you or deal with you any more, because you don't exist. That's Joe's superiority.

"One day last week," she went on, "I either had a dream, or else I was just daydreaming, that for the past few weeks Joe had become friendly with the Devil, and was having fun arguing with him and playing tennis with him, to test his own strength. Don't laugh."

"I'm not laughing."

"I thought Joe had invited the Devil to test me, too—probably it was because you mentioned *devil's advocate* that time. But this Devil scared me, because I wasn't that strong yet, and what was a game for Joe was a terrible fight for me." Here Rennie faltered a bit. "Then when Joe saw how it was, he told me that the Devil wasn't real, and that he had conjured up the Devil out of his own strength, just as God might do. Then he made me pregnant again so I'd know *he* was the one who was real and I wouldn't be scared, and so——"

(This pretty conceit Rennie had started calmly, but as she told it she grew more and more emotional—it was a thing she'd obviously worked out for herself with care to salve the hurt of her lying—until at the end her apparent new control was gone, and she shook with tears.)

"—and so I'd grow to be just as strong as he is, and stronger than somebody who isn't even real!"

But she wasn't. I stroked her hair. Her teeth were actually chattering.

"Oh, God, I wish Joe was here!" she cried.

"You know what he'd say, Rennie. Crying is one of the things that are beside the point: you're just evading the question. This Devil business is too easy. It lets you get rid of me on false pretenses."

"You're not *real* like Joe is! He's the same man today he was yesterday, all the way through. He's genuine! That's the difference."

She was sitting on the ground, her head on her knees, and still I stroked her hair.

"But not me," I said.

"No!"

"How about you?"

For answer she whipped her head from side to side shortly.

"I don't know. Joe's strong enough to take care of me, I guess. I don't care."

This was absurd and we both knew it. I confined my argument to stroking her hair, which made her shudder. We sat thus for perhaps five minutes without saying anything. Then Rennie got up.

"I hope to Christ you know what you're doing to us, Jake," she said.

I made no reply.

"Joe's real enough to handle you," she said. "He's real enough for both of us."

"Nothing plus one is one," I said agreeably.

Now Rennie was tight-lipped, and rubbed her stomach nervously. "That's right," she said.

But a most curious thing happened shortly afterwards. We took the horses back to the stable and drove home, neither of us saying an unnecessary word. It was as though a great many things were suspended in delicate equilibrium—the rapid crowding on of dusk upon an entirely empty summer sky, with its attendant noiseless rush as of the very planet plunging, doubtless helped—and one felt hushed, for a word might knock the cosmos out of kilter. It was dark when we parked in front of the Morgans' apartment and I escorted Rennie across the deep lawn.

"Joe's home," I said, observing a light behind the closed blinds of the living room. I heard Rennie, beside me, sniff, and realized that she'd been crying some more.

"We'd better wait a minute before you go in, don't you think?"

Rennie made no answer, but she stopped and we stood quietly

just outside the door. I had no desire to touch her. I bounced idly on my heels, singing to myself *Pepsi-Cola hits the spot*. I noticed that although the venetian blind was closed, it was not lowered completely: a bar of light streamed across the grass from an inch-high slit along the window sill.

"Want to eavesdrop?" I whispered impulsively to Rennie. "Come on, it's great! See the animals in their natural habitat."

Rennie looked shocked. "What for?"

"You mean you never spy on people when they're alone? It's wonderful! Come on, be a sneak! It's the most unfair thing you can do to a person."

"You disgust me, Jake!" Rennie hissed. "He's just reading! You don't know Joe at all, do you?"

"What does that mean?"

"*Real* people aren't any different when they're alone. No masks. What you see of them is authentic."

"Horseshit. Nobody's authentic. Let's look."

"No."

"I am." I tiptoed over to the window, stooped down, and peered into the living room. Immediately I beckoned to Rennie.

"What is it?" she whispered.

"Come here!" A sneak should snicker: I snickered.

Reluctantly she came over to the window and peeped in beside me.

It is indeed the grossest of injustices to observe a person who believes himself to be alone. Joe Morgan, back from his Boy Scout meeting, had evidently intended to do some reading, for there were books lying open on the writing table and on the floor beside the bookcase. But Joe wasn't reading. He was standing in the exact center of the bare room, fully dressed, smartly executing military commands. About *face!* Right *dress!* 'Ten-*shun!* Parade *rest!* He saluted briskly, his cheeks blown out and his tongue extended, and then proceeded to cavort about the room—spinning, pirouetting, bowing, leaping, kicking. I watched entranced by his performance, for I cannot say that in my strangest moments (and a bachelor has strange ones) I have surpassed him. Rennie trembled from head to foot.

Ah! Passing a little mirror on the wall, Joe caught his own eye.

What? What? Ahoy there! He stepped close, curtsied to himself, and thrust his face to within two inches of the glass. Mr. Morgan, is it? Howdy do, Mr. Morgan. Blah bloo blah. *Oo-o-o-o* blubble thlwurp. He mugged antic faces at himself, sklurching up his eye corners, zbloogling his mouth about, glubbling his cheeks. Mither Morgle. Nyoing nyang nyumpie. Vglibble vglobble vglup. Vglig-*gybloo!* Thlucky thlucky, thir.

He jabbed his spectacles back on his nose. Had he heard some sound? No. He went to the writing table and apparently resumed his reading, his back turned to us. The show, then, was over. Ah, but one moment—yes. He turned slightly, and we could see: his tongue gripped purposefully between his lips at the side of his mouth, Joe was masturbating and picking his nose at the same time. I believe he also hummed a sprightly tune in rhythm with his work.

Rennie closed her eyes and pressed her forehead against the window sill. I stood beside her, out of the light from the brilliant living room, and stroked and stroked her hair, speaking softly in her ear the wordless, grammarless language she'd taught me to calm horses with.

6. *In September It Was Time to See the Doctor*

IN SEPTEMBER IT WAS TIME TO SEE THE DOCTOR AGAIN: I drove
out to the Remobilization Farm one morning during the first week
of the month. Because the weather was fine, a number of the
Doctor's other patients, quite old men and women, were taking
the air, seated in their wheel chairs or in the ancient cane chairs
along the porch. As usual, they greeted me a little suspiciously
with their eyes; visitors of any sort, but particularly of my age, were
rare at the farm, and were not welcomed cordially. Ignoring their
stony glances, I went inside to pay my respects to Mrs. Dockey,
the receptionist-nurse. I found her in consultation with the Doctor
himself.

"Good day, Horner," the Doctor beamed.

"Good morning, sir. Good morning, Mrs. Dockey."

That large, masculine woman nodded shortly without speaking
—her custom—and the Doctor told me to wait for him in the
Progress and Advice Room, which, along with the dining room,
the kitchen, the reception room, the bathroom, and the Treatment Room constituted the first floor of the old frame house.
Upstairs the partitions between the original bedrooms had been
removed to form two dormitories, one for the men and one for the
women. The Doctor had his own small bedroom upstairs too, and
there were two bathrooms. I did not know at the time where Mrs.
Dockey slept, or whether she slept at the farm at all. She was a
most uncommunicative woman.

I had first met the Doctor quite by chance—a fortunate chance
—on the morning of March 17, 1951, in what passes for the grand

concourse of the Pennsylvania Railroad Station in Baltimore. It happened to be the day after my twenty-eighth birthday, and I was sitting on one of the benches in the station with my suitcase beside me. I was in an unusual condition: I couldn't move. On the previous day I had checked out of my room in the apartment hotel owned by the university. I had roomed there since September of the year before, when, half-heartedly, I matriculated as a graduate student and began work on the degree that I was scheduled to complete the following June.

But on March 16, my birthday, with my oral examination passed but my master's thesis not even begun, I packed my suitcase and left the room to take a trip somewhere. Because I have learned to be not much interested in causes and biographies, I ascribe this move to simple birthday despondency, a phenomenon sufficiently familiar to enough people so that I need not explain it further. Birthday despondency, let us say, had reminded me that I had no self-convincing reason for continuing for a moment longer to do any of the things that I happened to be doing with myself as of seven o'clock in the evening of March 16, 1951. I had thirty dollars and some change in my pocket: when my suitcase was filled I hailed a taxi, went to Pennsylvania Station, and stood in the ticket line.

"Yes?" said the ticket agent when my turn came.

"Ah—this will sound theatrical to you," I said with some embarrassment, "but I have thirty dollars or so to take a trip on. Would you mind telling me some of the places I could ride to from here for, say, twenty dollars?"

The man showed no surprise at my request. He gave me an understanding if unsympathetic look and consulted some sort of rate scales.

"You can go to Cincinnati, Ohio," he declared. "You can go to Crestline, Ohio. And let's see, now—you can go to Dayton, Ohio. Or Lima, Ohio. That's a nice town. I have some of my wife's people up around Lima, Ohio. Want to go there?"

"Cincinnati, Ohio," I repeated, unconvinced. "Crestline, Ohio; Dayton, Ohio; and Lima, Ohio. Thank you very much. I'll make up my mind and come back."

So I left the ticket window and took a seat on one of the

benches in the middle of the concourse to make up my mind. And it was there that I simply ran out of motives, as a car runs out of gas. There was no reason to go to Cincinnati, Ohio. There was no reason to go to Crestline, Ohio. Or Dayton, Ohio; or Lima, Ohio. There was no reason, either, to go back to the apartment hotel, or for that matter to go anywhere. There was no reason to do anything. My eyes, as Winckelmann said inaccurately of the eyes of the Greek statues, were sightless, gazing on eternity, fixed on ultimacy, and when that is the case there is no reason to do anything—even to change the focus of one's eyes. Which is perhaps why the statues stand still. It is the malady *cosmopsis*, the cosmic view, that afflicted me. When one has it, one is frozen like the bullfrog when the hunter's light strikes him full in the eyes, only with cosmopsis there is no hunter, and no quick hand to terminate the moment—there's only the light.

Shortsighted animals all around me hurried in and out of doors leading down to tracks; trains arrived and departed. Women, children, salesmen, soldiers, and redcaps hurried across the concourse toward immediate destinations, but I sat immobile on the bench. After a while Cincinnati, Crestline, Dayton, and Lima dropped from my mind, and their place was taken by that test pattern of my consciousness, *Pepsi-Cola hits the spot*, intoned with silent oracularity. But it, too, petered away into the void, and nothing appeared in its stead.

If you look like a vagrant it is difficult to occupy a train-station bench all night long, even in a busy terminal, but if you are reasonably well dressed, have a suitcase at your side, and sit erect, policemen and railroad employees will not disturb you. I was sitting in the same place, in the same position, when the sun struck the grimy station windows next morning, and in the nature of the case I suppose I would have remained thus indefinitely, but about nine o'clock a small, dapper fellow in his fifties stopped in front of me and stared directly into my eyes. He was bald, dark-eyed, and dignified, a Negro, and wore a graying mustache and a trim tweed suit to match. The fact that I did not stir even the pupils of my eyes under his gaze is an index to my condition, for ordinarily I find it next to impossible to return the stare of a stranger.

"Weren't you sitting here like this last night?" he asked me sharply. I did not reply. He came close, bent his face down toward mine, and moved an upthrust finger back and forth about two inches from my eyes. But my eyes did not follow his finger. He stepped back and regarded me critically, then suddenly snapped his fingers almost on the point of my nose. I blinked involuntarily, although my head did not jerk back.

"Ah," he said, and regarded me again. "Does this happen to you often, young man?"

Perhaps because of the brisk assuredness of his voice, the *no* welled up in me like a belch. And I realized as soon as I deliberately held my tongue (there being in the last analysis no reason to answer his question at all) that as of that moment I was artificially prolonging what had been a genuine physical immobility. Not to choose at all is unthinkable: what I had done before was simply choose not to act, since I had been at rest when the situation arose. Now, however, it was harder—"more of a choice"—to hold my tongue than to croak out something that filled my mouth, and so after a moment I said, "No."

Then, of course, the trance was broken. I was embarrassed, and rose quickly and stiffly from the bench to leave.

"Where will you go?" my examiner asked with a smile.

"What?" I frowned at him. "Oh—get a bus home, I guess. See you around."

"Wait." His voice was mild, but entirely commanding. I stopped. "Won't you have coffee with me? I'm a physician, and I'd be interested in discussing your case with you."

"I don't have any case," I said awkwardly. "I was just—sitting there for a minute or so."

"No. I saw you there last night at ten o'clock when I came in from New York," the doctor said. "You were sitting in the same position. You *were* paralyzed, weren't you?"

I laughed shortly. "Well, if you want to call it that, but there's nothing wrong with me. I don't know what came over me."

"Of course you don't, but I do. My specialty is various sorts of physical immobility. You're lucky I came by this morning."

"Oh, you don't understand——"

"I brought you out of it, didn't I?" he said cheerfully. "Here."

He took a fifty-cent piece from his pocket and handed it to me
—I accepted it before I realized what he'd done. "I can't go into
that lounge over there. Get two cups of coffee for us and we'll sit
here for a minute and decide what to do."

"No, listen, I——"

"Why not?" he laughed. "Go on, now. I'll wait here."

Why not, indeed?

"I have my own money," I protested lamely, offering him his
fifty-cent piece back, but he waved me away and lit a cigar.

"Now hurry up," he ordered calmly, around the cigar. "Move
fast, or you might get stuck again. Don't think of anything but the
coffee I've asked you to get."

"All right." I turned and walked with dignity toward the
lounge, just off the concourse.

"Fast!" the doctor laughed behind me. I flushed, and impulsively quickened my step.

While I waited for the coffee I tried to feel the curiosity about
my invalidity and my rescuer that it seemed appropriate I should
feel, but I was too weary in mind and body to wonder at anything. I do not mean to suggest that my condition had been unpleasant—it was entirely anesthetic in its advanced stage, and even
a little bit pleasant in its inception—but it was fatiguing, as an
overlong sleep is fatiguing, and one had the same reluctance to
throw it off that one has to finally get out of bed when one has
slept around the clock. Indeed, as the Doctor had warned (it was
at this time, not knowing my benefactor's name, that I began to
think of him with a capital D), to slip back into immobility at the
coffee counter would have been extremely easy: I felt my mind
begin to settle into rigidity, and only the clerk's peremptory
"Thirty cents, please," brought me back to action—luckily, because
the Doctor could not have entered the white lounge to help me.
I paid the clerk and took the paper cups of coffee back to the
bench.

"Good," the Doctor said. "Sit down."

I hesitated. I was standing directly in front of him.

"Here!" he laughed. "On this side! You're like the donkey between two piles of straw!"

I sat where ordered and we sipped our coffee. I rather expected to be asked questions about myself, but the Doctor ignored me.

"Thanks for the coffee," I said uncertainly. He glanced at me impassively for a moment, as though I were a hitherto silent parrot who had suddenly blurted a brief piece of nonsense, and then he returned his attention to the crowd in the station.

"I have one or two calls to make yet before we catch the bus," he announced without looking at me. "Won't take long. I wanted to see if you were still here before I left town."

"What do you mean, catch the bus?"

"You'll have to come over to the farm—my Remobilization Farm over near Wicomico—for a day or so, for observation," he explained coldly. "You don't have anything else to do, do you?"

"Well, I should get back to the university, I guess. I'm a student."

"Oh," he chuckled. "Might as well forget about that for a while. You can come back in a few days if you want to."

"Say, you know, really, I think you must have a misconception about what was wrong with me a while ago. I'm not a paralytic. It's all just silly, really. I'll explain it to you if you want to hear it."

"No, you needn't bother. No offense intended, but the things you think are important probably aren't even relevant at all. I'm never very curious about my patients' histories. Rather not hear them, in fact—just clutters things up. It doesn't much matter what caused it anyhow, does it?" He grinned. "My farm's like a nunnery in that respect—I never bother about why my patients come there. Forget about causes; I'm no psychoanalyst."

"But that's what I mean, sir," I explained, laughing uncomfortably. "There's nothing physically wrong with me."

"Except that you couldn't move," the Doctor said. "What's your name?"

"Jacob Horner. I'm a graduate student up at Johns Hopkins——"

"Ah, ah," he warned. "No biography, Jacob Horner." He finished his coffee and stood up. "Come on, now, we'll get a cab. Bring your suitcase along."

"Oh, wait now!"

"Yes?"

I fumbled for protests: the thing was absurd.

"Well—this is absurd."

"So?"

I hesitated, blinking, wetting my lips.

"Think, think!" the Doctor said brusquely.

My mind raced like a car engine when the clutch is disengaged. There was no answer.

"Well, I—are you sure it's all right?" I had no idea what my question signified.

The Doctor made a short, derisive sound (a sort of "Huf!") and turned away. I shook my head—at the same moment aware that I was watching myself act bewildered—and then fetched up my suitcase and followed after him, out to the line of taxicabs at the curb.

Thus began my *alliance* with the Doctor. He stopped first at an establishment on North Howard Street, where he ordered two wheel chairs, three pairs of crutches, and certain other apparatus for the farm, and then at a pharmaceutical supply house on South Paca Street, where he also made some sort of order. Then we went to the W.B.&A. bus terminal on Howard and Redwood streets and took the Red Star bus to the Eastern Shore. The Doctor's Mercury station wagon was parked at the Wicomico bus depot; he drove to the little settlement of Vineland, about three miles south of Wicomico, turned off onto a secondary road, and finally drove up a long, winding dirt lane to the Remobilization Farm, an aged but clean-painted white clapboard house in a clump of oaks on a knoll overlooking some creek or other. The patients on the porch, senile men and women, welcomed the Doctor with querulous enthusiasm, and he returned their greeting. Me they regarded with open suspicion, if not hostility, but the Doctor made no explanation of my presence—for that matter, I should have been hard put to explain it myself.

Inside I was introduced to the muscular Mrs. Dockey and taken to the Progress and Advice Room for my first interview. I waited alone in that clean room, bare, but not really clinical-looking—just an empty white room in a farmhouse—for some ten minutes, and then the Doctor entered and took his seat very much in front of me. He had donned a white medical-looking jacket and appeared entirely official and competent.

"I'll make a few things clear very quickly, Jacob," he said, leaning forward with his hands on his knees and rolling his cigar around in his mouth between sentences. "The farm, as you can see, is designed for the treatment of paralytics. Most of my patients are old people, but you mustn't infer from that that this is a nursing home for the aged. It's not. Perhaps you noticed when we drove up that my patients like me. It has happened several times in the past that for one reason or another I have seen fit to change the location of the farm. Once it was outside of Troy, New York; another time near Fond du Lac, Wisconsin; another time near Biloxi, Mississippi. And we've been other places, too. Nearly all the patients I have on the farm now have been with me at least since Fond du Lac, and if I should have to move tomorrow to Helena, Montana, or Far Rockaway, most of them would go with me, and not because they haven't anywhere else to go. But don't think I have an equal love for them. They're just more or less interesting problems in immobility, for which I find it satisfying to work out therapies. I tell this to you, but not to them, because your problem is such that this information is harmless. And for that matter, you've no way of knowing whether anything I've said or will say is the truth, or just a part of my general therapy for you. You can't even tell whether your doubt in this matter is an honestly founded doubt or just a part of your treatment: access to the truth, Jacob, even belief that there is such a thing, is itself therapeutic or antitherapeutic, depending on the problem. The reality of your problem itself is all that you can be sure of."

"Yes, sir."

"Why do you say that?" the Doctor asked.

"Say what?"

" 'Yes, sir.' Why do you say 'Yes, sir'?"

"Oh—I was just acknowledging what you said before."

"Acknowledging the truth of what I said or merely the fact that I said it?"

"Well," I hesitated, flustered. "I don't know, sir."

"You don't know whether to say you were acknowledging the

truth of my statements, when actually you weren't, or to say you were simply acknowledging that I said something, at the risk of offending me by the implication that you don't agree with any of it. Eh?"

"Oh, I agree with *some* of it," I assured him.

"What parts of it do you agree with? Which statements?"

"I don't know: I guess——" I searched my mind hastily to remember even one thing that he'd said. He regarded my floundering coldly for a minute and then went on as if the interruption hadn't occurred.

"Agapotherapy—devotion therapy—is often useful with older patients," he said. "One of the things that work toward restoring their mobility is devotion to some figure, a doctor or other kind of administrator. It keeps their allegiances from becoming divided. For that reason I'd move the farm occasionally even if other circumstances didn't make it desirable. It does them good to decide to follow me. Agapotherapy is one small therapy in a great number, some consecutive, some simultaneous, which are exercised on the patients. No two patients have the same schedule of therapies, because no two people are ever paralyzed in the same way. The authors of medical textbooks," he added with some contempt, "like everyone else, can reach generality only by ignoring enough particularity. They speak of paralysis, and the treatment of paralytics, as though one read the textbook and then followed the rules for getting paralyzed properly. There is no such thing as *paralysis*, Jacob. There is only paralyzed Jacob Horner. And I don't *treat* paralysis: I schedule therapies to mobilize John Doe or Jacob Horner, as the case may be. That's why I ignore you when you say you aren't paralyzed as the people out on the porch are paralyzed. I don't treat your paralysis: I treat paralyzed you. Please don't say, 'Yes, sir.'"

The urge to acknowledge is almost irresistible, but I managed to sit silent and not even nod.

"There are several things wrong with you, I think. I daresay you don't know the seating capacity of the Cleveland Municipal Stadium, do you?"

"*What?*"

The Doctor did not smile. "You suggest that my question is

absurd, when you have no grounds for knowing whether it is or not—you obviously heard me and understood me. Probably you want to delay my learning that you *don't* know the seating capacity of Cleveland Municipal Stadium, since your vanity would be ruffled if the question *weren't* absurd, and even if it were. It makes no difference whether it is or not, Jacob Horner: it's a question asked you by your doctor. Now, is there any ultimate reason why the Cleveland Stadium shouldn't seat fifty-seven thousand, four hundred eighty-eight people?"

"None that I can think of," I grinned.

"Don't pretend to be amused. Of course there's not. Is there any reason why it shouldn't seat eighty-eight thousand, four hundred seventy-five people?"

"No, sir."

"Indeed not. Then as far as Reason is concerned its seating capacity could be almost anything. Logic will never give you the answer to my question. Only Knowledge of the World will answer it. There's no ultimate reason at all why the Cleveland Stadium should seat exactly seventy-seven thousand, seven hundred people, but it happens that it does. There's no reason in the long run why Italy shouldn't be shaped like a sausage instead of a boot, but that doesn't happen to be the case. *The world is everything that is the case,* and what the case is is not a matter of logic. If you don't simply *know* how many people can sit in the Cleveland Municipal Stadium, you have no real reason for choosing one number over another, assuming you can make a choice at all—do you understand? But if you have some Knowledge of the World you may be able to say, 'Seventy-seven thousand, seven hundred,' just like that. No choice is involved."

"Well," I said, "you'd still have to choose whether to answer the question or not, or whether to answer it correctly, even if you knew the right answer, wouldn't you?"

The Doctor's tranquil stare told me my question was somehow silly, though it seemed reasonable enough to me.

"One of the things you'll have to do," he said dryly, "is buy a copy of the *World Almanac* for 1951 and begin to study it scrupulously. This is intended as a discipline, and you'll have to pursue it diligently, perhaps for a number of years. Informational Therapy is one of a number of therapies we'll have to initiate at once."

I shook my head and chuckled genially. "Do all your patients memorize the *World Almanac*, Doctor?"

I might as well not have spoken.

"Mrs. Dockey will show you to your bed," the Doctor said, rising to go. "I'll speak to you again presently." At the door he stopped and added, "One, perhaps two, of the older men may attempt familiarities with you at night up in the dormitory. They're on Sexual Therapy, and I find it useful and convenient in their cases to suggest homosexual affairs rather than heterosexual ones. But unless you're accustomed to that sort of thing I don't think you should accept their advances. You should keep your life as uncomplicated as possible, at least for a while. Reject them gently, and they'll go back to each other."

There was little I could say. After a while Mrs. Dockey showed me my bed in the men's dormitory. I was not introduced to my roommates, nor did I introduce myself. In fact (though since then I've come to know them better), during the three days that I remained at the farm not a dozen words were exchanged between us, much less homosexual advances. When I left they were uniformly glad to see me go.

The Doctor spent two or three one-hour sessions with me each day. He asked me virtually nothing about myself; the conversations consisted mostly of harangues against the medical profession for its stupidity in matters of paralysis, and imputations that my condition was the result of defective character and intelligence.

"You claim to be unable to choose in many situations," he said once. "Well, I claim that that inability is only theoretically inherent in situations, when there's no chooser. Given a particular chooser, it's unthinkable. So, since the inability *was* displayed in your case, the fault lies not in the situation but in the fact that there was no chooser. Choosing is existence: to the extent that you don't choose, you don't exist. Now, everything we do must be oriented toward choice and action. It doesn't matter whether this action is more or less reasonable than inaction; the point is that it is its opposite."

"But why should anyone prefer it?" I asked.

"There's no reason why you should prefer it," he said, "and no reason why you shouldn't. One is a patient simply because one chooses a condition that only therapy can bring one to, not because any one condition is inherently better than another. All my therapies for a while will be directed toward making you conscious of your existence. It doesn't matter whether you act constructively or even consistently, so long as you act. It doesn't matter to the case whether your character is admirable or not, so long as you think you have one."

"I don't understand why you should choose to treat anyone, Doctor," I said.

"That's my business, not yours."

And so it went. I was charged, directly or indirectly, with everything from intellectual dishonesty and vanity to nonexistence. If I protested, the Doctor observed that my protests indicated my belief in the truth of his statements. If I only listened glumly, he observed that my glumness indicated my belief in the truth of his statements.

"All right, then," I said at last, giving up. "Everything you say is true. All of it is the truth."

The Doctor listened calmly. "You don't know what you're talking about," he said. "There's no such thing as truth as you conceive it."

These apparently pointless interviews did not constitute my only activity at the farm. Before every meal the other patients and I were made to perform various calisthenics under the direction of Mrs. Dockey. For the older patients these were usually very simple—perhaps a mere nodding of the head or flexing of the arms—although some of the old folks could execute really surprising feats: one gentleman in his seventies was an excellent rope climber, and two old ladies turned agile somersaults. For each Mrs. Dockey prescribed different activities; my own special prescription was to keep some sort of visible motion going all the time. If nothing else, I was constrained to keep a finger wiggling or a foot tapping, say, during mealtimes, when more involved movements would have made eating difficult. And I was told to rock from side to side in my bed all night long: not an unreasonable request, as it happened, for I did this habitually anyhow, even in my sleep —a habit carried over from childhood.

"Motion! Motion!" the Doctor would say, almost exalted. "You must be always *conscious* of motion!"

There were special diets and, for many patients, special drugs. I learned of Nutritional Therapy, Medicinal Therapy, Surgical Therapy, Dynamic Therapy, Informational Therapy, Conversational Therapy, Sexual Therapy, Devotional Therapy, Occupational and Preoccupational Therapy, Virtue and Vice Therapy, Theotherapy and Atheotherapy—and, later, Mythotherapy, Philosophical Therapy, Scriptotherapy, and many, many other therapies practiced in various combinations and sequences by the patients. Everything, to the Doctor, is either therapeutic, anti-therapeutic, or irrelevant. He is a kind of super-pragmatist.

At the end of my last session—it had been decided that I was to return to Baltimore experimentally, to see whether and how soon my immobility might recur—the Doctor gave me some parting instructions.

"It would not be well in your particular case to believe in God," he said. "Religion will only make you despondent. But until we work out something for you it will be useful to subscribe to some philosophy. Why don't you read Sartre and become an existentialist? It will keep you moving until we find something more suitable for you. Study the *World Almanac:* it is to be your breviary for a while. Take a day job, preferably factory work, but not so simple that you are able to think coherently while working. Something involving sequential operations would be nice. Go out in the evenings; play cards with people. I don't recommend buying a television set just yet. If you read anything outside the *Almanac,* read nothing but plays—no novels or non-fiction. Exercise frequently. Take long walks, but always to a previously determined destination, and when you get there, walk right home again, briskly. And move out of your present quarters; the association is unhealthy for you. Don't get married or have love affairs yet: if you aren't courageous enough to hire prostitutes, then take up masturbation temporarily. Above all, act impulsively: don't let yourself get stuck between alternatives, or you're lost. You're not that strong. If the alternatives are side by side, choose the one on the left; if they're consecutive in time, choose the earlier. If neither of these applies, choose the alternative whose name begins with the earlier letter of the alphabet. These are the principles of Sinistrality, Antecedence, and Alphabetical Priority—there are others, and they're arbitrary, but useful. Good-by."

"Good-by, Doctor," I said, a little breathless, and prepared to leave.

"If you have another attack, contact me as soon as you can. If nothing happens, come back in three months. My services will cost you ten dollars a visit—no charge for this one. I have a limited interest in your case, Jacob, and in the vacuum you have for a self. That *is* your case. Remember, keep moving all the time. Be *engagé*. Join things."

I left, somewhat dazed, and took the bus back to Baltimore. There, out of it all, I had a chance to attempt to decide what I thought of the Doctor, the Remobilization Farm, the endless list of therapies, and my own position. One thing seemed fairly clear: the Doctor was operating either outside the law or on its very fringes. Sexual Therapy, to name only one thing, could scarcely be sanctioned by the American Medical Association. This doubtless was the reason for the farm's frequent relocation. It was also apparent that he was a crank—though perhaps not an ineffective one—and one wondered whether he had any sort of license to practice medicine at all. Because—his rationalizations aside—I was so clearly different from his other patients, I could only assume that he had some sort of special interest in my case: perhaps he was a frustrated psychoanalyst. At worst he was some combination of quack and prophet—Father Divine, Sister Kenny, and Bernarr MacFadden combined (all of them quite effective people), with elements of faith healer and armchair Freud thrown in—running a semi-legitimate rest home for senile eccentrics; and yet one couldn't easily laugh off his forcefulness, and his insights frequently struck home. As a matter of fact, I was unable to make any judgment one way or the other about him or the farm or the therapies.

A most extraordinary Doctor. Although I kept telling myself that I was just going along with the joke, I actually did move down to East Chase Street; I took a job as an assembler on the

line of the Chevrolet factory out on Broening Highway, where
I operated an air wrench that bolted leaf springs on the left side
of Chevrolet chassis, and I joined the U.A.W. I read Sartre but
had difficulty deciding how to apply him to specific situations.
(How did existentialism help one decide whether to carry one's
lunch to work or buy it in the factory cafeteria? I had no head
for philosophy.) I played poker with my fellow assemblers, took
walks from Chase Street down to the waterfront and back, and
attended B movies. Temperamentally I was already pretty much
of an atheist most of the time, and the proscription of women was
a small burden, for I was not, as a rule, heavily sexed. I applied
Sinistrality, Antecedence, and Alphabetical Priority religiously
(though in some instances I found it hard to decide which of those
devices best fitted the situation). And every quarter for the next
two years I drove over to the Remobilization Farm for advice. It
would be idle for me to speculate further on why I assented to this
curious alliance, which more often than not is insulting to me—I
presume that anyone interested in causes will have found plenty
to pick from by now in this account.

I left myself sitting in the Progress and Advice Room, I believe,
in September of 1953, waiting for the Doctor. My mood on this
morning was an unusual one; as a rule I am almost "weatherless"
the moment I enter the farmhouse, and I suppose that weatherlessness is the ideal condition for receiving advice, but on this morning, although I felt unemotional, I was not without weather. I felt
dry, clear, and competent, for some reason or other—quite sharp
and not a bit humble. In meteorological terms, my weather was
sec Supérieur.

"How are you these days, Horner?" the Doctor asked affably
as he entered the room.

"Just fine, Doctor," I replied breezily. "How's yourself?"

The Doctor took his seat, spread his knees, and regarded me
critically, not answering my question.

"Have you begun teaching yet?"

"Nope. Start next week. Two sections of grammar and two of
composition."

"Ah." He rolled his cigar around in his mouth. He was studying me, not what I said. "You shouldn't be teaching composition."

"Can't have everything," I said cheerfully, stretching my legs out under his chair and clasping my hands behind my head. "It was that or nothing, so I took it." The Doctor observed the position of my legs and arms.

"Who is this confident fellow you've befriended?" he asked. "One of the other teachers? He's terribly sure of himself!"

I blushed: it occurred to me that I *was* imitating Joe Morgan. "Why do you say I'm imitating somebody?"

"I didn't," the Doctor smiled. "I only asked who was the forceful fellow you've obviously met."

"None of your business, sir."

"Oh, my. Very good. It's a pity you can't take over that manner consistently—you'd never need my services again! But you're not stable enough for that yet, Jacob. Besides, you couldn't act like him when you're in his company, could you? Anyway I'm pleased to see you assuming a role. You do it, evidently, in order to face up to me: a character like your friend's would never allow itself to be insulted by some crank with his string of implausible therapies, eh?"

"That's right, Doctor," I said, but much of the fire had gone out of me under his analysis.

"This indicates to me that you're ready for Mythotherapy, since you seem to be already practicing it without knowing it, and therapeutically, too. But it's best you be aware of what you're doing, so that you won't break down through ignorance. Some time ago I told you to become an existentialist. Did you read Sartre?"

"Some things. Frankly I really didn't get to be an existentialist."

"No? Well, no matter now. Mythotherapy is based on two assumptions: that human existence precedes human essence, if either of the two terms really signifies anything; and that a man is free not only to choose his own essence but to change it at will. Those are both good existentialist premises, and whether they're true or false is of no concern to us—they're *useful* in your case."

He went on to explain Mythotherapy.

"In life," he said, "there are no essentially major or minor characters. To that extent, all fiction and biography, and most historiography, are a lie. Everyone is necessarily the hero of his own life story. *Hamlet* could be told from Polonius's point of view and called *The Tragedy of Polonius, Lord Chamberlain of Denmark.* He didn't think he was a minor character in anything, I daresay. Or suppose you're an usher in a wedding. From the groom's viewpoint he's the major character; the others play supporting parts, even the bride. From your viewpoint, though, the wedding is a minor episode in the very interesting history of *your* life, and the bride and groom both are minor figures. What you've done is choose to *play the part* of a minor character: it can be pleasant for you to *pretend to be* less important than you know you are, as Odysseus does when he disguises as a swineherd. And every member of the congregation at the wedding sees himself as the major character, condescending to witness the spectacle. So in this sense fiction isn't a lie at all, but a true representation of the distortion that everyone makes of life.

"Now, not only are we the heroes of our own life stories—we're the ones who conceive the story, and give other people the essences of minor characters. But since no man's life story as a rule is ever one story with a coherent plot, we're always reconceiving just the sort of hero we are, and consequently just the sort of minor roles that other people are supposed to play. This is generally true. If any man displays almost the same character day in and day out, all day long, it's either because he has no imagination, like an actor who can play only one role, or because he has an imagination so comprehensive that he sees each particular situation of his life as an episode in some grand over-all plot, and can so distort the situations that the same type of hero can deal with them all. But this is most unusual.

"This kind of role-assigning is myth-making, and when it's done consciously or unconsciously for the purpose of aggrandizing or protecting your ego—and it's probably done for this purpose all the time—it becomes Mythotherapy. Here's the point: an immobility such as you experienced that time in Penn Station is possible only to a person who for some reason or other has ceased to participate in Mythotherapy. At that time on the bench you were neither a major nor a minor character: you were no character at all. It's because this has happened once that it's necessary for me to explain to you something that comes quite naturally to everyone else. It's like teaching a paralytic how to walk again.

"Now many crises in people's lives occur because the hero role that they've assumed for one situation or set of situations no longer applies to some new situation that comes up, or—the same thing in effect—because they haven't the imagination to distort the new situation to fit their old role. This happens to parents, for instance, when their children grow older, and to lovers when one of them begins to dislike the other. If the new situation is too overpowering to ignore, and they can't find a mask to meet it with, they may become schizophrenic—a last-resort mask—or simply shattered. All questions of integrity involve this consideration, because a man's integrity consists in being faithful to the script he's written for himself.

"I've said you're too unstable to play any one part all the time—you're also too unimaginative—so for you these crises had better be met by changing scripts as often as necessary. This should come naturally to you; the important thing for you is to realize what you're doing so you won't get caught without a script, or with the wrong script in a given situation. You did quite well, for example, for a beginner, to walk in here so confidently and almost arrogantly a while ago, and assign me the role of a quack. But you must be able to change masks at once if by some means or other I'm able to make the one you walked in with untenable. Perhaps—I'm just suggesting an offhand possibility—you could change to thinking of me as The Sagacious Old Mentor, a kind of Machiavellian Nestor, say, and yourself as The Ingenuous But Promising Young Protégé, a young Alexander, who someday will put all these teachings into practice and far outshine the master. Do you get the idea? Or—this is repugnant, but it could be used as a last resort—The Silently Indignant Young Man, who tolerates the ravings of a Senile Crank but who will leave this house unsullied by them. I call this repugnant because if you ever used it you'd cut yourself off from much that you haven't learned yet.

"It's extremely important that you learn to assume these masks wholeheartedly. Don't think there's anything behind them: *ego* means *I*, and *I* means *ego*, and the ego by definition is a mask. Where there's no ego—this is you on the bench—there's no *I*. If you sometimes have the feeling that your mask is *insincere*—impossible word!—it's only because one of your masks is incompatible with another. You mustn't put on two at a time. There's a source of conflict, and conflict between masks, like absence of masks, is a source of immobility. The more sharply you can dramatize your situation, and define your own role and everybody else's role, the safer you'll be. It doesn't matter in Mythotherapy for paralytics whether your role is major or minor, as long as it's clearly conceived, but in the nature of things it'll normally always be major. Now say something."

I could not.

"Say something!" the Doctor ordered. "Move! Take a role!"

I tried hard to think of one, but I could not.

"Damn you!" the Doctor cried. He kicked back his chair and leaped upon me, throwing me to the floor and pounding me roughly.

"Hey!" I hollered, entirely startled by his attack. "Cut it out! What the hell!" I struggled with him and, being both larger and stronger than he, soon had him off me. We stood facing each other warily, panting from the exertion.

"You watch that stuff!" I said belligerently. "I could make plenty of trouble for you if I wanted to, I'll bet!"

"Anything wrong?" asked Mrs. Dockey, sticking her head into the room. I would not want to tangle with her.

"No, not now," the Doctor smiled, brushing the knees of his white trousers. "A little Pugilistic Therapy for Jacob Horner. No trouble." She closed the door.

"Shall we continue our talk?" he asked me, his eyes twinkling. "You were speaking in a manly way about making trouble."

But I was no longer in a mood to go along with the whole ridiculous business. I'd had enough of the old lunatic for this quarter.

"Or perhaps you've had enough of The Old Crank for today, eh?"

"What would the sheriff in Wicomico think of this farm?" I

grumbled uncomfortably. "Suppose the police were sent out to investigate Sexual Therapy?"

The Doctor was unruffled by my threats.

"Do you intend to send them?" he asked pleasantly.

"Do you think I wouldn't?"

"I've no idea," he said, still undisturbed.

"Do you dare me to?"

This question, for some reason or other, visibly upset him: he looked at me sharply.

"Indeed I do not," he said at once. "I'm sure you're quite able to do it. I'm sorry if my tactic for mobilizing you just then made you angry. I did it with all good intent. You *were* paralyzed again, you know."

"Horseshit!" I sneered. "You and your paralysis!"

"You *have* had enough for today, Horner!" the Doctor said. He too was angry now. "Get out! I hope you get paralyzed driving sixty miles an hour on your way home!" He raised his voice. "Get out of here, you damned moron!"

His obviously genuine anger immediately removed mine, which after the first instant had of course been only a novel mask.

"I'm sorry, Doctor," I said. "I won't lose my temper again."

We exchanged smiles.

"Why not?" he laughed. "It's both therapeutic and pleasant to lose your temper in certain situations." He relit his cigar, which had been dropped during our scuffle. "Two interesting things were demonstrated in the past few minutes, Jacob Horner. I can't tell you about them until your next visit. Good-by, now. Don't forget to pay Mrs. Dockey."

Out he strode, cool as could be, and a few moments later out strode I: A Trifle Shaken, But Sure Of My Strength.

7. The Dance of Sex: If One Had No Other Reason for Choosing to Subscribe

THE DANCE OF SEX: IF ONE HAD NO OTHER REASON FOR CHOOSING TO SUBSCRIBE to Freud, what could be more charming than to believe that the whole vaudeville of the world, the entire dizzy circus of history, is but a fancy mating dance? That dictators burn Jews and businessmen vote Republican, that helmsmen steer ships and ladies play bridge, that girls study grammar and boys engineering all at behest of the Absolute Genital? When the synthesizing mood is upon one, what is more soothing than to assert that this one simple yen of humankind, poor little coitus, alone gives rise to cities and monasteries, paragraphs and poems, foot races and battle tactics, metaphysics and hydroponics, trade unions and universities? Who would not delight in telling some extragalactic tourist, "On our planet, sir, males and females copulate. Moreover, they enjoy copulating. But for various reasons they cannot do this whenever, wherever, and with whomever they choose. Hence all this running around that you observe. Hence the world"? A therapeutic notion!

My classes commenced on the seventh of September, a tall blue day as crisp as the white starched blouses of the coeds who filed into my classroom and nervously took their seats. Standing behind the lectern at eight o'clock sharp, suit fresh-pressed and chin scraped clean, I felt my nostrils flare like a stud's at the nubby tight sex of them, flustered and pink-scrubbed, giggling and moist; my thighs flexed, and I yawned ferociously. The boys, too, lean and green, smooth-chinned and resilient, shivered and stretched at the mere nearness of young breasts and buttocks as hard as new

pears. In a classroom on the first day of a new term the air's
electric with sex like ozone after a summer storm, and all sensed
it, if all couldn't name it: the rubby sweet friskies twitched in
their seats and tugged their skirts down dimpled white knees; the
springy fresh men flexed and slouched, passed quick hands over
crew cuts; I folded arms and tightened hams, and leaning against
the desk, let its edge press calmingly against my trouser fly like a
steadying hand. Early blue morning is an erotic time, the commencement of school terms an erotic season; little's to be done
but nod to Freud on such a day.

We looked one another over appraisingly. What I said, with
professorial succinctness, was: "My name's Jacob Horner; my
office is in Room Twenty-seven, around the corner. There's a list
of my office hours on the door." I assigned texts and described
the course; that was all, and that was enough. My air of scholarly
competence, theirs of studious attention (they wrote my name and
office number as frowningly as if I'd pronounced the Key to the
Mystery) were so clearly feigned, we were all so conscious of
playing school, that to attempt a lesson would have been pre-
posterous. Why, confronted with that battery of bosoms and be-
hinds, a man cupped his hands in spite of himself; the urge to
drop the ceremonious game and leap those fine girls on the spot
was simply terrific. The national consternation, if on some September morn every young college instructor in the land cried out what
was on his mind—"To hell with this nonsense, men: let's take
'em!"—a soothing speculation!

"That's all for today. Buy the books and we'll start right off
next time with a spelling test, for diagnostic purposes."

Indeed! One hundred spelling words dictated rapidly enough to
keep their heads down, and I, perched high on my desk, could
diagnose to my heart's content every bump of femininity in the
room (praised be American grade schools, where little girls learn
to sit up front!). Then, perhaps, having ogled my fill, I could get
on with the business of the course. For as a man must grow used
to the furniture before he can settle down to read in his room, this
plenitude of girlish appurtenances had first to be assimilated before
anyone could concentrate attention on the sober prescriptions of
English grammar.

Four times I repeated the ritual pronouncements—at eight and nine in the morning and at two and three in the afternoon. Between the two sessions I lounged in my office with a magnificent erection, wallowing in my position, and watched with proprietary eye the parade of young things passing my door. I had nothing at all to do but spin indolent daydreams of absolute authority—Nerotic, Caligular authority of the sort that summons up officefuls of undergraduate girls, hot and submissive—leering professorial dreams!

By four o'clock, when my first working day ended, I had so abandoned myself to the dance that I was virtually in pain. I tossed my empty brief case into the car and drove directly across town to the high school, to seek out Miss Peggy Rankin; after some inquiry at the principal's office I caught up with her just as she was leaving the teacher's lounge.

"Come on!" I said urgently. "I have to see you right away!"

She recognized me, blushed, and fumbled for protests.

"Come on!" I grinned. "I can't tell you here how important it is!" I took her arm and escorted her swiftly outside.

"What's the matter, Jake? Where are we going?"

"Wherever you want to," I said, holding the car door open for her.

"Jake, for God's sake, are you just picking me up again?" she asked incredulously.

"What do you mean, just? There's nothing just about this, girl."

"There certainly isn't! It's fantastic! What do you think I am, for heaven's sake?"

I stepped on the accelerator. "Shall we go to your place or to mine?"

"Mine!" she said furiously. "And just as fast as you can! I've never in my life met such a monster as you are! You're simply a monster!"

"I'm not simply a monster, Peggy: I'm also a monster."

"You're an incredible cad! That exactly describes you—you're a complete cad! You're so wrapped up in yourself that you don't have a shred of respect for anyone else on earth! Turn left right here."

I turned left.

"The fourth house up on the right-hand side. Yes."

I parked the car.

"Now look at me, Jake. *Look* at me!" she cried. "Don't you realize I'm just as much of a human being as you are? How in the *world* could you even look me in the eye again after last time? I'd have been shocked if you'd even had the gall to face up and apologize to me, but *this*——"

"Listen, Peggy," I said sharply. "You say I don't respect you. Is that because I didn't bother to flatter you at Ocean City, or apologize afterwards, or call up yesterday to make a date for today?"

"Of course it is! What do you *think* I mean? You haven't got the slightest bit of common courtesy in you; not even common civility! I'm—I'm astonished! You're not a man at all."

"I'll explain this only once," I said solemnly; "I assumed you were mature enough to understand it without explanation, as these things should be understood."

"What on earth are you getting at?"

"I'm afraid I overestimated you, Peggy," I declared. "I thought after I met you that you might actually be the superior woman you give the first impression of being. But you know, you're turning out to be one hundred per cent ordinary."

She was speechless.

"Don't you understand," I smiled, my testicles aching, "that I'm probably less interested in sex than any other man you've ever met?"

"Oh, my *God!*"

"I enjoy it, all right, just as I'd enjoy having a lot of money, but I'm not willing to put up with any nonsense to get either."

"Not even a common respect for a woman's dignity!"

"That's it, right there," I said soberly: "a common respect, a common courtesy, a common this, a common that. Add it all up and what it gives you is a common relationship, and that's a thing I've no use for. You don't seem to be my kind of girl, Peggy, and I could have sworn you were. My kind of girl doesn't want common respect; she wants uncommon respect, and that means a relationship where nobody makes the common allowances for anybody else."

"I don't believe you," Peggy said, aghast and troubled.

"You're testifying against yourself, then," I said quietly. "Don't you understand that all this rigmarole of flattery and chivalry—the whole theatrical that men perform for women—is *disrespect?* Any lie is disrespect, and a relationship based on that nonsense is a lie. Chivalry is a fiction invented by men who don't want to be bothered with taking women seriously. The minute a man and woman assent to it they stop thinking of each other as individual human beings: they assent to it precisely so they won't have to think about their partners. Which is completely useful, of course, if sex is the only thing that's on your mind. I may as well tell you, Peggy, now that it's too late, that you're the only woman I ever dared try to respect before, and take completely seriously, on my own terms, just as I'd take myself. No lies, no myths, no allowances, no hypocrisy. That's the only kind of relationship with a woman that I could ever stay interested in vertically as well as horizontally."

Peggy burst into nervous laughter.

"You mustn't laugh at that, Peggy," I said gravely.

"Oh, my God!" she laughed. "Oh, my *God!"*

I turned from the wheel and very carefully socked her square on the cheek. The blow threw her head back against the window, and immediately she began crying.

"As you see, I'm still taking you seriously," I said.

"Oh!"

"Try to understand, Peggy, that I'm *just not that interested* in laying women. I can do without. But I will not have my Deepest Values thrown in my face! I'm not a man who strikes girls. To hell with girls. What I want is a female human being that I can take as seriously as myself. If you're not interested, get out, but don't laugh at the only man who's ever taken you seriously in your whole life."

"Jake, for God's sake!" Peggy sobbed, embracing my lap. Fresh tears. "What a horrible spot a woman's in!"

I patted her head. "Our society makes sincerity sound like the greatest hypocrisy of all."

"Jake?"

"What?"

Because she'd lost her summer tan, her red eyes looked redder than they had in July.

"I'll die if you say it's too late."

I smoothed her hair. "I socked you, didn't I? Nothing's less chivalrous than that."

"Thank God you did!" She inspected the welt on her cheek in the mirror. "I wish it would never go away."

"I really *was* just bringing you home, you know, Peggy," I smiled, playing the kicker at the end of my hand. "When can I see you?"

She was properly amazed. "Jake?"

"What?"

"Oh, Jake, *now!* You've got to come up to my apartment right now!"

I made a mental salute to Joseph Morgan, *il mio maestro,* and another to Dr. Freud, caller of the whole cosmic hoedown: up to Miss Peggy's flat we tripped. A *pas de deux,* an *entrechat,* and that was that. I left on promises of greater things to come, which I had no special plans to keep.

He having stood me in such excellent stead that afternoon, it was rather a pity that, come nightfall and my first really clandestine visit to Rennie, I was no longer prepared to be Joe Morgan or any other sort of dancer. I was never highly sexed. For me the intervals between women were long, as a rule, and I was not normally disturbed by doing without sexual intercourse. A condition of erotic excitement such as I'd entertained during most of this first school day was almost as rare as a manic with me, and almost as easily dissipated. After the one game I was good for, I was as unarousable as a gelding.

That, I think, is not how Rennie had found me on the evening of our first adultery, shortly after we'd played Peeping Tom on Joe—the sheer energy required to be the spirited lover is difficult, but not impossible, for me to muster—but that's how I felt on this evening when I went to her. I was neither bored nor fatigued nor sad, nor excited nor fresh nor happy: merely a placid animal.

The initial act had been a paradigm of assumed inevitability.

Three days after our eavesdropping Joe went to Washington to do research in the Library of Congress, and before leaving he asked me to keep Rennie company during his absence—a very Morganesque request. I went out there and spent the afternoon playing with the boys. It was not *necessary* for me to do this at all, but neither was it obviously compromising. Rennie quite un-suggestively invited me to stay for dinner, and I did, though I had no special reason not to eat as usual in a restaurant. We scarcely spoke to each other. Rennie said once, "I feel lost without Joe," but I could think of no appropriate reply, and for that matter I was not certain how extensive was the intended meaning of her observation. After dinner I volunteered to oversee the boys' bath, spun them a bedtime story, and bade them good night. I could have left then, but my staying to drink ale with Rennie during the evening certainly had no clear significance. We talked im-personally and sporadically—much of the time nothing was said, but mutual silences were neither unusual nor uncomfortable with Rennie—and I truly remember little of our conversation, except that Rennie mentioned being weary and thanked me for having helped with the children that day.

The point I want to make is that on the face of it there was no overt act, no word or deed that unambiguously indicated desire on the part of either of us. I shall certainly admit that I found Rennie attractive that day. Her whole manner was one of ex-hausted strength: throughout the afternoon her movements had been heavy and deliberate, like those of a laborer who has worked two straight shifts; in the evening she sat for the most part without moving, and frequently upon blinking her eyes she would keep them shut for a full half minute, opening them at last with a wide stare and a heavy expiration of breath. All this I admired, but really rather abstractly, and any sexual desire that I felt was also more or less abstract. We spoke little of Joe, and not at all about what we'd seen through the living-room window.

Then at nine-thirty or thereabouts Rennie said, "I'm going to take a shower and go to bed, Jake," and I said, "All right." To reach the bathroom, she had to go through a little hallway off the living room; to get my jacket, I had to go to an open closet in this same hallway, and so it is still not quite necessary to raise an eyebrow at the fact that we got up from our chairs and went to the hallway together. There, if she turned to face me for a slight moment at the door to the bathroom, who's to say confidently that good nights were not on the tips of tongues? It happened that we embraced each other instead before we went our separate ways—but I think a slow-motion camera would not have shown who moved first—and it happened further (but I would not say *consequently*) that our separate ways led to the same bed. By that time, if we had been consciously thinking of first steps— and I for one certainly wasn't—I'm sure we both would have assumed that the first steps, whoever made them, had already been made. I mention this because it applies so often to people's reasoning about their behavior in situations that later turn out to be regrettable: it is possible to watch the sky from morning to midnight, or move along the spectrum from infrared to ultraviolet, without ever being able to put your finger on the precise point where a qualitative change takes place; no one can say, "It is exactly *here* that twilight becomes night," or blue becomes violet, or innocence guilt. One can go a long way into a situation thus without finding the word or gesture upon which initial responsibility can handily be fixed—such a long way that suddenly one realizes the change has already been made, is already history, and one rides along then on the sense of an inevitability, a too-lateness, in which he does not really believe, but which for one reason or another he does not see fit to question.

I could illustrate this phenomenon, in the case at hand, clear up to the point—well, up to the point where the cuckolding of Joe Morgan was pretty much an accomplished fact; but delicacy, to which I often incline, forbids. We spent a wordless, tumultuous night together, full of tumblings and flexings and shudders and such, exciting enough to experience but boring to describe; for the neighbors' sake I left before sunrise.

It is with reason that I say no more than this about our adultery: the whole business was without significance to me. I had no idea what was on Rennie's mind—and no wish to penetrate until afterwards her characteristic taciturnity—but I know that my own was empty. It was not a case of weatherlessness; my mood was one of first general and later specific desire, combined with a definite but not inordinate masculine curiosity: in other words, first I wanted to copulate, then I wanted to copulate with Rennie and in addition to learn not only "what she was like in bed," but also what the intimate relationship (I do not mean sexual relationship) would be like which I presumed would be established by our intercourse. Although I was not often gregarious or even very sociable, I could maintain a thoroughgoing curiosity about one or two people at a time.

That was all. Other than these half-articulated sentiments there was nothing on my mind. Rennie, a bed partner rather too athletic for my current taste, more than satisfied my desires, both general and specific, and my curiosity was satisfied that it would be satisfied as time went on. I cannot call my share in the act gratuitous in the sense of its being unmotivated—I knew why I went along with it—but I would call it both specifically (if not generally) unpremeditated and entirely unreflective. The fellow who committed it was not thinking ahead of his desire.

The next day I became engrossed in reading several volumes of plays that I'd borrowed from the college library at the Doctor's behest, and gave the matter no more thought of any sort. It was insignificant, unimportant, and, as far as I was concerned, inconsequential. I didn't read often, but when I got a fit on I read voraciously; for the next four days I scarcely left my room except to eat, and I read seven collections of plays—some seventy or eighty plays in all. The day after I finished the last volume was the first day of the school term, the day of this chapter, and it was, I think, not at all my love-making of five days earlier, but the release from my heavy diet of vicarious emotions, that induced my highly erotic mood.

In the evening, after supper, I felt tortoise-like, even lichen-like, and, left to myself, I'd have sat rocking in my chair, buried in comfortable torpidity, until bedtime. This inertia, which must be distinguished from both weatherlessness and Penn Station-type immobility, is mildly euphoric—my mind is neither empty nor still, but disengaged, and the idle race of fugitive thoughts that fill it spins past against a kind of all-pervasive, cosmic *awareness*, almost palpable and audible, which I can compare only to the text "I feel the breath of other planets blowing," from Schönberg's

Second String Quartet, or, less esoterically but about as accurately, to the atmospheric rustle on a radio receiver when the volume is turned on full. It is a state from which I can remove myself at will, but I'm usually reluctant to do so. It turned out that, as in the case of my July manic, a telephone call from Rennie dispelled it.

"Jake, I think you'd better come over here," she said. "I have to see you."

"All right." I had no feeling about going, except the special, non-urgent curiosity previously mentioned. "When?"

"Now. Joe's at his Scout meeting."

"All right."

I readily assumed that what was in the offing was a polishing of the crown of horns we'd already placed on Joe's brow; as I drove out to the Morgans' I attempted, halfheartedly, to be pleased by the irony of my friend's being at a Boy Scout meeting at the time. But it didn't work. Indeed, I was somewhat irritable, not a bit desirous; felt commonplace, conventional; *wanted* to feel conventional; didn't want to think about myself. Perhaps as a result, for the very first time since I'd met the Morgans, I experienced a sudden, marvelous sensation of guilt.

And, following immediately on this sensation, the guilt poured in with a violent shock that slacked my jaw, dizzied me at the wheel, brought sweat to my forehead and palms, and slightly sickened me. What in heaven's name was I doing? What, for God's sake, had I done? I was appalled. Does Jacob Horner betray the only man he can think of as a friend, and then double the felony by concealing the betrayal? I was anguished, as never before in my life. What is more, my anguish was pretty much unself-conscious: I was not aware of watching Jacob Horner suffer anguish. Had I been, I believe I'd have seen a face very like Laocoön's.

The instant assumption of this burden of guilt crushed me. I wanted to turn back, or, better, keep on going, out of Maryland, and not come back. This was a new feeling for me, and I had not the strength or courage, or the complexity, even to be curious about it, as I usually am about my rare moments of intense feeling. But I hadn't nerve enough to escape. I parked in front of Rennie's house, and after a while went inside. I had no idea what to do: certainly I was incapable of repeating the offense.

Rennie answered the door, dead white. As soon as she saw me she tried to say something, choked on it, and burst into tears.

"What's the matter, Rennie?" I took her shoulders and would have embraced her, only to steady both of us, but she jerked away, horrified, and fell into a chair. The intensity of her agitation increased my nausea: cold sweat ran under my clothes; I felt weak-kneed and ready to vomit.

"It's incredible, Rennie!" I cried. She looked up at me but couldn't speak, and tears sprang to my eyes. I had to sit down.

"God, I feel *weak!*" I said. The enormity of the injury I'd done Joe was almost too painful to bear. He never looked finer or stronger to me than at that moment when I thought of him at the Boy Scout meeting. "What in the world was I *thinking* of? Where in hell *was* I?"

Rennie closed her eyes and whipped her head from side to side. After a moment she calmed herself somewhat and wiped her eyes with the top of her wrist.

"What are we going to do, Jake?"

"Does he know yet?"

She shook her head, pressing the butt of her hand against her brow.

"He worked terribly hard in Washington, to get enough material to last him awhile, and then when he came home"—she choked on it—"he was sweeter to me than he's ever been before. I wanted to die. And when I thought—how I was carrying his child when it happened——"

I burned with shame.

"Do you know what I did? I went to our doctor this morning and asked him for Ergotrate to abort it. He was terrible to me. He's known me since I was little, and he got angry and told me I should be ashamed."

"Oh, God."

"Then it turned out I didn't need it. This afternoon I started menstruating. I wasn't even pregnant; I was just late."

She broke down again; apparently the fact that she wasn't pregnant somehow made things worse.

"Will you tell Joe?" I asked.

"I don't know," she said dully. "I can't imagine *never* telling him. God, the last thing we'd do is hide anything from each other! These five days have been terrible, Jake. I've had to pretend to be gay and alert all the time. I swear, the only reason I haven't killed myself is that that would just be cheating him more."

"How would he take it?"

"I don't know! That's the terrible thing. I can imagine him doing anything from just laughing to shooting both of us. What's terrible is that I don't know *what* he'd do, and that's because neither of us would ever dream of doing anything like this to the other! Do you think I should tell him?"

"I don't know," I said, but so unnerved was I by my guilt that the prospect terrified me.

"You're afraid of him, aren't you?" Rennie asked.

It was fortunate that she asked this, because although the taunt in her voice was slight—the real sense being that she too was afraid—nevertheless it was fundamental, perhaps the most fundamental taunt one human being can throw at another. I steadied at once.

"I'm afraid of violence," I said. "I'm always afraid of any kind of violence, even violent emotions. But you have to understand that when anything that matters is concerned, I wouldn't go an inch out of my way to avoid violence. Fear is different from cowardice. If I don't want you to tell Joe it's because I'm afraid of possible violence, but I'd never say a word to talk you out of telling him. There's nothing a man can do about fear, but he has to choose to be cowardly."

This was pretty much true; at least I felt it was at the time. I would not normally be cowardly unless taken by surprise. But I felt weak, pitifully weak: weak to have gone to bed with Rennie in the first place; weak not to have told Joe at once afterwards; weak now at being so afraid of his finding out. The violence was one thing; just as intense was my fear of his disappointment in me, his disapproval of me, and his disgust with me—I felt weak at being afraid of these things, which ordinarily would not bother me. I could account for all except the original weakness in having unthinkingly betrayed Joe, because one weakness spawns other weaknesses as one strength spawns other strengths; but there was no excusing that original one. I was miserable.

After a while Rennie said, "Joe will be coming home in a few minutes."

I rose to leave.

"Rennie—God, I'm sorry. Do whatever you think is best."

She didn't look at me.

"I don't know what to do. Sometimes I wake up in the morning feeling wonderful: he—we always sleep with our arms around each other——" This overwhelmed her for a moment. "Then I remember it, against my will, and I want to die. I wish I'd never waked up. I hardly believe it happened. I guess I don't really believe it *did* happen. It *couldn't* have happened, Jake: I couldn't have hurt him like that."

"That's how I feel," I said. I almost reminded her how much it would hurt him to find out, and checked myself just in time, afraid that if I said it she'd think I was trying to talk her out of telling him—precisely the truth—and therefore tell him. With all my heart I didn't want her to tell him.

"Do whatever you have to do," I said. "Be strong as you can."

I left and drove back to my room. It was useless to try to read or sleep: there was no slipping into someone else's world or otherwise escaping my own, which had me by the throat. All I could think of was Rennie there in the house with Joe, perhaps in bed with him; I wondered how long her strength would last against his embraces, his sleeping with her in his arms, his new sweetness. My heart was filled equally with profound sympathy for Rennie, whom I felt I'd placed in that position, and with fear that she'd tell him what we'd done. He must have walked in about ten minutes after I left—I perspired to think I'd got out just in time.

It occurred to me that, granted all this profound sympathy, tenderness, and general concern for Rennie, I could have stayed to face Joe directly myself and tell him everything. Every passing minute added to my deception. So, then, it seemed I had to admit that I *was* a coward after all: an adulterer, a deceiver, a betrayer of friends, and a coward. And now I was self-conscious again; I watched myself refuse to recognize that beside my bed was a telephone by means of which one could call Joe Morgan; that parked out front was a Chevrolet by means of which one could drive out there. Cowardice, apparently, is as proliferous as is weakness. The act of will required to make the tiny motion of lifting the telephone was beyond me.

My curiosity returned with my self-consciousness. I placed my hand on the telephone and for some time studied with interest the blushing, uncomfortable fellow who would not pick it up.

8. *Such Guilt as I Felt Could Not Be Sustained, nor Could Such Self-Contempt*

SUCH GUILT AS I FELT COULD NOT BE SUSTAINED, NOR COULD SUCH SELF-CONTEMPT. Killing it with sleep was out of the question, because I couldn't sleep, except fitfully. No great activity or overwhelming new mood appeared, to remove it from my mind. The loathing that I felt for myself soured my digestion, so that food lay like clay in my stomach; poisoned my consciousness, so that attempts at diversion—books or movies—were agonizing, and acting the professor was a bitter farce. As though to complement my mood, it rained for the next three days: one got soaked running from cars to buildings and from buildings to cars; the classrooms smelled of wet clothing, chalk dust, and stale air; students stared sullenly out the windows. To hear my own voice, prating of adverbs and prepositions like an insane parrot, sickened me; no one paid attention. Penned in my room alone with myself, I was frantic.

I believe a week of such self-revulsion would have brought me to suicide: certainly that was what occupied my mind a great deal of the time. I envied all dead things—the fat earthworms that lay squashed upon the wet sidewalks, the animals whose fried bodies I chewed at mealtimes, people decomposing in muddy cemeteries—but I had at hand no means of self-destruction that I was courageous enough to use.

Stendhal claims to have once postponed suicide simply out of curiosity about the contemporary political situation in France: he wanted to see what would happen next. And, apart from cowardice, there was a similar thing that stayed my hand—since the

evening of my last interview with Rennie, Joe had not been to
school. Shirley, Dr. Schott's secretary, announced that Mr. Morgan was ill, but was expected to return to work any day. The
suspense involved in his absence was torturous, to be sure: was
he actually ill, or had Rennie confessed her adultery? What was
the specific connection between her confession and his absence?
Most important of all, what would his reaction be? These were
terrifying questions, but while they made me shrink at the thought
of finally coming face to face with him, they also worked counter
to any suicidal impulses; I could not kill myself at least until they
were answered, if no other reason than that from one very
special point of view I would never learn whether doing away
with myself had been *called for*.

On the third day, after lunch, Joe appeared at school and taught
his afternoon classes. I paled when accidentally I met him in
the main hallway between periods; my nervousness was made more
excruciating by the fact that we had time to do no more than
say hello to each other. He was entirely calm, but my feelings
must have shown all over my face. I've no idea how I managed
my last two classes.

At four o'clock I went to my office to grade my first batch of
compositions, and a few minutes later Joe walked in. The two men
who shared the office had gone home. Joe sat on the edge of the
desk next to mine.

"How's it going?" he asked.

I shook my head, aching to tell him everything before he could
tell me he already knew; but by this time I was so demoralized
and confirmed in my weakness that all I could see was the
remote possibility that he still didn't know. As long as this possibility existed I was not strong enough to confess, and yet I knew
very well that whatever happened to remove it would at the same
time render my confession pointless.

"First batch of themes," I said, keeping my eyes on them. "How
do you feel? Shirley said you've been sick."

"I have," Joe said. No doubt his face would have told me how
to understand this reply, but I couldn't look him in the face.
I pretended to examine a theme paper, and clutched at the hope
that he was speaking literally.

"How about you?" he asked; there was no sarcasm in his voice, only curiosity. My heart lifted.

"Oh, as usual."

"No colds from all this rain?"

"Nope. I don't take cold easily." I could have laughed aloud with relief! Shame I would doubtless feel later, but just then the narrowness of my escape exhilarated me. He didn't know! Silently I thanked Rennie with all my heart—almost loved her at that moment.

"What'd you have?" I asked, more steadily and cheerfully. "Mononucleosis or gonorrhea?" Now I even dared glance at him to see his response to my slight joke.

"Horner," he said painfully, "why in the name of Christ did you fuck Rennie?"

The question was like a blow to the head: I grew dizzy; my stomach knotted up. For a moment it was impossible to talk. He waited, regarding me with, I think, fascinated disgust.

"Lord, Joe——" I croaked. At the first sound of my voice, at the sheer effort of speaking, tears filled my eyes, and I blushed and sweated. I had nothing to say.

Joe pushed his glasses back on his nose.

"Why'd you want to do it? What was your reason?"

"Joe, I can't talk now."

"Yes, you can," he said evenly. "You talk now, or I'll knock the crap out of you."

This, I should say, while entirely in keeping with his frank nature, was a double tactical error on Joe's part. In the first place, although the threat of violence frightened me, it also put me immediately on the defensive, and if defensiveness is an indication of guilt feelings, it is at the same time a release from them: a murderer bent on escaping punishment has little time to contemplate the vileness of his deed. Second, it seems to me that, generally speaking, the only way for a person to get truly honest answers from another person, and be confident of their honesty, is to create the suggestion that any answer will be received cordially, without punishment.

"I didn't *want* to do it, Joe. I don't know why I did it."

"Horseshit. Maybe you don't *approve* of what you did, but you obviously wanted to do it, or you wouldn't have done it. What a man ends up doing is what he has to take responsibility for having wanted to do. Why did you *think* you were doing it?"

"I wasn't thinking, Joe. If I'd been thinking I wouldn't have done it."

"Did you think I'd like the idea? What kind of a guy did you think I was?"

"I didn't think, Joe."

"You're being deliberately obtuse, Horner, and that irritates me."

"Maybe obtuse, but not deliberately. I don't know what unconscious motives I might have had, Joe, but whatever they were, they were unconscious, so I can't know anything about them." And, I was thinking, can't be held responsible for them. "But I swear I had no conscious motives at all."

"Don't you *want* to be held responsible?" Joe asked incredulously.

"I do, Joe, believe me," I said halfheartedly. "But I can't give you reasons when I didn't have any. Do you want me to make up reasons?"

"What kind of picture did you have of Rennie and me, for God's sake?" Joe said, exasperated. "The thing that appalls me most is what you must have thought of our relationship, to pull a stunt like that! I know you made fun of a lot of things about us—I always had to excuse a lot of your crap because I was interested in you. Did you decide that Rennie was easy game because I was driving her hard, or what? And don't you draw any distinctions between easy game and fair game? Did you really think you could split her off from me to the point where she'd keep something like that a secret?"

"Joe, for God's sake, I know it was a hell of a thing to do! I'm not defending adultery and deception."

"But you committed them. Why did you do it? Do you think I care what you think about the seventh commandment? I'm not objecting to adultery and deception as sins, Horner; I object to your screwing Rennie and then trying to get her to hide the fact from me. Listen, I don't give a damn about you. You've already forfeited any claims you might have thought you had to my friendship. On that level I'm through with you. It may be that

I'm through with Rennie, too, but I can't tell until I've heard the whole story. I want to hear your version of the business, if you've got one. I've already heard Rennie's—that's what I've been doing for the last three days. But her memory's not perfect, and like anybody else's it's selective. Naturally, what I've heard puts the best possible interpretation on what she did, and perhaps the worst possible on what you did. Remember, boy, *I wasn't there.* Rennie's not playing innocent, but I want all the facts and all the interpretations of the facts."

"What can I say, Joe?"

He sprang down lightly from the desk. "I'll be up to see you after supper," he said. "I'd rather hear what you have to say without Rennie around. Don't worry," he added with some contempt; "I won't shoot you, Jake. I wouldn't have mentioned violence if Rennie hadn't said you expected it."

Well, I ate an uneasy meal. Nevertheless, the notion of suicide no longer entered my head. As if to symbolize my weather change, the rain let up during the late afternoon, and by six o'clock ceased altogether, though the sky was still overcast. Indeed, I even found myself adding my former intense guilt feeling to the list of my other weaknesses, and consequently regretting it along with the rest. I felt no better about what I'd done—fornicating with their wives behind my friends' backs and then deceiving them about it were evils in terms of my own point of view whenever I could be said to have a point of view—but I felt *differently* about it. Now that it was out in the open I felt truly relieved, and dealing concretely with Joe shifted the focus of my attention from my guilt to what I could do toward salvaging my self-respect. If I was going to live, I had to live with myself, and because much of the time I was a moral animal, the salvage job was the first order of business. What had been done had been done, but the past, after all, exists only in the minds of those who are thinking about it in the present, and therefore in the interpretations which are put upon it. In that sense it is never too late to *do* something about the past. Not that I wanted to recreate the incident, *à la* Moscow, in a way favorable to myself: my difficulty, precisely, was that I hadn't the desire to defend what I'd done, or the ability to explain it. The Jacob Horner that I felt a desperate desire to defend was not the one who had tumbled stupidly on Joe Morgan's bed with Joe Morgan's wife or the one who had burned in shame and skulking fear for days afterwards, but the one who was now the object of Joe's disgust—the Horner of the present moment and all the Horners to come. And, for better or worse, the fellow who rose to the defense was still contrite—profoundly contrite—but no longer humble.

Joe came up to my room shortly after seven and sat not quite at ease in one of my grotesque chairs. The very fact of his coming there instead of asking me to come to his place, while no doubt the only way to operate, was, it seemed to me, another tactical error—at least his manner was more subdued than it had been that afternoon. But, as he would have observed at once had I been in a position to point this out, Joe by his very nature had no tactic. It was, of course, the simple fact that he wasn't interested in prosecuting any case against me which made the job of defending myself more difficult, if not impossible.

"Let me explain my position in this, Jake," he began.

"God, Joe, yours is the only position that doesn't need it!"

"That's not right. The fact that you don't realize it's not right is part of your misunderstanding of Rennie and me."

"Joe, I realize perfectly well that you'd have been completely justified in beating the daylights out of me or even shooting me. I don't question my guilt."

"And I'm not interested in your guilt," he said. "This business of harping on your guilt and my right to be outraged is an oversimplification of the problem. By pretending that all the fuss is over broken commandments, you allow yourself not to take any of it very seriously, because you know as well as I do that those things aren't absolutes. I'm not interested in blaming anybody for anything. If you really understood us you'd realize that—but of course if you really understood us this wouldn't have happened."

"I wish to Christ it hadn't," I said fervently.

"That's silly. If anything I'm glad it did happen, because it uncovered real problems that I didn't know existed. Try to remember that I'm not the least bit interested in or concerned about you. If that hurts your pride, all I can say is that your pride isn't the most important thing on my mind right now. If I can explain our problem to you, maybe you'll understand what's relevant and what isn't."

And so he explained it:

"The most important thing in the world to me—one of my absolutes, I suppose—is the relationship between Rennie and me. Rennie's already told me all the stuff she could remember having told you about us during your horseback rides. The fact that she told you is one of my problems, but since she did it's probably best to hear my end of it too.

"You know I met Rennie in New York while I was at Columbia. What attracted me to her was that she was the most *self-sufficient* girl I'd ever met; maybe the only one—our culture doesn't turn them out too generously. She was popular enough, but she didn't seem to need popularity or even friendship at all. If she ever felt lonely back then, I believe it was because she didn't always understand her own self-sufficiency—certainly she didn't feel lonely very often. That's what attracted me. I had been in the Army before Columbia, and in a college fraternity before that, and I'd done plenty enough horsing around with women not to confuse one kind of attraction with another. Have you laid very many women, Jake?"

"Not very many," I replied modestly.

"I only asked because I wonder if that mixing-up of attractions might not be involved in your part of this business. Possibly it was in Rennie's: she'd never slept with any man but me before."

I squirmed with contrition.

"It was because of this self-sufficiency I thought I saw in her that I was able to imagine having the kind of relationship with her that she described to you—a more or less permanent relationship. It would only be possible between two pretty independent people who had a complete respect for each other's self-sufficiency. The fact that we didn't *need* each other in any of the ordinary 'basic' ways seemed to me to mean that we could be damned good for each other in all kinds of other ways. But I think you've heard all this. It explains, incidentally, why Rennie's telling you all that stuff in the pine grove surprised me and bothered me—not that privacy is so important in itself, but it's an indication of the kind of independence we thought we had.

"Now you must realize that I don't have any theories about sexual morality, for Christ's sake. Rennie and I never talked about it at all. But I believe we both tacitly assumed that any kind of extramarital sex was out of the question for us in the same way that lying or homosexuality was out of the question: we hadn't the slightest need for it. Not only don't I have any philosophy about sexual morals; I don't seem to have any automatic feelings about them, either. But Rennie did. Very strong ones. I'm sure she couldn't have defended them rationally—no ethical program can be defended rationally clear down the line. Probably it was a carryover from her home life. But the fact that she felt strongly about marital fidelity was enough to make it our way of operating: her feeling didn't conflict with any private notions of my own, and for that matter it kind of suited the relationship we wanted, because it kept everything intramural.

"So that was my ideal of Rennie: self-sufficiency, strength (I could tell you a lot about her strength), and privacy. And there's our problem. According to my version of Rennie, what happened couldn't have happened. According to her version of herself, it couldn't have happened. And yet it happened. That's why even now we have a hard time believing it really *did* happen: we not only have to accept the fact that she did what she did, but also the fact that she *wanted* to do it—don't think I'm accusing you of rape. Accepting those facts makes it necessary to correct our version of Rennie, and right now we can't see how any version that allows for what happened would also allow for the kind of relationship we thought we had. And that relationship was the orientation post that gave every other part of our lives—everything we did—its values. It's more important to me than being a great scholar or a great anything else. If we have to scrap it, all these other things lose their point. There's nothing emotional about all this—it's as coherent a picture as I can make of the way I see what Rennie and I were doing, and why everything's got to be held in suspension now until we decide the significance of what happened. Rennie feels the same way. It's what we've been talking about for the last three days, and it's what we'll talk about for a long time to come, if she doesn't do away with herself while I'm up here with you."

My heart went out to him.

"I'm sorry, Joe."

"But that's beside the point!" he laughed, not humorously. "The only reason I'm interested in your share of this—the reason I keep asking you why you did it and what you thought of Rennie and me to give you the idea of trying her out—is that I have to know to what extent your actions influenced her actions."

"Joe, I swear, I take full responsibility for everything that happened."

"But I see you're not willing to help me. Do you take full responsibility for the fact that she was on top the first time? Was it you that bit yourself on your own left shoulder? Damn it, I told you Rennie wasn't playing innocent! What she and I want out of each other isn't possible unless we assume that we're free agents—*pretend* we are even when we suspect we aren't. Why do you insist on playing games like this, Jake? I'm obviously being as honest as I can. Just once, for God's sake, drop all the acting and be straight with me!"

"I'm doing my best, Joe," I declared uncomfortably.

"But you refuse to forget about yourself even for a minute! What do you want? If you're trying to make me feel good about you, I swear this isn't the way. I don't know whether anything you say will work that way, but the only chance at all is to be absolutely honest now."

"Well, it seems to me that you won't accept anything as honest except whatever it is that you want to hear, and I'm not sure what that is or I'd say it. Ask me questions, and I'll answer them."

"Why'd you screw Rennie?"

"I don't *know!*"

"What reasons do you think you might have had?"

"I couldn't give any reason that I think would be true."

"Hell, Horner, you don't just *do* things. What was on your mind?"

"Nothing was on my mind."

Joe began to show anger.

"Listen, Joe," I pleaded. "You've got to allow for the fact that people—maybe yourself excluded—aren't going to have conscious motives for everything they do. There'll always be a few things in their autobiography that they can't account for. Now when that happens the person could still make up conscious reasons—maybe in your case they'd spring to mind the first time you thought about an act after you did it—but they'd always be rationalizations after the fact."

"That's all right," Joe insisted. "If I went along with everything you just said, I'd still have to say that even the rationalizing after the fact has to be done, and the person has to be held responsible —has to hold *himself* responsible—for his rationalizings, if he wants to be a moral actor."

"Then you'll have to go further still and allow that sometimes a man won't even be able to rationalize. Nothing comes to mind. You don't accept it when I take full responsibility for everything that happened, and you won't accept it if I don't take any responsibility. But in this business I don't see what's in between."

I lit a cigarette. I was nervous, and happy and unhappy at the same time about the fact that despite my nervousness I felt pretty good, pretty sure of my mind, pretty satisfied at my ability to play a role that struck me as being at once somewhat abhorrent and yet apparently ineluctable. That is, I felt it to be a role, but I wasn't sure that anything else wouldn't also be a role, and I couldn't think of any other possible roles for me anyhow. If, as may be, this is the best anyone can do—at least the best I could do—why, then, it's as much as can ever be signified by the term *sincerity*.

"That's all beside the point," Joe said. "I'm not interested in how much responsibility you're willing to assume. What I want to know is what happened, so I'll know how much responsibility to hand out all around, whether you accept it or not. When did you get the idea you could make out with Rennie?"

"I don't know. Maybe not till we were in bed, maybe as soon as I met you all, maybe sometime in between. I wasn't aware of getting the idea."

"What did she do or say that gave you the idea?"

"I'm not sure I *had* the idea. The afternoon and evening I was out there, while you were gone, I could interpret everything she said and didn't say as evidence that she was prepared to make love with me, or I could interpret none of it as evidence. At the time I don't believe I was interpreting at all."

"What was said?"

"God, I can't remember conversations! Didn't Rennie tell you?"

"Sure she did. Can't you remember, or are you playing obtuse again?"

"I can't remember."

"Well, what the hell am I going to do?" Joe cried. "You claim you didn't have any conscious motives. You aren't aware of any unconscious motives. You won't rationalize. You didn't make any conscious interpretations of anything Rennie did. And you can't remember any conversations. Have I got to agree with Rennie that you don't even exist? What else makes a man a human being except these things?"

I shrugged. "I could add some more things to the list of my inabilities."

"Don't bother. Don't you see, Horner, if you could convince me that very much of what Rennie did was under your influence, it wouldn't be good, because she shouldn't have been in a position to be influenced very much. And if you convinced me that very little if any of it was your influence it still wouldn't be good, because by our picture of her she couldn't have chosen to do it. So it's not that I'm trying to solve the problem by passing the buck. The thing is, I can't be sure just what the problem is that has to be solved until I know just what happened and why each thing happened."

I felt strong enough by this time to say, "I don't think you'd have as much of a problem if you had more respect for the answer 'I don't know.' It can be an awfully honest answer, Joe. When somebody close to you injures you unaccountably, and you say, 'Why in the world did you do that?' and they say, 'I don't know,' it seems to me that that answer can be worthy of respect. And if it's somebody you love or trust who says it, and they say it contritely, I think it could even be acceptable."

"But once they've said it," Joe said, "once they're in a position to *have* to say it, how do you tell whether the love and trust that make it acceptable were justified?"

How indeed? All I could have replied is that I personally couldn't imagine ever having to reach that question, but I could certainly imagine Joe reaching it.

"Well, that could never do, Jake," Joe said, getting ready to go. "If that has to be your answer, I can't see how to deal with you, and if it's got to be Rennie's I can't see how to deal with her either. That answer simply doesn't come up in the Morgan cosmos. Maybe I'm in the wrong cosmos, but it's the only one I can see setting up serious relationships in. You ought to know, boy, that Rennie blames you for nearly everything that happened."

I was a little surprised, but I simply wrinkled my forehead and made a quick *tch* in the left corner of my mouth.

"I don't see why you shouldn't believe her," I declared.

"But you think it's pretty ordinary of her, don't you? The kind of thing you'd expect a *woman* to do?"

"I don't have any opinion," I said. "Or rather, I have both opinions at once."

This observation nearly clenched Joe's fists in disgust, and he left my room.

I could say that this conversation left me disturbed, but it seems more accurate to say that it left me stimulated: my disturbance was the disturbance of stimulation more than of guilt, the same disturbance that a complicated argument always produces—the disturbance, neither pleasant nor unpleasant, but invariably exhilarating, effected by any duel of articulations, where the duelists have things of sufficient value at stake to make the contest, if after all a game, at least a serious game.

Articulation! There, by Joe, was *my* absolute, if I could be said to have one. At any rate, it is the only thing I can think of about which I ever had, with any frequency at all, the feelings one usually has for one's absolutes. To turn experience into speech—that is, to classify, to categorize, to conceptualize, to grammarize, to syntactify it—is always a betrayal of experience, a falsification of it; but only so betrayed can it be dealt with at all, and only in so dealing with it did I ever feel a man, alive and kicking. It is therefore that, when I had cause to think about it at all, I responded to this precise falsification, this adroit, careful myth-making, with all the upsetting exhilaration of any artist at his work. When my mythoplastic razors were sharply honed, it was unparalleled sport to lay about with them, to have at reality.

In other senses, of course, I don't believe this at all.

9. *One of the Things I Did Not See Fit to Tell Joe Morgan*

ONE OF THE THINGS I DID NOT SEE FIT TO TELL JOE MORGAN (for to do so would have been to testify further against myself) is that it was never very much of a chore for me, at various times, to maintain with perfectly equal unenthusiasm contradictory, or at least polarized, opinions at once on a given subject. I did so too easily, perhaps, for my own ultimate mobility. Thus it seemed to me that the Doctor was insane, and that he was profound; that Joe was brilliant and also absurd; that Rennie was strong and weak; and that Jacob Horner—owl, peacock, chameleon, donkey, and popinjay, fugitive from a medieval bestiary—was at the same time giant and dwarf, plenum and vacuum, and admirable and contemptible. Had I explained this to Joe he'd have added it to his store of evidence that I did not exist: my own feeling was that it was and was not such evidence. I explain it now in order to make as clear as I can what I mean when I say that I was shocked and not surprised, disgusted and amused, excited and bored, when, the evening after the conversation just recorded, Rennie came up to my room. I'd had a brilliant day with my students, explaining gerunds, participles, and infinitives, and my eloquence had brought me around to feeling both guilty and nonchalant about the Morgan affair.

"Well, I'll be damned!" I said when I saw her. "Come on in! Have you been excommunicated, or what?"

"I didn't want to come up here," Rennie said tersely. "I didn't want to see you again at all, Jake."

"Oh. But people want to do the things they do."

"Joe drove me in, Jake. He told me to come up here."

This was intended as a bombshell, I believe, but I was not in an explodable mood.

"What the hell for?"

Rennie had started out with pretty firm, solemn control, but now she got choky and couldn't, or wouldn't, answer the question.

"Has he turned you out?"

"No. Can't you understand why he sent me up here? Please don't make me explain it!" Tears were imminent.

"Honestly, I couldn't guess, Rennie. Are we supposed to re-enact the crime in a more analyzable way, or what?"

Well, that finished her control; the head-whipping began. Rennie, incidentally, looked great to me. She'd obviously been suffering intensely for the past few days, and, like exhausted strength, it lent her the sexual attractiveness that tormented women occasionally have. Tender, lovelike feelings announced their presence in me.

"Everything that's happened wrenches my heart," I said to her, laying my hand on her shoulder. "You've no idea how much I sympathize with Joe, and how much more with you. But he sure is making a Barnum and Bailey out of it, isn't he? This sending you up here is the damnedest thing I ever heard of. Is it supposed to be punishment?"

"It's not ridiculous unless you're determined to see it that way," Rennie said, tearfully but vehemently. "Of course *you'd* say it was, just so you won't have to take Joe seriously."

"What's it all about, for heaven's sake?"

"I didn't want to see you again, Jake. I told Joe that. He told me everything you said to him last night, and at first I thought you were lying all the way. I guess you know I've hated you ever since we made love; when I told Joe about it, I didn't leave out anything we did—not a single detail—but I blamed you for everything."

"That's okay. I don't have any real opinion on the subject."

"I can't blame you any more," Rennie went on. "It's too easy, and it doesn't really solve anything. I guess I don't have any opinion either—and Joe doesn't either."

"He doesn't?"

"He's heartbroken. So am I. But he's determined not to evade the question in any way, or take a stand just to cover up the hurt. You don't realize what an obsession this is with him! Sometimes I've thought we'd both lose our minds this past week. This thing is tearing us up! But Joe would rather be torn up than falsify the trouble in any way. That's why I'm here."

"Why?"

She hung her head.

"I told him I couldn't stand to see you again, whether you were responsible or not. He got angry and said I was being melodramatic, evading the question. I thought he was going to hit me again! But instead he calmed down and—even made love to me, and explained that if we were ever going to end our trouble we'd have to be extra careful not to make up any versions of things that would keep us from facing the facts squarely. If anything, we had to do all we could to throw ourselves as hard as possible against the facts, and as often as possible, no matter how much it hurt. He said that as it stands now we're defeated, and the only possible chance to save anything is never to leave the problem for a minute. I told him I'd die if I had to live with it much longer the way I've been doing, and he said he might too, but it's the only way. I guess you think this is ridiculous."

"No opinion," I said, meaning I felt contradictory opinions.

"One of the things he thinks we mustn't do is drop you yet, or let you drop us. That's why he brought me up here. Refusing to see you again is—evading the issue."

"Well, I'm happy as hell to see you, but I must say I'm all in favor of evading any issue if it's both painful and insoluble. Aren't you?"

With all her heart, I could see, she was indeed.

"No," she said determinedly. "I agree with Joe completely."

"Well, what are we supposed to do? Talk philosophy?"

Head-whipping. "Jake, for Christ's sake, tell me *honestly* what you think of Joe."

"I honestly have a number of opinions," I smiled.

"What are they?"

"Well, in the first place—not first in order of intensity—he's noble as the dickens."

Rennie laughed and cried at once.

"He's noble, strong, and brave, more than anybody I've ever seen. A disaster for him is a disaster for reason, intelligence, and civilization, because he's the quintessence of these things. There's nobody else like him in the United States. I believe this."

Rennie so melted that, had I chosen, I could have embraced her at that moment without protest.

"In the second place," I said, "he's completely ridiculous. Contemptible. A buffoon, a sophist, and a boor. Arrogant, small, intolerant, a little bit cruel, and even stupid. He uses logic and this childish honesty as a club and a shield at the same time. Or you could say he's just insane, a monomaniac: he's fixed in the delusion that intelligence will solve all problems."

"But you know very well he could reply to that!"

"Sure, he can defend his position and his method, but he can't solve this problem happily in terms of it. But you know, all these versions of him are complimentary, because they're extreme. My last opinion, which I don't hold any more strongly than the others, is that he's a little bit of all these things, but mainly just a pretty unremarkable guy, more pathetic than tragic, and more amusing than contemptible. Faintly grotesque and in the last analysis not terribly charming or even pleasant. Kind of silly and awfully naïve. That's our Joseph. Not a man to take too seriously, because he simply doesn't represent his position brilliantly enough or even coherently enough. I should add that I feel all these things about myself, too, and some more besides."

"Jake, you know he could answer all those charges."

"Sure. The beauty of it is that it doesn't make any difference whether he can or not. They're not charges: they're opinions. Hell, Rennie, don't get the wrong idea: I like Joe all right."

"You're acting awfully superior."

I laughed. "One of my opinions, along with the one that I'm inferior to Joe in most ways, is that I'm superior to him in most ways. You be honest with me now: what does Joe really have on his mind in sending you up here?"

"We've had to agree that even if you're the one who started the whole thing, I couldn't have allowed you to influence me if I hadn't wanted to be influenced. You took advantage of a weak time in my life, but you didn't rape me. I can't deny Joe's statement that if I ended up in bed with you it's because when all's said and done I *wanted* to, no matter how repugnant the idea is now. So Joe insists that all my dislike for you now is beside the point. He asked me how I'd have felt three weeks ago if he'd suggested that I make love to you, and I had to say, 'I don't know.' Then he asked me how I'd feel if he suggested it now, and I told him I was horrified and repelled by the idea. He said that's the sort of reaction we have to guard against, because it obscures the problem. We have to be as honest as possible about what we really believe, and not confuse it with what we think is safe or prudent to believe, and we have to act on our real beliefs so we can know where we stand. And apparently—this is what Joe said—I believe it's all right for me to make love to other men, at least to you, whether I want to admit it to myself or not, since I did it."

"Good Lord!"

"Jake—he sent me up here to do it again."

"But you disagree with him about this, don't you?"

She did, of course, as much as she'd disagreed about the necessity of not evading the whole issue, but she'd already committed herself to agreeing with him on that, and for that matter on everything else. It took her a moment to answer.

"I hate the idea, Jake! Everything in me recoils at the idea. But that hate is just like my feelings about you. Nobody has to point that out to me. I'm lost, Jake! I'm not as strong as Joe or even you. I'm not strong enough to get caught in this!"

Well, now. It occurred to me that Joe's position, while entirely illogical (Rennie's single adultery, of course, did not at all necessarily imply that she believed extramarital sex was *generally* "all right" with either other men in general or me in particular: at most it implied that she'd been willing to do it just once), afforded me a chance to really persecute her if I wanted to. It was a great temptation to cut short the conversation and say, "Okay, there's the bed"; but I was not in a Rennie-torturing mood.

"Are you willing to do it, then?" I asked her.

"No! God, it's the last thing in the world I could ever do again!"

"Joe's insane. You know, I could say this strikes me as being perverted on his part."

"Go ahead and say it. Then you won't have to try to understand him."

"That's a wonderful line," I laughed. "It cancels out any possible criticism anyone could ever make of him! That line and the one about his being strong enough to be a caricature of himself—those two defenses make anybody unassailable."

"But in his case they're true," Rennie insisted.

"What time is he picking you up?"

"We assumed you'd drive me home afterwards," she said glibly.

"After we'd finished?"

"Stop it, please!"

"Well, are you ready to go? Home, I mean?"

She looked at me, bewildered.

"He's not going to examine you each time, is he?" I grinned. "He couldn't tell anyhow. All you have to do is swear on your scout's honor we did our duty."

Now for the first time she saw the real nature of her dilemma: she had to choose between going to bed with me, which was repugnant to her, and lying to Joe, which was also repugnant to her, since the third alternative—asserting her own opinion by simply refusing to comply with his policy decisions at all—was apparently beyond her strength.

"Oh, God! What would you do if you were me, Jake?"

"I'd have told him to go to hell!" I said cheerfully. "I wouldn't have come up here in the first place. But since you did, if I were you I wouldn't hesitate to lie to him. Give him a string of gory details. Tell him we made love five times and committed sodomy twice. He's asking for it. I'll bet he won't send you up here again if you make it sound hot enough. It's the old trick of getting rid of a bad law by overenforcing it."

Rennie bit her knuckle and whipped her head shortly.

"I can't lie to him. I can't ever do that again."

"Then tell him to go to hell."

"You don't understand how this thing has affected him, Jake. He's not insane; I couldn't even call him neurotic. I believe he's thinking more clearly and intensely than he ever has in his life.

But this is a life-and-death business with him. With both of us. It's the biggest crisis we ever had."

"What could he do if you just said you won't string along with him on this one thing?"

"I can imagine him walking out flat, for good, or killing himself or all of us. I can even imagine him bringing me right back up here and coming up himself to make sure——"

"To make sure you do what you're supposed to want to do? God, this is funny!"

"He'd think I was letting him down completely. Throwing up my hands."

"Well, then, for Christ's sake let's go to bed. If you can't pretend to take him seriously, let's really take him seriously. I guarantee he won't send you up here again." I stood up. "Come on, girl: you can tell him all the things I said before and be telling the truth. We'll give old Joe an object lesson."

"How can you even *think* of it?" Rennie cried.

To tell the truth, my feelings were ambivalent as usual. Rennie's conflict was the classical one between what she liked and what she approved of—rather, between her dislike of further adultery and her disapproval of lying to Joe—but mine was between two things that I approved of and also between two things that I liked. I approved of disengaging myself from any further participation in the business that had so disrupted the Morgans' extraordinary relationship (which, I might as well add, I regarded as an admirable one, as a matter of fact, but which I knew better than to think I could have enjoyed personally in very many of my moods) yet at the same time I approved of the idea of going along with Joe on this point, both because I had pledged my co-operation and because I really believed that one good dose of his medicine would make him change his prescription. Also, though I was at times entirely capable of enjoying sexual sadism, I was not just then in a frame of mind to like an intercourse that would be pure torture for Rennie; nevertheless, as I mentioned earlier, her suffering exerted a powerful physical attraction on me. My guilt feelings, incidentally, although I'd still have agreed to their propriety, had got lost in the melodrama of Joe's new step.

I was too entirely astonished and intrigued by his action to devote much attention to feeling guilty.

"I'm not taking a stand," I declared. "I'm an issue evader from way back. I'll go along with you any way you want."

"I can't do it!" Rennie wailed.

"Let's go home, then."

"I *can't!* Please, *please,* either throw me out or rape me, Jake! I can't do anything!"

"I'm not going to make up your mind," I said.

This too, I suppose, was sadistic, but it was pretty much honest; I really couldn't have done very wholeheartedly either of the things she requested, and it is easier to sit still halfheartedly than to do dramatic things halfheartedly. Rennie sobbed for a full two minutes, huddled in her chair: this affair was indeed tearing her up.

Ah me, and there were so many other ways it could have been handled. Perhaps, I reflected, what would eventually destroy both Morgans, after all, was lack of imagination. I glanced up at Laocoön: his agony was abstract and unsuggestive.

10. *The Disintegration of Rennie That September Was Not Often an Entertaining Spectacle*

THE DISINTEGRATION OF RENNIE THAT SEPTEMBER WAS NOT OFTEN AN ENTERTAINING SPECTACLE to observe, for although, as she pointed out, it is not self-evident that every personality is valuable simply because it's unique, nevertheless I could seldom enjoy contributing to the unhappiness of people whom I'd come to know at all well. There is no humanitarianism in this fact: for humankind in general I had no feeling one way or the other, and the plight of some specific people, Peggy Rankin for example, I must say concerned me not at all. This is merely a description of my reactions—I wouldn't attempt to defend it as an assumed position.

The trouble, I suppose, is that the more one learns about a given person, the more difficult it becomes to assign a character to him that will allow one to deal with him effectively in an emotional situation. Mythotherapy, in short, becomes increasingly harder to apply, because one is compelled to recognize the inadequacy of any role one assigns. Existence not only precedes essence: in the case of human beings it rather defies essence. And as soon as one knows a person well enough to hold contradictory opinions about him, Mythotherapy goes out the window, except at times when one is no more than half awake.

There were such times, but they were few. The latter part of the evening just described was one: when at length I carried Rennie to the bed (excited by her heaviness) I was able to do so only because, for better or worse, enough of my alertness was gone to permit me to dramatize the situation as part of a romantic contest between symbols. Joe was The Reason, or Being (I was using Rennie's cosmos); I was The Unreason, or Not-Being; and the two of us were fighting without quarter for possession of Rennie, like God and Satan for the soul of Man. This pretty ontological Manichaeism would certainly stand no close examination, but it had the triple virtue of excusing me from having to assign to Rennie any essence more specific than The Human Personality, further of allowing me to fornicate with a Mephistophelean relish, and finally of making it possible for me not to question my motives, since what I was doing was of the essence of my essence. Does one look for introspection from Satan?

As for Rennie, she had by that time very nearly reached the condition of paralysis, and it was, I believe, with something like relief that she allowed me to cast her in the role of Mankind; what drama was on *her* mind I couldn't say. I took her home afterwards.

"Aren't you going to come in for a while?" she asked numbly.

But my little play had dissipated with my sexual ardor, and I was vegetable.

"Nope. I'll see you around."

For the rest, I felt mostly a generalized pity for the Morgans, especially for Rennie. Joe, after all, was behaving pretty consistently with his position, and that knowledge can be comforting even in cases where the position leads to defeat or disaster, as when a bridge player plays out a losing hand perfectly or an Othello loves not wisely but too well. But Rennie no longer had a position to act consistently with, not even the position of acting inconsistently, and yet, unlike my own, her personality was such that it seemed to require a position in order to preserve itself.

She came to my room three times during September and once in October. The first visit I've already described. The second, on Wednesday of the following week, was quite different: Rennie seemed warm, strong, even gay and a little wild. We made love zestfully at once—she went so far as to tease me for being a less energetic lover than her husband—and afterwards she talked animatedly for an hour or so over a quart of California muscatel she'd brought with her.

"Lord, I've been silly lately!" she laughed. "Mooning and crying around like a schoolgirl!"

"Oh?"

"How in the world could I have taken this business so seriously? You know what happened to me last night?"

"No."

"I popped awake at three in the morning—wide awake, like I've been doing every night since this business started. Usually I get the shakes when that happens, and either sit up the rest of the night shivering and sweating or else wake up Joe and go over the whole thing with him again. Well, last night I woke up as usual, and the moon was shining in and I could see Joe lying there asleep—he looks adolescent when he's asleep!—and for some reason or other while I was watching him he started picking his nose in his sleep!" She giggled at the memory and burped slightly from the wine. "Excuse me."

"Certainly."

"Well, that reminded me of that night we peeked in on him through the living-room window, only this time instead of hurting me it just struck me funny! The whole thing struck me funny, and how we were taking it. Joe seemed like a teen-ager trying to make a tragedy out of nothing, and you just seemed completely ineffectual. Does this make you angry?" She laughed.

"Of course not."

"And I've been being a runny-nose little girl myself, crying all over the place and letting you two bully me around about such a stupid thing. I felt just like I feel when I let the kids get me down. Lots of times when the kids scream and fight all day I get so worked up at them I end up screaming and crying myself, and I always feel silly afterwards and a little bit ashamed. How can grown people make so much fuss over something so silly? Especially married people with kids?"

"Poor little coitus," I smiled. In fact, Rennie's high spirits produced a contrary feeling in me: the happier she grew, the more glum I became, and the more she professed to take the matter lightly, the graver it seemed to me.

"Such a completely insignificant thing to take seriously! It's hardly worth thinking about, much less breaking up a marriage over! I could sleep with a hundred different men and not feel any different about Joe!"

"Well, now," I protested snappishly, "of course nothing's significant in itself, but anything's serious that you want to take seriously. There's no reason to make fun of another man's seriousnesses."

"Oh, stop it!" Rennie cried. "You're as bad as Joe is. I think all our trouble comes from thinking too much and talking too much. We talk ourselves into all kinds of messes that would disappear if everybody just shut up about them." She drank another glass of wine—her fourth or fifth—while I still nursed my first one. "You know what I think? I think none of this would have happened if we all didn't have so much time on our hands. I really do. You claim you don't know how you could ever have begun the whole business, but I think you did it because you're bored."

"Is that so?"

"You don't have any ambitions, you're not very busy or very handsome, you live by yourself. I think of you up here all day long, rocking in your rocking chair, daydreaming and cooking up schemes, just because you're bored. I think the key to your whole character is that you're just bored."

"I'm not just anything," I said without conviction. "Maybe *also* bored, but never *just* bored." Rennie, it was clear, was practicing a little layman's Mythotherapy herself: anybody who starts talking in terms of keys to people's characters is making myths, because the mystery of people is not to be explained by keys. But I was too glum just then to take more than perfunctory note of her playwriting.

"Well, *I* think you're just bored; I don't care what you think. I don't care what you or Joe either one thinks about this mess or about me any more: I've stopped taking it seriously. I've even stopped thinking about it."

"Good for you."

"That gets under your skin, though, doesn't it?" she laughed. "It takes the fun out of it when I stop being hurt. Well, the devil with you! I've stopped being hurt. Look how down in the mouth you are. You look like you've messed your pants or something." The idea amused her; she giggled vinously. "That's just

how Joe looked this morning—gloomy as a prophet. You're pouting because your game is spoiled. Now cheer up and get drunk
with me or else take me home."

I emptied my glass and refilled it. "You realize, of course, that
I don't believe a word of this. It's brave, but it's not convincing."

"You don't dare believe it," Rennie taunted.

"I don't dare to, and you couldn't if your life depended on it."

"I don't care," Rennie declared. "I don't give a damn."

"I don't believe Joe knows anything about it either."

"I don't care."

"He wouldn't get gloomy. He'd walk out."

"That's what you think. We're tied tighter than that. I don't
know why I worried in the first place; no piece of nonsense like
this could break Joe and me up. It would take a stronger person
than you, Jake. You don't really know anything about Joe and
me. Not a damned thing."

"I said last time you should tell him to go to hell."

"Maybe I'll tell you both to go to hell."

"Okay, girl, but watch that left hook of his when you do."

This remark canceled the effects of at least three glasses of
muscatel.

"I don't think Joe would ever hit me again," she said seriously.

"Then skip home with that quart of muscatel in you, tweak
his nose for him, and tell him you can't think seriously any more
about anything as silly as your sex life," I suggested. "Tell him the
whole trouble is he thinks too much."

"He wouldn't hit me, Jake. He'd never do that again."

"He'd fracture your damn jaw for you. Tell him he's acting like
a high-school boy! He'll lay you out cold and you know it. Come
on, I'll go along with you. If you're right we'll all three chuckle
and chortle and snot our noses. We'll shake hands all around and
our troubles will be over."

Rennie was entirely sober now.

"I hate you," she said. "You won't let me even try to be halfway happy again for a minute, will you? I can't even pretend
to be happy."

And (*mirabile dictu*) as soon as she assumed my glumness, I was free of it—took up her lost gaiety, in fact, and poured myself another glass of muscatel.

"You feel great, don't you?" Rennie cried.

"Happy human perversity. I'm genuinely sorry, Rennie."

"You're genuinely cheerful!" she said, whipping her head from side to side.

But such precarious good spirts as these of Rennie's and such unnecessary cruelty as this of mine were rare. Just as the second visit had borne little resemblance to the first, the third (and last in September) was nothing at all like the second. By this time I was involved enough in teaching so that my moods more and more often had their origin in the classroom. On this particular day, the last Friday in September, I felt acute, tuned-up, razor-sharp, simply because in my grammar class that morning I'd explained the rules governing the case forms of English pronouns: it gives a man a great sense of lucidity and well-being, if not downright formidability, to be able not only to say, but to understand perfectly, that predicate complements of infinitives of copulative verbs without expressed subjects go into the nominative case, whereas predicate complements of infinitives of copulative verbs *with* expressed subjects go into the objective case. I made this observation to my assemblage of young scholars and concluded triumphantly, "I was thought to be *he,* but I thought John to be *him!* Questions?"

"Aw, look," protested a troublesome fellow—in the back of the room, of course—whom I'd early decided to flunk if possible for his impertinence, "which came first, the language or the grammar books?"

"What's on your mind, Blakesley?" I demanded, refusing to play his game.

"Well, it stands to reason people talked before they wrote grammar books, and all the books did was tell how people were talking. For instance, when my roommate makes a phone call I ask him, 'Who were you talking to?' Everybody in this class would say, 'Who were you talking to?' I'll bet ninety-nine per cent of the people of America would say, 'Who were you talking to?' Nobody's going to say, 'To whom were you just now talking?'

I'll bet even you wouldn't say it. It sounds queer, don't it?" The class snickered. "Now this is supposed to be a democracy, so if nobody but a few profs ever say, 'To whom were you just now speaking?', why go on pretending we're all out of step but you? Why not change the rules?"

A Joe Morgan type, this lad: paths should be laid where people walk. I hated his guts.

"Mr. Blakesley, I suppose you eat your fried chicken with your fingers?"

"What? Sure I do. Don't you?"

The class tittered, engrossed in the duel, but as of this last rather flat sally they were not so unreservedly allied with him as before.

"And your bacon at breakfast? Fingers or fork, Mr. Blakesley?"

"Fingers," he said defiantly. "Sure, that's right, fingers were invented before forks, just like English was invented before grammar books."

"But not *your* fingers, as the saying goes," I smiled coolly, "and not your English—God knows!" The class was with me all the way: prescriptive grammar was victorious.

"The point is," I concluded to the class in general, "that if we were still savages, Mr. Blakesley would be free to eat like a swine without breaking any rules, because there'd be no rules to break, and he could say, 'It sounds queer, don't it?' to his heart's content without being recognized as illiterate, because literacy—the grammar rules—wouldn't have been invented. But once a set of rules for etiquette or grammar is established and generally accepted as the norm—meaning the ideal, not the average—then one is free to break them only if he's willing to be generally regarded as a savage or an illiterate. No matter how dogmatic or unreasonable the rules might be, they're the convention. And in the case of language there's still another reason for going along with even the silliest rules. Mr. Blakesley, what does the word *horse* refer to?"

Mr. Blakesley was sullen, but he replied, "The animal. Four-legged animal."

"*Equus caballus,*" I agreed: "a solid-hoofed, herbivorous mammal. And what does the algebraic symbol x stand for?"

"*x?* Anything. It's an unknown."

"Good. Then the symbol *x* can represent anything we want it to represent, as long as it always represents the same thing in a given equation. But *horse* is just a symbol too—a noise that we make in our throats or some scratches on the blackboard. And theoretically we could make it stand for anything we wanted to also, couldn't we? I mean, if you and I agreed that just between ourselves the word *horse* would mean *grammar book,* then we could say, 'Open your horse to Page Twenty,' or 'Did you bring your horse to class with you today?' And we two would know what we meant, wouldn't we?"

"Sure, I guess so." With all his heart Mr. Blakesley didn't want to agree. He sensed that he was somehow trapped, but there was no way out.

"Of course we would. But nobody else would understand us— that's the whole principle of secret codes. Yet there's ultimately no reason why the symbol *horse* shouldn't always refer to grammar book instead of to *Equus caballus:* the significances of words are arbitrary conventions, mostly; historical accidents. But it was agreed before you and I had any say in the matter that the word *horse* would refer to *Equus caballus,* and so if we want our sentences to be intelligible to very many people, we have to go along with the convention. We have to say *horse* when we mean *Equus caballus,* and *grammar book* when we mean this object here on my desk. You're free to break the rules, but not if you're after intelligibility. If you *do* want intelligibility, then the only way to get 'free' of the rules is to master them so thoroughly that they're second nature to you. That's the paradox: in any kind of complicated society a man is usually free only to the extent that he embraces all the rules of that society. Who's more free in America?" I asked finally. "The man who rebels against all the laws or the man who follows them so automatically that he never even has to think about them?"

This last, to be sure, was a gross equivocation, but I was not out to edify anybody; I was out to rescue prescriptive grammar from the clutches of my impudent Mr. Blakesley, and, if possible, to crucify him in the process.

"But, Mr. Horner," said a worried young man—in the front

row, of course—"people are always finding better ways to do things, aren't they? And usually they have to change the rules to make improvements. If nobody rebelled against the rules there'd never be any progress."

I regarded the young man benignly: he would survive any horse manure of mine.

"That's another paradox," I said to him. "Rebels and radicals at all times are people who see that the rules are often arbitrary—always ultimately arbitrary—and who can't abide arbitrary rules. These are the free lovers, the women who smoke cigars, the Greenwich Village characters who don't get haircuts, and all kinds of reformers. But the greatest radical in any society is the man who sees all the arbitrariness of the rules and social conventions, but who has such a great scorn or disregard for the society he lives in that he embraces the whole wagonload of nonsense with a smile. The greatest rebel is the man who wouldn't change society for anything in the world."

So. This troubled my bright young man no end, I'm sure, and to the rest of the class it was doubtless incomprehensible, but its effect on me was to add to my already-established sense of acumen the delicate spice of slightly smiling paradox. The mood persisted throughout the day: I left school with my head full of the Janusian ambivalence of the universe, and I walked through the world's charming equipoise, its ubiquitous polarity, to my room, where at nine o'clock that evening Rennie found me rocking in my chair, still faintly smiling at my friend Laocoön, whose grimace was his beauty.

She was nervous and quiet. We said hello to each other, and she stood about clumsily for a minute before sitting down. Clearly, some new stage had been reached.

"What now?" I asked her.

She made no answer, but ticked her cheek and gestured vacantly with her right hand.

"How's Joe?"

"The same."

"Oh. How're you?"

"I don't know. Going crazy."

"Joe hasn't been giving you a hard time, has he?"

She looked at me for a moment.

"He's God," she said. "He's just God."

"So I understand."

"All this week he's been wonderful. Not like he was just after he got back from Washington—that wasn't normal for him. You'd think it was all over and done with."

"Why shouldn't it be? That's how I felt the day after it happened."

She sighed. "So, I just mentioned offhand that I didn't feel like coming up here any more—didn't see any point to it."

"Good."

"He didn't say a word. He just gave me a long look that made me wish I was dead. Then tonight he said he'd pretty much come to accept this as a part of me, even though he couldn't understand why it had started, and he'd respect me more if I was consistent than if I repudiated what I'd done. Then he said he didn't see any need to talk about it any more, and that was that."

"Well, by God, then, the trouble's all over with, isn't it?"

"Except that I don't particularly believe him, and even if I did, I don't recognize myself any more."

"That's not so awful. I almost never do."

"But Joe always does. So nothing's solved as long as I can't be as authentic as he is, and see myself in what I do as clearly as I see him in what he does. Joe's always recognizable."

I smiled. "Almost always."

"You mean that time we spied on him? Oh, Jesus!" She shook her head. "Jake, you know what? I wish I'd been struck blind before I looked in that window. That's what started everything."

Sweet paradox: "Or you could say that's what ended everything. But it would start or end anything only for a Morgan. Certainly not for a Horner. In my cosmos everybody is part chimpanzee, especially when he's by himself, and nobody's terribly surprised by anything the other chimpanzees do."

"Not Joe, though."

"Maybe the guy who fools himself least is the one who admits that we're all just kidding."

Sweet, sweet paradox!

"Joe and I have done a Marcel Proust on this thing," Rennie said sadly. "We've taken it apart from every point of view we could think of. Sometimes I think I've never understood anything as thoroughly in my life as I do this, and other times—like after I was up here last time, and now—I realize I don't understand any more than I ever did. It's all still a mystery. It tears me up even when I don't see anything to be torn up about."

"What does Joe think of me lately?"

"I don't know. I don't think he hates you any more. Probably he just doesn't care to deal with you. He thinks your part in it was probably characteristic of you."

"Which me, for heaven's sake?" I laughed. "How about you?"

"I still despise you, I think," Rennie said unemotionally.

"Clear through?"

"As far as I can see."

This thrilled me from head to foot. I had been not interested in Rennie this night until she said this, but now I was acutely interested in her.

"Has this been just since we slept together?"

"I don't know how much of it is retroactive, Jake; right now I think I've disliked you ever since I've known you, but I guess that's not so. I've had some kind of feeling about you at least since we started the riding lessons, and as far as I can see now it was a kind of dislike. Abhorrence, I guess, is a better word. I don't believe in anything like premonitions, but I swear I've wished ever since August that we'd never met you, even though I couldn't have said why."

I felt way high on a mountaintop, thinking widely and un-cloudedly; hundred-eyed Argus was not more synoptic.

"I'll bet I know one point of view you and Joe didn't try, Rennie."

"We tried them all," she said.

I felt like the end of an Ellery Queen novel.

"Not this one. And by the Law of Parsimony it's good, because it accounts for the most facts by the fewest assumptions. It's simple as hell, Rennie: we didn't just copulate; we made love. What you've felt all along and couldn't admit to yourself was that you love me."

"That's not right," Rennie breathed, looking at me tautly.

"It could be. I'm not being vain. At least I'm not *just* being vain."

"That's not what I meant," Rennie said, and she had some difficulty saying it. "I meant—it's not right that I've never admitted it to myself."

Now her eyes showed real abhorrence, but it was not clear in them what or whom she abhorred. I grew very excited.

"Well, I'll be damned!"

"That's one of the things that destroys me," Rennie said. "The idea that I might have been in love with you all the time occurred to me along with all the rest—along with the idea that I despise you and the idea that I couldn't really feel anything about you because you don't exist. You know what I mean. I don't know which is true."

"I suppose they're all true, Rennie," I suggested. "While we're at it, did you ever consider that maybe Joe's the one who doesn't exist?"

"No." She whipped her head slowly. "I don't know."

"I don't think you have to be afraid of the idea that you feel some kind of love for me. Certainly it doesn't imply anything one way or the other about your feeling for Joe, unless you want to be romantic about it. In fact, I don't see where it implies anything, except that the whole affair is less mysterious than we'd supposed, and maybe less sordid."

But Rennie clearly accepted none of this.

"Jake, I can't make love to you tonight."

"All right. I'll take you home."

In the car I kissed her gently. "I think this is great. It's funny as the devil."

"That's about right."

"Did you tell Joe you suspected this along with the rest?"

"No." She lowered her eyes. "And I can't ever tell him. That's the thing, Jake," she said, looking at me again. "I still love him more than he or anybody else suspects, but what we had before is just out. This makes it impossible. Even if it's actually not true that I love you, the possibility that I might—the fact that I'm not sure I don't—kills everything. It doesn't solve any problems: it *is* the problem. Can you imagine how it makes me feel when he says he's accepted my relationship with you, and tries to act as if nothing had happened? The whole damned thing's a lie from now on—has been ever since I first admitted to myself that I might love you."

"Nothing has to be wrecked, Rennie."

"It's already wrecked, what Joe and I had before, and it was the finest thing any man and woman ever had. There's no room in it for lies or divided affections. I feel like I've been robbed of a million dollars, Jake! If I'd shot him I couldn't feel worse!"

"Do you want me to come inside with you?" I asked.

"No."

"Aren't you just postponing things?"

"I'm postponing as much as I possibly can," she said, "for as long as I possibly can. I'm desperate, and that's the only thing I can think of to do."

"Joe might have allowed for the same possibility all along," I offered. "He's not afraid to look at all the alternatives."

"It wouldn't make any difference."

"I just don't see where the situation is desperate. It wouldn't be in my world."

"I'm not surprised," Rennie said. I wasn't sure whether she was crying or not, since it was dark in the car. I daresay she was. We sat for some minutes without speaking, and then she opened the door to get out.

"God, Jake, I don't know where all this will lead to."

"Neither does Joe," I said lightly. "Those were his very first words."

"For Christ's sake try to remember one thing, anyhow: if I love you at all, I don't *just* love you. I swear, along with it I honestly and truly hate your God-damned guts!"

"I'll remember," I said. "Good night, Rennie." She went in without replying, and I drove home to rock a bit and contemplate this new revelation. I was flattered beyond measure—I responded easily and inordinately to any evidence of affection from people whom I admired or respected in any way. But—well, perhaps this is specious, but the connoisseur is by his very nature a hair-splitter. The thing is that even in my current mood I

couldn't see much of a paradox in Rennie's feelings, and I was
piqued that I could not. The connoisseur—and I had been one
since nine-thirty that morning—requires of a paradox, if it is to
elicit from him that faint smile which marks him for what he
is, that it be more than a simple ambiguity resulting from the
vagueness of certain terms in the language; it should, ideally, be
a really arresting contradiction of concepts whose actual compat-
ibility becomes perceptible only upon subtle reflection. The apparent ambivalence of Rennie's feelings about me, I'm afraid, like
the simultaneous contradictory opinions that I often amused myself by maintaining, was only a pseudo-ambivalence whose source
was in the language, not in the concepts symbolized by the language. I'm sure, as a matter of fact, that what Rennie felt was
actually neither ambivalent nor even complex; it was both single
and simple, like all feelings, but like all feelings it was also completely particular and individual, and so the trouble started only
when she attempted to label it with a common noun such as
love or *abhorrence*. Things can be signified by common nouns
only if one ignores the differences between them; but it is precisely
these differences, when deeply felt, that make the nouns inadequate and lead the layman (but not the connoisseur) to believe that he has a paradox on his hands, an ambivalence, when
actually it is merely a matter of *x*'s being part horse and part
grammar book, and completely neither. Assigning names to things
is like assigning roles to people: it is necessarily a distortion, but
it is a necessary distortion if one would get on with the plot, and
to the connoisseur it's good clean fun.

Rennie loved me, then, and hated me as well! Let us say she
x-ed me, and know better than to smile.

During this month I had of course seen Joe any number of
times at school, even though our social relationship had ended. If
it had been possible I'd have avoided him altogether, not because
I felt any less warmth, admiration, or respect for him—on the
contrary, I felt more of all these things, and sympathy besides—
but because the sight of him invariably filled me with sudden
embarrassment and shame, no matter what feelings I had at other
times. To feel, as Joe did, no regret for anything one has done

in the past requires at least a strong sense of one's personal unity, and such a sense is one of the things I've always lacked. Indeed, the conflict between individual points of view that Joe admitted lay close to the heart of his subjectivism I should carry even further, for subjectivism implies a self, and where one feels a plurality of selves, one is subject to the same conflict on an intensely intramural level, each of one's several selves claiming the same irrefutable validity for its special point of view that, in Joe's system, individuals and institutions may claim. In other words, judging from my clearest picture of myself, the individual is not individual after all, any more than the atom is really atomistic: he can be divided further, and subjectivism doesn't really become intelligible until one finally locates the subject. I shall say that, if this did not seem to me to be the case, I should assent wholeheartedly to the Morgan ethics. As it is, if I say that sometimes I assent to it anyway and sometimes not, I can't really feel that this represents any more of an inconsistency than can be found in the statement "Some people agree with Morgan and some don't." In the same way, when upon confronting Joe in the hallways, in the cafeteria, or in my office I felt terribly ashamed of the trouble I'd caused him—when in my mind I not only regretted but actually repudiated my adultery—what I really felt was that *I* would not do what that Jacob Horner had done: I felt no identity with that stupid fellow. But as a point of honor (in which some Horner or other believed) I would not claim this pluralism, for fear Joe would interpret it as a defense.

Only once in September did we have what might be called a conversation. It was very near the end of the month, when, happening to see me alone in my office, he came in to talk for a few minutes. As always, he looked fresh, bright, clean, and sharp.

"Mr. MacMahon's complaining that his horses are getting too fat," he said. "How come you quit your riding lessons?"

I blushed. "I thought the course was finished, I guess."

"You want to pick them up again? It's right much trouble for him to take time to exercise them as much as they need."

"No, I guess not. I've kind of lost interest, and I don't think Rennie would enjoy it very much."

"Don't you? Why shouldn't she?"

I should say there was no malice evident in his voice, but I couldn't help thinking I was being embarrassed purposely.

"You know why not, Joe. Why do you even suggest it?" I was suddenly indignant on Rennie's behalf. "I feel uncomfortable as hell criticizing you, but I don't see why you're so determined to make her feel worse than she does already."

He jabbed his spectacles back on his nose.

"Don't worry about Rennie."

"You mean it's a little late for me to start being thoughtful. I agree. But unless you're out to punish her I don't know why you make her come up to my room and all."

"I'm not out to punish anybody, Jake; you know that. I'm just out to try to understand her."

"Well, don't you understand that she's pretty much shot these days? I'm surprised she's held up this long."

"She's pretty strong," Joe smiled. "You probably don't realize that in a way Rennie and I have been happier in the last few weeks than we've been for a long time."

"How come?"

"For one thing, since this started I've shelved the dissertation for a while, so we've had more time together than usual. We've talked to each other about ourselves more than we ever did before, necessarily, and all that."

I was appalled. "You can't say she's been happy."

"Not in the way you probably mean, I guess. We certainly haven't been *carefree*; but you can be pretty much happy without being carefree. The point is we've been dealing with each other pretty intensely and objectively—exploring each other as deep as we can. That part of it's been fine. And we've been outdoors a lot, because we didn't want to ruin our health over it. We've probably felt a lot closer to each other than ever, whether we've solved anything or not."

"Do you think you have?"

"Well, we've certainly *learned* some things. For one thing we've found all kinds of ties that we weren't aware of before, so that we probably wouldn't break up even if the thing doesn't straighten itself out. I doubt if I respect her as much as before—how could I? At least not for the same things. But she's been awfully good in this. Pretty damned strong most of the time, and I appreciate that. What do you think of my friend Rennie these days?"

"Me?" I hadn't been especially thinking about what I thought of her, at least since her revelation of two nights earlier. Now I had to think about it quickly. "Oh, I don't know," I stalled.

"You must have had a strange picture of us both before. I'd like to know what you think of her now. Are you disgusted with her for not knowing how she feels?"

I leaned back in my chair and regarded the red pencil with which I'd been correcting grammar exercises.

"As a matter of fact," I said, "I might be in love with her."

"Is that right?" he asked quickly, bright with interest.

"I wouldn't be surprised. It was right a couple of days ago, anyhow. I don't feel it very strongly now, but I don't feel that I'm not, either."

"That's great!" Joe laughed: what he meant, I believe, was *That's interesting*. "Is that what you felt when you went to bed with her the first time? You could have said so."

"No. I didn't feel that way then."

"Does Rennie know about this?"

"No."

"How does she feel about you?"

"Not long ago she despised me. A week or so ago she said she didn't give a damn."

"Does she love you?" he asked, smiling.

Now I've said all along that Joe was without guile, but it's almost impossible really to believe that a man is without guile. It is perhaps a great injustice that I couldn't entirely trust that open smile and clear forehead of Joe's, but I confess I did not.

"I'm pretty sure she despises me," I said.

Joe sighed. He was sitting in the swivel chair next to mine, and now he put his feet on the desk in front of him and clasped his hands behind his head.

"Did you ever consider that maybe I'm to blame for all of this? A lot of things could be explained neatly if you just said that for some perverse reason or other I engineered the whole affair. Just a possibility, along with the rest. What do you think?"

"Perversity? I don't know, Joe. If I see anything perverse it's your sending Rennie up to my place now."

He laughed. "I guess you could call all my encouragements of you two perverse now that we know what happened, but if any of it was really perverse it was unconsciously so. But you can't really believe it's perversity that makes me insist on her going up to your place. That business really is a matter of testing her. She's got to decide once and for all what she really feels about you and me and herself, and you know as well as I do that if it weren't for those trips to your place she'd repress that first business as fast as she could."

"Don't you think you're just keeping the wounds open?"

"I guess so. In fact, that's exactly what I'm doing. But in this case we've got to keep the wound open until we know just what kind of wound it is and how deep it goes."

"It seems to me that the important thing about wounds is healing them, no matter how."

"You're getting carried away with the analogy," Joe smiled. "This isn't a physical wound. If you ignore it, it might seem to go away, but in a relationship between two people wounds like this aren't healed by ignoring them—they keep coming back again if you do that." He dropped the subject. "So you love Rennie?"

"I don't know. I've felt that way once or twice."

"Would you marry her if she weren't married to me?"

"I don't know. Honestly."

"How would you take it if it turned out that the best answer to this thing was some kind of a permanent sexual relationship between you and her? I mean a triangle without conflicts or secrecy or jealousy."

"I don't think that's an answer. I'm the kind of guy who could probably live with that sort of thing, but I don't believe either Rennie or you could." As a matter of fact, I was interested to notice that at the very mention of marriage and permanent sexual attachments I began to grow tired of the idea of Rennie. Happy human perversity! There was little of the husband in me.

"I don't either. What's the answer, Jake? You tell me."

I shook my head.

"Shall I shoot you both?" he grinned. "I already own a Colt forty-five and about a dozen bullets. When Rennie and I first got going on this thing, the time I was out of school for three days or so, I dug the old Colt out of the basement and loaded it and put in on the shelf in the living-room closet, in case either of us wanted to use it on ourselves or anybody else."

That statement thrilled me. Perhaps it was Joe Morgan, after all, that I loved. He stood up and clapped me amiably on the shoulder.

"No answers, huh?"

I shook my head. "Damned if I know what to say, Joe."

"Well," he said, stretching and walking out the door, "it's still there in the closet. Maybe we'll use it yet."

The Colt .45 used as a sidearm by the United States military is a big, heavy, murderous-looking pistol. Its recoil raises the shooter's arm, and the fat lead slug that it fires strikes with an impact great enough to knock a man off his feet. The image of this weapon completely dominated my imagination for the next three or four days after Joe had mentioned it: I thought of it, as Joe and Rennie must have thought of it, waiting huge in their living-room closet all through the days and nights during which they had dissected and examined every detail of the adultery—waiting for somebody to reach a conclusion. Little wonder that Rennie's nights were sleepless! So were mine, once that machine had been introduced so casually into the problem. Even in my room it made itself terrifically present as the concrete embodiment of an alternative: the fact of its existence put the game in a different ball park, as it were; flavored all my reflections on the subject with an immediacy which I'm sure the Morgans had felt from the first, but which my isolation, if nothing else, had kept me from feeling.

I dreamed about that pistol, and daydreamed about it. In my imagination I kept seeing it as in a photographic close-up, lying hard and flat in the darkness on the closet shelf, while through the door came the indistinct voices of Joe and Rennie talking through days and nights. Talking, talking, talking. I heard only the tones of their voices—Rennie's calm, desperate, and hysterical by turns; Joe's always quiet and reasonable, hour after hour, until its quiet reasonableness became nightmarish and insane. I'm sure nothing has ever filled my head like the image of that gun. It took on aspects as various as the aspects of Laocoön's smile, but infinitely more compelling and, of course, final. It was its finality that gave the idea of the Colt its persistence. It was with me all the time.

So it was like the realization of a nightmare when, shortly afterwards, I was confronted with the weapon itself in my room, which it had already tenanted in spirit, and that's why I paled and went weak, for I have no abstract fear of pistols. Rennie came in at eight o'clock, after telephoning an hour earlier to say she wanted to see me, and to my surprise Joe came with her, and with Joe came the Colt, in a paper bag. Rennie, I thought, had been crying—her cheeks were white and her eyes swollen—but Joe seemed cheerful enough. The first thing he did after acknowledging my greeting was take the pistol out of the bag and lay it carefully on a little ash-tray stand, which he placed in the center of the room.

"There she is, Jacob," he laughed. "Everything we have is yours."

I admired the gun without touching it, laughed shortly along with Joe at the poor humor of his gesture, and, as I said before, paled. It was a formidable piece of machinery, as large in fact as it had been in my imagination and no less final-looking. Joe watched my face.

"How about a beer?" I asked. The more I resolved not to show my alarm—alarm was the last thing I wanted to suggest was called for—the more plainly I could see it in my voice and manner.

"All right. Rennie? Want one?"

"No thanks," Rennie said, in a voice something like mine.

She sat in the overstuffed chair by the front window, and Joe on the edge of my monstrous bed, so that when I opened the beer bottles and took the only remaining seat, my rocking chair, we formed most embarrassingly a perfect equilateral triangle, with the gun in the center. Joe observed this at the same instant I did, and though I can't vouch for his grin, my own was not jovial.

"Well, what's up?" I asked him.

Joe pushed his spectacles back on his nose and crossed his legs. "Rennie's pregnant," he said calmly.

When a man has been sleeping with a woman, no matter under what circumstances, this news always comes like the kick of a horse. The pistol loomed more conspicuous than ever, and it took me several seconds to collect my wits enough to realize that I had nothing to be concerned about.

"Congratulations!"

Joe kept smiling, not cordially, and Rennie fixed her eyes on the rug. Nobody spoke for a while.

"What's wrong?" I asked, not knowing for certain what to be afraid of.

"Well, we're not sure who to congratulate, I guess," Joe said.

"Why not?" My face burned. "You're not afraid *I'm* the father, are you?"

"I'm not particularly afraid of anything," Joe said. "But you might be the father."

"You don't have to worry about that, Joe; believe me." I looked a little wonderingly at Rennie, who I thought should have known better than to complicate things unnecessarily.

"You mean because you used contraceptives every time. I know that. I even know how many times you had to use them and what brand you use, Jacob."

"What the hell's the trouble, then?"

"The trouble is that I used them every time too—same brand, as a matter of fact."

I was stunned. There was the pistol.

"So," Joe went on, "if, as my friend Rennie tells me, this triangle was never a rectangle, and if her obstetrician isn't lying when he says rubbers are about eighty per cent efficient, the congratulations should be pretty much mutual. In fact, other things being equal, there's about one chance in four that you actually are the father."

Neither Joe's voice nor his forehead indicated how he felt about this possibility.

"How sure are you that you're pregnant?" I asked Rennie. To my chagrin my voice was unsteady.

"I'm I'm pretty late," Rennie said, clearing her throat two or three times. "And I've been vomiting a lot for the last two days."

"Well, you know, you thought you were pregnant once before."

She shook her head. "That was wishful thinking." She had to wait a second before she said anything else. "I wanted to be pregnant that time."

"There's not much doubt," Joe said. "No use to hope along those lines. The obstetricians never commit themselves for a month or so, but Rennie knows her symptoms."

I sighed uncertainly; Joe still gave no hint of his feelings. "Boy, that complicates things, doesn't it?"

"Well, does it or not? How would you say it complicates things?"

"I guess that depends on how you all feel."

"Why is that? Look, Horner, you ought to decide what your point of view is going to be. Rennie's the same distance from me as she is from you."

"We should have allowed for the possibility, I guess," I suggested carefully.

"Aren't you actually saying that I should have allowed for the possibility when I sent Rennie up here? I allowed for all possibilities. That doesn't necessarily mean I like the idea of her being pregnant with your kid. I don't like that possibility a single God-damned bit, if you want to know, and I didn't really look for it to happen. But I did allow for the possibility right from the time I first heard you'd laid her. If you all didn't, you're stupid."

"It's a possibility I'd never allow for at the time." I smiled ruefully. "A bachelor would lead a lonely life if he did."

"Which heaven forbid."

I shrugged. I wasn't sure to what extent I was justified in being annoyed by his manner: the thing was too complicated. There was silence for a while. Joe chewed his thumbnail idly, Rennie still stared at the rug, and I tried to keep the gun out of my eyes and thoughts.

"What do you suggest, Joe?"

"Don't say that, now," he protested. "It's not all my baby. What do *you* suggest?"

"Well, I can't say anything until I know whether you want to keep the child or put it up for adoption or what. You know I'd pay for the obstetrician and the hospital and all, and the kid's support, if you decide to keep it, or help all I can with an adoption. If I could raise the child myself I'd do it."

"But you can't vomit for Rennie or split up the labor pains with her."

"No, I can't do that."

"You're oversimplifying even when you say *if I decide to keep the kid.* That makes it my responsibility. You say you're willing to take on the expense, but that doesn't mean a thing and you know it. Making it a practical problem, like a money problem, is too easy. I'd be a lot happier if you'd take on your share of responsibility. You don't have to take any shit off of me. That's too easy too."

"How do I go about taking on responsibility?" I asked. "I'm willing."

"Then for Christ's sake take a position and stick to it so we'll know who we're dealing with! Don't throw everything in my lap. What the hell do *you* think I should do? Tell Rennie what you want her to do and what you want me to do, and we'll tell you the same thing. Then we can work on the problem, for God's sake!"

"I don't have opinions, Joe," I said flatly. Of course the trouble was that I had, as usual, too many opinions. I was on everybody's side.

Joe jumped from the bed, snatched up the pistol, and aimed it at my face.

"If I told you I was going to pull this trigger, would you have any opinions about that?"

I was sick. "Go ahead and pull it."

"Horseshit: you'd never have to face up to anything then." He put the pistol back on the smoking stand. Rennie had watched the scene with tears in her eyes, but she wasn't weeping for either of us.

"What do *you* want to do?" Joe said roughly to her, and when she whipped her head I saw his eyes water also, although his expression didn't change. There was no alliance against me.

"I don't care about anything," Rennie said. "Do whatever you want to."

"I'll be damned!" Joe shouted, with tears on his cheeks. "I'm not going to do your thinking or his either. Think for yourself, or I don't want anything to do with you! I mean it!"

"I don't want the baby," Rennie said to him.

"You want to put it up for adoption?"

She shook her head. "That wouldn't work. If I carried it for nine months I'd love it, and I don't want to love it. I don't want to carry it for nine months."

"All right, there's the pistol. Shoot yourself."

Rennie looked at him sadly. "I will if you want me to, Joe."

"God *damn* what I want!"

"Did you mean you want an abortion, Rennie?" I asked.

Rennie nodded. "I want to get rid of this baby. I don't want to carry this baby."

"Where in hell are you going to find an abortionist around here?" Joe asked disgustedly. "This isn't New York."

"I don't know," Rennie said. "But I'm not going to carry this baby. I don't want it."

"Are you going to go to Dr. Walsh like last time and let him insult you?" Joe demanded. "He'd throw you out! I don't believe there's an abortionist in this county."

"I don't know," Rennie said. "I'm going to get an abortion or shoot myself, Joe. I've decided."

"Well, that sounds brave, Rennie, but think clearly about it: you don't know any abortionists around here, do you?"

"No."

"And you don't know any in Baltimore or Washington or anywhere else. And you don't know anybody who's ever had an abortion, do you?"

"No."

"Well, you say you're going to get an abortion or shoot yourself. Suppose you started tomorrow: what are you going to do to find an abortionist?"

"I don't know!" Rennie cried.

"Damn it, if there was ever a time when we've got to think

straight, this is it, but you're not thinking straight. You're setting up alternatives that aren't actually open to you."

Rennie gave a little cry and rushed to the smoking stand, but because I had seen as clearly as Joe that that was what she was being driven to I was ready when she made her move. I dived headlong from my rocker for the gun. I fell short (physical coordination was not my forte), but my fingers closed on the edge of the stand and I pulled stand, gun, and all down on top of me. Rennie, in her rush, struck my head with her shoe, a stunning blow, and fell to her knees. She scrabbled for the pistol, which had landed on my left shoulder blade and slid down beside my armpit. By rolling over on it I kept it from her long enough for me to get my own hands on it, and then fended her off until I was able to get to my feet again. She made no attempt to take it from me, but went back to her chair and buried her face in her hands. Very much shaken, I left the smoking stand where it lay and kept the gun.

"You people are insane!" I said.

Joe hadn't moved, although he too was obviously shaken.

"Explain why, Horner," he demanded, with considerable emotion.

"The hell I will," I said. "Do you want her to blow her damned head off?"

"I want her to think for herself," Joe said. "Since you stopped her, you must have some other opinion. Or is that you just don't want your room messed up? Would you rather we go home and do our shooting?"

"For Christ's sake, Joe, do you love your wife or not?"

"You're begging the question. Do *you* love her? Is that why you stopped her?"

"I don't love anybody right now. I think you're both insane."

"Stop saying things you can't explain. Would you rather force her to have a baby she doesn't want?"

"I don't give a damn what you all do, but I'm going to hold on to this pistol."

"You're talking nonsense," Joe said angrily. "You refuse to think. You're still talking about *us all*, and you know that's a distortion. You say you don't give a damn what Rennie does, but you take away her ability to choose. You're doing all you can to confuse everything."

"What the hell do you want?" I shouted.

"I want you to forget about everything except what's to the point and what's beside the point!" Joe said fiercely. "People act when they're ready whether they've thought clearly or not, and if there's one thing I'd kill you for, Horner, it's for screwing up the issues so that we have to act before we've thought, or taking something as important as this out of the realm of choice. Don't think I'm just talking: I'd kill you for it."

"What's beside the point, then?"

"Your oversimplifying is beside the point, for one thing: asking me *as the husband* what my position is; referring to Rennie and me together as if this were a conspiracy against you; blocking her actions; talking about perversity and insanity."

"Damn it, Joe, if I hadn't jumped she'd be *dead* right now! Would you be satisfied with that?"

"We're not playing games, Jake! Forget all the movies you ever saw and all the novels you ever read. Forget everything except this problem. Everything else obscures and confuses it. Stop looking at me as if I'm a monster!" he shouted, losing his temper. "If you ever knew a guy who's thought straight about these things it's me, God damn it! If you're interested, I'll tell you that you and I would probably be dead by this time too, if Rennie had shot herself; but I wouldn't have stopped her. Nobody else you ever met ever loved a female human being, Horner: they just love pictures in their heads. If I didn't love Rennie do you think I could have sat here when she went for the gun? In the name of Christ, Horner, *open your eyes!* Just this one time open your God-damned eyes and try to understand somebody!"

"Do you want me to put this pistol back on the table?"

"*Stop asking me what I want!*"

I was lost.

"Here," I said, handing Joe the Colt. "If you're so set on acting by your ideas, you put it back."

Joe took the gun and unhesitatingly offered it to Rennie.

"Here," he said gently, gripping the back of her chair for support. "Do you want it?"

Rennie shook her head without looking at him.

"Maybe she'd like to have you do it for her," I said, as acidly as possible, but I was so moved I was dizzy.

Joe glanced at me. "Do you want me to shoot you, Rennie?" he asked sarcastically. She shook her head again. Joe picked up the smoking stand, replaced the pistol on it, and went to his seat on the bed.

"So, Jake, you've decided we'll have the baby. Do you have any more opinions?"

I couldn't speak. Like Rennie, I shook my head. It is a demoralizing thing to deal with a man who will see, face up to, and unhesitatingly act upon the extremest limits of his ideas.

"Apparently you don't," Joe said contemptuously. He rose and began putting on his topcoat. "Do you want to come home now?" he asked Rennie.

Rennie rose and put on her coat. At the last minute Joe slipped the Colt into his pocket. He was extremely upset.

"Look, Joe," I called out as they left. "If Rennie *could* find an abortionist, what would you say?"

"What do you mean? What difference would it make what I said?"

"I mean how would you feel about the idea of her going through with an abortion?"

"I don't like it," Joe said flatly. "If it was a really competent abortion done in a good hospital by a good obstetrician it wouldn't matter, but it couldn't possibly be that. Rennie's in perfect health, and the only abortion she could get even in the city would be a half-ass job by some half-ass doctor who could mess her up for the rest of her life." He turned to go.

"I'll see if I can find somebody to do it," I said, "and if I can find somebody decent I'll pay for it."

"Horseshit," Joe said.

11. *The Next Morning, Early, My Eyes Opened Suddenly*

THE NEXT MORNING, EARLY, MY EYES OPENED SUDDENLY, and I leaped in a sweat from my bed with a terrible feeling that Rennie was dead. I called the Morgans at once, and could scarcely believe it when Rennie herself answered the telephone.

"I'm sorry I woke you up, Rennie. God, I was afraid you'd shot yourself already."

"No."

"Listen," I begged. "Promise me you'll wait awhile, will you?"

"I can't promise anything, Jake."

"You've got to, damn it!"

"Why?"

"Well, if for no other reason, because I love you." This, I fear, was not true, at least in the sense that any meaningless proposition is not true, if not false either. I'm not sure whether I knew what I was saying when I told Joe I loved Rennie, but at any rate I couldn't see any meaning in the statement now.

"So does Joe," Rennie said pointedly.

"Yes, all right, let's say he loves you more than I could ever love anybody. He loves you so much he's willing to let you shoot yourself, and I love you so little that I'm not."

Rennie hung up. I dialed her number again. This time Joe answered.

"Rennie doesn't want to talk to you," he said. "That was a stupid thing you said a minute ago—stupid or malicious."

"I'm sorry. Listen, Joe, do you think she'll commit suicide?"

"How the hell do I know?"

"Will you stay home with her today and see that she doesn't? Just today?"

"Of course not. For one thing, I can't think of anything more likely to make her to do it tomorrow."

"Then you *don't* want her to, do you?"

"That's beside the point."

"Just today, Joe! Look, I might be able to get hold of somebody for her if you won't let her do anything today."

"Do you know an abortionist? Why didn't you say so last night?"

"I'm not sure. I don't know any myself, but I know several people in Baltimore who might know of one. I'm going to call them now. Make her promise to sit still till I see."

"Rennie doesn't take orders from me."

"She will, and you know it. Tell her I know a doctor but I've got to call him to make arrangements."

"We don't operate that way."

"Just today, Joe!"

"Hold on," he said. "Rennie?" I heard him call to her. "Did you intend to kill yourself today?"

I heard Rennie ask why I wanted to know.

"Horner says some of his Baltimore friends might know of an abortionist," Joe said. I was furious that he told her the truth. "He's going to call them and see."

Rennie said something that I couldn't make out.

"She says she doesn't want to talk about anything," Joe said.

"Look, Joe, I'll call around. Maybe it won't even be necessary to have an abortion. I'll try to get hold of some Ergotrate. That ought to do it. Tell Rennie I'll stop out there today or tonight and either bring the Ergotrate with me or else have something definite arranged."

"Yeah, I'll tell her," Joe said, and hung up.

Now it wasn't quite true—in fact it wasn't at all true—that I had friends in Baltimore who might know abortionists, for I had no friends in Baltimore or anywhere else. What I did next was telephone every doctor in Wicomico, in alphabetical order. To the first one I said, "Hello. My name is Henry Dempsey. We're new in town and we don't have any regular doctor. Say, listen, my wife's in a terrible predicament: we have two kids already, and she thinks she's pregnant again. She's not a healthy girl—physically okay, you know, but not *psychologically* healthy. In fact she's under psychiatric care right now. I frankly don't think she could stand the strain of another pregnancy."

"Really?" said the doctor. "Who's her psychiatrist?"

"You might not know him," I said. "He's in White Plains, New York, where we used to live. Banks. Dr. Joseph Banks."

"Does your wife commute to White Plains for treatment?" the doctor asked innocently.

"We just moved, sir, as I said, and we haven't been able to find another psychiatrist yet."

"Well, that's out of my line."

"I know, sir; I didn't mean that. I'm afraid my wife might commit suicide over this pregnancy, before I can get her to another psychiatrist. She's in a terrible state. Frankly, I was wondering if you wouldn't prescribe Ergotrate or something for her. I know it's out of line, but this is a desperate case. In a year, two years, she could very well be adjusted enough to have all the kids we want —we don't want a *large* family, but we'd like to have three or four. A pregnancy now will mess her up completely."

"I'm sorry, Mr. Dempsey," the doctor said coldly. "I can't do that."

"Please, Doctor! I'm not asking you to go outside the law. I'll get a sworn affidavit from Dr. Banks in White Plains. Will that be okay? He'll take all the responsibility."

"No, Mr. Dempsey. I appreciate your dilemma, but my hands are tied."

"Doesn't the law allow you to take measures when the woman's life is in danger?"

"It's not what the law says, I'm afraid: it's what the people in town *think* the law says, and frankly the people around here are as opposed to abortions as I am, whether they're done by drugs or surgery. Besides, if your wife's trouble is mental, it's not that clearly a matter of life or death."

"It is! Dr. Banks will tell you so!"

"I'm sorry, Mr. Dempsey. Good-by."

I tried the same story on the other doctors whom I found listed in the telephone book—those who would speak to me at all—only

I located my mythical psychiatrist in Philadelphia instead of White Plains, in case I had to drive up there to get the proper postmark on a fake letter. Also, after consulting the Philadelphia directory in the lobby of the Peninsula Hotel, I changed the psychiatrist's name from Joseph C. Banks to Harry L. Siegrist, the name of a bona fide psychiatric practitioner whom I picked at random from the book. But all the doctors turned me down. My nerve began to flag: so predisposed was I to obeying laws, and so much did I fear, as a rule, the bad opinion even of people whom I neither knew nor cared about, it was all I could do to tell my elaborate fiction just once, and with each refusal it became harder to repeat. The effort was demoralizing.

Doctor #7, to my inexpressible relief, seemed not quite so unreceptive to my story. His name was Morton Welleck, and he sounded like a younger man than his colleagues.

"Now, Mr. Dempsey," he said, when I'd finished my piece, "you realize that any doctor who agrees to help your wife is assuming considerable responsibility, don't you?"

"Indeed I do, Dr. Welleck. If there's any way for me to legally assume all the responsibility, I'll do it gladly."

"But unhappily there isn't. I sympathize with your problem, though, and the law does provide that where there's clear danger to the patient's life, certain measures can be taken at the physician's discretion. You admit that Mrs. Dempsey is in good physical condition, so the question is whether her psychological condition is as serious as you believe it is. That would be a difficult thing to prove if anybody wanted to make an issue out of it, and I may as well tell you that certain of my older colleagues in Wicomico would jump at the chance to make an issue out of a thing like this. Frankly, I'm not the martyr type."

But I saw the shadow of a chance in Dr. Welleck's tone.

"Wouldn't a sworn affidavit from Dr. Siegrist do the trick?" I pleaded. "He'd be glad to provide one."

"It might," Dr. Welleck admitted. "Of course, I'd have to examine Mrs. Dempsey myself, if only to make sure she's pregnant!" We both laughed, I more tightly than he. "And I'd want to ask her a few questions, you know, even though I'm not a psychiatrist."

"Certainly. I'll have her come right down to your office." I hoped fervently that Dr. Welleck was new in town.

"Do that," he said, "and have Dr. Siegrist call me from Philadelphia, would you? We can decide whether it's advisable to get the affidavit or not, and he can explain Mrs. Dempsey's problem in more detail."

The prospect of driving to Philadelphia at once and impersonating a psychiatrist appalled me, but it seemed my only hope.

"All right," I agreed. "I'll telephone him as soon as I can and have him call you."

"That will be fine," Dr. Welleck said. He paused a moment. "You realize, Mr. Dempsey, that I can't promise anything. Like a lot of small towns, Wicomico is dead set against frustrating Mother Nature. Mainly, I'll admit, it's the older doctors here who are responsible: I doubt there's been a legal abortion here for years and years. Professional ethics aside, they're a collection of old sticks-in-the-mud. If they and some of the religious groups in town got wind of anything like this they'd crucify the poor fellow who did it. We can't always be as liberal as some of us might like to be."

"I understand perfectly, Doctor, but this really is a matter of life or death."

"Well. We'll see what we can do."

Dr. Welleck's manner gave me some confidence that he could be swindled. For one thing, he talked too much: three of the doctors I'd called had refused to discuss anything at all over the telephone, and none of the others had been anything like so garrulous as young Dr. Welleck. Also, from the nature of the conversation I gathered that he was finding it difficult to compete with the older practitioners, perhaps because he was new in town. Any professional man who would criticize his colleagues to a perfect stranger on the telephone was, I guessed, a man with whom arrangements could be made.

But Philadelphia! To fake a letter was one thing—I could be anybody in a letter—but I found it almost insuperably difficult to be even Henry Dempsey on the telephone: how could I be Dr. Harry L. Siegrist? There was no time to waste; already it was ten o'clock, and Philadelphia is two and a half hours from Wicomico.

Luckily it was Saturday—I had no classes to teach, but the college library was open. I drove out there at once, borrowed the first textbook on abnormal psychology that I could find, and set out for Philadelphia without delay. I'd gone no more than ten miles before I realized that if an affidavit had to be mailed from Philadelphia, it would certainly have to be a typewritten document, and I'd never be able to find a typewriter in a strange city. Back home I went, breaking the speed limits, and rushed up to my room. It was after eleven when I got there.

To whom it may concern, I wrote, scratching desperately for sentences: *Susan Bates Dempsey, age twenty-eight, wife of Henry J. Dempsey of Wicomico, Maryland, was a patient of mine between August 3, 1951, and June 17, 1953, shortly after which time Mr. and Mrs. Dempsey left Philadelphia to live in Wicomico. Mrs. Dempsey became my patient on the advice of her husband and her physician, Dr. Edward R. Rice of this city, after suffering frequent periods of acute despondency. During two of these periods she threatened to take her own life, and once even slashed her wrists with a kitchen knife. Examination indicated that Mrs. Dempsey had pronounced manic-depressive tendencies, the more dangerous because during her most acute depressions her two young sons often became the objects of her hostility, although at other times she was a competent, even a superior, mother. Mrs. Dempsey suffered markedly from the fear that she might lose her husband's affections: in her depressive states she was inclined to believe that the birth of her sons had detracted from her beauty, and this belief tended to focus her resentment upon her children. However, because she felt only hostility and not persecution, and because her periods of despondency alternated with periods of intense exuberance, even jubilation, my diagnosis was subacute manic-depressive psychosis rather than paranoia.*

During the period of her treatment, the amplitude of Mrs. Dempsey's manic-depressive cycle showed an appreciable decrease, and at no time after becoming my patient did she threaten to take her life or the lives of her children. She

*responds satisfactorily to competent psychotherapy, and with
continued treatment I believe her condition can be stabilized.
When the Dempseys left Philadelphia I recommended that
her treatment be continued if possible, but suggested to Mr.
Dempsey that immediate resumption was not urgent. However, I also recommended that Mrs. Dempsey avoid pregnancy until completely cured, since her former pregnancies
had been largely responsible for her condition.*

*I believe that an accidental pregnancy at this time may
produce a critical recurrence of her despondency; that she
may again threaten to take her life, rather than carry the
fetus; and that she may very well carry out her threat even
if psychiatric treatment were resumed at once. I unhesitatingly recommend, even urge, that for the protection of her
other children and herself, Mrs. Dempsey's pregnancy be
aborted at the earliest possible moment.*

I signed the letter, "Harry L. Siegrist, M.D.," put it into an
envelope, and hurried back to my car. I stopped along the road
to eat lunch and bone up on the manic-depressive psychosis, and
by shortly after three o'clock I was in a telephone booth in a Penn-
Whelan drugstore on Walnut Street in Philadelphia, placing a
long-distance call to Dr. Welleck in Wicomico. My hands shook;
I sweated. When I heard Dr. Welleck's receptionist answer, and
the operator asked me to deposit sixty cents, I dropped a quarter
on the floor: my courage barely sufficed to retrieve it and ask for
Dr. Welleck.

"I'm sorry, Dr. Siegrist," the receptionist said after I'd introduced myself. "Dr. Welleck is at the hospital just now."

"Oh, that's too bad!" I exclaimed in gruff disappointment. "I
don't suppose you could reach him?"

"I'm afraid not, sir; he's in surgery this afternoon."

"What a bother!" I was immensely relieved, almost joyous,
that I wouldn't have to speak to him, but at the same time I
feared for my plan.

"I'll have him call you as soon as he comes in, if you like."

"Oh, now, I'm afraid that won't do," I said peevishly. "My
vacation started today, and Mrs. Siegrist and I will be in Bermuda

all through October. Mr. Dempsey reached me just as we were closing up the house—thank heaven! Another hour and we'd have been gone. You know, this is something of an emergency, but my plane leaves two hours from now and I couldn't say where I'd be between now and then. Dr. Welleck *will* administer Ergotrate, won't he? This could turn into a nasty thing."

"He wanted to talk to you, Dr. Siegrist."

"I know, I know. Well, see here, I'll have my secretary type up an affidavit before I leave—this is quite a routine thing, you know—and I'll have it notarized and sent special delivery and all that. What a nuisance that I can't talk to Dr. Welleck personally!" I said with some heat. "I can't emphasize too much the seriousness of this sort of thing with a manic-depressive like Mrs. Dempsey. She could behave perfectly normally one moment and shoot herself the next, if she hasn't already. Really, Dr. Welleck should give her the Ergotrate at the earliest possible moment. Tonight if possible; tomorrow at the very latest. I've already arranged with Mr. Dempsey to place his wife under the care of one of my colleagues until I get back, but this thing really must be taken care of first."

"I'll tell Dr. Welleck at once," the receptionist said, clearly impressed.

"Please do, and he'll get the affidavit tomorrow morning."

"Could you give me your Bermuda address, sir, in case Dr. Welleck wants to get in touch with you?"

Great heavens! "Mrs. Siegrist and I will be stopping at the Prince George Hotel," I said, hoping there was such a place.

"The Prince George. Thank you, sir."

"And please, tell Dr. Welleck to get that Ergotrate into Mrs. Dempsey as soon as he can. I'd hate to lose a patient over something as silly as this. I don't blame the man for being cautious, but I must say that if it were I, she'd be aborted by this time. A layman could tell she's manic-depressive, and her suicidal tendencies stick out all over. Good-by, now."

I hung up, and very nearly fainted. A big obstacle was behind me, but there was a still bigger one ahead. I found a notary public in a loan office two blocks down Walnut Street (which I prayed Dr. Siegrist didn't happen to patronize) and went in quickly before my nerve failed. It is my lot to look older than my years, but I could scarcely believe anyone would seriously take me for a certified psychiatrist. Besides, it is even more difficult to act out a fiction face to face with the man you're lying to than it is to do it on the telephone. Finally, I wasn't at all sure that notaries didn't demand identification before administering the oath and seal. Assuming the most worldly manner I could muster, I asked a clerk where the notary public was, and he directed me to the assistant manager's desk across the room.

"Howdy do," smiled the assistant manager, a squat, bald-headed, cigar-chewing little man with steel-rimmed glasses.

"My name's Siegrist," I said genially: "Harry Siegrist. I've a paper here somewhere to be notarized, if I haven't left it at the office." I smiled and made a leisurely search of my pockets. "Oh yes, here you are, you little rascal." I fetched the letter from my inside coat pocket, opened it, and casually scanned it. "Mmm-*hmm*. There you go, sir."

The assistant manager read the document carelessly.

"Boy oh boy," he said. "She's a real bat, isn't she, Doc?"

"Not as bad as some we get," I chuckled.

"Ha!" said the notary. "You ought to see some of the boobies we get in here. You could make a fortune."

I waited to be asked for my credentials.

"I swear," the notary mused absently, "I think it's all in their heads. Well——" He began fumbling in his desk drawer. "Raise your right hand a little bit, will you, Doc?"

I did, and he likewise.

"Now, then, d'you swear before God that the blah blah blah blah and all that?" he asked, still digging around in his desk with the other hand.

"I do."

"Won't make no difference whether you do or not if I can't find my seal," he said cheerfully. My head reeled—after my good luck in finding a notary as cynical as he was credulous, could my scheme hang on such a mischance?

"Ah, there she blows," he said, fishing out the seal. He clamped the official impression on my letter and signed it. Then he called two nearby clerks over to sign as witnesses. "Don't mind reading it," he told them. "Just put your John Hancock where it says." They did. "All right, Doctor: buck and a half."

I paid him with a bill from my wallet, holding my identity card from view, and left with my letter, which I dropped into the first deposit box I encountered. So much for Philadelphia—it was four o'clock, and I had to get home fast. In general I was amazed at the success of my plan, but four distressing things were on my mind. First, I had no idea whether Dr. Welleck would be convinced by my completely non-technical affidavit, which for all I knew any M.D. might be able to recognize as spurious at first glance; at any rate, it was entirely possible that if any doubt remained in his mind the coincidence of Dr. Siegrist's taking so immediate a vacation might turn that doubt into skepticism: should Welleck at any time be dubious enough to call the office of the real Dr. Siegrist, the jig was up. Second, I had deliberately not left a telephone number with Welleck, and of course there was no Henry Dempsey in the Wicomico directory; despite the fact that there are human beings without telephones, Welleck's inability to reach me, should he try before I got home and called him, could add to his suspicion. The third unknown was even more worrisome: even if everything else worked out perfectly and Welleck consented to administer the Ergotrate, it was quite possible that he was not new in town at all and might know Rennie. Finally, even if he didn't, there was one more danger: so innocent was I of the business of abortion that, for all I knew, Welleck might require that Rennie go to the hospital for something or other, since the thing was going to be legal, and even if Welleck himself didn't know her, someone at the hospital surely would.

As soon as I reached my room again I called Welleck at his house.

"Oh, Mr. Dempsey," he said, a little coldly. "I've been trying to telephone you."

"I'm sorry, Doctor. We haven't had a phone put in yet, and I have to use my landlord's. I'd have called you earlier, but I've been driving my wife around in the country today, to sort of keep her mind off things."

"Well, Dr. Siegrist called from Philadelphia."

"Did he? Good! I barely caught him before he left on his vacation. Did you get anything straightened out?"

"I didn't talk to him. I was in surgery. He talked to my receptionist, and he's sending down an affidavit. My understanding is that he strongly recommends the abortion."

"Whew!" I laughed. "You don't know how relieved I am."

"Yes. Now he said something to my receptionist about giving the Ergotrate tonight, but I'm afraid I can't do it until I have the affidavit in my hands. If he mailed it special delivery this afternoon, I should get it at least by Monday morning."

"That's wonderful."

"You give me your landlord's number and I'll let you know when the affidavit comes so you can bring Mrs. Dempsey in to the office."

"Well, now, my landlord's right touchy about receiving calls for me, and frankly this is none of his business. I'd rather he knew nothing about it, because he's a terrible gossip. Couldn't I call you?"

"Perhaps that would be better. Despite the fact that this won't be illegal, we'd just as well keep it quiet. Call me around noon on Monday, and if I have the affidavit I'll give you an appointment for after lunch."

"That's fine."

"Oh, one more thing. I have a standard authorization form that I use for sterilizations, abortions, and the like. Both you and your wife will have to sign it, and you'll have to get it notarized. You could do that Monday morning if you like. Just pick up the form from my receptionist."

"Okay. Swell. Good night, Doctor."

Another document, another notary, another hurdle to clear— but by this time I was past caring. I drove in weary triumph out to the Morgans' house to announce my success. On their doorstep I got the cold shudders: I'd been out of town most of the day—what if I was already too late? Joe answered the door.

"Oh, hello, Jake. You look sick."

"Is Rennie okay?"

"She's still with us, if that's what you mean. Come on in."

Rennie was waxing the kitchen floor. She scarcely acknowledged my presence.

"Well, I think it's all set," I said, feigning tranquillity. "If you want an abortion, Rennie, you can get a shot of Ergotrate Monday afternoon."

Joe showed no reaction to the news. Rennie came to the kitchen doorway, waxing rag in hand, and leaned against the doorframe.

"All right. Where do I have to go? Baltimore?"

"Nope. Right here in town. Just don't tell me you know Dr. Morton Welleck."

"Dr. Welleck. No, I don't know him. Do you, Joe?"

"I know of him. He's been here about two years. You mean the damned fool's an abortionist?"

"Nope," I said, not a little proudly. "He's a completely legitimate doctor, and a pretty good one, so I hear. And everything's going to be completely legal. You don't have to feel guilty or afraid of going to him at all."

"How come?" Joe asked.

"As a matter of fact, I told him pretty much the truth. I said you had two kids already and wanted more later, but you were so despondent about getting pregnant just now that I was afraid you were on the verge of suicide. Of course it was a little more elaborate than that."

"How was it more elaborate, Jake?" Rennie asked wonderingly.

"Well, I had to jazz it up a little. You're my wife these days, for one thing: Mrs. Henry J. Dempsey, of the Philadelphia Dempseys."

"What?"

I warmed to the the story then, exhilarated by my day's adventures, and told them in detail about the telephone calls, the trip to Philadelphia, the letter, the impersonations of Dr. Siegrist, and the assistant manager of the loan office. They listened in astonishment.

"So, all Mr. and Mrs. Dempsey have to do now is sign an authorization Monday morning and get it notarized, and we're set. You don't have to act crazy or anything, and once you've had the shot you can forget the whole business."

Joe watched Rennie with interest.

"That's absurd," she said at once.

"Isn't it fantastic?" I grinned, not wanting to believe she meant what I feared she meant.

"It's horrible!"

"You'll do it, won't you?"

"Of course not. It's out of the question."

"Out of the question! Good Christ, Rennie, I've run my ass off today getting it set up, and you say it's out of the question. Nothing will happen, I swear!"

"That isn't the point, Jake. I'm through lying. Even if I didn't have to sign anything or say anything it would still be lying. You should've known I wouldn't want anything to do with it."

The whole edifice came down. Joe's expression didn't change, but I felt a great unanimity of spirit between him and Rennie. I was out of it.

"Shoot yourself then, damn it!" I cried. "I don't know why I bothered to sweat my tail off for you today anyhow, if you don't really want an abortion. Obviously you were just being melodramatic last night."

Rennie smiled. "I *am* going to shoot myself, Jake, as soon as it's clear that you can't arrange an abortion. I wasn't just being dramatic. I don't care who does the job or where it's done or under what circumstances, but I won't tell lies or assent to lies, and I won't pretend to be anybody but myself. I don't know anybody and Joe doesn't either. If you hadn't said you thought you did, I wouldn't have waited this long." She rubbed her hand once across her stomach. "I don't want this baby, Jake. It might be yours."

She was clearly sincere. I looked desperately to Joe for support, but he was noncommittal. Again I felt their unanimity. It occurred to me to accuse them of romanticism; to make fun of their queer honor—God knows it needed poking fun at, and a great part of me longed to do the job wholeheartedly—but I no longer trusted this strategy: it might only confirm what was already evidently a pretty fixed resolve.

"Don't do it yet, Rennie," I said wearily. "I'll think of something else."

"What will you think of, Jake? If you had any real ideas you wouldn't have started with something as fantastic as this business today. If you think I'll change my mind if you stall long enough, you're wrong."

"What about the boys? Have you given them a thought, or are you going to plug them too?"

"You're asking questions you don't have to ask," Joe said.

"Don't play games, Jake," Rennie said. "Do you have anything on your mind or not?"

"Yes, I do," I said. "I know a woman in town who's had a couple of abortions. I'd have thought of her before if I hadn't been so excited. I'll see her tomorrow and find out where she had them done."

"I don't believe you," Rennie said.

"It's the truth, I swear it."

"What's her name, then? Don't make up one."

"Peggy Rankin. She teaches English at the high school."

Rennie went to the telephone at once and looked for the name in the directory.

"8401," she said. "I'll call her and ask her."

"Don't be silly! She's not married. Would she admit something like that to a stranger?"

"You call her then. Right now. You must not be a stranger if you know that about her."

"You're making it impossible. Women don't work that way— other women, anyhow. I'll see her tomorrow and let you know tomorrow night."

"I think you're stalling, Jake."

"Well, think it, damn it! Are you so trigger-happy you can't wait twenty-four hours?" I felt as though I'd explode from desperation, but still Joe watched us impassively. There were books and notebooks open beside the telephone on the writing table: he'd been working on his dissertation! Rennie thought a moment.

"I'll wait till tomorrow night," she said, and went back to waxing the floor.

Rennie had stated the matter exactly when she accused me of stalling in hopes that she'd change her mind, but I could no longer entertain such hopes. Certainly I hadn't the slightest idea whether

Peggy Rankin had ever had an abortion, and I had no reason to expect that she'd help me even if she could, for I'd not seen her since the time early in September. She had telephoned me—first hopefully, then angrily, and at last pleadingly—a number of times in the past few weeks, but I'd received her calls without encouragement. The next morning, Sunday, I telephoned her.

"Jake Horner, Peggy. I have to see you about something important."

"Well, I don't want to see you," she said.

"This is something awfully serious, Peggy, believe me."

"Yes. It has been about a month, hasn't it?"

"Listen, it doesn't have anything to do with that. I'm trying to help somebody who needs help very badly."

"You're a real humanitarian."

"Peggy, for God's sake! I won't pretend I've been thoughtful of you, but this is a pretty desperate thing. I realize there's no reason why you should do me any favors."

"That's right."

"Look, you've got me over a barrel. You might not be able to help these friends of mine even if you wanted to, but they're in such a spot that I'd do absolutely anything to help them out. Name your own conditions."

"What do you want me to do?"

"All I want you to do is let me talk to you for a few minutes. As I said, you might not be able to help at all, but there's just a chance that you might."

"Who are the friends?"

"I can't talk over the phone. Can I see you today?"

"Jake, if this is another line I'll kill you."

"It's no line!" I said vehemently. "This doesn't have anything to do with me. When can I see you? The sooner the better."

"Well. All right, then. Come on over now. But God, Jake, be straight this time."

"This is straight."

I drove over to her place immediately, and she received me with great suspicion, as though she expected to be assaulted at any moment.

"I don't even like to have you in here," she said nervously. "What is it?"

"The wife of one of the guys at school is pregnant, Peggy, and she's going to kill herself if she can't get an abortion."

Peggy's face went hard. "What a monster you are! And you come to me for help!"

"You don't understand yet. They're both good friends of mine, and they don't know where to get the abortion."

"Am I supposed to know? Why doesn't she have the kid, if she's married?" This last with some bitterness.

"She's got two already, and frankly there's some question about who's the father of this one. That's why she's desperate. Her husband knows all about it. She just made one slip."

"Jake, are you the one?"

This I took to be a crucial question: her willingness to help might hinge on my answer, and I had no idea which answer she wanted to hear.

"That's right, Peggy." I looked her straight in the eye, putting all my money on honesty. "It was the stupidest thing I ever did in my life, and now she's going to shoot herself. I've messed them up completely. All I can do now is try to clean up as much of the mess as I can."

"When did you start cleaning up your messes?"

"Two days ago. If I can't find a way to help them by tonight, it'll be too late. That's all the time I've got."

"She won't kill herself," Peggy said contemptuously. "If women killed themselves out of remorse I'd have been dead at least since July."

"She will, Peggy. She'd be dead now if I hadn't stopped her, and she'll be dead tomorrow if I can't help her."

"What do you care?"

I still looked her straight in the eye. "I said I'm trying to clean up my messes."

"You mean *this* mess."

"I mean all my messes."

"Some of them it's too late to clean up."

"Maybe. But I'm going to do my best."

"What's that?"

"I don't know, Peggy. I'm new at this. Right now I'm doing whatever people want me to do. I said you could name your conditions."

Peggy stared at me awhile.

"Who's this girl?"

"Rennie Morgan. Her husband teaches history at the college."

But obviously Peggy was more concerned about herself.

"Do you think I've had abortions before? I guess you'd assume that, though, wouldn't you?"

"I'm not assuming anything. I hoped maybe you'd know somebody who has had one, or that maybe you'd have heard of an abortionist."

"Suppose I did know of one?"

"I said already there's no reason why you should help me, and I take it you don't feel one way or the other about Rennie Morgan —or maybe you dislike her, I don't know. All I can say is that this is my last chance to keep her from committing suicide, and I'll do absolutely anything to get your help."

"You must love her a lot."

"If I do I don't know it. Do you know of an abortionist, Peggy?"

After a while she said, "Yes, I do. I had to find one myself, two years ago."

"Who was it?"

"I haven't decided yet that I'm going to help you, Jake."

"Look," I said, in the straightest tone I could manage, "you don't have to assert your position; I'm aware of your position. You don't have to hold out for anything; I've already told you to write your own ticket."

"I could help you," Peggy said; "this man's still around, and he'd do the job. His price is two hundred dollars."

I thought it would be effective if I stood close in front of her, laid my hands on her shoulders, and leaned down to look into her eyes. And so I did.

"What's yours?" I asked, with appropriate calm.

"Oh, Jake, I could name a high price! You've been desperate for a day or two, but I've been desperate for fifteen years!"

"Name it."

"Why? Once she'd had the operation, you'd leave me."

"You want me to marry you, Peggy?"

"That would be my price," she said.

"I'll do it."

"You probably would. Then which would you do afterwards? Leave me flat, or torture me for the rest of my life?"

"Neither one of those sounds like a good way to clean up messes," I grinned.

"You couldn't possibly do anything but hate me. No man ever loved a woman he was coerced into marrying."

"Try me."

Peggy was extremely nervous, excited by the position she had me in, a little afraid of her temerity.

"How can I believe you, Jake? You haven't done one single thing to make me believe you can be trusted."

"I know it."

"And yet you say you're being sincere this time?"

"That's right."

"You don't love me."

"I don't love anybody. But I've been a bachelor a good while, and even without this abortion thing I owe you enough to last a right long time."

Peggy shook off my hands and whipped her head in a manner quite like Rennie's.

"What is it about you? Even when you're being kind you put me in a false position—a humiliating position."

"Well, you be quiet, then. Let me propose to you. I've decided that I want to marry you. If I ever said an honest thing in my life, that's it."

"You never did say an honest thing to me, did you?"

"I just said one. I'd marry you today if we could get the license on Sunday. We'll get it tomorrow and get married on Wednesday."

"You said she had to know tonight."

"That's right. All you have to do is tell her you know a guy. You can call her right now. I think that'll do it. Tell her that for personal reasons or something you can't give his name until Wednesday. If she agrees to wait, I'm satisfied."

"But if she doesn't, that's that?"

Another crucial question, but the proper answer was obvious.

"If she doesn't, there's nothing else I can do for her, but I don't see where that would change my obligation to you. You'd have done all I asked, and I'd do everything I promised."

Now Peggy began to cry, squirming with indecision.

"I'll marry you and love you as much as I can ever love anybody, for the rest of my life," I swore.

She wept for a while without replying, until I began to grow apprehensive. Something else had to be done, immediately. I considered embracing her: would that turn the trick, or spoil everything? I was aware that every move was critical now; any word or action—or any silence or inaction—could convince her suddenly of my sincerity or insincerity. Peggy Rankin! I was cursed with an imagination too fertile to be of any use in predicting my fellow human beings: no matter how intimate my knowledge of them, I was always able to imagine and justify contradictory reactions from them to almost anything. A kiss now: would she regard it as evidence that I was overplaying my hand, or as evidence that I was too sincere to care whether she thought me insincere? If I made no move, would she think my inaction proof that I couldn't carry the fraud further, that I was so sure she was hooked that no further move was necessary, or that in my profound sincerity I was afraid to move for fear she'd think my proposal a mere stratagem after all?

I took her head in my hands and turned her face up to me. She hesitated for a moment and then accepted a long kiss.

"Thank God you believed me, Peggy," I said quietly.

"I don't."

"*What?*"

"I don't believe a single lying word you've said since you walked in here. I should have hung up on you when you called. Please get out."

"Good Christ, Peggy! You've got to believe me!"

"If you don't get out I'm going to scream. I mean it."

"Don't you believe Rennie Morgan's going to shoot herself?" I shouted.

She let out a yell, and I had to clap my hand over her mouth to stop her. She kicked and pummeled me, and tried to bite my hand. I forced her back into her chair, sat on her lap to keep her legs still, and clamped my other hand around her throat. She was fairly strong, and it was all I could do to hold her—with Rennie it would not have been possible at all.

"I'm more desperate than you think, damn it! I meant it when I said I'd marry you, and I mean it when I say I'm going to throttle you right this minute if you don't help me."

Her eyes got round, I took my hand off her mouth, and as soon as she tried to holler again I squeezed her windpipe hard—really hard, digging my thumb and forefinger into the sides of her neck.

"Stop it!" she squeaked. I let up, afraid I'd really damaged her. The breath rushed into her lungs with a great croak.

"Who's the abortionist?" I demanded.

"There isn't any," she said, clutching her throat. "I don't know any! I was just trying to——"

I slammed her as hard as I could and ran out of the place.

There was nothing else to do: whether I had been sincere or not, whether she had been lying or not, made no difference now. I went home and sat in the rocking chair. It was already eleven-thirty in the morning. I was out of straws to clutch at, and out of energy, beaten clear down the line. I tried to force my imagination to dream up another long shot, but all I could think of was Rennie, eight or ten hours from that moment, going to the living-room closet without a word. Joe, perhaps, would be bent over a note-book on the writing table. He might hear Rennie put down—her newspaper?—and go to the closet. I could imagine him then either continuing to stare at the notebook, but no longer seeing the words he'd written, or maybe turning his head to watch her open the closet door. The boys would be asleep in their room. I didn't believe Rennie would come back into the living room to do it. There in the closet, where the half-open door would stand be-tween her and Joe, she'd reach the Colt down from the shelf, move the safety catch off, put the muzzle to her temple, and pull the trigger at once, before the feel of the barrel against her head made her vomit. I believed she might sit down on the closet floor to do it.

That was as far as I could imagine with any clarity, for I'd never seen a bloody corpse. For perhaps two hours—that is, until about one-thirty—this sequence of actions repeated itself over and over in my imagination, up to the moment of the explosion. Drastic courses: I could go out there and—try to rush for the gun? But what would I do with it? They'd simply look at me, and Rennie would use something else later. Grab Rennie and hold her, if possible. Forever? Call the police and tell them—that a woman was about to commit suicide. What could they do? She'd be sitting home reading the paper, Joe working at the writing table. Tell her I've arranged an abortion—with whom? For when? Tell her—what?

My rocking slowed to a nearly imperceptible movement. Except for the idea of the gun against Rennie's temple, the idea of the lead slug waiting deep in the chamber—which was not an image but a tenseness, a kind of drone in my head—my imagination no longer pictured anything. My bladder was full; I needed to go to the bathroom, but I didn't go. After a while the urgency passed. I decided to try to say *Pepsi-Cola hits the spot*, but after the first couplet I forgot to say the rest. The urge to urinate returned, more sharply than before. I couldn't decide to get up.

Someone downstairs turned a radio on loud, and I jumped to my feet. It was three o'clock: the half-minute that I thought I'd spent not getting up to go to the bathroom had been an hour and a quarter! A moment later I hurried downstairs to the car; I drove out past the Morgans' at sixty miles an hour, out in the country to Vineland, and to the Remobilization Farm. I found Mrs. Dockey in the entrance hall, tying up large corrugated boxes with rope.

"Where's the Doctor? I have to see him right away."

She jerked her head toward the back of the house. As I went through the reception room I noticed rolled carpets, disarranged furniture, and more paper boxes.

"You're upset," the Doctor observed as soon as he saw me. Dressed in a black wool suit, he was reading the Sunday paper on the back porch, which in cold weather was converted into a sun parlor. He was, fortunately, alone: most of the patients were either taking the air out front or lounging in the reception room. "Sit down."

"I had a touch of my trouble this afternoon," I said.

"Immobility?" He put down his paper and looked at me more carefully. "Then you haven't been applying the therapies."

"No, I'll confess I haven't. I've been awfully busy lately."

It was cool outside, even chilly, but the sun shone brightly, and out over a marshy creek behind the farmhouse a big gray fish hawk hung motionless against the wind. I didn't know where to start.

"If that's so," the Doctor said critically, "I don't understand why you were immobilized."

"I think I can explain it. What I've been doing is trying to straighten out some problems that have come up."

"Well. This time I'm afraid I'll have to know the problem, since it developed after you started therapy. Maybe we'd better go into the Progress and Advice Room."

"I can tell you right here. It won't take long."

"No. Let's go into the Progress and Advice Room. You go on in—tell Mrs. Dockey so she'll know where we are—and I'll be there in a minute."

I did as he said, and a little while later he came in and took his position facing me. He'd changed into a white medical jacket.

"Now, what is it?"

With my knees straight in front of me and my arms folded across my chest, I told him the story of my brief affair with Rennie, and its consequences. To my surprise it came rather easily, so long as I stuck to the actual events and made no attempt to explain anybody's motives. The most difficult thing was to handle my eyes during the telling: the Doctor, as usual, leaned forward, rolling his unlit cigar around in his mouth, and watched my face the whole time; I focused first on his left eye, then on his right, then on his forehead, the bridge of his nose, his cigar—and it became disconcerting that I couldn't hold my eyes still for more than a few moments. I told him all the details of my search for an abortionist, and even my interview with Peggy Rankin. It was enormously refreshing to articulate it all.

"There's no question at all about Rennie's resolve," I said at last. "She'll commit suicide tonight if I can't tell her something definite, and I ran out of possibilities at eleven-thirty this morning. It was after that that the paralysis set in, and it lasted until an hour or so ago, when somebody downstairs from me turned a radio on. She'll shoot herself five or six hours from now."

"Is this your idea of a tranquil existence?" the Doctor demanded irritably. "I told you to avoid complications! I told you specifically not to become involved with women! Did you think your therapies were just silly games? Were you just playing along with me to amuse yourself?"

"I don't know, sir."

"Of course you do. For a long time you've considered me some kind of charlatan, or quack, or worse. That's been clear enough, and I allowed you to go on thinking so, as long as you did what I told you, because in your case that sort of attitude can be therapeutic itself. But when you begin to disregard my advice, then that attitude is very dangerous, as I trust you see now."

"Yes, sir."

"Do you understand that if you'd kept up with your treatment you wouldn't be here right now? If you'd studied your *World Almanac* every day, and thought of nothing but your grammar students, and practiced Sinistrality, Antecedence, and Alphabetical Priority—particularly if you thought them absurd but practiced them anyway—nothing that happened would have been a problem for you."

"Frankly, Doctor, I've been more concerned about the Morgans lately than about myself."

"And you see what's happened! I didn't tell you to make friends! You should have been thinking of nothing but your immobility."

It was time to tell him why I had come out to see him, but he went on talking.

"Now clearly this paralysis you just had is a different sort from what you had before. In Penn Station it was inability to choose that immobilized you. That's the case I'm interested in, and that's the case I've been treating. But this was a simple matter of running yourself into a blind alley—a vulgar, stupid condition, not even a dilemma, and yet it undoes all I'd accomplished."

"Doctor, excuse me—that girl's going to shoot herself!"

"It would serve you right if the husband shot you. Mythotherapy—Mythotherapy would have kept you out of any involvement, if you'd practiced it assiduously the whole time. Actually you did practice it, but like a ninny you gave yourself the wrong part. Even the villain's role would have been all right, if you'd been an out-and-out villain with no regrets! But you've made yourself a penitent when it's too late to repent, and that's the best role I can think of to immobilize you. Well!" he exclaimed, really disturbed. "Your case was the most interesting I've treated for years, and you've all but ruined it!"

For a full two minutes he chewed his cigar in angry silence. I was terribly conscious of time slipping by.

"Can't you——"

"Be quiet!" he said impatiently. After a while he said, "The girl's suicide will be entirely anti-therapeutic. Even disastrous. For one thing, the husband might shoot you, or you might even shoot yourself, you've relapsed so badly. These two eventualities I could prevent by keeping you here on the farm, but he might get the police to hunt for you when he finds out you're gone, and I don't want them out here. You've completely botched things! You've spoiled two years of my work with this silly affair."

"Can't you give her a shot of Ergotrate, Doctor?" I asked quickly.

The Doctor removed the cigar from his mouth for a moment in order to look at me the more caustically. "My dear fellow, for what earthly reason would I have Ergotrate here? Do you think these ladies and gentlemen conceive children?"

I blushed. "Well—could you write a prescription?"

"Don't be any more naïve than you have to. You could just as well write one yourself."

"God. I don't know what to do."

"Horner, stop being innocent. You came out here to ask me to abort the fetus, not to talk about your immobility."

"Will you do it?" I begged him. "I'll pay anything you want to charge."

"An empty statement. Suppose I wanted to charge seven thousand dollars? What you mean is that you'll pay up to maybe five hundred dollars. And since you'd renege on payments after the thing was done, the possible price couldn't be more than one or two hundred. Unless I'm greatly mistaken you haven't more than that on hand."

"I've got about two seventy-five, Doctor. I'll give it to you gladly."

"Horner, I'm not an abortionist. I've aborted perhaps ten fetuses in my career, and that was years ago. If I performed an abortion now I'd jeopardize this whole establishment, the future welfare of my patients, and my own freedom. Is two hundred and seventy-five dollars enough for that? Or five thousand, for that matter?"

"I can't offer you anything else."

"Yes, you can, and if you do I'll abort the girl's fetus."

"I'll agree to anything."

"Certainly. But whether you keep your agreement is another matter. I'm preparing to relocate the farm—no doubt you noticed the things in the entrance hall and the reception room. For a change, we're moving because we want to and not because we have to; I've found a better location, in Pennsylvania, and we're leaving Wednesday. Mrs. Dockey would have contacted you tomorrow if you hadn't come out here today. Now, then, if it weren't for this, the abortion would be out of the question; since we're moving anyway, I'll perform it tonight."

The shock brought tears to my eyes, and I laughed sharply.

"What I'd like to do is simply give you a catheter for the girl. If she walked around with that in her for a day or two it would induce labor and abort the fetus. She'd hemorrhage a lot, but the hospital would have to accept her as an emergency case. This would be better because she wouldn't have to come out here at all, but it takes too long; she might not even start labor until Wednesday, and she'd be so miserable with the catheter in her uterus that she'd probably kill herself anyway. Bring her out here tonight, and I'll scrape the uterus and get it over with."

"I will! Lord, that's wonderful!"

"It's not. It's sordid and disgusting, but I'll do it as a last resort to save your case. What you have to do in return is not only give me all the money you've got to help move the farm to Pennsylvania, but quit your job and come with us. I require this for two reasons: first, and most important, I want you on hand twenty-four hours a day so I can establish you on your schedule of therapies again; second, I'll need a young man to do a great deal of manual labor while the new farm is being set up. That will be your first therapy. Perhaps my fee is too high?"

I remembered the old men in the dormitory.

"Don't dawdle, Horner," the Doctor said sternly, "or I'll refuse. Your case is a hobby with me, but it's not an obsession, and you annoy me as often as you entertain me."

"I'll do it," I said.

"Very well. Tonight I'll do the abortion. You'll have to bring a check for the money, since it's Sunday. Tomorrow you let the college know you're quitting, and Wednesday morning be at the Greyhound terminal in Wicomico at eight-thirty. You'll meet Mrs. Dockey and some of the patients there and go up with them on the bus."

"All right."

"Do you want me to explain all the things I can do to make sure you keep your promise, or at least make you awfully sorry you broke it?"

"You don't have to, Doctor," I said. "I'm exhausted. I'll keep it."

"I'm sure you will," he smiled, "whether you are or not. All right, that's all." He stood up. "The patients go to bed at nine. Bring the girl out at nine-thirty. Don't shine your headlights on the house, and don't make noise; you'll alarm everybody upstairs. And bring your check and your bankbook, so I'll know the check's as large as possible. Good-by."

As I went out, I found Mrs. Dockey still stolidly tying up boxes in the entrance hall.

"The Doctor told me about moving," I said to her. "It looks like I'll be going along with you, for a while, anyhow."

"Okay," she growled, without looking at me. "Be there at eight-thirty sharp. Bus leaves at eight-forty."

"I will," I said, and half ran to the car. It was then close to five o'clock.

12. I Stood in the Morgans' Living Room with My Coat Still On, for It Was Not Suggested That I Stay

I STOOD IN THE MORGANS' LIVING ROOM WITH MY COAT STILL ON, FOR IT WAS NOT SUGGESTED THAT I STAY for dinner or anything else. Both Joe and Rennie were in the kitchen, leisurely preparing supper for the boys. They seemed in good humor, and had apparently been joking about something.

"Where have you been this time?" Rennie asked.

"Everything's settled," I said.

"All you have to do is catch the next plane to Vatican City," Joe told her, mocking the weariness and relief of my voice, "and tell the man you're the Pope's concubine."

"I said once and for all I won't lie," Rennie laughed.

"I'll pick you up at nine o'clock," I said. "The appointment's for nine-thirty. It won't be Ergotrate."

Rennie's smile faded; she paled a little.

"Have you really found somebody?"

"Yes. He's a retired specialist who runs a convalescent home out near Vineland."

"What's his name?" Joe asked unsmilingly.

"He wants to stay anonymous. That's understandable enough. But he's a good doctor. I've known him for several years, before I came here. In fact, I took this teaching job at his suggestion."

They showed some surprise.

"I've never heard of a convalescent home out that way," Rennie said doubtfully.

"That's because he keeps the place private, for his patients'

benefit, and because he's a Negro doctor with an all-white
clientele. Not many people know about him."

"Is he safe?" Joe asked, a little suspiciously. They were both
standing in the kitchen doorway by this time.

"That doesn't matter," Rennie said quickly, and went back to
the stove.

"Will you be ready at nine?" I asked her.

"I'll be ready."

"You'll want to come too, won't you?" I asked Joe.

"I don't know," he said dully. "I'll decide later."

It was as though I'd spoiled something.

Back in my room, the pressure off, I experienced a reaction not
only against the excitement of the days just past but against my
whole commitment. It was not difficult to feel relieved at having
finally prevented Rennie's suicide, but it was extremely difficult to
feel chastened, as I wanted to feel chastened. I wanted the adventure to teach me this about myself: that regardless of what shifting
opinions I held about ethical matters in the abstract, I was not so
consistently the same person (not so sufficiently "real," to use
Rennie's term) that I could involve myself seriously in the lives of
others without doing damage all around, not least to my own
tranquillity; that my irrational flashes of conscience and cruelty, of
compassion and cynicism—in short, my inability to play the same
role long enough—could give me as well as others pain, and that
the same inconsistency rendered it improbable that I could remain
peacefully in painful positions for very long, as Joe, for example,
could remain. I didn't consistently need or want friends, but it was
clear (this too I wanted to learn) that, given my own special
kind of integrity, if I was to have them at all I must remain uninvolved—I must leave them alone.

A simple lesson, but I couldn't properly be chastened. My
feelings were mixed: relief, ridiculousness, embarrassment, anger,
injured pride, maudlin affection for the Morgans, disgust with
them and myself, and a host of other things, including indifference
to the whole business.

Also, I was not a little tired of myself, and of my knowledge
of my selves, and of my personal little mystery. Although I had,

in fact, no intention of keeping my pledge to go to Pennsylvania with the Doctor, I composed a brief note to Dr. Schott, informing him of my resignation: my play for responsibility had indeed exhausted me, and I was ready to leave Wicomico and the Morgans. In a new town, with new friends, even under a new name—perhaps one could *pretend* enough unity to be a person and live in the world; perhaps, if one were a sufficiently practiced actor . . . Maybe I would marry Peggy Rankin; take her surname; father a child on her. I smiled.

At a few minutes before nine o'clock I went to get Rennie, and found her and Joe just finishing a late dinner by candlelight.

"Big occasion," Joe said dryly. He flicked on the light at once and blew out the candles, and I saw that they'd been eating hot dogs and sauerkraut. Allowing Rennie to put her coat on by herself, he started carrying dishes to the sink.

"How long does this take?" he asked me.

"I don't know, Joe," I said, acutely uncomfortable. "I shouldn't think it would take very long."

"I'm ready," Rennie said. She looked bad: white and shaky. Joe kissed her lightly and turned the sink faucet on to wash the dishes.

"You're not coming?" I asked him.

"No."

"Well——" I said. Rennie was already headed for the door. "See you after a while."

We went outside. Rennie bounded gracelessly ahead of me down the sidewalk, and opened the car door before I could do it for her. She sniffed a little, but held back the tears. I drove out the highway toward Vineland.

"This really turned into a mess, didn't it?" I said sympathetically. She stared out the window without answering. "I'm terribly sorry that any of it happened."

She gave no clue to her feelings. The thing that I was sharply conscious of was her loneliness in what had happened and what was about to happen—the fundamental, last-analysis loneliness of all human beings in critical situations. It is never entirely true, but it's more apparent at some times than at others, and just then I was very much aware of her as apart from Joe, myself, values, motives, the world, or history—a solitary animal in a tight spot. And Joe, home, washing the dishes. Lonely animals! Into no cause, resolve, or philosophy can we cram so much of ourselves that there is no part of us left over to wonder and be lonely.

"This fellow's really a fine doctor," I said a minute later.

Rennie looked at me uncomprehendingly, as if I'd spoken in a foreign language.

"Rennie, do you want me to take you home?"

"If you do I'll shoot myself," she said hoarsely.

When we came to the end of the driveway leading to the farmhouse, I cut out the headlights and drove quietly into the yard. I explained to Rennie that the Doctor didn't want me to disturb his patients, but I'm afraid the theatricality of it did her nerves no good. As I ushered her into the farmhouse I felt her trembling. Mrs. Dockey and the Doctor were waiting for us in the reception room. They both scrutinized Rennie frankly, and some contempt was evident in Mrs. Dockey's expression.

"How do you do, Mrs. Morgan," the Doctor said. "We can begin right away. Mrs. Dockey will take you to the Treatment Room.

Wordlessly Mrs. Dockey walked toward the Treatment Room, and Rennie, after a second's uncertainty, jumped to follow that formidable woman. My eyes watered. I didn't know how to go about distinguishing compassion from love: perhaps it was only compassion I felt for her.

"Did you bring the check and the bankbook?" demanded the Doctor.

"Yes." I handed them to him. On the next-to-last check stub the balance read two hundred eighty-seven dollars and thirty-two cents, and the next check was made out to that amount and signed. "I didn't know who to pay it to."

"I'll write that in. Very well, come along. I want you to watch this, for your own good."

"No, I'll wait out here."

"If you want the abortion done," the Doctor said, "then come along and watch it."

I went, most unwillingly. The Doctor donned his white jacket, and we went into the Treatment Room. Rennie was already on the examination table with a sheet up to her neck. I was afraid she'd object to my presence, but she gave no sign of approval or disapproval. Mrs. Dockey stood by impassively. The Doctor washed his hands and drew up the sheet from Rennie's abdomen.

"Well, let's see if you're pregnant, first."

When his fingers touched her to begin the examination, she jumped involuntarily. A minute or so later, when the Doctor slipped his hands into rubber gloves, greased the fingers, and began the internal examination, she started sobbing.

"Now stop that," the Doctor said irritably. "You've had children before." After a while he asked, "How old do you think the fetus is?" Rennie made no answer, and he didn't ask her anything else.

"All right, we may as well get to work. Hand me a dilator and a curette, please," he said to Mrs. Dockey, and she went to the sterilizer nearby to get them. The surgical instruments clinked in the sterilizer, and Rennie's sobbing became looser and louder. She twisted a little on the examination table and even began to raise herself.

"Lie down and be quiet!" the Doctor ordered sharply. "You'll wake everybody up."

Rennie lay back again and closed her eyes. I began to be sick as soon as the Doctor accepted the bright curette from Mrs. Dockey; I resolved to keep my eyes on Rennie's face instead of the operation.

"Fasten the straps," the Doctor said to Mrs. Dockey. "You should have done that before." A wide leather strap was secured across Rennie's diaphragm. "Now, then, hold her right leg, and Horner, you hold the other one. Since we don't go in much for obstetrics here I didn't bother to buy a table with stirrups on it."

Rennie's legs were drawn up and spread wide in the lithotomy position. Mrs. Dockey gripped one, pressing the calf against the thigh, and I, very reluctantly, held the other.

"I'm sorry, Rennie," I said.

Rennie whipped her head and moaned. A few moments later —I would guess that the Doctor had applied his curette, but I wasn't looking to find out—she began screaming, and tried to kick free.

"Hold those legs!" the Doctor snapped. "She's cutting herself to pieces! Shut her up, Horner!"

"Rennie——" But I couldn't say anything else. She was terrified; I think she no longer recognized me. Her face swam through my tears. For an instant she relaxed, fighting for control, but almost at once—another scrape of the curette?—she screamed again, and struggled to raise herself.

"Okay," the Doctor said disgustedly to Mrs. Dockey. "The curette's out. Let go of her leg and shut her up."

Mrs. Dockey pushed Rennie's head down and clamped a hand over her mouth. Rennie kicked wildly with her free leg; the Doctor jumped clear, upsetting his stool, and cursed. I inadvertently glanced away and saw blood on the sheet under Rennie's abdomen, blood on her upper thighs, blood on the Doctor's gloves. The vomitus rushed to my mouth, and I was barely able to swallow it down.

"She's already hemorrhaging," the Doctor said to Mrs. Dockey. "Keep her quiet for a minute, and I'll get an anesthetic."

I began to catch Rennie's fear. She lay quiet again for a moment, and her eyes pleaded with me.

"Take your hand off," I told Mrs. Dockey. "She won't holler." Mrs. Dockey removed her hand warily, ready to clap it back at once.

"Jake, I'm scared," Rennie cried softly, trembling all over. "He's hurting me. I don't like being scared, but I can't help it."

"Are you sure it's too late to quit, Doctor?" I called across the room, where he was fitting a rubber hose to two tanks of gas on a dolly.

"No use to now," he said. "I'd be finished by this time if she'd cut out her foolishness."

"Do you want to go home, Rennie?"

"Yes," she wept. "But let him finish. I want to hold still, but I can't."

"We'll take care of that," the Doctor said, no longer annoyed. He wheeled the gas tanks over to the head of the table. "The way you were jumping around I could very well have punctured your uterus. Relax, now."

Rennie closed her eyes. The Doctor handed the mask to Mrs.

Dockey, who with some relish held it down over Rennie's nose and mouth. The Doctor immediately opened valves, and the gases made a soft rush into the mask.

"Breathe deeply," the Doctor said, watching the pressure gauges.

Rennie inhaled deeply two, three, five times, as though anxious to lose consciousness. Her trembling subsided, and her legs began to go limp.

"Check the pulse," the Doctor told Mrs. Dockey.

But as she reached for Rennie's wrist with her free hand, Rennie's stomach jerked inwards, and she vomited explosively into the mask. A second later a horrible sucking sound came from her throat, and another. Her eyes half opened briefly.

"Bronchoscope!" the Doctor said sharply, jerking the mask away. Rennie's face was blue: the sucking noise stopped. "Take the strap off, Horner! Quick!"

I tore at the strap with my fingers; couldn't see it clearly for the water in my eyes. Another gurgling explosion came from Rennie's chest.

"*Bronchoscope!*" the Doctor shouted.

Mrs. Dockey ran back to the table with a long tubelike instrument, which the Doctor snatched from her hands and began to insert into Rennie's mouth. The vomitus was all over her face, and a small puddle of it lay under her head, in her hair. Her face darkened further; her eyes opened, and the pupils rolled senselessly. My head reeled.

"Get oxygen ready!" ordered the Doctor. "Horner, take the pulse!"

I grabbed Rennie's wrist. Maybe I felt one beat—anyway, no more after that.

"I don't feel any!" I cried.

"No," he said, less excitedly. He withdrew the bronchoscope from her windpipe and laid it aside. "Never mind the oxygen, Mrs. Dockey." Mrs. Dockey came over unhurriedly to look.

And so this is the picture I have to carry with me: the Treatment Room dark except for the one ceiling floodlight that illuminated the table; Rennie dead there now, face mottled, eyes wide, mouth agape; the vomitus running from a pool in her mouth to a pool under her head; the great black belt lying finally unbuckled across the sheet over her chest and stomach; the lower part of her body nude and bloody, her legs trailing limply and clumsily off the end of the examination table.

"So," the Doctor sighed.

"How'd it happen?" Mrs. Dockey asked.

"She must have eaten a big meal before she came out here." he said. "She should've known better. Vomited it up from the ether and then aspirated it into her lungs. What a mess this is!"

I was stunned past weeping. Shock set in at once, and I was forced to find a chair before I fell.

"Straighten up, Horner; this won't do."

I couldn't reply. I was fighting nausea and faintness.

"Go lie down on a couch in the reception room," he ordered, "and prop your feet up. It'll pass. We'll clean her up, and then you'll have to take her out of here."

"Where?" I cried. "What am I going to do?"

"Why, take her back home. Don't you think her husband wants the body?"

I lurched for the door, but fell flat before reaching it. When I revived I was lying in the reception room, and the Doctor was standing nearby.

"Swallow these," he said, giving me two pills and a glass of water.

"Now, then, pay attention. This is serious, but it'll be all right if you keep hold of yourself. We took her out to your car. Don't do anything silly like trying to dispose of her secretly. I've called the husband and explained that she'd be awhile coming out of anesthesia. The best thing for you to do is take her right to her house and tell the husband she's dead. Be in a panic. Tell him she seemed all right until you got halfway home, and then she started vomiting and got strangled—the autopsy will pretty much bear that out. He'll call the hospital ambulance, and they'll discover the abortion, but that's okay. You'll be asked questions; that's okay too. Don't tell them where it was done until tomorrow; after that it won't matter. I'm leaving tonight with a few of the patients in the station wagon, and Mrs. Dockey will stay here to handle things. The house and phone are in her name, and she'll say she's one of my patients who set up the home. You don't know my name, and she'll give them the wrong one and plead ignorance of the whole business. They can't hold you or her either, and they won't be able to find me. Here, take this." He gave me an envelope. "That's your bus fare and enough money to last you until Wednesday. Our plans are the same. Meet Mrs. Dockey and the other patients Wednesday morning at the Greyhound station, and she'll tell you then if there has to be any change in our plans. Do you feel able to drive now?"

I couldn't answer: all my grief had returned in a rush with consciousness.

"You look all right," he said curtly. "This thing was everybody's fault, Homer. Let it be everybody's lesson. Go on, now; get it over with."

The pills must have worked: when I stood up this time I didn't feel faint. I went out to the car and got in. Rennie was lying curled on the back seat, dressed, washed, her eyes closed. It was too big a thing to know what to think about it, to know how to feel. I drove mechanically back to the Morgans' house.

It was about eleven when I got there. The grounds and most of the house were dark, and there was no traffic on the highway. I rang the doorbell, and when Joe answered I said, "She's dead, Joe."

He winced and shoved his glasses back on his nose. Tears sprang into his eyes and ran at once down both cheeks.

"Where is she?"

"Out in the car. She vomited from the ether and strangled to death on it."

He walked past me out to the car. With difficulty he took her out of the back seat and carried her into the house, where he laid her gently on the daybed. Tears poured down his face, but he neither sobbed nor made any kind of noise. I stood by helplessly.

"What's the name of that doctor?"

"I don't know, Joe. I swear to Christ I'm not protecting him. I've been going to him, but he never told me his name. I'll explain it to you when you want to hear it."

"Where does he operate?"

"Out past Vineland. I'll tell the police—"

"You get out fast."

"All right," I said, and left at once.

I sat up through the rest of the night waiting to hear from either Joe or the police, but no one called. I wanted terribly to call the police, to call the hospital, to call Joe—but there was no reason to call anyone. What Joe was doing I had no idea; for all I knew he might have done nothing yet—might still be regarding her on the daybed, making up his mind. But I decided to let him take whatever action he wanted to—even killing me—without my interference, since he hadn't wanted my help. Unless he requested differently, I intended to answer everybody's questions truthfully, and I hoped the Doctor had been mistaken: I hoped with all my heart that there was some way in which I could be held legally responsible. I craved responsibility.

But no one called. I was presented in the morning with the problem of deciding whether to go to school or not, and I decided to go. I couldn't telephone Joe; perhaps someone at school would have heard some news.

When I reached the college I went directly to Dr. Schott's office on the pretext of looking for mail. Dr. Schott was in the outer office, along with Shirley and Dr. Carter, and it was apparent from their expressions that they'd heard of Rennie's death.

"Good morning," I said, uncertain how I'd be received.

"Good morning, Mr. Horner," Dr. Schott said distractedly. "We've just heard a terrible thing! Joe Morgan's wife died very suddenly last night!"

"What?" I said, automatically feigning surprise and shock. So, it seemed that they didn't suspect my part in her death: my feigned surprise was proper until I found out what was on Joe's mind.

"Terrible thing!" Dr. Schott repeated. "A young girl like that, and two little children!"

"How did it happen, sir?"

He blushed. "I'm not in a position to say, Mr. Horner. Joe naturally wasn't too coherent on the phone just now . . . A shock, you know—terrible shock to him! I believe she died under anesthesia last night in the hospital. Some kind of emergency operation she was having."

"That's awful, isn't it?" I said, shaking my head.

"Terrible thing!"

"Shall I call the hospital?" Shirley asked him. "Maybe they'd have some information."

"No, no," Dr. Schott said at once. "We mustn't pry. I'll telephone Joe later and ask if there's anything I can do. I can't believe it! Mrs. Morgan was such a fine, healthy young thing!"

It was evident to me that he knew more than he was telling, but whatever Joe told him must not have involved me. Dr. Carter noticed my eyes watering and clapped me on the shoulder. It was known that I was some kind of friend of the Morgans.

"You never know," he sighed. "The good die young, and maybe it's best."

"What'll he do about the children?" I asked.

"Lord knows! It's tragic!" It was not certain what exactly he referred to.

"Well, let's don't say any more about it than we have to," Dr. Carter advised, "until we hear more details. It's a terrible shock to all of us."

I guessed that Dr. Schott had confided to him whatever information he had.

So on Monday and Tuesday I taught my classes as usual, though in a great emptiness of anxiety. Tuesday afternoon Rennie was buried, but because the college could not declare a holiday on that account Dr. Schott was the only representative of the faculty at the funeral. A collection was taken by Miss Banning for a wreath from all of us: I gave a dollar from what little money the Doctor had given me. At the moment when Rennie was lowered into the earth, I believe I was explaining semicolons to my students.

It was given out at the college that Mrs. Morgan had not died from anesthesia after all, but had strangled when a morsel of food lodged in her throat, and had succumbed en route to the hospital. This is what appeared in Tuesday's newspaper as well —Dr. Schott must have been a power in the community. More-

over, it was rumored that Mr. Morgan had submitted his resignation; everyone agreed that the shock of his wife's death was
responsible—that Joe very understandably wanted a change of
scenery for a while. The boys were being cared for by Mr. and
Mrs. MacMahon, Rennie's parents.

But later Tuesday afternoon I heard the truth of the matter
from Dr. Carter, who accosted me as I was leaving school for the
last time.

"I know you were a friend of Morgan's," he said confidentially,
steering me away from the group of students nearby, "so you
might as well know the truth about this business. I'm sure it'll
go no further."

"Of course not," I assured him. "What is it?"

"Dr. Schott and I were terribly shocked, Horner," he said. "It
seems that Mrs. Morgan really died from the effects of an illegal
abortion someplace out in the country near here."

"No!"

"I'm afraid so. When he took her to the hospital they found
out she'd strangled under anesthesia, and there were obvious
signs of the abortion."

"That's a terrible shame!"

"Isn't it? Dr. Schott managed to keep everybody quiet, and
the police are investigating secretly, but so far they haven't had
any luck. Morgan claims he doesn't know who the doctor was
that did it or where the thing was done. Says his wife arranged
it on her own and he wasn't there when it happened. I don't
know whether he's lying or not; there's no way to tell."

"Good Lord! Can they punish him for anything?"

"Not a thing. But here's the unfortunate part: even though
Schott's kept everything hushed up, he decided he can't in good
conscience keep Morgan on the staff. It's a bad thing in itself, and
it would be worse if the students got wind of it. You know, a
small college in a little town like Wicomico. It could lead to a
great deal of unpleasantness. Frankly, he asked for Morgan's
resignation."

"Oh, the poor bastard!"

"Yes, it's a pity. You won't say anything, will you?"

I shook my head. "I won't tell a soul."

I was going to be denied, then, the chance to take public responsibility. Rennie was buried. I was still employed, my reputation was untouched, and Joe was out of a job.

Lord, the raggedness of it; the incompleteness! I paced my room; sucked in my breath; groaned aloud. I could imagine confessing publicly—but would this not be a further, final injury to Joe, who clearly wanted to deprive me of my responsibility, or at any rate wanted to hold his grief free from any further dealing with me? I could imagine carrying the ragged burden secretly, either in or out of Wicomico, married to Peggy Rankin or not, under my real name or another—but was this not cheating my society of its due, or covertly avoiding public embarrassment? For that matter, I couldn't decide whether marrying Peggy would be merciful or cruel; whether setting police on the Doctor would be right or wrong. I could not even decide what I should *feel*: all I found in me was anguish, abstract and without focus.

I was frantic. Half a dozen letters I started—to Joe, to the police, to Peggy, to Joe again—and could finish none. It was no use: I could not remain sufficiently simple-minded long enough to lay blame—on the Doctor, myself, or anyone—or to decide what was the right course of action. I threw the notes away and sat still and anguished in my rocking chair. The terrific incompleteness made me volatile; my muscles screamed to act; but my limbs were bound like Laocoön's—by the serpents Knowledge and Imagination, which, grown great in the fullness of time, no longer tempt but annihilate.

Presently I undressed and lay on the bed in the dark, though sleep was unthinkable, and commenced a silent colloquy with my friend.

"We've come too far," I said to Laocoön. "Who can live any longer in the world?"

There was no reply.

Sometime during the night the telephone rang. I was naked, and since the window curtains were open I answered the phone in the dark. Joe's voice came strong, clear, quiet, and close over the wire.

"Jake?"

"Yes, Joe." I tingled in every nerve, thinking, among other things, of the big pistol in his closet.

"Are you up to date on everything?"

"Yes. I think so."

There was a pause.

"Well. What are your plans? Anything special?"

"I don't know, Joe. I guess not. I was going to follow your lead, whatever it turned out to be."

Another pause.

"I might leave town too," I said.

"Oh yes? Why?"

No alteration in his voice, no hint of his attitude at all.

"I don't know. How about you, Joe? What'll you do now?"

He ignored the question.

"Well, what's on your mind, Jake? What do you think about things?"

I hesitated, entirely nonplused. "God, Joe—I don't know where to start or what to do!"

"What?"

His voice remained clear, bright, and close in my ear. Tears ran in a cold flood down my face and neck, onto my chest, and I shook all over with violent chills.

"I said I don't know what to do."

"Oh."

Another pause, a long one; then he hung up and I was left with a dead instrument in the dark.

Next morning I shaved, dressed, packed my bags, and called a taxi. While I waited for it to come, I rocked in my chair and smoked a cigarette. I was without weather. A few minutes later the cabby blew his horn for me; I picked up my two suitcases and went out, leaving the bust of Laocoön where it stood on the mantelpiece. My car, too, since I saw no further use for it, I left where it was, at the curb, and climbed into the taxi.

"Terminal."

John Barth was born on May 27, 1930, in Cambridge, Maryland. As a student at Johns Hopkins University he was fascinated by Oriental tale-cycles and medieval collections, a body of literature that would later influence his own writing. He received his B.A. from Johns Hopkins in 1951 and his M.A. in 1952. He has held professorships at Pennsylvania State University, the State University of New York at Buffalo, and Boston University. He presently teaches in the English and Creative Writing programs at Johns Hopkins.

Barth's first novel, *The Floating Opera* (1956), was nominated for the National Book Award. *The End of the Road* (1958) was also critically praised. In 1960, *The Sot-Weed Factor*—a comic historical novel—established Barth's reputation. *Giles Goat-Boy* (1966) was a huge critical and commercial success, after which he revised and republished his first three novels. *Lost in the Funhouse*, a book of interconnected stories, earned him a second nomination for the National Book Award. His other works are *Chimera* (1972), a collection of three novellas, which won the National Book Award; *Letters* (1979), an epistolary novel; *Sabbatical: A Romance* (1982); and *The Friday Book* (1984), a collection of essays. His latest work is *Tidewater Tales* (1987).